# NIGHTWALKER

# Nightwalker

## The World of Nightwalkers

**Jacquelyn Frank**

INTEGRATED MEDIA
NEW YORK

ISBN: 979-8-3372-0549-6

This edition published in 2026 by Open Road Integrated Media, Inc.
180 Maiden Lane
New York, NY 10038
www.openroadmedia.com

*To my sister Laraine,*
*You're always there for me. No matter what.*
*I'm a very, very lucky sister.*

# NIGHTWALKER

# THE LOST SCROLL OF KINDRED

. . . And so it will come to pass in the forward times that the nations of the Nightwalkers will be shattered, driven apart, and become strangers to one another. Hidden, by misfortune and by purpose, these twelve nations will come to cross-purposes and fade from each other's existence. In the forward times these nations will face toil and struggle unlike any time before, and only by coming together once more can they hope to face the evil that will set upon them. But they are lost to one another . . . and so will remain lost, until a great enemy is defeated . . . and a new one resurrects itself . . .

# CHAPTER 1

Kamenwati awoke with a sharp intake of breath. He exhaled when he realized that the dream was just that . . . a dream. He sat up in his bed and turned on the light on the nightstand beside him. The room still felt alien to him. Probably because it was not really *his room* and it was not meant to be comfortable. It was meant to be something just shy of a prison cell.

So be it. Considering the unforgivable nature of his crimes against his hosts and against humanity in general, he should have gotten much worse than this comfortable bed, a room of his own, and three exquisite meals a day. In truth, very little had changed about his daily life since coming to this place. He spent his days studying ancient texts, scrolls, and papyrus that were brittle to the touch and on the verge of crumbling to dust. He studied new spells and magic, studied histories and old languages. Just as he had done before.

But while these were things that had once given him great pleasure and devoured much of his time, his pleasure had since crumbled to dust, just like an old parchment. And rightfully so. For it was in one of these scrolls that he'd uncovered the spell that allowed him to inadvertently unleash the deadly and dangerous imp god, Apep.

Intentionally or not, he had done it. He was responsible. And therefore it was he who must find the means to destroy the god he had brought forth. He had walked into the "enemy" camp, the Bodywalker Politic, and thrown himself on their mercy. Then he had thrown himself into studying every piece of ancient text he could find to discover the way to destroy the god. There had to be a way. It was simply a matter of whether they could find the solution.

Kamen turned and threw his legs over the bed. He let the sheets pull away, leaving his bare legs exposed to the chill air. The inside of the New Mexico stronghold was climate controlled for the most part, but he always found it to be a little too cold for his liking. But since he was more a prisoner than a guest, it wasn't as though he could complain. He stood up, feeling the need to move. He had grown very restless of late, which thankfully coincided with his jailors allowing him more freedom to move about. He was no longer confined to his quarters—although that had been a rather loosely adhered to policy from the beginning. In truth, these people were really lucky he was honestly trying to reform himself. He could have caused a great deal of damage to them had he been of a mind to. He knew more than enough spells to wreak havoc if he wished to.

For centuries, he had been gathering spells like a child gathers wildflowers from a field. Each time he was reborn into a new host body, he would learn more, and that knowledge stayed with him throughout his many lives, even in the Ether, that bodiless state of being where a Bodywalker spirit resides for the one hundred years in between lives.

For he was indeed a Bodywalker: a soul that had originated during the long lost dynasties of ancient Egypt. He had been born, he had lived a life, and he had died. And like many noble Egyptians, he had been mummified and buried with all of his wealth, intending to take it with him into the afterlife. But apparently, the hubris of such an act, of trying to force the hand of the powers of life and death, had instead given the Egyptians' souls life everlasting . . . in the Ether. Knowing no eternal rest, no heaven or hell, no life other than to exist and watch the years unfold on the earthly plane.

Until one day one soul thought to ask a living soul on earth who was on the cusp of death if he wished to share his body in exchange for being returned to full health, as well as having the powers of immortality and extraordinary self-healing. The living man had agreed and both souls returned to the living man's body. The souls eventually Blended and become as one, harmonious inside the human host. And once one soul was able to do so, all the other souls followed suit and began to share the bodies of human mortals who would have died otherwise.

Only, some Bodywalkers wanted full control without having to answer to the original soul, so they did as little Blending as possible, suppressing the human soul until its voice became nearly nonexistent. These were the Templars. The Politic Bodywalkers were of an opposing mentality. They respected the original soul by sharing its body on equal footing and honoring the agreement they had made.

Kamen had been the second most powerful Templar there was, the favorite of their leader, the most powerful Templar, Odjit. And in turn, Kamen had loved Odjit. Not as a man loves a woman, but as a devoted follower loves his master. He thought it was Odjit's plan to do away with the animosity between the two sides of the Bodywalker race so they could all live in harmony one day. He had believed in her cause—in *their* cause.

He had been blind, he thought as he pulled on a pair of slacks. He had discovered that she just wanted power for herself at any cost. Kamen was a very smart man, but he had been very stupid when it came to Odjit. He had spent far too much time engrossed in his books and spells and not enough time living in the real world and seeing truths for what they were.

Kamen pulled on a collared shirt but did not button it. He knew he was likely to be the only one up at this time of the day so he didn't bother. He looked out of the windows, their polarized glass keeping all hint of sunlight from touching anyone in the house. Bodywalkers were paralyzed by the touch of the sun. All Nightwalkers, in fact, had a weakness to sunlight. Djynns blistered and burned unless they turned to their smoke form, Night Angel skin turned from ebony to albino and their natural abilities became muffled. From what he had read, Mysticals were forced to be in their mystical form rather than their human form. Phoenixes burst into flame at the touch of the sun, leaving only ash from which they would be reborn once darkness fell, and one touch of the sun made Wraiths—who spent the darkness in their ghostly forms that could phase right through solid objects—instantly solid, which was deadly if they happened to be phasing through something at the time.

He had found out about all of these weaknesses during his hours of study. What he did not know was what the weaknesses of the other six Nightwalkers were, the new Nightwalkers they had only just discovered: Demons, Lycanthropes, Mistrals, Vampires, Druids, and Shadowdwellers. He wanted to learn about them, but so far, it had proven next to impossible. Nothing in their written languages made sense to him, and, in fact, without a human translator, there wasn't even any way of speaking with them. It was as if they weren't there at all. Besides, Kamen didn't think they would be all that willing to share information about their weaknesses in any event, never mind sharing it with the likes of him.

Still, Kamen had spent hours in conversation with the Druid called Bella, whose talent was the ability to read any language put before her. Any language, that is, written by humans or the six Nightwalker races she knew of. The Bodywalkers wrote in Egyptian or the language they were reborn into, plus any languages they had studied over their incarnations. Kamen himself could read and write and speak almost any language put in front of him. The product of having his nose constantly in a book whenever he had a body.

But while this Bella could read Egyptian, she could not read anything that referred to any of the six races she was not familiar with. Instead, the pages would simply be filled with the Egyptian alphabet. Something that might seem strange, but not strange enough to have gotten her to question it earlier. And when books in the Demon language were brought to Kamen, all he could see was gibberish that meant absolutely nothing and was completely indecipherable. If Bella wrote something in English about the other Nightwalkers, it just looked like pages filled with the English alphabet.

It was clear that whatever was keeping the two factions apart was determined to do it in such a way that they would never have questioned it. And yet, for all of this misdirection and codification, somehow a prophecy in the Demon language about the twelve Nightwalker nations had survived, giving a hint of what was out there. It had been useless with no context, until Bella, a half-breed Druid, had literally run into Kat, a half-breed Djynn. While they could not see each other nor speak to each other, they could write to each other and use humans as go-betweens when getting messages across.

It made for slow going, this communication process. It had been seven months now since they had first found each other and they were still trying to smooth out ways of communicating and transferring messages back and forth.

He had been working with Bella since he had a larger store of language capability than anyone else in the Portales, New Mexico, compound. If a solution was going to be found, it was going to be found by the two of them. They just had to hope it would happen sooner rather than later. Time was growing short.

For Apep was about to give birth.

In this incarnation, the imp god had taken over Odjit's body. He had then chosen a father from among the Nightwalker breeds, a powerful Night Angel named Dax, and had raped him in order to impregnate himself. Apep was due to deliver the child into the world any day now.

One god was nearly impossible to fight, but two? And while there was still hope they might stumble upon a text somewhere that would tell them how to get rid of Apep, the god's child would be something never seen before. There would be no telling how to be rid of it.

Apep had been quiet for the duration of his pregnancy, but after he gave birth, he would focus on destroying them—Kamen was certain of it. He suspected that the Nightwalkers were key to Apep's undoing, and that the god knew it. So he would destroy them as soon as he was able. Kamen believed that Apep's pregnancy made him vulnerable, and while they should probably strike before that weakness was gone from him, there were two problems. They didn't know how to attack him and they no longer knew where he was.

Actually . . . Kamen was fairly certain he had a spell that could locate him, only he hadn't mentioned it to the others as yet. He felt in his gut that they weren't ready to face Apep, that they were missing a key element that would allow them to defeat him at last. Bella agreed with him. And anyway, the surest way to defeat him would be if the two Nightwalker factions could coordinate their attacks, and until they figured out why they couldn't see each other, they wouldn't be able to enact that kind of coordination effectively.

It was a curse. It had to be a curse.

Kamen's head spun with these thoughts over and over again. It was no wonder he hadn't been able to sleep, sometimes for days at a stretch. These people were counting on him to fix the mess he had created, and if he failed . . . if he failed, every death Apep caused would be on his soul. A weight he would carry from now until the world ended and there were no more humans left to Blend with.

And when he did sleep, it was to have horrible nightmares. Nightmares about what he had set loose on the earth. He could end up being solely responsible for the destruction of all mankind, not just Nightwalkers. The only thing in their favor was that any written history about Apep they had found so far, as spare as it had been, had said he craved the adulation of his followers. Apep would no doubt prefer to enslave the world rather than destroy it.

Not that that was anything to feel better about.

Kamen walked to the bathroom and splashed some cold water on his face. Then he turned on the lights and picked up one of the ancient tomes he had been studying in hopes of finding a solution to any of his many daunting problems. And, failing that, he was searching for spells, both offensive and defensive—anything that would help protect the Nightwalkers when Apep's next attack took place.

He had been reading for several hours when, suddenly, something on a papyrus scroll jumped out at him—hieroglyphs of the figure of a god using some kind of power to divide a group of twelve beings into two halves.

Kamen knew instantly that the god was Apep and that he had used his power to sunder the Nightwalker nation into two. Then it showed that the god had died as a result of the curse. This was new information. He felt an emotion akin to excitement—if a man as jaded as he was could even feel excitement and hope any longer. If the god could die from the curse, then that meant he could die, period. That his mortal body was fragile enough to be destroyed. The question was, how did they go about destroying that mortal body when they hadn't even gotten close to doing so in spite of using strength and manmade weapons against him? He'd been shot directly in the heart and it hadn't even made him blink. If that couldn't kill him, then what could?

But the next hieroglyphs were even more important. They showed the god resurrecting, enslaving people, using his power to kill . . . and then they showed the twelve beings coming together to fight the god. Eventually destroying him.

Did that mean what he thought it meant? That if all twelve nations of Nightwalkers got together they could fight this god? If that were the case then it would be an impossible task. Not only because they couldn't see one another, but because the twelfth nation, the Wraiths, were enemies to all the other Nightwalkers. True, there had been an unspoken truce of sorts these past decades, more a case of neither making any moves against the other. But every Nightwalker on this side of the faction, known now as the Second Faction, knew the Wraiths were cold-blooded and would just as soon touch you with their instantly fatal deathtouch as not. The First Faction was lucky they knew nothing of the Wraiths. They made Nightwalker blood run cold.

But what if the Wraiths could be made to come to the table? Could be made to understand that it was best for all of them if they worked cooperatively against the god Apep? Surely they had just as much to lose.

But the glyphs showed no explanation as to how the twelve were able to coordinate an attack against the god. Hieroglyphs were notoriously open to interpretation and could only get across the most rudimentary of ideas. It wasn't as though you could glean great philosophical discussions from them.

He gingerly touched the aged papyrus. Simple they may be, those few succinct images were the closest they had gotten to some kind of history or explanation or suggestion as to how to end all of this. He put a marker in the page and continued on in search of more, but he went through all the other scrolls and found no hint of further explanation.

Twelve nations, working together.

It was worth considering at least. And it wasn't his place to agree or disagree with the concept. His only role was to report what he learned.

And so when dusk fell, that was what he would do.

# CHAPTER 2

Isabella Russ, known simply as Bella or Bella the Enforcer, had found herself living in New Mexico for the better part of seven months now. It was necessary for her to be there in order to work closely with Kamenwati, the Bodywalkers' most learned man. So she had moved and, with great reluctance, brought her children to the compound as well. The god Apep knew where the compound was and had already made an attack on it. It was dangerous to have them there.

But living apart from them for days at a time? Unacceptable. She would not be a ghost in her children's lives during the most important years of their development. True, Leah was ten now and more than capable of being independent of her mother for short stretches of time, but her son was not. He was just exiting his toddler years, having only recently learned all the basics of walking and potty training and other such milestones for a child of three going on four.

But she struggled constantly with the idea of them being potentially in the line of fire. Luckily their father was there and he had always been able to protect them. And several of their friends from the other Nightwalkers in the First Faction were there as well. There were Sagan and Valera, the former Shadowdweller priest and his natural Witch wife; Jasmine and Adam, the Vampire prince's most trusted aide and her Demon husband; Windsong, one of the Mistral leaders; and Jinaeri, a Lycanthrope scholar.

Together it meant that every member of the First Faction was represented. As for the Second Faction, so far there were numerous Bodywalkers, a Night Angel named Faith and her human husband, Leo, who often acted as a translator and who came with some mercenary skills of his own. There was a Djynn named Kat and her Gargoyle husband—although the Gargoyles were not technically members of the Second Faction because they were the scions of the Bodywalkers. She'd learned that Gargoyles had been created by Templars to be used as slaves. Other than that, there was no representation of the Mysticals, no one from the Phoenixes and no one from the Wraiths . . . although to hear the Second Faction tell it, this was a good thing.

But Bella couldn't escape the thought that they needed to have the Phoenixes and Mysticals there. As she got dressed for the night she thought about it more and more. If they were going to get out of this mess they needed all hands on deck.

An idea that was supported only an hour later when she met up with

Kamen and he revealed his discovery, via Leo who was interpreting between the two.

"But if what you're saying is true, then we have to get the Phoenixes and Mysticals on board. And the Wraiths."

"We'll have to do this without the Wraiths. Trust me, they are too deadly to be dealt with."

"Well, we'll have to deal with at least one of them according to this. I think it means we need a party of twelve to defeat Apep," Bella said.

"Surely you aren't thinking of sending just twelve people to fight a god?" Kamen was aghast.

"Of course not! But we have to have at *least* twelve. One from each nation. That means you have to make nice with a Wraith."

Kamen thought about this a moment. "Then it seems it's clear what we have to do here. We have to make contact with each of these groups and get representatives from each to come here."

"And who are you going to get to do that?" Leo asked. "The last time we met up with Wraiths they almost killed Faith and me."

"I don't know, but someone has to try," Kamen said.

"We should start with the Phoenixes and Mysticals first. Begin with the easy ones," Bella said.

"Easy? We've been trying to contact them and get them to cooperate for months now. They aren't all that interested," Kamen said.

"Well then, we need to send someone to make it interesting for them," Bella said.

Kamen grew quiet then said, "It should be me."

"You? Why you? We need you here, researching how to break this curse."

"I have to do this," Kamen said firmly. "I have to do something other than study books. You can take over doing it just as easily as I can for now. Let me go to the courts of the other three Nightwalkers."

"So you're going to reach out to the Wraiths?"

"We have to at least try to approach them. They might surprise us."

"Or they might kill you. No way. No way are you going alone. At the very least you should take Leo. He's human and immune to their deathtouch."

"Or so we believe," Kamen retorted. "There's no proof of that."

"You can't go alone. It would be suicide."

"It's homicide to risk more than one life . . . and it will look less threatening if one is sent as opposed to a cadre of Nightwalkers showing up on their doorstep."

"He has a point," Leo added. "One trained man can get in a lot better than six. I just don't know if I'd call Kamen a trained man."

"I can take care of myself," Kamen said harshly. "I was second only to Odjit when it came to Templar power. I can keep the Wraiths off me long enough to get them to talk and I can escape more quickly than anyone else. It would be better if I didn't have anyone else to worry about in the process."

"I'm convinced," Leo said. "I just don't think you're going to convince Jackson."

"If you want to convince the leader of the Politic Bodywalkers to let you do this," Bella said, "you better meet with him alone. There are too many people here who think the worst of you and will shoot you down before you can say boo about it."

"I am aware of that," Kamen said grimly. "But getting Jackson alone will not be an easy trick for me."

"It would be for me," Leo said. "He's my best friend after all. If I ask him to meet me alone, he'll come alone. Bella, you can stay here and work," Leo said, indicating the mounds of books that had been brought into the library for her and Kamen to go through together.

She nodded and let them go. She crossed her fingers though. There were too many variables that made it a bad idea all around. But she had a feeling Kamen was going to convince Jackson . . . or die trying.

When Jackson entered Leo's rooms, answering a summons to meet him alone, he was extremely curious. He was surprised to find Kamen there with Leo. As they laid out their plan and the reasoning behind it, Jackson found himself agreeing with them.

"So, you think it's a good idea?" Leo asked, shocked it had been so easy. For Jackson to trust Kamenwati . . . well, they had barely let the man leave the property since he had defected.

"Actually, I think it's a great idea—one a long time coming. Time is growing short, I think we all feel that. We have to convince these other Nightwalkers it's in their best interest to join us. Who better than the man who created the problem and who understands it better than any of us?"

"Well, when you put it that way," Kamen said wryly.

"It's the truth isn't it?"

"Very much so," Kamen admitted readily. "I know where my responsibilities lie. I have all along. It's why I came here in the first place. I am aware I have a lot to atone for . . . and not just this crime. Allow me to do it."

"All right, you have a deal. But take one of the house cellphones with you and check in every couple of hours like clockwork. This way we'll know if you've been wasted by the Wraiths as soon as possible and can start concocting a plan B. Actually, I think we'll concoct one anyway, just in case you fail at any aspect of this."

Kamen nodded in agreement.

Jackson continued. "So, we're straight then? Start with the Wraiths . . . they'll be the toughest and most deadly. Then you can go to Brazil and handle the Phoenixes. They're the farthest away. Then, while you're doing that, we'll get in touch with Grey. Last I checked he had a Mystical Pegasus in his stable. Maybe she can point us to where the leader of her people is."

"As I understand it, she *is* the leader of her people," Leo said. "At least I think that's what Grey said. Anyway, he went to a lot of trouble to rescue her from the Wraiths. She must be very important. That's provided she can be persuaded to change out of her Mystical form and into that of a speaking being. I know Grey's been trying to do exactly that but last I heard he wasn't having much luck. She doesn't seem to trust all that easily. Then again, would you if you'd been taken prisoner by the Wraiths? Grey's been treating her like gold ever since he organized that rescue, so hopefully that will count for something."

"Hopefully," Jackson said, before turning back to Kamen. "Do you know how you'll find the Phoenixes?"

"Their main colony is in Brazil, as you said, though no one really seems to know where," Kamen said. "But I have a locator spell that should allow me streak right to them. Or reasonably close. It takes me to a place with a high content of power located in one area. It was often how we located your Politic cell houses."

"Nice," Jackson said. "I wondered how you were able to do that. It seemed no matter where we moved you still found us."

"It only works for high concentrations of power. Phoenixes have a lot of power. I'm hoping that finding the colony will help lead me to the leaders."

"It should. So far we've had no luck getting to them. You'll have your work cut out for you."

"I'm not afraid of a little work."

"But you should be afraid of the Wraiths. They can phase right through you, wrap their hands around your heart and solidify, touching you from the inside out. Even without that, all it takes is a brush against your skin and you're done for. That deathtouch of theirs . . . there's no avoiding it."

"I am aware of the risks, Leo, thank you."

Leo frowned. "Just watch your back. Honestly, I don't see you succeeding here. I kind of think it's a death wish. But hey, you do what you feel you need to do. I'm not going to stop you on the off chance this crazy idea works. My wife is going to be on the front lines of this if and when it comes to an all-out battle. Her ability to shield and deflect is so powerful, it already hurt Apep once when she deflected his own power back on him. And so far it's the only thing that has hurt him. I don't see anyone else around here with the power of a god so we better come up with a game plan and fast."

"This is the game plan. When we get everyone else on board then we'll come up with the next stage. Meanwhile, I'm going to keep running our people through battle drills like we've been doing these past seven months. I want everyone battle ready," Jackson said.

"I think we are battle ready. The trouble is coordinating our attack with the attacks of a group of people you can't even see," Leo said.

"That means depending on humans to relay between the two sides and frankly, I don't want weak humans anywhere near that thing when it comes."

"Hey!" Leo said, taking offense at his best friend's words.

"You're a mercenary, Leo, which makes you good against human targets. The best even. But Apep isn't human. And if you think he is coming alone, you're wrong. He won't make that mistake twice. He's going to bring followers, and a lot of them."

"We'll need more Nightwalkers if that's the case," Leo said. "And the main house is already packed to the brim."

"We've got the two other houses on the property. They're much smaller, but they'll hold a few people. Leo, talk with the First Faction and see who else they can bring in. We'll fill one of the houses with First Faction and the other with Second Faction. Here's hoping we don't confuse the hell out of each other in the process."

"Between Max, Jackson's human assistant; myself; and Angelina, Marissa's human sister, you've got three interpreters going at all times. I can see if the First Faction has any humans they know of that can help as well. Anyone they trust."

"Good. We all know our tasks? Then let's get to it," Jackson said.

Kamen came away from the meeting feeling good about the choices he had made. Was it suicidal? Yes. Was it suicidal to *not* go? Yes. At least this way they had a chance, however remote it might be. Doing nothing guaranteed failure. At least he was doing *something*. He went to his rooms, frowning as he crossed the threshold. He had spent far too much time in these rooms since he had arrived at the compound nearly a year ago. He was tired of them. He was glad to be leaving, even if it did mean risking his life in the process. He had died before and would die again. He was not afraid of death. If he died his soul would simply go into the Ether for a hundred years, then he would be reborn again. But he *was* afraid of dying and leaving a mess behind, of having thousands of deaths on his conscience. And he made no mistake about it, there were going to be thousands if not hundreds of thousands of lives sacrificed to this god.

Maybe even more. Maybe even the majority of the human race.

There was something else at stake as well. Presently, the Nightwalker species were secreted from the human race. Very few humans knew about the Demons or Bodywalkers or that there were actual Vampires. To be honest, he had found the Vampires, Lycanthropes, and Demons' existence to be hard to believe and he *was* a Nightwalker. But once the humans found out these races indeed did exist . . . well it wasn't hard to imagine what would happen. When a human being was afraid of something, it lashed out and destroyed it without trying to understand it. If he were a human learning Vampires were real—what with all the frightening fiction having been written about them—he might want to eliminate the threat they posed too.

Well . . . maybe *he* wouldn't. He had found the idea of Vampires being real a bit daunting at first, but that had been his ignorance of the situation kicking up dust. It hadn't been easy learning to trust these new Nightwalkers. Nightwalkers they couldn't feel or touch or read. There were no faces to show their expressions as they spoke, there was no body language to hint at whether or not they were lying. This was, in a nutshell, blind trust.

But his other senses told him these races were worthy of his trust. Especially when the Demon King Noah had come clean about there being Vampire criminals killing Nightwalkers as a method of harvesting their power for themselves. That little bit of imperfection in their ranks made them a little more real. A little less saintly.

What he found intriguing was that none of the First Faction of Nightwalkers could wield magic without turning "corrupt." Magic blackened their souls and poisoned their minds—just as it did with humans who tried to wield it. He would have thought Nightwalkers of any breed strong enough to manage the power of magic. Apparently he was wrong. As it stood, the only races on their side of the factions that wielded magic were the Bodywalkers and the Djynn. Night Angels had a more inborn set of abilities that differed from one Angel to the next. The Wraith abilities all seemed to be uniformly innate, not magical, and the Phoenixes and Mysticals . . . well, they hardly knew anything about either of those species so he couldn't speak to it.

But none of this mattered at the present time. He had more important things to focus his attention on. He wondered at himself for insisting he go alone. Surely one other person wouldn't seem an intimidating presence to a Nightwalker breed. But he wouldn't risk anyone else. It was bad enough lives had already been lost and twisted because of him. He would avoid adding more deaths to his conscience wherever possible.

And clearly, by letting him go on this death mission alone, they felt it was his just reward for having brought this down on their heads in the first place.

Kamen packed a change of clothes in a backpack, along with some other essentials: his journal of spells, a few herbs and other components of more complex spell casting, and something to read and study up on in case he found himself with time on his hands. The journal of spells was not entirely necessary. Everything he needed to know was firmly entrenched in his memory. But the book he was reading might offer up some new spells and he liked to have a common place for them all to be as he familiarized himself with something new.

Kamen shrugged the pack onto one shoulder and turned to leave the room.

There was a mirror to his left and, as he passed, he caught sight of his reflection. He stopped and studied himself with a critical eye. If he was the lord of an alien culture, what would he make of this man before him?

Kamen could only hope they would have no way of knowing the truth.

# CHAPTER 3

Finding the Wraiths' nearest stronghold was easier than it should have been. He would have thought that they would at least have some kind of safeguards in place to prevent their enemies from finding them.

But they did not. To his fortune. He would have preferred to find where the head of the Wraiths' political structure was, if indeed they had one, and go directly there, but he had no way of doing that, so he would have to satisfy himself with whatever was closest.

Kamen could "streak"—a rapid-fire form of travel—from place to place using his magic. So combining the locator spell and the streak spell he was able to bring himself nearly to the Wraiths' doorstep. It was night, of course, since daylight would paralyze him. But night also meant that whatever was inside of the house he stood before had the advantage. And all it would take was a single touch and he would be dead. But he had a shield spell, one that formed a bubble around him that things would bounce off of if they came into contact with it. It expended a great deal of energy and focus, but as long as he kept calm it should work. He cast the spell as he looked around. The house was remotely located, in the middle of what appeared to be farmland. There were fields in every direction. He took a moment to magically discover he was in the middle of Iowa. Corn country. Corn as far as the eye could see.

As for the house, it was a quaint little farmhouse. Generations old, but it was well cared for. There was pretty landscaping around the front yard. Someone had taken their time gardening.

And no sooner had he thought that than a woman came around the side of the house, wearing gardening gloves and carrying a tray of seedlings.

It was instantly clear that she was a Wraith. She was pale—ghostly pale—her hair an iron gray length caught back in a perky ponytail atop her head. But she didn't look like any Wraith he'd met in the past. She was actually quite pretty, not gaunt-faced with prominent bones. She had high cheekbones, but other than that her face was soft and round.

She caught sight of him and froze midstep. The tray of seedlings nearly dropped from her hands, but she caught it, clutching at it as if it could somehow shield her from him.

"Wh-what do you want?" she demanded of him. "This is p-private property." She looked about furtively, casting a longing look at the front door to the house. Clearly she was judging whether she could make it past him before he could grab her.

"You don't look like any Wraith I've ever seen before," he said.

If she could have gone any whiter, she would have right then.

"Y-you know what we are?" She was incredulous. Then she was afraid. "What are you? Go away! I'll scream!"

"I am not here to hurt you. I am here to talk. To make contact between the Bodywalkers and the Wraiths. To perhaps come to some kind of truce—"

She cut him off by laughing in a hard burst.

"Bodywalkers? The Bodywalkers, like all the other Nightwalkers, want us dead and gone."

"Not true," he said. "Perhaps there has been animosity in the past, but the current regime of the Politic Bodywalkers is interested in a peaceful accord. Is there someone in charge that I should be discussing this with?"

"If you knock on that door"—she nodded to it—"you'll have a farmhouse full of Wraiths' attention. But you don't need them because all I would have to do is touch you and you'd be dead," she said.

Kamen thought about that a moment. "Then why are you so afraid of me?"

Her hands clenched around the seedlings tray.

"I'm not a-afraid of you. But you must be a very powerful Nightwalker for them to send you all alone into a den of Wraiths."

Well, at least she was smart. He had to give her that.

"I am a powerful Nightwalker, but I'm not interested in using that power unless I am forced to. I could have used it on you already but I didn't. And now we are talking. Which is all I wish to do today. Talk with Wraiths and let them know my purpose and why."

"Why?" she asked. "Why do you want peace with the Wraiths?"

He wasn't sure if he should jump into the details right away, but he did so anyway.

"Because an enormous danger, one that threatens every Nightwalker breed there is, is brewing and will attack at any time. It will start with the Bodywalkers and work its way down to the Wraiths. It's only a matter of when." He eyed her from head to toe. She was smaller than he was. Smaller by far. Petite but busty in the tank top she wore with a pair of worn denim jeans. She must be the thoughtful gardener of the house, seeing as though the knees of the jeans were stained with fresh soil. She had probably done every last bit of the landscaping. It bemused him, to think of a Wraith doing such a *normal* thing. To care about plants and the appearance of the house? It was all very . . . human.

"They won't believe you," she said, lifting her chin a little. "And you can't threaten a race of people who only need to touch you to kill you."

"I don't have time to explain it all to you. I need to speak with whoever is in charge here. I would prefer if it were the person in charge of all the Wraiths, but I'm willing to start lower down on the chain and work my way up. But I'm not going to explain it to you then repeat myself again later on. Let's start with you going into that house and bringing out whomever is in charge."

"In charge of all the Wraiths?" She dropped her jaw. "You want to speak with the Doyen?"

"Is that what you call him?"

"Yes."

"Then yes. I want to speak with your Doyen. How else am I to implement a peace accord?"

"I thought you were just trying to start with this cell. I didn't realize you were thinking you could do something like that all by yourself." She narrowed her eyes on him. "Why are you all by yourself? Seems to me a delegate for peace from the Bodywalkers would come with a group. For support or something."

"We felt it would come across less threatening if I were to come alone."

She shifted her weight from one foot to the other. Then she sucked her lower lip between her teeth and began to nibble on it.

"I'm supposed to kill any person who comes up to the house. We all are. I'm supposed to be killing you right now."

"But you're not," he observed.

"I don't want to drop my plants."

"I'll wait for you to put them down," he said politely.

"A-aren't you afraid? All I have to do is touch you." She slowly bent her knees, lowering herself so she could gently place the tray of seedlings down in the grass. She stood up straight, still nibbling on that lip. She looked far more adorable than she did threatening right then.

"Then touch me," he invited her softly.

She took off her gardening gloves, dropping them beside the seedlings, and rubbed together a pair of long fingered narrow palms.

"If I don't, I'll probably get in a lot of trouble," she explained, almost apologetically.

"I understand. Let's get on with it then, shall we?"

She came closer to him. About two steps closer.

"You'll have to get closer than that," he noted.

"What is wrong with you?" she cried then. "Why are you doing this?"

"Why *aren't* you?" he countered.

"B-because . . . because . . ." She floundered for a reason, clearly trying to avoid the true one.

"Because you've never killed anyone before?" he offered.

She looked at him in surprise. "How did you know that?"

"Call it intuition. So, you aren't going to kill me and I'm not going to kill you. That's a start anyway. How about we go inside the house next?"

Her eyes widened. "You don't want to do that. They *have* killed and they won't hesitate if you've invaded their territory. Besides, you have no idea the trouble I'd get into if I let you in the door."

"Then do you propose we just stand out here and stare at each other?" he queried.

She bit her lip again and he couldn't get over how ingenuous a gesture it was. It made her look so innocent and vulnerable. She was fortunate his intentions were good. Had they been otherwise she would be dead by now. The idea made him frown.

"I could . . . I could take you somewhere else. Somewhere they don't know me. I know! I can take you straight to the Doyen's offices! That's really where you want to go anyway, isn't it?"

*Interesting,* he thought. She would rather lead him into the heart of Wraith society than lead him into that house. He wondered at that.

"Very well. If you think that's possible then yes, I would prefer to get to the heart of the matter."

"I . . . I have to get cleaned up first. Can you meet me at the end of the drive in twenty minutes?"

He frowned. "You aren't going to try to ambush me with greater numbers are you? I'd be a fool to let you go in that house."

"Please . . . I promise it will be just me."

For some reason he believed her. He nodded and moved away down the driveway. It was a very long drive that turned through a small patch of tall corn. This wasn't part of the fields, but a hand-planted garden meant for personal use. But the corn was still high enough to hide him from the house and the house from him.

He kept his shield in place just to be safe. He didn't know what he would do if he found himself ambushed by a flock of Wraiths, but he'd prepared an escape plan. He could streak back to the ranch in New Mexico and then start all over again.

He ended up waiting thirty minutes before she came around the bend in the drive. It was worth the wait, he decided. She had let her hair down and held it back with a bejeweled headband. It looked almost like a tiara, he thought. Her hair fell in wavy curves along her shoulders and back, appearing to be much longer than he had thought when he'd seen it in the ponytail. He also realized her hair wasn't a flat iron gray. It was shades of gray, from slate to ash and all the tones in between.

Her skin was a soft powdery white and he realized she had put on eye shadow in soft pink pastels, lining her eyes in a blue liner and coloring her gray lashes black with mascara. She had put on a fair pink lipstick. She looked completely human, if a bit on the pale side.

She was wearing a maxi dress, its empire waist enunciating the bounty of her bosom and the floor-length skirt making her seem taller than she actually was. The dress was pink, apparently a favored color, in a soft fabric; cotton he assumed. It hid the curve of her waist, but the elegant dress made no secret of the fact that she was everything feminine.

She had dressed up. It bemused him. Did she do this whenever she went out? Or was it because she was taking him to the highest ranking member of their society? He assumed it was the latter, but he wouldn't be surprised if both were true. Now that she was out of her grubby jeans he could see there was a certain elegance to her. A measure of class.

She was unlike any Wraith he had come into contact with before. Then again, it had been at least a hundred years since he'd had contact with a Wraith. A lot could change in a century.

He should know. The last time he'd been alive it'd been the turn of the century, when women didn't have the vote and still wore long skirts and corsets.

"You clean up surprisingly well," he said honestly, if not thoughtfully. He wasn't one to pretty things up and be concerned with the delicate feelings of others. He was honest to a fault. If he said something it was exactly what he was thinking. Anyone could be assured of his sincerity if nothing else.

"Thank you . . . I think," she said. He couldn't tell if it was because she was wearing rouge, but she seemed to blush at the compliment. It was immediately clear she wasn't used to getting any attention. "It's a long trip to Nevada. Where's your car?"

"I do not travel with a vehicle," he said. "Where in Nevada?"

"If you don't travel by vehicle then how are we supposed to get there?" she asked with frustration.

"Why don't you let me worry about that? Do you have an address?"

"There's no address really. It's in the middle of the desert."

"A house? In the middle of a desert?"

"Well . . . sort of. More like a bunker. A very nice bunker."

"Envision the place in your mind," he said. Then more hesitantly. "I will need to touch you for this to work."

"You can touch me. I can control the deathtouch. It won't hurt you unless I mean for it to hurt you."

That was a piece of information he had not been privy to before this. It was interesting to know. With some trepidation, he reached out and touched her forehead. Her skin was baby soft and smooth, warm to the touch. For some reason he had expected her to feel cold. Cold as death. But that was his fear of her ability to kill him with a mere touch of her fingers. She could kill him right then if she wanted to. But if he had read her right, she wasn't really capable of killing him. It went against something inside her. He suspected that would change if she felt seriously threatened, but for now . . .

He closed his eyes and focused on her mind and the image she was projecting. He slipped them into the streak and they slid through the distance in a mere couple of heartbeats. They appeared at the edges of a fenced-in property in the next instant. The Wraith—he had not gleaned her name as yet—doubled over the minute they were out of the streak. She grabbed onto his arm and fought to retain whatever was in her stomach. The streak did that to an inexperienced rider. It made them nauseated beyond compare.

He was impressed when she took a deep breath and managed to keep from vomiting. She straightened and with a staggering step she looked around them. They were just inside a barbed-wire fence that rimmed a desolate bit of property. There was only one structure on the property . . . a small shed of sorts. There were sentries at the entrance to the shed and at the gate in the fence. They had avoided one, but could not avoid the others if they wished to progress. This was going to be tricky.

"What's your name?" he thought to ask when he went to address her and came up empty.

"Geneviève. But most people call me Viève."

"Viève. Well, Viève, I am open to any suggestions on how to proceed."

"This is your quest," Viève said. "If I were alone I would simple phase through the ground and into the bunker. But if I did that with you and suddenly appeared—"

"Wait . . . you can phase me through as well?"

"Well . . . yes. All I have to do is touch you."

"Those are very powerful hands," he remarked, duly impressed with the extent of her ability.

"Not as powerful as most," she muttered.

"What does that mean?" he asked.

"Nothing," Viève said quickly. "So do you want me to phase you through or not? It will be dangerous for us to show up unannounced."

"I don't see how we have much choice. Those sentries aren't about to let me pass." Kamen's mouth turned grim. "Phase us through. But you have to bring us directly to the Doyen. It's the only way."

"They will be able to see us go past them," she said. "I can phase, not turn invisible. But as long as you are phased they cannot touch you and perhaps that will give you the time you need." She bit at her lip a moment. "Please don't make me regret this," she said with imploring eyes. "If you try anything, I'll be the first to touch you."

"I don't believe that for a second," he countered. "But don't worry. I won't give you cause to touch me."

She reached out and wrapped her hand around his biceps. Her touch was delicate, more like a caress. Kamen felt something inside himself tense with interest. It surprised him. He simply didn't feel things like sensual pleasure any longer. And her touch was definitely a sensual pleasure. He didn't know why, it simply was.

Suddenly she was pulling him downward and he felt his body passing through sand and earth. Then he was passing through the cold of metal and suddenly, they dropped into a large, richly appointed room. There were thick Turkish rugs laid out over deep Brazilian cherrywood flooring. Expensive artwork hung from the terra-cotta style walls. The shining, mellowed furniture was cherry to match the floors.

"I don't know what room he would be in. But we are bound to run into someone—"

As she spoke, her voice came out a whisper, not because she was whispering but because it hardly held form in their disembodied state. No sooner did he hear the words then someone entered the room.

Now here was what he was used to a Wraith looking like. Gaunt and pale, washed of all color and, seemingly, life. There was a hollowness around his eyes. An emptiness in his pupils. He was thin and wiry. He wore a robe that draped to the floor over a pair of black slacks and a black button-down shirt, both of which came from a very expensive designer.

He spied them in the corner of the room and stilled. He shut the door and looked at them, not raising any alarm. He simply studied them for a moment.

"What can I do for you, half-breed?" he asked smoothly, his voice far richer than Kamen was expecting.

*Half-breed? Ah,* Kamen thought. That explained why she looked so different from the Wraith who stood before him now. She was not a fully bred Wraith.

"We are here to see the Doyen," she said shakily.

"And why would the Doyen want to waste his time on a little half-breed and . . . whatever this is you've brought to him." He nodded to Kamen.

"He's a Bodywalker," she said meekly. "He wishes to talk peace with the Wraiths."

He laughed, the sound filling the room. "Other Nightwalkers do not ask for peace with the Wraiths. We are hated by all and we hate them in return. If you were fully bred perhaps you would know this. You best be gone before someone touches you with death."

To Kamen's surprise, Viève grew stubborn. "No. He wants to talk peace and I . . . I believe him. Isn't it worth at least a few moments of the Doyen's time? What if he is telling the truth? What if he really does want to talk peace?"

"And what if he's using a silly little girl to get close enough to the Doyen to assassinate him?" the man countered.

"I may be a half-breed, but I am loyal. If he even thinks of hurting the Doyen, I'll be the first to deathtouch him."

She lifted her chin firmly and for a moment Kamen almost believed her.

Almost.

The other Wraith didn't believe her either. He laughed.

"All right then, convince me. Let him speak for himself before I let him through to see the Doyen."

Kamen stepped away from Viève, letting her touch fall away and becoming solid in the room. He kept his shield in place as he got closer to the other Wraith.

"There is a threat to all the Nightwalkers. A god named Apep has come to destroy all who stand in his way. Nightwalker . . . human . . . anyone. We must band together to fight this evil. It is the only way."

"Apep," the Wraith mused. "And would it surprise you to know that in the past the Wraiths have served the god known as Apep? That he has already approached us and demanded our loyalty once more?"

Cold dread sank into Kamen's bones. He had not even considered a possibility like this. A Nightwalker race working in tandem with Apep? That would be catastrophic. Especially if it kept the twelve Nightwalker races from coming together and ending the curse among them. From ending Apep's existence.

He took a step back, dropping his shield so he could reach back and take hold of Viève's hand. He then raised the shield around them both, protecting them from the Wraith if necessary.

"I would say you are fools to obey an imp god. He may need you now, but the moment he tires of you or grows angry with you he will strike you down without any thought. Everything is disposable to him and he produces carnage wherever he goes. The imp god brings only chaos with him. His goal is to create havoc for the sake of his own entertainment. How long before it is you providing that entertainment, Doyen?"

The Wraith smiled. "So, you know who I am? What gave me away?"

"Your demeanor. Your inside knowledge of the god." Kamen waved all of that off. "My offer of peace is genuine. All eleven of the other Nightwalkers wish to strike an accord with you."

"Eleven? There are only five."

"There are eleven. The other six are hidden from us by a curse. A curse that can only be broken with the Wraiths' cooperation. Please, Doyen, see reason."

"I am seeing reason. I am seeing that it is best we not get in the middle of all of this. If Apep strikes at us we will strike back. We will not serve him and we will not serve you."

"Surely you can see the danger in refusing to serve him?" Kamen said. "He will grow furious and attack you. It is better that you have the power of the joined Nightwalker races to protect you."

"And all of the Nightwalkers are banded together?"

"All but three. The Wraiths, the Mysticals, and the Phoenixes. They are next on my list. Once I convince you, I will move on to them. I thought I would start with the most difficult first."

"Wise choice. If we fail to strike this accord then it is fruitless for you to go to the others."

"No. I will go anyway. Eleven united races are better than nothing. But old testaments show that only together can we break this curse and defeat this god."

The Doyen moved farther into the room then took a seat on a chair. He crossed his legs and leaned back comfortably.

"I'll tell you what. If you get all eleven races together, then the Wraiths will join you as well. But I have no fear of this happening. The Mysticals and the Phoenixes are insular, selfish races. They will not want to join you any more than I do."

"That is your answer then? If I get all eleven races to come to the table you will join as well?"

The Doyen seemed to think on it a moment.

"You have a point, you know. When Apep hears we will not serve him he will attack us. I must do something to protect my people from this. If joining your band of merry men is the only way, then I am open to it. But it is as you say. We must all come together and I do not think you will be able to pull it off."

"I will. I will and I will prove it to you," Kamen said strongly.

"Take the half-breed with you on your journey to the Phoenix and Mystical courts. Half-breed, you will report to me when you verify all eleven races have come to the table. Do you understand? Fail me and there will be repercussions."

"I-I will not fail you," Viève said meekly.

"Good. Now get out of my house."

Viève didn't waste any time. She pushed off with her feet and before he knew it he was rushing upward . . . through metal, through earth, through sand. They popped up to where they had started and Kamen felt the need to let go of her hand and draw a full breath. Moving through earth like that was disconcerting.

Suddenly, Viève rounded on him.

"What have you gotten me into?" she spat at him.

"You have gotten yourself into this. You could have denied me at any time."

"You didn't give me much choice!"

"You had many choices. You made the right ones, Viève. This peace accord is vital to all of our species. Because of you we can begin to bring it together. We can begin to fight the god Apep. You have brought hope where before there was none. You have opened your people up to a new way of living."

Viève's mouth dropped open a little. "I've done all of that? All I did was bring you here."

"You've seen peace in me. You've imagined peace for your people. Otherwise you would never have brought me here."

Viève thought on that a moment, then she gave a reluctant nod. "I suppose that's true. If I didn't believe you none of this would have happened. And I do want there to be peace between our people. I would like to live in a world where we aren't afraid of one another. Maybe I would fit into a world like that a little better."

"You don't fit into the world now?"

She shook her head. "You heard him. I'm a half-breed. Half-breeds are not held in much esteem."

"Half-bred with what?"

"A Wraith and a human."

"And how did that work?"

"My mother was a Wraith, my father human. She says it was a moment of weakness. That she craved him at first sight and came to him as if in a dream. She says she wishes she had never done it because ever since she has been branded with her half-bred child. She would be quit of me if she thought any other house would have me. So . . . I keep my head down and try to make myself useful. The useful half-breed instead of the plain old derided half-breed."

"That is a terrible way to live," Kamen said.

"As long as I look different, it is the only way for me."

"But you have all the abilities of a Wraith. The only thing different about you is the way you look. That is all."

"It is enough," she said with a simple shrug.

# CHAPTER 4

Jasmine was lying indolently on her bed as she watched her husband, Adam, walk out of the bathroom, fresh from his shower. A cloud of steam followed him out of the bath and she smiled. He was a Water Demon, which meant that he had control over everything $H_2O$. He could create it out of thin air, he could manipulate it into any shape, he could make it rain or make it fog. Anything from mist to downpour—although not a hurricane. He would need to work in unison with a Wind Demon in order for that to happen. But he could freeze it or boil it.

That allowed him to make his shower as hot as he could possibly bear, which was pretty damn hot. It created a fair amount of steam.

He was tall and huge in comparison to most men. Much larger than his more athletically built brother Jacob, an Earth Demon. But the brothers shared the same brown—almost black—hair color and very similar, though far from identical, facial features. In Jasmine's opinion, Adam was the more handsome of the brothers, which included Kane, their youngest brother, who sported the same coloring and similar features.

Kane, a Mind Demon, and his Druid wife, Corrine, a curvaceous redhead who was sister to Jacob's wife, had arrived at the compound in Portales, New Mexico, only a week earlier. They had been sent there by Noah, the Demon King, who felt that there needed to be more of a showing of the Demon and Druid races just in case this god Apep decided to appear. Maybe next time they would have a sporting chance against him.

Jasmine sat up in bed, crossing her legs and propping herself up with straight arms behind her. She gave her husband a once-over, taking in his damp skin and the white towel slung low over his hips. She traced the provocative line of hair leading down from his navel until it was cut off by the white of the towel.

*Darn,* she thought.

"I know that look," Adam said with a grin.

"What look? I don't have a look."

"Yes, you do, my Vampire bride. You have that look that kept us in our room for the entire two weeks of our honeymoon."

She grinned. "And so what if I do?" She reached out and touched his taut belly, trailing manicured fingernails over the ridges of his abdomen. He hissed in a breath.

"Your fingers are like ice. You need to feed, my darling."

"Ugh. Don't call me that. We'll start sounding like one of those sappy little couples who are *so* in love with each other it makes everyone around them sick to their stomachs."

"But we *are* so in love with each other. It's a hard, freaky kind of love, but it's still love."

"Do you have to remind me?" she said with an eye roll. Then she looked at him and chuckled. "How did you ever convince me of this? This whole mating thing?"

"It wasn't easy," he said, bending down so he was nose to nose with her, their breath mingling. Jasmine's belly tightened with anticipation. "But I managed to get you eventually."

He leaned in and caught her mouth with his, kissing her deeply. Then he broke off with an "Ugh!"

"Ugh?" she cried indignantly.

"You're cold. You *need* to *feed*. How did you let it get so bad?"

"There aren't exactly a lot of humans floating around. I can't use the ones here . . . I'd drain them dry in a week. I have to go into town. And it's such a small town."

"Not that small. I'm sure there are plenty of buffet items to choose from."

"Female buffet only. You won't let me drink from any male except you."

"Well, as I see it you have two choices. You run into town or . . ." He bared his neck to her.

Jasmine went immediately wet with desire, her body screaming with two very different types of hunger.

"I can't keep feeding from you, even if you are a Nightwalker and can heal from it quickly. Nightwalker blood is very rich and very powerful. Too powerful. It's too easy to get addicted."

"I don't mind, as long as you are only addicted to me."

A slow smile curled her lips. "You do have a point. It's no different than being addicted to chocolate, except chocolate can make your ass fat."

"I'm not going to make your ass fat."

"Not yet . . . but give it another three or four months."

Adam frowned. "I don't like it. I don't like you being here when you're—"

"We talked about this. Like, a hundred times. I'm pregnant, not fragile."

"Yes, but . . ."

"Geez. First-time fathers are such a pain in the ass."

"First time mothers are stubborn as hell."

"I can't believe you talked me into this whole parenting thing."

"I didn't talk you into anything! We just . . . we've never exactly been careful about these things. I'm surprised it didn't happen sooner."

"I refused to allow my body to get pregnant. I'm a Vampire. I can do that."

This took him by surprise. "You can?"

"How do you think I managed to stay un-pregnant all these years?"

"So that means . . . this wasn't an accident? You planned for this?"

She bit her lip and looked unsure for the first time in a long time. "Is that all right?"

"Hell yes, it's all right! I just thought we were like Damien and Syreena, unable to conceive because . . . I don't know . . . because we're from different species."

"Damien and Syreena couldn't conceive because of a curse. But they have now, so all is right with the world."

"Any word yet? She was supposed to drop that kid a week ago."

"You know it's hard to tell about these things when it comes to cross-species reproduction. Lycanthrope pregnancies are almost as long as Demon pregnancies while Vampire pregnancies are about as long as human ones. He's a Vampire, she's a Lycanthrope, anything in between is possible. The same will happen for us."

"Us." He smiled. "Thank you. For us."

She smiled back at him. "I wouldn't want to do it with anyone else. And I haven't . . . for over five centuries. I never wanted to. Until you."

"But you won't change my mind about you being here. I don't like it. I can easily talk to Noah and have him send someone else in our stead."

"If you refuse an order from the Demon King, he's going to want to know why. And I don't want everyone to know just yet. Vampires miscarry a lot. Especially in the first few months. Once we get past the first trimester we'll tell everyone."

"You don't think you'll be showing by then?"

"There are ways of hiding that."

He snorted. "Not for you. You flaunt this tight ass and that belly chain as much as you can."

Jasmine pouted. "My belly chain. I'm going to miss it."

"So am I," he said with a little growl. "Now c'mon. Feed. It can't be good for the baby to let yourself get this cold."

"All right. I'll go into town." She pushed him back and got out of bed. "I'll see if anyone wants to come with me. I think some of us are going a little stir crazy."

"We're going to have a battle-readiness training session today. I'll whip the boredom right out of them."

"I'm sure you will. I look forward to it."

"Jas . . ." he complained.

"If I don't play with the others they'll wonder why. I'll be all right, I promise."

"You better be."

She waved at him over her shoulder and went into the bathroom to shower. The hot water helped to warm her extremities.

Vampire body heat worked like a bull's-eye. When they fed they warmed from the center of their bodies outward toward their extremities. As the day wore on, the extremities began to cool in slow degrees, the center of the body remaining warm the longest. She had not fed for the better part of two days, so she was pretty cold. Adam was right. She couldn't allow this to happen again. No one knew what caused Vampire pregnancies to fail so often, and she wasn't going to give hers any opportunity for weakness. She had been foolish. She wouldn't be again. This baby was too important to her. To them.

Once she was showered she went back into the bedroom. Her husband was now dressed, much to her disappointment. But it wouldn't be fair to ask him to make love to what amounted to a cadaver in coldness. All the passion in the world couldn't change the feeling of making love to a Popsicle.

She got dressed and gave him a quick kiss—one that lingered into the promise of something warmer later on—then left their rooms.

There were three houses in the compound. The main house had been set aside for Second Faction residents. The second house had been put aside for First Faction. The third was an overflow for Gargoyles, humans, and anyone else who needed rooms.

Technically the two factions could share space and not even know the other was there . . . except for the small detail of clothing and belongings. Those were not a part of the curse so they would end up sharing drawer space. It was a wonder the factions hadn't figured this out years ago, but it wasn't surprising. Each race of Nightwalkers seemed to have its own area of origin and they tended to stick to that area. None of the areas seemed to overlap between First and Second Factions. And since most Nightwalkers didn't associate with humans, it had never come up why two people couldn't see each other.

The Druid Bella had found the prophecy about the twelve races of Nightwalkers written in ancient Aramaic by human hands, which was why others had been able to read the scroll as well. If it had been written by anyone affected by the curse, there was a good chance they would never have found it at all.

Strange that human writings had found their way into the great Demon and Druid library. Stranger still that humans were accurately prophesizing about Nightwalkers. Bella had put it down to fate and the unexplainable . . . or an act of some very mischievous gods. Who knew why? It was what it was. And it was for the better. The writings Kamen had found yesterday had been written in ancient Egyptian. Also, presumably, by human hands. A bit of luck, that. Again, how had such works found their way into the Bodywalker archives? How had humans known?

But those were just two lines of writing in vast amounts of scrolls and literature. And it was all they had found. Now they were acting on just these two small references. What other choice did they have?

Jasmine went into the kitchen, the hub of the household, and found Corrine and Bella chatting over their morning coffee. Her sisters-in-law. She had never been the sorority type, having always been a loner with the exception of Damien, the Vampire Prince. They had moved through the centuries together for as long as she could remember.

But she found she liked these two women. They could be a little giggly and cute every once in a while, but Jasmine was willing to forgive that. She brushed a hand over her belly, her secret burning at her conscience. She probably ought to have at least shared the news with her family members, but she had to admit she was too afraid to. She had never been a superstitious person, but she didn't want to do anything to jinx herself.

"Hey," she greeted them, going for the coffeemaker. Hot coffee ought to warm her up at least a little bit. But the fact was the moon was high, she had risen late, and she was hungry. What were the odds she would find someone wandering around the streets of Portales in the middle of the night? She was used to living in or near cities where people were up at all hours. This small town living was the pits when it came to getting a decent meal.

"I'm headed into town, anyone want to come?" Jasmine said.

"Feeling peckish?" Bella asked knowingly.

"A touch," Jasmine said with a grin. "Has anyone else arrived from our faction? Noah and Damien and Siena, our lovely Lycanthrope Queen, keep sending warm and not so warm bodies," she said.

"They're doing what leaders should be doing in a case like this. The Mistrals don't have a leader, but they've sent the Siren Windsong and her protégée Lyric to represent them. Hopefully their ability to stun with the sound of their voices will come in handy in a pitched battle. You can bet Apep will bring all those Templars with him and who knows who else. Maybe even humans. God, what will we do then? What do we do to misguided and stupid humans? Kill them?" Bella shuddered. "I hope not."

"Let's worry about that when the time comes," Corrine said.

"Let's not. We need a game plan for all instances of battle," Jasmine said. "We need to know exactly what we are going to do and who we are going to do it to. Humans can be dangerous too you know. What if they're necromancers? Humans using magic can be very deadly."

Corrine and Bella nodded grimly. They knew that all too well. Necromancers could summon a Demon using its true Demon name and this gave them power over them. Those Demons then became corrupted and could be used to fight against their own brethren.

"I hope there are no necromancers. I hate those guys," Corrine said with a little shudder. "I don't think I should even be here. My ability is to find mates for other Nightwalkers. I'm basically useless."

"But Kane is not and you weren't about to let him come here alone. As a Mind Demon he has great mental powers and can teleport as well. That might come in very handy in a fight. Your job is to get to safety the minute you see the poo hit the fan," Bella said.

"Yeah, I know. I'm supposed to corral all the humans and get us the frick out of Dodge. That's my job."

"I think the humans already know to get the frick out of Dodge, but they're going to need organization and that's a knack you possess in spades," Bella complimented her sister.

"Gee thanks. So glad I could be useful," Corrine said dryly.

"Hey, everyone has a job. There are no small parts here," Jasmine said. "Now who's coming to town with me?"

"I'll go. I need to hit Walmart for some stuff," Bella said. "We're sending the kids to their siddahs. It's too dangerous for them here. I should never have brought them. But I couldn't bear the idea of being separated from my babies for such a long time."

Siddahs were Demon foster parents. When a Demon child reached a certain age and their power kicked in, Demons believed someone other than a parent should take over their care and training. Technically, Bella's eldest child, Leah, should have already been with her siddah. Her power had been apparent ever since she was a small child. But Bella wasn't ready to send her away. She and Jacob had agreed they would let her go on her sixteenth birthday. That was still a ways off, so Bella didn't have to start fretting over it yet.

But their siddahs were their safest bet for the time being. That meant sending Leah to the Russian court of the Lycanthrope Queen Siena, who was married to Leah's male siddah, the Wind Demon Elijah. Leah's female siddah was Legna, Noah's sister and the Demon ambassador to the Lycanthrope court, so she was also in Russia.

Her son would be going to the court of the Demon King. Noah and his queen, Kestra, were the young boy's siddahs. Kane would teleport the children later that night. No doubt after many tearful goodbyes. But it was for the best. They suspected the only reason Apep had not attacked them so far was because of his pregnancy. For all they knew, he'd already given birth and it was only a matter of time until the god got his bearings and came after them with guns blazing.

The thought pressed a sense of urgency onto Bella. She got up and abandoned her cup of coffee.

"Come on. The kids are almost all packed. I just need a few things. I want them out of here within the next couple of hours."

"All right. Let's go!" Jasmine levitated off the floor.

"Uh, Jas . . . we can't fly, remember? We have to take a car."

"Right." Jasmine frowned with consternation. "I keep forgetting. Fine then, we'll drive. Can we take the Cobra though? I want to drive a cool car."

"Yes, you can drive the Cobra," Bella said with an eye roll.

She snatched the appropriate keys off the Peg-Board by the kitchen door.

# CHAPTER 5

Viève couldn't believe what she had gotten herself into. Her mother had always told her she was nothing but trouble—that she was so stupid she wouldn't know what to do in any situation, that she was useless to the Wraith race.

Now she didn't know if all of that had just come true, or if she'd just proved all of that to be false.

She knew she wasn't stupid. She was actually well read. But would a smart person have gotten mixed up in this mess? And she wasn't useless; she tended the grounds and the garden with precision and grit. But she did get into a lot of trouble and this latest screwup was just one example.

If it *was* a screwup. This man . . . this Bodywalker . . . was telling her she was practically the savior of her whole race. She didn't know if she believed that much. Certainly not that much. But if this did work out, she would have been useful. And that was all she had ever striven to be.

Useful.

"I don't even know your name," she said softly.

He looked sheepish. He had asked for hers but had not given his in return and she hadn't thought to ask until right then.

"Kamenwati. Kamen is fine."

"Kamen. Well, Kamen, what do we do now? It seems you're kind of stuck with me. Sorry about that."

"Don't be sorry. I'm not."

"Surely you'd be better off doing this without a Wraith by your side? I mean, one look at me and everyone's going to go running. They'll never give you a chance. I think that's what the Doyen is counting on."

"Perhaps," Kamen said. "But we will foil that plan easily. You do not look like a Wraith right now. You look like a pale female human with gray hair. You don't look like what I expect when I see a Wraith."

"I know," she said with a frown. She had been called human so many times it was like an epithet. The curse of her existence. If only she had looked more like a Wraith, her life would have been very different.

"This is a good thing," he said intently, turning her to face him. He took the side of her jaw in his hand and tipped her head back. She found herself looking up into the brightest blue eyes she'd ever seen. They seemed . . . wise. Aged. Learned of the world dozens of times over. Which, if he was a Bodywalker, she supposed he was. He had black hair, cut crisply at the nape and the edges of his face. He was handsome in the way of humans, she supposed. He reminded her of one of those actors, only without the smile lines creasing his face. She got the feeling he did not smile often at all, because of that and because of his general demeanor.

It was a shame. With such a handsome face, he probably had a very attractive smile.

"You are very fair and quite beautiful. No one will be running from you in fear."

To a Wraith that should have been an insult. They lived to put fear into others. They sometimes entertained themselves by haunting humans, scaring the hell out of them. But mostly they just wanted to be considered the most frightening Nightwalkers around. The bad asses that no one should mess with.

That was one of the reasons she was so surprised by the Doyen's calm demeanor and even calmer negotiation. Wraiths were hotheaded. They reacted before they thought. It was one of the reasons why doing what he had done had made her really respect Kamen. For his bravery . . . or maybe his recklessness. She wasn't sure which one to pay homage to just yet.

But his touch on her face was nice, she thought. No one ever touched her. They weren't a touchy-feely race as a whole, except when it came to the deathtouch. But perhaps that was why they never touched. One bad mood and bam . . . dead.

Because the deathtouch worked on Wraiths just as well as it worked on all the other Nightwalker breeds. The only difference was a Wraith could avoid it by phasing his body, denying the ability to touch. But if a Wraith was taken by surprise in his solid form . . .

She shivered a little at the morbid thought.

"Are you cold?" he asked her thoughtfully. She wasn't used to such kindness. She shook her head, the action making her jaw brush against the hand cupping it. The inadvertent caress gave her little goose bumps down the side of her neck.

"I'm just not used to being touched," she admitted.

He immediately dropped his hand, making her feel instantly bereft. "I'm sorry. That was wrong of me."

"No! I liked it!" she exclaimed. Then she realized what she had said and promptly blushed. "I meant to say, it wasn't bothering me."

He frowned a little as he studied her. "Just the same, I will not touch you again without your permission."

"That's kind of a silly statement," she declared.

"How so?"

"Because on this little journey I take it we are going to have to touch for travel and touch for protection and touch for this and touch for that. Consider permission granted from now on," she said with a definitive nod.

"Very well," he said, again that thought-filled frown marring his mouth. She wondered why he frowned so much. Yes, they were in a serious situation, but surely one little smile . . . what would that hurt?

She smiled at him, hoping he would smile back. "Shall we get going then? Before those sentries catch sight of us?"

His face remained impassive. "Yes, of course. But that means streaking again."

She blanched. "Oh. Well. I guess it can't be avoided. Just remind me not to eat right before we go somewhere. So where are we going?"

"Somewhere neutral and safe for the moment. I have to cast a spell in order to locate the Phoenixes. I can find the ruler of the Mysticals quite easily if I can get in touch with a certain Djynn I know."

"So you're saying that the Djynn and the Night Angels are already on your side? And these six other Nightwalkers?"

"I am saying exactly that."

"What are the other six like?" she asked.

"Well, as far as I can tell, they are peaceful, intelligent, and politically sound."

"High praise coming from you, I guess."

"What do you mean by that?"

"I mean you strike me as the sort who doesn't give praise too often."

"I suppose not," he agreed. "I give it when and where it is deserved." He took her measure. "For instance, I think you should know I consider you to be a very brave young woman."

She snorted a laugh. "I'm fifty-two. I'm hardly young."

"You are young by my standards. You look as though you are twenty at most. Forgive me if I insulted you."

"Nah. All women like to hear that they look young." She smiled at him a little uncertainly, again hoping he would smile back.

He did not.

"You deflect compliments quite adroitly," he said in a musing tone.

She felt a flush creep up her neck and burn into her cheeks. Blushing. Another sign of her humanity. Another thing that set her apart from other Wraiths.

"We should get going," she said, turning her back to him.

He was silent a moment and she couldn't see his expression with her back to him, but after a long moment he said, "Very well. Give me your hand."

She held her hand out, waiting for him to grab it.

"Turn and face me and put your hand in mine," he said, enunciating the request softly and slowly.

She turned and faced him, her whole being focused on not flushing under his regard of her. He held out his hand and waited.

Why couldn't he just take her hand and go from there? Why was he making such a production out of it?

She sighed and slid her hand into his. His fingers immediately tightened around hers and she braced herself for the nauseating flight into the streak. But instead of that he lifted her hand to his lips and brushed them against her knuckles in a whispery kiss. She blushed then, straight to the roots of her hair.

"I like that," he said softly.

"Like what?" she asked dazedly.

"The way you blush. It brings color to your cheeks. A very pretty color."

His words broke the spell for her. She went to pull away, but to her consternation he held tight.

"What's wrong with what I just said?" he asked her.

"Nothing. Can we go please?"

"Not until you tell me what's wrong. Why can't you accept a simple compliment?"

"It's not simple," she said irritably. "Wraiths aren't supposed to blush. They're not able to. It's just another way I'm different than the rest of them."

He looked down into her eyes very intently and said, "Sometimes different is better."

"Yeah? Well, tell that to my family," she said wryly.

"There is more to life than pleasing family," he said.

"Not to my life," she said.

"Maybe before. But now all of that has changed. And, I think, it's for the best."

Then he whipped them into the streak.

Kamen didn't know what had possessed him to act the way he had before the streak. To kiss her hand? To pay her compliments? But it had really bothered him that she thought so little of herself. Thought herself undeserving. He didn't know why it should bother him, but it did. They came out of the streak and into his room at the New Mexico compound. He quickly grabbed for a trash can and held it out to her in case she needed it. But once again she impressed him with her ability to ride out the nausea of the streak. Soon she would get used to it, but for now it would continue to bother her.

While she composed herself he walked into the sitting room adjacent to his bedroom. All of the furniture had been pushed back earlier and the components of a location spell had been laid out. He had already used them once to locate the Wraiths. Now he would do it again to locate the Phoenixes. The Mysticals he would save for last since he deemed the Empress the easiest to make contact with.

He had already created an image of a phoenix which he would center the spell around. It was not an image of an actual Phoenix, but a representation of the bird most commonly associated with the term.

He lit a candle and seated himself in the center of the circle he'd drawn out using the ash of an apple tree. There were three covered jars seated at three of the four compass points and he was seated at the fourth. The south position. He took the lit rosemary candle and touched it to each jar and then to himself, rubbing a bit of wax off each time. Then he settled the candle into its holder once more. He was aware of Viève entering the room and watching him, but to her credit, she didn't say anything. She let him focus on the task at hand.

It was a simple spell overall. A few common components, herbs and such. But the price that was paid for the information was anything but simple. As he spoke the words of the spell pain began to lance through him. He began to feel as though he were being pulled apart in four directions, north, east, south, and west. He ground his teeth together to keep from shouting out. He didn't want to disturb his guest with the details of the spell. She was skittish enough as it was.

But he was hiding nothing from Viève. She could see he was in pain however much he tried to hide it. She twisted her hands together anxiously, wanting to make him stop. It wasn't worth it, she kept thinking. And then she would remember what was at stake and understood why he was willing to go through the pain. It was so strange, she thought. She had never known such a selfless individual before. Wraiths were notoriously selfish, always wanting to know what was in it for them. The Doyen's behavior exemplified that. He would only help as long as there was something to be gained for himself and the Wraith race. It didn't matter what the consequences were to anyone else if he refused. All that mattered to him was what way would benefit him the most.

Yet here was this man . . . a man who had taken nothing for himself and strove with all he had to give, searching for answers and solutions to the danger he said was coming.

But how did she know it was true? How did she know he wasn't simply blowing the seriousness of the situation out of proportion?

Well, the Doyen's response for one. He would never have entertained Kamen's presence if there wasn't something serious involved. And he would never have sent her with him, for all she was a half-breed. She had this much to say about the Wraiths, they protected their own—no matter how diluted their blood.

No. The Doyen was worried. He wanted to be left alone, left out of the whole business entirely. That would be the safe thing to do . . . only he had come to realize there would be no neutral ground in this battle. The Wraiths would be the deciding factor and it would all come down to which side they chose.

Kamen realized this, she was aware. He understood that sacrifices would have to be made, and he was willing to make them. So if he was willing, then she had to be willing too. And she *would* be willing. No matter how much it all frightened her, she would give no less than he did.

She didn't know why exactly. It wasn't as though the Wraiths had ever been kind to her or made her feel welcome. But she wouldn't wish harm on anyone. If something she did could protect her mother and those of her cell, well she owed them that much for giving her a place to live, didn't she? She may not have been welcome, but she had been fed and clothed and housed in safety and relative comfort all these years.

The spell ended with a sudden whoosh of air punching out from the center of the circle, blowing out the candle. Kamen sagged for a moment, then picked himself up, getting to his feet with only the slightest hint of unsteadiness. He straightened and tugged on the sleeves of his button-down shirt, organizing himself in appearance as well as mentally and physically.

"Did it work?" Viève asked anxiously.

"It worked. There is a large group of Phoenixes in Brazil, in an area just west of the Rio Braco do Potinga. I can streak us there in a matter of minutes."

He took a step toward her and suddenly pitched forward. She hastily crossed into the circle and thrust her body up beneath his arm and against his side to support him.

"Not now you aren't! You need to rest first!"

"There isn't time," he said, giving in a little and leaning into her as she brought him to a couch nearby. He dropped onto it and sighed with relief. He was frustrated that he had shown and given in to weakness. He meant it, there wasn't time for weakness. Enough time had been wasted as it was. Soon that monster would give birth, regain his strength, and then he would come gunning for the one thing that could potentially stop him in his tracks. The one thing that might somehow find a way to send him back to the hell that had birthed him.

The Nightwalkers.

They couldn't allow his victory. They had a responsibility to see to it that Apep was driven back to that hell. If they didn't succeed, the imp god would cut a swath through the earth and the human race unlike anything ever seen before.

On top of that was the wild card. The infant that would be born to the god. Would it mature at the rate of a normal infant or would it be born fully fledged as in myths of old? It may have a Nightwalker father, but with a god as its mother anything was possible.

They had to stop it. If they could get to Apep before he gave birth, presumably in a weakened state, then they might have a chance.

That is presuming, he was weakened. They were making this assumption based on the fact that he hadn't attacked them in all these months, that perhaps he was conserving his strength or protecting his weak underbelly.

It was a sign of weakness they couldn't ignore. It had taken too many months to gather the two factions of Nightwalkers together into one place and still they weren't complete. But soon they would be. He would see to it that they were.

"I'm all right," he insisted after a moment of catching his breath. He went to push up but it was a testament to his weakened state that her delicate hands on his shoulders kept him firmly seated.

"You will take a moment and rest," she commanded him. Then she dropped to her knees between his feet and looked at him imploringly. "Another hour or two won't make that much of a difference."

"You can't know that," he said. He explained his theories on why the god had not attacked them again like it had all those months ago. Then he explained just how powerful that attack had been, how Apep had swatted at them as easily as one would swat a fly. Only luck had saved them that time. They would not be so lucky again. In the next confrontation lives would be lost.

"Here's what I do know," she said softly. "We're going to do this. We're going to get all these Nightwalkers together and convince the Wraiths it's the only way. But we're going to do it when you're up to it and not a moment sooner. I won't let you." She set her chin stubbornly, just so he could see how serious she was.

And for some reason it made him laugh.

He was not a man prone to finding or expressing humor. He rarely cracked a smile. There was really nothing worth smiling about anymore. But she made him chuckle softly and it felt good. It felt so good to leave the seriousness of the situation behind for that brief collection of seconds.

She smiled at the sound of his laugh. She looked infinitely pleased with herself. She should be, he thought. It was quite an achievement.

"So since you have me trapped here," he said, reaching out to touch her face along its pronounced cheekbone. "Tell me something about yourself." Why was it, he wondered, that he couldn't seem to keep himself from touching her. And, like the laugh, it felt good.

"There's nothing to tell. You already know everything about me there is to know."

"Tell me about the gardening," he pressed.

A special sort of light entered her eyes. "Oh, I love gardening," she breathed. "Making things live, nurturing them, bringing them back from sickness, making everything look so pretty. And the food . . . it's the best thing in the world to eat something you've grown from a little seed yourself. My favorites are the strawberries and the corn. A strawberry patch hides the berries until you push the leaves aside and find these little red gems and they're so sweet. And corn grows so high and strong and its treasure is hidden too until you shuck it and expose it."

"So you like to be surprised. You know it's going to be there, but it still surprises you to see it every time." Kamen felt a smile twitching at his lips. She had such an innocence about her. But he wouldn't call her naïve. The world she circulated in had been too hard on her for her to be naïve.

"Yes. Exactly like that. What about you? What do you do that gives you pleasure?"

"Nothing," he said. And sadly, it was the truth. He had only one hobby: researching and practicing new spells. But that was more a calling than a hobby. "I do a lot of reading, but it's not like gardening is for you."

"Why not? Aren't there ever any surprises when you read?"

Actually, there were. Often he would come across a little gem or come to an understanding he wasn't expecting.

"There are some," he admitted.

"And does reading give you any pleasure?"

"It gives me satisfaction," he said. "But I have lost the joy I used to find in it. Ever since . . ." Ever since he'd used a spell that had accidentally brought an imp god to their world. "It's been a long time and I don't expect it to change any time soon."

"That's so sad," she said softly, reaching to touch one of her pale hands to his face, her fingers caressing him along his jaw. "Maybe one day you will be able to change that."

"Perhaps," he said softly. But he doubted it. He couldn't explain to her why. He didn't want to see the change that would come over her once she realized he was to blame for all of this.

There was an extreme intimacy to the moment though. He was touching her face and she was touching his. He felt connected to her for that instant, grounded. For those brief moments he felt like he belonged somewhere.

It was a feeling he wanted to hold on to for all he was worth. A feeling he had not experienced in so long. Certainly not in this lifetime. He had left the pleasures of the flesh and soul behind him in his last lifetime on this planet. Since his resurrection into this body he had known cerebral pleasure, but never physical.

For just a moment, he wanted to change that. He didn't know why, couldn't explain the strange impulse interrupting his well-ordered existence, but he felt the overwhelming urge to kiss her.

Kamen surged forward and caught her mouth with his. He entered it analytically at first, trying to decipher the urge and the feelings that came with it, but his analytical mind was slammed shut as the pure pleasure of the sensation of her lips against his overwhelmed him. Her mouth was soft, compliant. Welcoming. She let him kiss her, let him deepen the kiss as it urged him to do. She tasted of those strawberries she so loved, and smelled just as sweet. Her skin was like cream beneath his fingertips as he cradled her face in his hand. Had he been more like himself he would have stopped, pulled back, apologized for whatever it was that had come over him . . . but he did none of those things. Instead, he touched his tongue to her lips and begged entrance to the warmth of her mouth. She drew a breath and then released it on a sigh as she parted her lips and bade him to enter.

Kamen drew her up tight into the sudden heat that boiled into the kiss. His tongue tangled with hers, and his heartbeat tripled in cadence. His usually smooth and refined and logical aura was decimated by a sudden need to feel her all over his body. To that end his arms wrapped around her and he pulled her in tight against him, her breasts crushed against his chest. She was still on her knees before him, his legs bracketing her body as he sat up to the edge of the couch so he could feel her against himself more thoroughly.

He broke from the kiss, panting hard for breath as he searched her face for answers to his own behavior. All he learned was that she was beautiful and tempting and he wanted more of her.

The desire shocked him to his core, jolting him into reality. And the reality was that he did not deserve her. He did not deserve the pleasure he was feeling with her. All he deserved was the cold, lonely existence he had known for months now.

He pulled away from her, standing up and putting distance between them. His breathing was ragged and harsh, and his body still hummed with the feel of her against him. She had been so willing. Would she still be if she knew the truth about him?

He didn't fool himself about that. One day she would learn the truth, and on that day she would no longer look at him the way she was looking at him right then. With soft longing. With desire and passion.

Kamen ran a hand over his face and turned his back to her. He couldn't bear looking into those warm, forgiving eyes.

"Kamen . . . did I do something wrong?" she asked. She had gotten to her feet and when he looked at her he saw honest puzzlement and distress on her face. She thought this was her fault? No. He would not have that.

"No. It has nothing to do with you. I . . . I simply do not partake of these kinds of pleasures. I am sorry. I don't know what came over me."

"Why don't you take part in pleasures like this?" she asked with honest curiosity. "What's wrong with it? Is it because I am a Wraith? I would understand if it was. Wraiths are not known for their sexual attractiveness."

"Enough!" he barked, startling her. "I said it has nothing to do with you and I meant it. You are not the problem here."

"Then what is the problem?" she wanted to know.

"It is too complex a thing to explain and we don't have time. I am feeling better now and we should move on to our next target."

Viève licked her lips, the flavor of him, a hot, heady taste on her tongue, still lingered. She had not expected his kiss, but it did not follow that it was unwelcome. In fact, it was the first time anyone had touched her with such a passionate need. Wraiths were so cold and she had always wanted more from them than they were able to give. It had been a failing of her human half, she believed. Had she been fully bred she wouldn't have wanted anything more than what she had.

But as it stood, she had always craved more—like what she had just received from Kamen. For the first time she had felt whole and wanted. It had to be the most glorious feeling she had ever known. She hadn't wanted it to end after so brief a knowing.

She chased after him, even as she told herself she shouldn't. But she had felt something more in his touch and his caress. She had felt kinship . . . felt someone who was seeking just as desperately as she was for a place to be wanted and accepted.

She reached out and touched him, longing for more contact, but he jerked away from her. It was enough to quiet her longings. He said it wasn't her, but how could it be anything else? She wasn't good enough. She wasn't wanted.

She backed away from him and fought a sudden surge of tears. She shouldn't cry. Wraiths did not cry. A full-bred Wraith didn't even have tear ducts. But she did, and she had often fought the urge to give in to tears. The only thing that had kept her from it was the idea of facing the ridicule that would come. Ridicule for her failings and weaknesses as a half-breed.

"Very well," she said hoarsely. "You are right. We should go if you are up to it. There is no time to waste on trivial mistakes."

Kamen turned to face her. He realized then that she didn't believe him when he said it wasn't her fault he had pulled away. The only way he could convince her would be to tell her the truth, but . . . he was quickly becoming a coward as far as that was concerned. He had readily accepted the fault and blame he deserved for his actions to date, but for some reason it was different with her. He didn't want her to look at him with the same judgmental eyes everyone else did.

He reached for her then, curling his hands around her upper arms and drawing her in close to his body. A part of him sighed with relief at the simple contact with her warmth and softness. But he struggled to rein that in.

"Viève . . . sweet little Viève . . . you deserve better than me," he said softly as he looked down into her dove gray eyes.

"That's so funny. I was thinking the same thing . . . that you deserve better than me," she said.

"No. Do not think that. I am a man of no passion. Your passion, as divine as it is, is wasted on a man like me."

"For a man with no passion, you certainly acted with intense passion a little while ago."

"Perhaps it was your beauty that inspired it," he said.

She snorted out a laugh. "I highly doubt that! I am not the sort of woman who inspires great feeling in others. I am a Wraith. Wraiths have no feelings."

"You are a half-breed, and you very much have feelings. I have seen them for myself."

"Well there's no need to throw it in my face!" she cried suddenly. Damn those tears; they were going to come anyway. Then what would he think of her?

"Viève . . ." His tone softened as he cupped her face in both hands and tipped her head back. He made certain there was complete eye contact so she would know and feel his sincerity. "I do not care if you are a half-breed. You are Wraith enough to get this job done and that is all that matters. And when it comes to the rest . . . you are more than woman enough to satisfy even the rusted over desires of an undeserving man." He dropped his head and gently kissed her full and inviting mouth. It was just a gesture of comfort, of reassurance, but he craved more instantly and he had to fight back that powerful hunger. He pulled away and met her eyes again. "And trust me when I say I am an undeserving man. You deserve far better than me."

Viève licked her lips and suddenly jumped in with both feet, risking her fragile ego. "But I don't want better. I want you."

That hunger ramped up to full on craving for Kamen. He didn't understand it, didn't understand why it was so strong. What was it about this woman that made him feel so alive? It was a wickedly tempting sensation.

"Believe me," he whispered a fraction of an inch away from her mouth, "there is no one I want more than you."

"But then why. . . ?"

"It's simply the way it must be."

She realized she was going to have to accept that . . . for now. But the feeling of inadequacy had flown away on rapid wings. He wanted her. He had said so himself. But something was making him feel like he didn't deserve to feel good. She would have to discover what it was . . . why he wanted to punish himself rather than pleasure himself. If she did that then maybe . . . maybe there could be more than just that wildly wonderful kiss.

"We should go," she said softly.

He let go of her face and reached down to take her hands in his. With a nod he frowned a little and said, "Brace yourself. The longer the streak the more unsettling it becomes."

"Luckily I haven't eaten anything today," she quipped, hoping to make him smile.

He did not. Instead he closed his eyes and they were swept into the streak.

# CHAPTER 6

Apep was heavily pregnant. He was uncomfortable, cranky, and craving pizza with an alarming intensity. He wanted this to be over with already. He had things to do, people to conquer and he couldn't do any of that while bogged down with the weight of a baby.

Whose idea had this been anyway? Had it been his? What kind of foolish logic had that been? This baby was sucking away half of his godly power. It was keeping him from making his presence known in the world. He needed to be at full strength if he was going to manipulate the world of man.

And before he did that he had to destroy the only beings on earth who could potentially stop him.

The Nightwalkers.

True, the curse kept them from joining forces. And true, the Wraiths were on his side and that would keep them from being able to break the curse, but his reception with the Wraith Doyen had been lukewarm at best and nothing like the instant adulation he had expected. But he couldn't demonstrate his power and all the reasons why the Wraiths should fall on their knees with adulation and fear.

Not like this.

Damn it all anyway, when would this thing be over with? When he had decided to procreate, to use the uterus of the Bodywalker female he had inhabited in this incarnation, he had thought it would be fun and in his best interest to create a son who would share in his power. A god and his heir. What could be more worthy of adulation?

But now he was thinking about what it would mean to share that adulation. He didn't want his son to get all of the attention. After all, he would only be a demi-god. His father was a powerful Night Angel it was true, but still he was little better than a human. Just like this body he now possessed.

He would simply have to set some rules. Make certain the people understood who was more deserving of their attention. He would let his son have a little attention of his own, but in the end Apep would garner most of it. And the best way to do that was through fear. He would make them fear him and then he would make them adore him.

After he got rid of this thing holding him down!

He tried using his godly power to hasten the birth but found that it would not work. The child would come only when it wanted to and for some reason there was nothing he could do to change that.

It was completely unfair. Perhaps he could turn to human medical methods? They could surely induce labor. But that carried risks with it. He had to be sure the baby was fully formed. He would not give birth to a fragile, weakling child. What would the people think of him if he did that? No, he must produce a fat, healthy infant to show to the world. It would be yet another way to display his own magnificence.

"Asutept!" Apep whined. "Get me some pizza! And not that generic delivery kind! I want a good pizza . . . with extra cheese and pepperoni!"

"Yes, mistress, whatever you desire."

Mistress. These fools were still laboring under the delusion that he was Odjit, the female Bodywalker in charge of the Templar clique. Well, once he was free of the burden of the child he would change all of that. For now it served him best to let them think he was this female Nightwalker. It had given him ready-made followers. The Templar sect was devoted to this woman, and so they were devoted to him. Eventually they would know the truth and it would be an easy transition. After all, they had been serving him already for the better part of a year.

Apep sat back in his bed, elevating his swollen feet. *Soon,* he thought. Soon everything would change. Soon he would let his power be known. His power and the power of his scion would be enough to rule the world. And there would be no one to stop him.

He would see to that.

After the nausea of traveling so fast wore off, Viève found herself in the damp, humid wilds of a Brazilian rain forest. The first thing that struck her was the noise. There was a cacophony of sounds: the sound of buzzing insects, the sound of a rushing river, the sound of living things swinging about in the canopy and sliding into the water. Something slithered past her feet and with a squeal she practically jumped up into Kamen's arms. For the second time that night, she made him chuckle.

"You know you can phase and nothing can touch you, right?" he said.

"Oh. Right. I forgot." But she didn't want to phase as long as she could be pressed up against him like this. He felt so strong and he was so self-assured. He knew what he was doing, where he was going, and he did it all with single-minded purpose. There was something inherently attractive about that. Call her a fool for feeling that way, but she felt it just the same.

And she realized that now that she'd had a small part of him, he could not take it back from her. He could not color her experience with him, however much he might have rejected her afterward. She had felt something in those fleeting moments of their kiss and she was sure he had felt something too.

Maybe that made her a fool.

The air was hot, heavy, and sultry—the dampness settling immediately on her dry skin. But as she drew in a breath she thought she had never smelled anything so . . . so alive in her life. There had to be hundreds of varieties of plants just within the quick sweep of her eyes. This was nature's landscaping and it was beautiful.

"We have company," he said, looking up at the canopy.

There, flying between the branches of the soaring trees were flame colored birds, their red and orange feathers obvious in the darkness.

"Phoenixes?" she whispered.

"That would be my guess. But I imagine they aren't interested in making the first move."

Kamen cast a spell and suddenly they began to levitate off the ground. With a squeak of surprise, she wrapped herself tightly around him as they went up into the canopy, leaving the ground far below. She could have phased right then, since she was just as capable of flying in phased form as he was in this form. But, again, she didn't want to let go of him.

The feel of him was fast becoming an addiction. And was it any wonder? He was strong and vital and everything she wasn't. Of course she would be attracted to that.

They reached the arm of a tree and he put his hands around her waist and hoisted her up onto it. Her feet were left dangling over what felt like hundreds of feet of air.

Then he turned into the canopy and shouted out, "The Bodywalker court wishes to address the Phoenix court on a matter of extreme urgency."

At the sound of his voice things were startled into movement all around her. There was the flutter of wings and the rustle of vines and leaves. The humming sounds of the rain forest paused briefly, but picked up again after only a few moments of quiet.

"Now what do we do?" she asked.

"We wait," he said. "We wait for them to realize we aren't going anywhere until we get the meeting we are looking for."

"But that could be hours. Days even." She swatted at a mosquito on her neck.

"This is true. If they don't respond immediately I will see about making things more comfortable for us."

"How will you do that?" She swatted again.

"Well, for one I can keep the insects away." He mumbled something in a hushed tone and suddenly a green light limned her entire body, hugging her skin perfectly. It left her looking like a pale, glowing emerald, but it was keeping the insects off her. She could feel the difference immediately and when a mosquito landed, it appeared to alight a full inch away from her skin. Frustrated, it flew away.

"They won't even know you're here in another moment. As soon as your scent drifts away."

"My scent?"

"You smell sweet like strawberries. That would attract anything." His voice dropped an octave as he looked at her intensely for a long moment. She felt her heart flutter in her chest under his penetrating regard.

"Does it attract you?" she blurted out, before she could think better of it.

His mouth tightened into a grim sort of line. "More than you know," he said, though he did not look happy about the admission.

Well, it was something at least. He was attracted to her. He simply didn't think he had any right to be. It was a curious reaction. What was it, she wondered, that held him back so tightly? What was it that made him feel so undeserving, even of someone as insignificant as she was?

"Why . . ." She broke off. Perhaps it was best not to press the matter. He had not grown angry with her thus far, but it was only a matter of time. She always made everyone angry eventually. They lost patience with her or she earned their contempt in one fashion or another. She didn't want to earn his contempt. "Do you think they'll answer you soon?" she asked instead of asking him why he was so hard on himself or why he didn't allow himself even the smallest of comforts or pleasures. He didn't even allow himself the pleasure of a hobby. There had to be a reason why.

"I doubt they will answer right away." He moved to sit beside her on the tree branch. He looked around for a moment and took in a deep breath. "This is a beautiful place. I can see the appeal."

"But there's no one here. It's so isolated."

"They have each other. Perhaps that is all they need."

"Perhaps," she said. She could understand that. The Wraiths were a very insular society. They lived in cells, each house containing multiple generations from the same family. It was only at the Kinua, the gatherings of the cells, that they were exposed to other Wraiths. Where they could find mates if they so desired. Even so, Wraiths did not get married and did not move into the family houses of other Wraiths. Not usually. They merely mated if they wished to and got pregnant, the females keeping the child in their houses and freeing the males of all responsibility toward that child. It was a cold transaction, just like all the other transactions between Wraiths. If not for their sex drive there would be no new generations of Wraiths. But while the Wraiths had no real emotions to speak of, they did have an intense sex drive. They were not sexually attractive, did nothing to attract a mate, but they did want to rut and rut hard when the mood fell on them.

"If they only have each other, I imagine they don't have things like half-breeds in their society."

"Perhaps. There could be indigenous tribes around here that might attract their attention."

"I hadn't thought of that."

He paused a beat. "What is so bad about being a half-breed?" he asked gently, knowing it was a touchy subject.

She winced. "It's a testament to the weakness of the mother. A living testament. It's worn like a scarlet *A* on the chest."

"The mother? What about half-breed children sired by the father?"

"We don't have those. In our society the mother rears the child. If a male strays from his race . . . well, he leaves the product of it behind if there is any. Just like they would with a Wraith female."

"But then that's leaving a human woman with the rearing of a Nightwalker child. A child that can't go out in daylight."

"Oh, we can go out in daylight. We just can't phase in daylight. It turns us solid. Takes away all of our preternatural abilities. Makes us . . . in a word . . . human."

"But surely they look different."

"You mean like me? I'm sure they do. But there are ugly humans all over the world. It's not really given a second thought."

"You are not ugly," he snapped at her. "Far from it."

"I'm ugly to a Wraith. And isn't that all that matters? Unless I want to find a mate from the human world, which I don't. I wouldn't do that to a child—Raise it up in a house where it would be spit upon and ridiculed."

"Not every mating ends up in a child." He paused. "So you don't have children?" It was a question he hadn't thought to ask. Had he forced her to leave her family behind?

"No. I haven't . . . I'm not . . ." She set her chin. "I am not what you would call an ideal choice for a Wraith male. Perhaps one day there will be a male who won't care that I'm a half-breed, but that day hasn't come yet."

"Do you mean to tell me you've never had sex? Fifty years on this planet and you've never had sex?"

"No Wraith has ever wanted me. My only other choice would be a human male, and I already told you why I won't do that."

"But surely you've wanted to . . ."

"Of course I have! Sometimes so badly I ache all over from it! Luckily for me the craving—the overwhelming urge to have sex that Wraiths experience—hasn't hit me so hard that I am blinded by it, as happens with the rest of my people. Thankfully my sex drive is one of the things affected by my being a half-breed. I have seen Wraiths go mad from being denied a resolution to the craving. Can you imagine what would have happened to me if I'd been a half-breed with a full-bred dose of the craving? No one would have wanted me so if I didn't choose a human partner I would go crazy with need."

"Your society sickens me," he said with heat, his hand wrapping around the side of her neck, his thumb feathering along the length of her jaw. "I'm sorry, but it does. It's cold and callous and prejudiced beyond reason."

She nodded and whispered, "But it's all I know."

"You could easily pass for human. You could live in the human world."

"I wouldn't know how. And it would cut me off from all the Wraith resources. Money, comfort."

"Comfort! What about the way you live is comforting?"

"Well . . . there's my gardening."

"You could easily garden in the human world."

"Well why don't you live in the human world?" she rounded on him. "You are practically human!"

"Only the touch of the sun paralyzes me."

"So? Humans live their lives in the night too."

He got her point. But his existence wasn't an abused one. Not really.

Or was it? Nowadays most hated the sight of him. But he had given them good cause. She had done nothing to deserve the contempt of her peers besides being born. It was different. She didn't deserve it. He did.

"But maybe in the human world you could find people to accept you. To love you," he insisted.

"I'm a Wraith," she said quietly. "We don't need love."

"You're a half-breed, and I can see that you do need it."

He saw tears well up suddenly in her eyes. "I don't want to. I wish I had been born without these emotions. It would have made life so much easier."

"But you weren't born without them. You have them and you have to accept them. You have to accept that you have needs that the Wraiths aren't fulfilling for you. If you do that then maybe you can move on to a situation that is far healthier for you."

"I'd be an outcast for the rest of my life," she whispered.

"You already are an outcast," he said gently.

He was right. She was an outcast. She always had been and always would be. She would never belong anywhere. It was a saddening thought and it made her heart feel heavy in her chest.

But the sensation was swept away in the next instant as his mouth touched gently to hers. He kissed her with little passion, but with plenty of comfort. She drew in a sharp breath.

"Don't do that," she said, turning her face away from him. "Don't feel sorry for me. I don't want your pity."

He caught her head in his hands and turned her eyes back up to his.

"I do feel sorry for you. Someone has to because you won't do it for yourself. You simply accept it and move on with your daily life as though you don't deserve more. But you do."

"So do you!" she blurted out. "You deserve more too but you don't think you do any more than I do."

"It's different. I've done terrible things, Viève. Things you don't understand or you wouldn't even want to talk to me. You wouldn't want me to touch you. You certainly wouldn't want me to kiss you. And I'm being selfish by not telling you what those things are because for just a little while I want to be around someone who doesn't hate me."

"I don't hate you. I wouldn't hate you."

"You would," he breathed as he touched his forehead to hers. "You would."

A sound to their right caught their attention, as a large orange and red bird came to roost on the branch next to theirs. There was a sudden burst of blinding, hot flame and then a man was sitting on the branch. He was dark skinned, with a pair of dark brown eyes, flame-red hair, a wide flat nose, and a full, plush mouth. His skin was an even brown, the complete antithesis to any redhead Kamen had ever known. He was naked, of a wiry build and every muscle could be seen beneath the smooth dark color of his skin.

"Who seeks to speak to the Chieftain?" he asked in a heavily accented voice.

"My name is Kamenwati. I represent the Bodywalkers and the united tribes of the Nightwalker nations. They have sent me here to seek your help in dealing with a problem that threatens us all."

The man laughed. "We have no problems here. Now go away."

"I can't," Kamen said quickly before the man could turn into a bird again and fly away. "There is a creature on this earth that will seek the destruction of all of the Nightwalker races. Including the Phoenixes."

"Who then?" the Phoenix countered. "Who threatens us in our peaceful forest far away from the rest of the world?"

"His name is Apep. He is an imp god brought forth onto this planet by a foul deed. Even now he is gathering strength. And when he is at full strength he will attack us because he knows that only the joined races of the Nightwalkers can stop him from running rampant throughout this world—he will kill or enslave any man or Nightwalker that gets in his way. So far all of the Nightwalker races save the Phoenixes, Mysticals, and Wraiths have joined our cause. The Wraiths will join, but only once all the others have. I implore you, we must see the Chieftain as soon as possible. Time grows very short." He drew a breath. "And there is more. Much more. Would you rather live in ignorance or will you hear me out?"

The man seemed to contemplate that for a moment, and Viève held her breath. He had to say yes. He simply had to. She didn't know what they would do if he didn't.

"My name is Cembo," he said after a moment. "I am the Chieftain of this Nightwalker tribe. Anything you have to say, say it now, because I am not certain yet if I believe you."

Kamen did so, and quickly. He explained first about the curse and the two factions of Nightwalkers. Then he explained every other detail, save the one about how he personally was responsible for bringing Apep to this world.

"This sounds like a Bodywalker problem, not a Nightwalker one. You have made an enemy of this god. We have not. We will not expose ourselves to the outside world when we do not have to."

"This is beyond a Bodywalker problem. Surely you can see how it affects all Nightwalkers."

"I do not see that," Cembo said stubbornly. But then, "However, I do think it deserves further study. I will send representatives to the outside world. They will make a judgment and send word to me." Cembo called out in a cawing sound and a pair of brightly plumed birds alighted on the branch next to him.

"This is Cordo and Ceara. They will come with you to the outside world."

"I will have to bring them on two separate trips," Kamen said. "I can only carry a maximum of two passengers and I will not Viève behind."

Cembo gave him a nod. "Return here and Cordo will be waiting. Take Ceara now."

The bird on the left exploded into flame, a light dusting of ash drifting over Kamen and Viève in its wake. After the burn of the flame eased from their retinas, they could see a pretty, Amazonian woman with skin as dark as the Chieftain's and hair a slightly fairer shade of red.

"Ceara and Cordo are my voice. Whatever they decide is what I decide. They are my most trusted advisors."

"I understand. Thank you. They will quickly come to see the importance of this."

"I pray not. I pray that you are blowing this out of proportion and that it has nothing to do with us. The alternative is unthinkable."

"But the unthinkable is real. Your aides will see that. Ceara, come take my hand," Kamen said, reaching to grip hold of Viève's hand with one hand and extending the other to Ceara. She looked at it a moment as though she were perplexed by what to do, but then she held out her hand so Kamen could take it.

They jumped into the streak a second later.

# CHAPTER 7

They appeared on the grounds of a sprawling ranch with several empty stone platforms lining the drive and a nicely manicured front garden. There were cacti and stone, deep red earth and well-tended flowers. The house had three stories to it at least, with great soaring windows by the front door.

Ceara fell to her knees when they came out of the streak and vomited violently. Strangely enough, this time it didn't feel so bad for Viève. She was actually beginning to grow used to the unnerving, unsettling streak.

Feeling for the Phoenix, she got to her knees beside the young woman and patted her back consolingly.

"It will pass in a second," she said.

Ceara merely nodded and made an obvious effort to keep from heaving again. Meanwhile, Kamen disappeared from sight, in a streak of movement. Ceara was just getting to her feet when he returned with Cordo in tow. Cordo's reaction to the streak was just as violent as Ceara's had been, but when Ceara and Viève went to help him, he put up a hard hand to keep them at bay. He regained his composure with a few swift breaths, then got to his feet.

Both Phoenixes were naked, and Viève found herself discomforted by the fact. Cordo was a very well-endowed male and much larger than the Chieftain had been. More muscular. Overall he was a very handsome male, in a savage sort of way. And Ceara was only slighter in build than her counterpart, but she was very much all curves and all female. With their matching broad features, red hair, and dark skin, they could have been brother and sister. Viève wondered if they were.

"Welcome to the house of the Politic Bodywalkers . . . and the commune of almost all the known Nightwalker races. With your arrival and Viève's presence, that leaves only one group of Nightwalkers not represented here. The Mysticals."

"We are here as seekers of knowledge. We have come to examine your claims. Nothing more," Ceara said.

"Of course," Kamen said. But the fact was, he felt calmer knowing they were here. Now he was desperate for the Mysticals to get on board. If he could just get one of each member of the Nightwalkers there, maybe he could devise a way of breaking the curse. It certainly seemed as though that would be the key component. Then, perhaps, with a little magical assistance . . .

But he was getting ahead of himself. Having them represented was only a small part of it. The races all needed to come together, to be a part of this wholeheartedly. That would mean convincing the Phoenixes that there was trouble worth their attention. He had to figure out how to achieve that shy of Apep attacking them again.

That was it! He could cast a witness spell! He quickly ushered them all into the house. There he found Jackson and his wife, Marissa, as they were entering the living room. The couple came to a surprised halt when they saw their naked guests. Viève as well.

"Menes," Kamenwati said, "this is Ceara and Cordo, representatives of the Phoenix tribe."

Jackson's Bodywalker soul was known as Menes, a great Egyptian pharaoh of the past and now Pharaoh of all the Politic Bodywalkers. He went by either name, but usually was known as Jackson.

Jackson moved forward and extended a hand toward the male Phoenix. The Phoenix looked at the hand then looked up into his eyes.

"This one says there is a threat to the Phoenixes. We are here only to assess that threat."

"Well, we can help with that," Jackson said. "But first we should introduce you to the others in the house."

"We do not have time for such things. Nor does it matter who is here in this house. All that matters is the threat. You do not look threatened at present. You look quite at ease." Cordo narrowed suspicious eyes on them all.

"If you give me a few moments to recover from the streak that brought you here," Kamen said, "I think I can show you what you need to see."

Jackson lifted a brow. "How will you do that?"

"You will have to place a small amount of trust in me." Kamen knew just how difficult that was for the Pharaoh. "This is Viève. She is a Wraith representative."

That elicited gasps from the two Phoenixes. "You ally with the Wraiths? They are wicked creatures!" Ceara said.

"We are allying with *all* the Nightwalkers," Kamen said harshly. "Including the Wraiths. And she has done nothing wicked, I assure you. Indeed, she has been most accommodating and understanding of the plight we are all facing." Which was more than he could say for them. But he didn't blame them. He was asking a lot of them in a short period of time. Still he would not have them denigrating Viève. She did not deserve that. Other Wraiths perhaps, but not Viève.

"Well, you are all welcome here," Jackson said, running a hand back through his crisp, short black hair. "We have a lot of Nightwalkers in this house and in the two other houses on the property. Some of them you can't see, but believe me when I say they are there. We've got the laundry to prove it."

"What other proof do you have?" Ceara asked curiously. "How do you know they are there?"

"The humans on the property can see and speak to them. They act as our interpreters. If you have anything to say to any of the First Faction you have to go through them." Kamen quickly explained who the members of the First Faction of Nightwalkers were.

"You allow humans to know about you?" Cordo asked, clearly appalled at the notion. "Where we come from the humans only speak of us in legend."

"They speak of Vampires and Lycanthropes and Demons in legend. Djynn as well. But if we are to communicate with each other, humans are essential. Humans and half-breeds."

"Half-breeds?" Viève asked, perking up.

"Nightwalkers bred with humans can write to one another. Or that has been our experience so far. They can feel each other as well. But they can't see each other any more than we can," Kamen said.

"So you mean they're useful to you?" she asked. "To communicating, I mean."

"Yes. Very useful," Kamen said. He reached out and touched her face briefly.

Jackson's eyes widened at the gesture. Was that *affection* he had just seen from Kamenwati? The coldest, most analytical and calculating man he knew . . . showing *affection*? It boggled the mind.

Jackson put that aside and focused on all of his new guests. "Would you like some clothes? We keep clothing in many sizes and styles for guests such as yourselves."

"We don't wear clothing."

"Usually," Ceara spoke up giving Cordo a hard look. "But in this case we are willing to do so."

"Why? To make them more comfortable?" Cordo scoffed. "We are not here to make friends."

"Yes, you are," Kamen said harshly. "You are here to assess the need to strike an accord between our peoples. To do that means you have to get along with everyone here. You might make an effort to that end. Especially since, once you see the threat in question, you will need us as much as we need you."

"That remains to be seen," Cordo said coldly. "Very well, bring us these *clothes*."

Marissa gestured for them to follow her and they didn't seem to understand.

"Follow me," she said, clarifying the gesture. Cordo frowned but did so, pulling on Ceara's hand and leading her with them. Once they were out of the room, Viève sighed. "They are very unpleasant," she said.

"There are those who would say the same about your race," Jackson said candidly.

"And they would be right," she replied grimly. "The Wraiths are not ones to make friends, not even amongst themselves. We gather just once a year, more to mate than anything else. But I've never . . . I hear they're grim affairs."

"You've never gone to one of these gatherings?" Jackson asked.

"No."

"Why not?"

"I wouldn't be well received. You see, I am a half-breed. That is not looked upon with a kind eye amongst Wraiths."

"But it is looked upon with a kind eye amongst us," Jackson said quickly. "The more people who can communicate with the other Nightwalkers the better."

"Are you sure I can do it?"

"All the other half-breeds can."

"Oh. Well, I would like to try."

"Perhaps later," Kamen said. "Right now I need to go to my room and gather some spell components together. I need to read up on something called a witness spell. And I will need you, Jackson, and Marissa for the spell. You will be a key component."

Jackson frowned. "We do not like magic," he said hesitantly.

"Why not?" Viève asked defensively. "It has allowed him to make great strides in this peace accord you are so keen on."

"It's just . . . it has always meant something negative for the Politic. It is hard to change that way of thinking."

"Well now you have more than one magic-using Templar that has defected to your side. It might be wise to open your mind to it a little. It may be key to breaking this curse and defeating Apep," Kamen said.

"I realize that," Jackson said grimly. "It's just habit. There are a lot of people here who feel the same way. The Politic have been fighting the Templars for so long . . . but I have great hopes that one day there will no longer be Templars and Politic. It will just be Bodywalkers as a whole. And there will be no First Faction or Second Faction of Nightwalkers; it will just be Nightwalkers, fully united."

"That sounds almost like a dream." Viève sighed. "Everyone finally getting along with everyone else. Wouldn't that be nice?" But then she said, "But I wouldn't count too heavily on the Wraiths. They are very selfish."

"And you? Are you selfish?" Jackson asked, a tease to his tone.

"I can be, I suppose. Aren't we all in our way? We all want what's best for ourselves. In this case, we hope what's best for us is understood by everyone to be us all working together."

"To that end, I must go to my rooms. Jackson, will you see to it Viève is introduced around the estate?"

"Of course. Viève," Jackson said, holding out an inviting elbow. It was a gesture of pure trust, she realized. He had to know that a Wraith's touch could kill him. But he had seen Kamen touch her with no ill effect and was assuming there would be no malice to her touch. She took his arm with a shy smile.

Kamen studied them critically a moment then, with a short nod, he left to go up to his rooms.

Viève followed Jackson around the huge house. They first entered an enormous living room, where she met Ahnvil's wife, Kat.

"This is my blushing bride," Ahnvil said, his thick Scottish burr as deep and warm as the look in his eyes when he gazed at Kat. It was a study in contrasts. The huge Gargoyle male was extremely tall and buff; his muscles seemed to have muscles. Kat was small and petite, lost completely in his loving hug as it swallowed her whole. "We got married last week to the day. 'Tis our one week anniversary. And I've something special in mind, make no mistake about that, Kat lass."

"Stop it!" she cried, blushing a pretty shade of pink. "Do you have to tell everyone?"

"And anyone. The whole world's to know how I feel about you, Kat lass, and I doona want to change that."

She sighed, clearly put upon, but she smiled fondly at him and patted him on his bulging biceps. "Don't mind us," she said. "What were we saying? Oh yes, I was the first half-breed to make contact with the First Faction of Nightwalkers. It was quite by accident, although Bella, the Druid whom I ran into, says a premonition drove her to be exactly there at the exact time she needed to be there. You see, she has these super intense premonitions. Oh, and she's an Enforcer. Which is like a cop. A real bad-ass kick-ass cop that keeps Demons in check. And if you knew how powerful these Demons are, you'd know keeping them in check ain't easy."

"I can't wait to meet her."

"But enough about us, let's talk about you," Kat said, leaning forward with interest. "Tell us all about yourself."

Viève paled. If there was one thing she didn't want to do, it was talk about herself. She suddenly missed Kamen's protection and she found herself a little stunned by the feeling. Since when had she started thinking of him as her protector? They hadn't even known each other for more than a few hours. Why was she suddenly so dependent on him?

Because she was completely out of her element. She was not the right choice for an assignment such as this. She knew nothing about diplomacy. She didn't even like to talk to people. She had learned to keep quiet and not ask any questions. She had never even travelled away from her house, not even for the Kinua. All she did was work in her garden or, in the winter months, read and sew. She did her share of chores . . . more than her share. But no one in the cell, not even her mother, went out of their way to talk to her. There were days when she didn't speak a single word to anyone. And that was just the way they liked it.

She wondered why the Doyen would give such an important job to someone like her. He had clearly known she was a half-breed. Why would he even trust her? According to her cell she wasn't worthy of trust. By nature of her human side she was prone to be a deceiver and a liar.

"There's nothing to tell. Just that I'm a half-breed Wraith and I've been sent here to see if you can get all eleven Nightwalkers together before we agree to become the twelfth."

"And if we can't do that, the Wraiths won't join us? What will they do when Apep goes gunning for them?" Kat asked.

"Apep has already made contact with the Wraiths," Viève said quietly. "He demands that they serve him as they have done in the ancient past."

Kat paled. "And will they do that? I don't know what we'll do if a race full of Nightwalkers who can simply kill us by touch were to fight against us."

"Oh no, I don't think the Doyen wants that either. If it were up to him we'd just remain neutral."

"Apep won't allow that. He will demand obedience," Jackson said.

"And that's why I'm here," Viève said.

"Well, we are glad you are," Jackson said. "Come. Meet everyone else."

She followed him. She met the humans Max, a longtime Bodywalker associate; Angelina, Marissa's sister; and Leo, a tough-looking man, the sort any human would be a fool to mess with. His bride, Faith, was much more open and easygoing. She laughed easily and her eyes shone with warmth and welcome. Then she met Ram and Docia, a blond god of a man and a petite but curvy brunette, who was Jackson's sister.

It was a lot to keep track of, but Viève prided herself on doing it well. If she was going to be thrust into this position, she was going to do the best she possibly could.

Jackson then used Max to introduce her to the First Faction of Nightwalkers that were about. She couldn't see any of them, but Max had gotten used to describing the two sides to one another so he gave brief descriptions. There was Jacob and Bella. A Demon and a Druid respectively, the male tall and tanned and dark-haired and the female short and sassy with long black hair. There was Sagan, the Shadowdweller male who apparently couldn't tolerate even the smallest amount of light, so he spent his time in his rooms with his wife, Valera, a natural born Witch. Apparently she could do magic, as long as it was in self-defense or with good intentions; otherwise it would stain and corrupt her. Sagan was dark-skinned, tall, and black haired. Valera was a redhead of average height and build for a woman.

Then she was introduced to Jasmine, the black-haired slender Vampire, and her mate, Adam, who was a Demon. Like his brethren he too was tall and well-built and black-haired.

Then she met Windsong, a Mistral, whose song could entrance anything that heard it. She was a small-boned woman who could turn into a bird on command, her soft brown hair becoming soft brown feathers.

Last she was introduced to Jinaeri, a slender brunette Lycanthrope who could apparently turn into a lemur at any given moment. The idea tickled Viève. The idea of anyone being able to change at will to an animal—how much fun that must be! So liberating. She had seen it with the Phoenixes and had marveled at it then. To think there were those who could become any animal on the planet. Although, as she understood it, each Lycanthrope could change into only one of three forms. Their human selves, a specific animal, and a human-sized cross between human and animal. So basically Jinaeri's third form was that of an ape-woman type of appearance.

She was exhausted by the time she met Jinaeri. Jackson could see her fatigue so he steered her toward the stairs.

"Let's get you back to Kamen," he said. "It seems you are comfortable with him."

She flushed a little. What did that mean exactly? Had she done something to give away the fact that she was attracted to Kamen? If so she couldn't remember what it was. Did that matter to them? She didn't see why it should, but she wasn't sure. She didn't want to do something wrong after only being there for less than an hour. Her role here was very important. The Doyen believed there was a threat because Apep himself had already approached him, so she did not require proof as the Phoenixes did. She was there to see everyone joined for the good of her own species. The Doyen had not said as much, but she felt it was true.

That and she felt surprisingly welcome here in just this short amount of time and she didn't want to do anything to ruin that. It was a good feeling, a feeling she had never really known before. But Jackson had explained to her the difference between Politic and Templar Bodywalkers, and how the Templars had been the enemies of the Politic for so long. Would they frown upon her for liking their once-enemy, a Templar Bodywalker? She wondered what crimes they thought him guilty of in specific. Was he even guilty of any crimes at all? Or was he like her? Guilty of just being different?

But there were so many different people here, all being accepted, that she found that hard to believe. They were even accepting *her* . . . so far. They hadn't really gotten to know her yet, and she hadn't gotten into any trouble yet. But she would work very hard at not upsetting anyone. Maybe here she would succeed when before she had failed.

She followed Jackson up two flights of stairs and into the depths of a hallway. The house was huge and it must have been quite an undertaking to have it built out there in the middle of nowhere. Jackson opened a door and Viève found herself standing in the room she had been in with Kamen earlier. She could tell by the ashen circle on the floor and the bits of herbs that had been strewn about. There, on the chair, was where he had kissed her.

She blushed at the thought and covered her cheeks self-consciously and out of habit to hide it. But then she remembered she wasn't with Wraiths and these people wouldn't care if she blushed like a human or not. She dropped her hands and swallowed bravely. She felt exposed, but refused to cover up again.

Jackson didn't even seem to notice, a fact that relieved her. Kamen was in the room, seated at a desk in the far corner. He had a worn journal in his hands and was alternately thumbing through it and through some old tomes he had opened up before him. He didn't even glance their way, instead staying focused on his task.

"I feel Viève is more comfortable in your company," Jackson announced to him, making Viève blush again. "So I will leave her with you for now. Viève, should you need anything just ask any person in this house. We are all here for the same purpose and we will all help whenever and however we can. If that means making you more comfortable, then that is what we will do."

"Thank you," she said politely.

Jackson nodded to her, then looked at Kamen with a little frown on his lips. "Your plan . . . will it succeed?"

"There is no knowing that until it is done," Kamen said shortly. "But if you mean can I execute the spell, then yes, I can. There are not many who could. Though I may need a little help from Tameri."

"I'm sure she'd be happy to help." Jackson would feel far better about whatever course of action Kamen was thinking of taking if Tameri, the Bodywalker half of his sister Docia, was involved. At least he could be assured of her honesty and her trustworthiness. He could be assured of her motives. With Kamen, even after almost a year he still was not certain. One year on their side did not make up for centuries on the opposing side. Although, if he were to be fair, most of those centuries had been spent in the Ether waiting to be reborn. Being in a position of high import, Kamen had often been a target and his lifespan on earth had been relatively short each time. Jackson's own Bodywalker Menes had been personally responsible for taking Kamen out on two separate occasions.

All the more reason why it felt strange to be living in peace with the man. But he was willing to give it a shot and he would make a genuine effort to believe him.

He only hoped his faith wasn't being misplaced. If Kamen turned on them at a crucial moment, all could be lost.

But then Jackson recalled that oddly affectionate little caress Kamen had given the Wraith. For the first time he saw Kamen as being more like the rest of them . . . instead of this highly disciplined and highly unapproachable creature. That single sign of tenderness had made him seem instantly more approachable . . . more fallible and more real. More *normal*.

"I would like to help too," Viève said eagerly.

"I'll leave you to it then," Jackson said. He swept his eyes between Kamen, who had returned to studying, and Viève, who had moved over to him to help. She reached out to touch his shoulders, squeezing them as she leaned against his back to peer over his shoulder. Kamen didn't shrug her off or complain about the intimacy, and Jackson took heart in the act. There was definitely something going on there. Only time would tell what it was exactly, but for now . . . for now he turned and left the room, leaving the couple alone. Sometimes these things were better left to grow slowly with time.

So he did just that.

# CHAPTER 8

Kamen was deep in thought one moment, then thoroughly distracted the next. Viève's hands were on his shoulders, absently massaging the tense muscles there. When he'd been with the Templars he'd had full body massages on a regular basis, along with manicures and pedicures and other such luxuries that came with wealth, power, and position.

But he had none of those things now. He had no wealth and was completely dependent on the good graces and wealth of the body Politic. He had no power other than the power of his magic. And his position amongst these former enemies was the lowest it could possibly have been.

*How the mighty have fallen,* he thought wryly.

But he had made this choice. He could easily have chosen to continue to serve Odjit/Apep, probably even maintaining a position of wealth and comfort in the process. But that would only have been until he did something to displease Apep. Then he would be as easily discarded as a used tissue.

Yet it wasn't fear of that that had motivated him to switch sides. He had been a blind fool when it came to Odjit. And he had to right all of his wrongs . . . if such a thing were even possible.

So he gladly accepted his lack of means and position. It was as he deserved. But that had meant leaving behind such treasures as a simple massage.

And yet this was no simple massage. This massage stirred him, swept heat over his shoulders and made him aware of her weight, slight as it was, pressing into his back. He felt her breasts against his spine as her fingers worked absently on his shoulders. She was looking over his shoulder at the pages of the journal he held in his hands. He gripped it tightly to keep himself from turning in his chair and grabbing hold of her. He fantasized dragging her into his lap, settling her backside against his growing erection.

The sensation took his breath away. He couldn't even remember the last time he had been sexually aroused by a woman. Certainly not in his present lifetime . . . maybe not even in the one before it either. True, he had only been in this body for ten years, but that was plenty of time to nurture a need if it had come. Only it had never come and he had never sought it. He had deemed himself above such base pleasures of the flesh.

And yet, here he was. And with, of all things, a Wraith. A race notoriously cold and callous. A race, according to Viève, with no sexuality except a mating drive that struck once every few years. Whatever a few years meant. Three? Five? Ten? More? The Wraiths were just as immortal as all the Nightwalker races and could live for centuries under the right conditions. The drive to mate every decade would not be so inconceivable in the grand scheme.

But she was no normal Wraith. They had established that from the beginning. What did that mean for her sex drive?

Wait. What was he thinking? This should not matter to him! None of this should even be making any kind of impression on him. He was well beyond such animalistic behaviors!

"What can I do to help?" she asked in a whisper near his ear. Her warm breath washed against him and his resolve weakened even as his body tightened further. He stood up suddenly, nearly knocking her over backward, as he took several steps and put distance between them. He began to glare at her, but her honest puzzlement made him realize she had no idea what she had done to affect him. These had not been calculated acts of seduction.

It made him feel twice as foolish. Imagine, he thought, what she could do to him if she were to put her mind to it!

"Is something wrong?" she asked.

He floundered for a response. Honesty sprang to the forefront, but he held the reaction in check. He did not wish to encourage her, and honesty might do exactly that.

"I am not used to being crowded as I work," he said. Honest yet not entirely. It would have to do.

"Oh. I am sorry. I won't do it again."

He couldn't keep himself from thinking what a pity that was. But he brushed the sentiment aside.

"Very well," he said, edging back toward the desk and watching her warily. She moved back a step to give him room and he took a tense seat. He began to thumb through the pages of his journal again slowly, but quickly realized he wasn't seeing the pages; he was too concerned with the woman hovering back behind his left shoulder. She was giving him room, yet he felt her as if she were still leaning against him.

He went back a few pages and tried to focus once again. Before her arrival, he had been focused on three books at once. Now it was a chore to focus on the one. He redoubled his efforts. He must find the witness spell. He was certain he had seen it, almost certain he had written it into his journal of spells. But his journal spanned volumes. He was guessing it was in the volume before the one he was presently recording spells into. Recent, but not too recent.

He looked at the spell compendiums also laid open on his desk. He knew it was in one of these three books. But it was hard to remember things from a lifetime ago.

As he thought of these things, he began to feel centered again. He was still aware of her . . . very much so . . . but she kept her distance as she had agreed to do and that helped.

"Surely there's something I can do?"

"Only if you can read Arabic, for that is what I write in." He showed her his journal, written in very neat Arabic. "These others are in Sanskrit and French. I am having trouble deciding if the spell is very old or if it was of a newer bent. I know it is in one of these volumes."

"Well, I don't know about Arabic or Sanskrit, but I can read French."

He looked at her, his brow shooting up. "Really? It's an old version of French, probably as easy to read as old English."

"I think I can manage. I may be only half a century old, but I am well read. Self-taught, but good enough. What am I looking for?" She reached across him for the volume in French and her scent, the scent of sweet strawberries, assaulted him. He took a deep breath, unable to help himself, his eyes closing as the pleasure of the smell wended into him.

"It's called the Witness Reflection," he said, willing himself not to breathe deeply again.

She moved away from him, thank the gods, and sat down on the couch, pulling up her skirt so she could cross her legs Indian style. She settled the book into the well of her lap and promptly began to thumb through the pages.

"This is very clearly written. If it's in here it should be easy to find," she said. "Too bad there isn't a table of contents."

"That would be too easy," he said wryly in response.

"I suppose so. But this will be easier than Sanskrit. Or Arabic."

"Arabic is easy once you get the trick of it. Perhaps I'll teach you," he said. The words were out of his mouth before he could stop them and she immediately beamed at him.

"Would you? I'm a very fast learner."

"I'm sure you are. Let's focus on the task before us for the moment."

"Of course," she agreed, and then buckled down to her reading.

Kamen tried to do the same, but he could swear he could smell her from across the room. As a Nightwalker his senses were very keen. His eyesight in the dark was perfect, his palate refined, his hearing acute. But was his sense of smell so keen that he could smell her from such a distance . . . or was it only his imagination?

He decided it was just a matter of keen senses. Why would he imagine such a thing? He was a man of cold hard facts. He was not given to fanciful notions.

They studied together in silence for a good half an hour, each making slow progress through their works; though his was somewhat slower because he was constantly distracted by her smell. How did she manage to smell like that? Was it some kind of perfume? A body wash perhaps? Whatever it was it was delectable; it made him think about whether or not her skin would taste like strawberries as well.

He was doing it again! Allowing himself to get wrapped up in ridiculous fancy! What was it about her that had him fantasizing about her in the most peculiar ways?

"I found it!" she cried suddenly. "At least, I think I did. Is this it?"

She leapt up and hurried over to him, shoving the book and the scent of strawberries under his nose.

He didn't even look at the book. He grabbed hold of her arm as he surged out of his seat, towering over her.

"What is this spell?" he asked accusatorily. "What magic have you used?"

"Magic? I-It's the spell you're looking for . . ."

"I want to know what you've done to me!"

"D-done? I haven't done anything!"

"Oh yes, you have. You touch me and my body burns with heat, you come close to me and I am assailed by your scent and the desire to lick you from head to toe. This is some kind of spell! A lust spell or something. What is it?" His grip on her arm tightened and he jerked her body up against his. He pressed his face to the side of her neck and drew a deep breath.

"I've never cast a spell in my life!" she cried.

"Then what is this?"

"I don't know! I . . . I feel it too! You . . . you smell like bergamot. Every time I come near you I smell bergamot and it smells so good." She moaned when his lips stroked the side of her neck. "Please . . . please . . ."

"Please what? Please break this spell or please throw myself into it? Which shall I do?" he demanded to know.

"There's no spell! I swear, I would never do that."

"So this is naturally occurring? I find that hard to believe. I am not a man prone to lust. And that is what I feel when you are near me like this. Unadulterated lust."

She gasped when his tongue came to touch the soft side of her neck and then licked its way slowly upward. When he reached her hair he cursed sharply. "You even fucking taste like strawberries."

He had not struck her as a man who swore so baldly, so like everything else, it shocked her to her core. But she didn't have time to process his hard words because his hard mouth was crushed against hers in the very next moment. There were no niceties, no preamble. He thrust his tongue into hot hard contact with hers, tangling them together. She moaned at the rawness of it, at the deep pleasure it sent whipping through her. She had never known such heat, such intensity. She had never even come close. She had never even kissed a man until she had kissed him. None had wanted her. Not even as a curiosity.

His hands came to her back, dragging her up against him, pressing his body flush to hers. She was instantly aware of his erection through the soft material of his slacks. She blushed hotly and as habit went to cover her cheeks. But his hands suddenly gripped her wrists and pulled them forward, wrapping her arms around his lean, muscular body. She pressed her palms to his back, feeling the play of muscles there as he wrapped his arms around her and dragged her deep into the bend of his body.

Kamen's heart was racing, as though it would bolt out of his chest if given the chance. His body was hard with desire for her, his tongue full of the sweet taste of her. He devoured her like a man starved for food would devour even the smallest morsel. That was how she made him feel. As if he had been parched for a lifetime and she, finally, was his drink.

He stroked her back, satisfying his craving for the feel of her only minutely. Then he swept his touch to the front of her body, filling his hand with the warm weight of her breast. She wasn't wearing a bra, he realized instantly. The dress she wore had a built-in shelf bra. That left her next to bare, allowing him to feel the puckering of her nipple when it happened. He groaned, feeling himself harden even more because of it. He could tell she was being swept away, just as he was. He wondered how far she would let him take her.

He broke from her mouth, panting hard as he pressed their foreheads together. "What have you done to me?" he asked her in a hoarse whisper.

"Nothing. I swear!" she said.

"Little liar," he said, but it was a soft accusation. "You may not have meant to, but you have definitely done something to me. So now I'm going to do something to you."

He reached to curl his fingers around the strap of her maxi dress and pulled it down her arm. Slowly he pulled, making her breath catch in her chest as her breast was exposed to the cool air of the room. She swallowed noisily, her gaze worried as it focused on his eyes, which were focused on the flesh he was uncovering. When her nipple was exposed he took in a soft breath.

"Good enough to eat," he said, his voice tight with unspent passion. A shiver walked down her spine at his words and she flushed warmly under his regard of her. Then his hand drifted toward her breast and he cupped her fully in his warm, strong palm; his long, tapered fingers wrapping around her intently. He kneaded her. Weighed her. Then he pulled her nipple between his fingers until she gasped from the sensation. Never having been touched like this before, she didn't know the sensation would be so overwhelming. And making her even dizzier, he kissed her mouth again with ferocious hunger.

Then he let her breathe for barely a moment before he dropped his mouth to her breast. He kissed the upper swell of it first. Tongued her there wetly. Then he moved his hand aside so he could take her nipple into his mouth. Viève surged up onto her toes, her hands tangling into his hair. She moaned with pleasure, her head tipping back, her eyes closing tight. He sucked on her, taking her nipple deep into his mouth and she went wet between her thighs. It was a glorious sensation. All of it. She felt more alive in those few seconds than she had in the whole half decade she'd been living.

The next thing she knew she was on the floor, the thick carpeting beneath her shoulders and his hand at her ankle, dipping beneath her skirt. His smooth fingers ran up along her calf, tracing it lovingly, then moving up to her knee where he tickled her in the sensitive spot behind it. He pulled the skirt of her dress up further as he stroked her outer thigh, climbing all the way to her hip. Then his fingers were curving over the swell of her backside, toying at the edge on her bikini panties. He swept around her hip and suddenly he was touching her right between her legs, his fingers gliding over the fabric of her underwear where it covered the most secret heart of her.

Viève was overwhelmed. She had never thought she could feel like this . . . that she *would* feel like this. She had long ago resigned herself to the fact that sex would never be a part of her life. And yet now here she was, doing sexual things she never thought she would be doing. All because of this man. Where was all her caution? All the things she should be worrying about?

It didn't matter. It couldn't possibly matter in the face of feelings as good and wondrous as these. To be wanted! Oh, how miraculous it was. How easily it changed her perspective on everything. And she was grateful for this new way of looking at things.

He lifted his head from her breast and met her eyes as he stroked the hot core of her through a barrier of damp cotton. Sensation ripped through her and she clutched at him blindly with her legs, drawing him deeper between her thighs until she could feel his erection against the core of her. He ground out a passionate groan as her hands gripped his backside and pulled him ever deeper against her.

Then her hands were suddenly on his shirt, ripping through the buttons in bursts of frenzied energy until the fabric parted and exposed his chest to her touch. She looked at him, at the warmth of his flesh exposed to her, at the two flat discs of his nipples and she longed to taste him as he had tasted her.

As if he had read her mind he braced his free hand against the floor and surged up her body, as if he had thrust inside of her, and brought his left nipple to her mouth. She eagerly touched her tongue to him . . . and then her teeth. She heard him hiss in pleasure just as his fingers slipped past the edge of her panties and sank into wet, hot flesh.

Viève cried out, throwing her head back as he sought for, and found, the little nub of flesh that would be the key to her pleasure. He found her mouth again as he swirled his touch around that sensitive spot over and over again. She cried out into his mouth, gasping in his breath, devouring his tongue.

She had only ever reached orgasm by her own hand, and even that had been an empty sort of pleasure compared to this. She launched into orgasm within what seemed like only moments; coming hard, every nerve on fire, caught like tinder to his flame.

"Yes," he said on a sibilant *s*. "Oh yes . . . I like that. I like it a great deal. Must do it again."

She moaned, swept up in his kiss and the redoubled efforts of his touch. She clutched at him with hands and legs, holding him as though she were afraid he would escape. Not until she was done with him. Not until then.

This time as he stroked her he slipped a finger inside her. She gasped at the sensation, at the profundity of someone other than herself breeching her body.

"Please," she begged him, though she didn't really know what she was begging for.

"I will do as I please. Yes, I will take as I please." He lowered his head to her exposed breast and fell on the pointed nipple. Sucking it strongly and in tandem to the stroking of his fingers. It wasn't long before she was launching into a second orgasm. "Gods above I could come just listening to you," he said heatedly as her cries filled his ear . . . filled the room.

"Please don't," she said shakily. "N-not until you're inside me."

"Oh, don't worry, little dove, I'll not disappoint you."

He gripped the side of her panties and began to pull them down her legs, lifting his body away from hers to do so, laughing when she tried to clutch him close.

"Would you rather I tear them off?" he asked.

"Anything. Just don't leave me." She was so afraid he would leave her. That he would end it all, bring her world suddenly crashing down around her. She didn't want to come down. She wanted to ride this incredible high for all it was worth. It mustn't end too soon.

"As you wish," he said, snapping the fragile fabric of her panties, lace and cotton giving way to their ardor.

"Now you," she insisted, pushing his shirt down his broad shoulders, her hands shaping to the flexed muscles of his arms as she swept by. He pulled his shirt free and tossed it into the room somewhere. Neither cared where. Then her hands dropped to the buckle of his belt and here she hesitated.

"Take what you want," he whispered against her ear. "Without fear. Without regret. Simply take what you want. What you feel you deserve."

She did deserve this. She was owed this a thousand times over. The hundreds of times she'd been sneered at, told she wasn't good enough, would never be good enough. Well, here was a man who thought she was more than good enough. He was on fire for her. For her. No one else. The thought was empowering, and she unbuckled his belt, pulling the leather strap out of his belt loops. Then she went straight for the button and zipper of his pants.

She was gaining momentum, gaining in eagerness. She wanted to see him. Wanted to feel him. She had never come so close before . . . had never even wanted to before. But now she wanted. As she cupped him through the fabric of his underwear, she wanted.

He hissed in pleasure at the feel of her small hand fondling him. Her touch was awkward and unsure, as if she were afraid to touch him yet her desire was overriding her fear. And for a brief moment he wondered if she should be afraid. If they both should be. He feared only two things in life. His own failure and his own hubris. Were either of those coming into play here?

He didn't think so. He prayed not.

Her hand slipped inside the material of his boxer briefs, wrapping around his painfully hard shaft. All outside thoughts flew away. He could only focus on the moment and all he could think about was that it had been so long since he had been touched by a woman. And far longer since he had been touched by a woman like her. She was so open, so pure, so curious. He ground his teeth together as she stroked him, discovered him, shaped her hand to him however she liked.

"You're so hard . . . and so hot. Are all men so hot?" she asked.

The question stilled him inside, tried to calm his racing heart with its importance. He suddenly realized . . .

"That's right . . . you've never done this"—he indicated their nearly joined bodies—"before?"

She looked suddenly frightened, her lip going between her teeth and her eyes wide with worry.

"It doesn't matter," she said.

"It does matter," he insisted strongly.

"Please . . . please don't stop. I don't want this to end."

He absorbed that a moment. "Why would it end?" he asked her. "Do you think I will suddenly stop wanting you? After all the barriers this desire has knocked down, do you think the idea of one more barrier will suddenly make me come to my senses?"

"I don't want to take that chance," she whispered. She gnawed at her lip a moment. "I've never had sex before. I'd never even been kissed until you kissed me. No one wanted me because I was a—"

"Half-breed," he finished for her. "I see. I am clear enough in my thoughts to tell you that something like that will not stop me from wanting you, will only make the craving stronger. To think I will give you what no one else has . . . it makes me burn ever hotter with need." He gave her a hard look. "But are you sure? This is all so sudden and—"

"Yes! I'm sure!" she hastened to say.

He chuckled. "Very well then. Let's proceed. You may resume stroking me," he said intently, "and I shall resume stroking you." With those words he slipped two fingers inside her, making her gasp. He scissored his fingers inside her, stretching her as much as he could, the touch serving a dual purpose for him. To give her pleasure, and to make her ready for him.

Meanwhile she was stroking him in earnest, eager for the feel of him, wanting to learn everything about how to please him. He pressed a kiss to her mouth and said, "Easy, little dove. We have all the time in the world." It wasn't true and they both knew it, but it did slow her down a little.

"Take off your pants," she said. "I want to feel all of you."

"Likewise. This dress must go. I would see you free of everything save your skin."

They came apart and each undressed swiftly. She laid back on the carpet once she was naked and held her arms out to him, demanding he return at once. He wanted to, but he needed a moment to drink her in. She was so small, so petite and so pale compared to him—she made him look practically tanned up against her. Her ivory skin was broken up only by a thatch of gray curls at the apex of her thighs and the two lightest pink nipples on her full breasts.

"You're beautiful," he uttered, running his hand down over that white skin from shoulder to hip to ankle.

"I'm not," she argued, a pink blush appearing on her cheeks. She lifted her hand to cover it up, but he stayed her.

"Don't. There's no need to hide from me. Your blushes please me. Your shyness delights me. Your courage astounds me. Now come and kiss me. Let me find my way inside of you. I find it is the place I most want to be at present."

"Oh. I'm so glad," she whispered fiercely. It made him chuckle. "I like it when you laugh," she said. "It's such a nice sound."

One he wasn't prone to making. But he found his heart felt infinitely lighter around her, making it come much more easily. For her. Only for her. His life and his crimes were far too serious for levity to enter any other part of his life.

And that thought made him hesitate. She didn't know what he was. Didn't know what his crimes were. He should tell her now, so she would know the monster she was thinking of bedding. That would be the right thing to do. The unselfish thing to do. He opened his mouth to say something, but she filled his parted lips with her mouth and her tongue and all of his words flew away. Far too easily, he thought. But he did not want this to end. Not just the sex, but the part where she didn't look at him with contempt. He selfishly did not want that to happen.

Not yet.

Kamen kissed the side of her neck. Her shoulder, her breast. He moved on to her belly, her navel, her curls. There were clearly many things she had not experienced, and he was determined to be the one to introduce her to every pleasure she deserved. He kissed the inside of one thigh and then the inside of the other. The smell of her tickled his senses. Strawberries and sex. Her arousal was sharp and he hungered for her. Holding her thighs apart, feeling her fingers clutching the strands of his hair, he touched his tongue to her. He licked her and she gasped. He found her clit with his tongue and toyed with it in quick little flicks and slow, sensual teases. His tongue danced against her highly sensitized flesh. She moaned with ecstasy, her hands in his hair steering him to what pleasured her most. He heard every sigh and whisper. Every hint of passion. He chased it all down until she was crying out in long, sustained moans of pleasure. Then, when she was nearly at the top, he sucked her clit into his mouth and sent her shooting over like a burning star in the night sky. She cried out her pleasure loud and long and he thrust his fingers into her to feel the spasms he had created from the inside.

He took the opportunity to stretch her some more, listening to her pant, feeling her hands fumbling to find him. But listening to her had put him at the razor's edge. He didn't think he could bear her curious touch right then. So he surged up her body, took her hands and placed them on his chest as he set his hips between her open and wet thighs. He took a moment to speak a Word, waited for the brief spell to settle, then he slid himself through the slick track of her folds, groaning at the feel. Did she understand how responsive she was? Did she understand what it was doing to him?

"I'm going to take you now," he said through his teeth. "Right now!"

"Yes! Please!" she cried as he notched himself to her and made his opening thrust.

She was so tight. So untried. He attempted to go slowly, but he failed miserably. Where had all his lauded control gone? Where was the man who had not been stirred to passion for ages? He was gone. So far gone. Because of her. He thrust deeper, his pace all the more hurried as he finally found full seat inside her. He took a moment to take stock of her, to make certain there was no pain. To make certain she was still with him.

"Don't stop," she whispered hotly against his ear. "Never stop."

He didn't. He surged into her hard, making her draw in a wild breath. Then he thrust again, and again. Until he had found an almost frantic rhythm inside her.

"I'm going to come for you," he said. "Would you like that?"

"Yes. Very much so. Please," she said.

He chuckled. "Well, since you're being so polite about it, I must make it a point to do so more than once."

"Oh yes. That would be wonderful." She began to pant in time to his thrusts. She started to moan, her pleasure obviously building. But this time would feel different for her. This time her orgasm would be from the inside out. He would see to it.

He hit into her harder. Harder and faster. She gloved around him, tight and wet and he couldn't make himself hold back. When she came he went right along with her, shouting out as he ejaculated into her. It was like a catharsis for his soul. Years of staid control had burst apart at the seams. And he was glad of it. Had anyone asked him hours ago how he felt about sex he'd have said he had no desire to do so whatsoever. Now the opposite was true.

Now, he wanted more.

# CHAPTER 9

Apep was seated on the exam table, a little strip of paper under his butt and a dressing gown in his lap. He had been instructed to change, leaving the gown open to the front and, of course, the nurse had said with a chuckle, panties off.

He didn't even wear panties, so that was a moot point, but the rest of it . . . he was a *god*. Gods don't get naked for others, others get naked for them. Besides, he didn't see the point. He was only there for one thing. He had shown up at this random doctor's office without an appointment and had dropped an insane amount of money on the front desk, stating that the doctor would see him now. That it was a matter of life and death. He failed to mention that it was the doctor's life in the balance and his death he was talking about. He would get to that part later, but only if necessary. He wasn't ready to expose himself to the adulation of these puny mortals. For the duration of his pregnancy having the Templar Bodywalkers as his lackeys had been more than adequate. They were sufficiently cowed by him, subservient to him, scared to death of him. Sure, one or two had tried to escape the compound where they had moved in order to wait out the remainder of his enceinte state, but they had been caught and dealt with accordingly, making nice examples for anyone else who thought to do so.

Apep impatiently plucked at the tie to the robe. Really, where was this doctor? He'd been waiting a whole three minutes already.

The door to the exam room opened right then and a woman in scrubs with short, pixie curls and a man just past middle age with a balding head entered the room. He had a thunderous look on his face.

"Now see here, Ms. . . . Ms. . . ." He glanced down at the chart which had not been filled out to anyone's satisfaction.

"Odjit," Apep supplied.

"Ms. Odjit, you can't simply stride into a doctor's office, throw your money around and expect him to heel to your command."

"Yes. I can. But, as I said, this is a matter of life and death."

"Is there something wrong?" he asked, switching gears. "You have not changed."

Apep laughed. "Oh, of course not. Let's not be silly. And yes, something is very wrong. You need to take this thing out of me." He pointed to his swollen belly.

"Your child? You want me to remove your child from your womb? How far along are you?" Again he looked at the chart.

"Far enough. I've had it with this whole impending motherhood shtick. It's time to move on to bigger and better things. And I cannot do that with this thing sucking half the life out of me. You have no idea what a drain on the resources this has been!"

"Pregnancy can be very taxing," the doctor said, looking suddenly uneasy. "But you can't rush to the end of it just because you want to. These things must conclude in their own time. You can't have that much further to go. Who has been your doctor to date?"

"You are my doctor," Apep said, as though talking to a not-too-clever child.

"I've never seen you before!"

"Of course not! You aren't the brightest bulb in the package are you?"

"You mean to say you've had no prenatal care until *now*?" The doctor was incredulous. He exchanged a glance with his nurse.

"I took very good care of myself. There was no need for doctors then. But there is a need now. Now, I'm losing patience. What can you do to get this *thing* out of me?"

"You need tests! A sonogram! We need to find out how far along you are. We have to make certain the baby is healthy."

"Oh, it's healthy all right. You won't find a healthier baby, believe you me. It's half god after all. Demi-gods are notoriously hearty."

"D-Demi—?" The doctor's face screwed up into a strange expression. "I see. Well, we'll have to run a battery of tests and perhaps have you sit down with our staff psychologist."

"Screw your tests!" Apep roared, his patience at an end. He leapt from the table and grabbed the doctor around his throat. He slammed the annoying little man back against the door and held him there as his feet flailed and his face turned purple from a lack of oxygen.

Apep sighed and straightened his clothing with his free hand. "Now see what you've done? You made me pee myself a bit. My damned bladder can only hold a teaspoon of liquid these days, and one little sneeze or if I move too quickly . . ." He shrugged. "And you!" he snapped, looking hard at the nurse. "Don't move. I have one free hand. If you cause me any trouble . . ." he trailed off meaningfully and she of the pixie curls cowered in the far corner of the exam room. "Now listen to me very carefully," Apep said to the doctor, speaking slowly as the doctor suffocated. "You are going to do whatever is necessary to remove this child from my body. Is that clear? You have no other purpose on this planet until that is done. Cancel all your other patients, call your wife and tell her you won't be home. If you don't I will break your body one small bone at a time until you are screaming in agony. As I understand it there are two hundred and six of them. Shall I start with your pinky?" Apep grabbed for the doctor's finger with his free hand and the doctor cried out in a garbled sound. Apep smiled his prettiest smile. "Good. We have an understanding then. Yes?" He waited for the man's strained nod then finally let go of him. He crumpled to the floor in a heavy fall of bones and flesh, his head thumping noisily against the door. The nurse didn't so much as budge from her corner to help him. Apep was pleased. He liked her immediately. He loved when his worshippers were appropriately awed and frightened by him.

"Where shall we do this then? Here?" Apep bent down and kindly picked the doctor up, settling him on his feet and supporting him with a single hand as he reached out to brace himself.

"Hospital," he croaked.

"Hmm. No need for that. In fact, I think it would be best if you gathered all the supplies you need and come with me. Bring your nurse too. I like her."

The nurse's eyes widened and she shook her head wildly. Apep couldn't resist tormenting her. "And, sweetness, if you even think of running or calling for help, there will be a price to pay. Whether it be by you . . . or by the good doctor here. Now, you wouldn't want to be responsible for a man's death, would you?"

The nurse began to cry.

"Pull yourself together," Apep said in his kindest tone. He really was feeling benevolent now that he knew relief was at hand. "And remember, I'll kill anyone you think to ask for help. Now send everyone home and let's get back to my compound." Apep sighed. "My own personal doctor. Why didn't I think of this sooner?"

Apep sat down in a chair and watched the doctor and the nurse scramble to leave the room. He hoped beyond hope that they tried to tell someone what was happening, but they didn't, much to his consternation. He would have liked to kill someone right about then. Maybe he would do it anyway. He was having such a craving . . .

But he realized that he would best control the doctor through intimidation, not through out and out terror. If he saw one of his coworkers die he might be reduced to a babbling ball of fear, and then where would that leave Apep? Back at square one.

He was not going back to square one. He refused.

It was far past time to end this.

He had an enemy to destroy and a world to conquer.

Kamen had rolled to the side, his back hitting the carpet as he panted for breath. He felt starved for oxygen, and yet was replete in every other way. He ringed an arm around Viève's shoulders and drew her close, pressing her head to his chest as he dipped down and kissed her on her crown. She was struggling for breath too, her hands gripping at him. She curled up to his side and shivered a little. He immediately teleported a blanket from the bed and let it fall over them where they lay. He should have brought her to the bed. She deserved a bed. He was about to get up and carry her into the next room when she sat up with a squeal. Panic flooded her features.

"What is it?" he asked, immediately concerned.

"We . . . we didn't used a condom! I'm a Wraith female! Wraith females get pregnant every time they have sex! Every time. Without fail! Unless a condom is used. And we didn't. Use one."

Kamen relaxed. "Is that all? You had me worried for a minute there."

"Is that all? Is that *all*? I don't want a half-breed child! I won't put a child through what I've gone through! Never!"

"Relax, little dove, I would never treat you with such lack of respect and forethought. You were protected against pregnancy."

"I . . . I was?" She looked perplexed. "How?"

"If you can recall . . . right before I came into you I spoke a Word of magic."

Viève wracked her memory, then realized she did remember something like that.

"I think so . . ." she said hesitantly.

"I was rendering myself infertile. The spell will last for twenty-four hours. You cannot get pregnant by me."

"Really?" she was both stunned and impressed. "You can do that?"

"I can. If I couldn't I would have made certain to use a condom. I would never have done anything to harm you. I have done enough harmful things in my life. I do not wish to compound my errors."

She sat there a moment, pushing strands of her dove gray hair behind her ear, the bareness of her upper body attracting him. He reached out and drifted his long fingers over her shoulder.

"We're supposed to be looking for a spell."

He frowned. She had a point. He had allowed himself to be thoroughly distracted from what was most important. He sat up and glanced at the book of French spells she had left open on his desk before he had taken leave of his senses and lost himself in her.

But he wouldn't have changed a thing, he thought. Not a single second of it. Perhaps that made him selfish, selfish when he didn't deserve to be selfish, but he couldn't force himself to regret it.

He stood up and walked naked to the desk, feeling her eyes upon him the entire way. He turned the book so he could read it and there it was, the witness spell, just as she had said.

"This is it," he said.

"It is? That's wonderful!" She was excited. She stood up, wrapping the cover around herself as she hurried to his side. She began to read the spell aloud, but he silenced her with fingertips to her lips.

"Careful," he said. "This spell needs no herbal components. It only needs to be spoken. Remember, anyone can cast magic, but not everyone can handle the consequences."

"But you do it with such ease."

"I am a very powerful Egyptian priest who has been spellcasting through over a dozen resurrections. There is only one spellcaster more powerful than I am and she is no more."

"All right. So what do we do now?"

"Now? Now we get dressed, for I find it hard to think when I know you are so readily naked."

She laughed at him. "I could say the same!"

He looked down at his bare body. "Although, it might make the Phoenixes feel right at home."

"True!" She lifted her chin and dropped the coverlet to the floor. "Let's go!"

He got his first real look at her fully naked body and his reaction was instant and blinding. She was pale perfection, only the tips of her fair pink nipples providing color on an otherwise monochromatic theme. But her paleness suited her, like the white of a living marble statue, all alabaster curves made warm and inviting; crafted by an artist's loving touch. All of this tempted him beyond reason. He could smell her still . . . only now she smelled of him and the knowledge was provocative.

He still did not know what had come over him; how he had managed to find himself with a lover after so many years of abstinence. And it wasn't as though he had put any effort into that abstinence. It had just come to be. It had suited him well. Sex was such a messy thing.

And now he wanted to get messy. With her.

His aroused thoughts were reflected onto his body and she went prettily pink along her cheeks as she noticed.

"No," he said, turning to face her and touching long fingers to the delicate curve of her collarbone. "None will see you like this save me." He traced the bone to the hollow at the base of her throat and touched that vulnerable spot. "Are we agreed on that?"

"I . . . I don't want anyone else to see me like this except for you," she said.

"Then we are of like mind on this. I hope it is a sign we will be of like mind on other things as well." His words were loaded with sensual promise, and it was not lost on her.

"And I can see you . . ." She reached out and fingered the tattoo on the back of his shoulder, a twisting together of snakes each devouring the tail of the other. "What is this?" she asked him.

"It is the ouroboros. It appears on the skin when a Bodywalker enters the body of a human. It can show up in a variety of places. For me, it is there."

"It's very pretty."

He smiled at that. "Thank you," he said.

Then she bent to fetch her dress from the floor. His eyes didn't miss a single millimeter of movement. She slipped the dress on, hiding almost all of her pale prettiness from view.

"Your turn," she said. She picked up his boxer-briefs and shyly handed them to him. He found himself resisting the urge to chuckle. What was it about her that made him feel so much lighter? Light enough to laugh even when things were so damned serious?

He took the underwear from her and put it on. He then fetched the rest of his clothes and in short order was impeccably dressed once more, as though their liaison had never happened. But it had happened and the proof of it was in the delicious way she smelled. His mark was all over her.

And it wasn't enough, he realized immediately. Not for a day. Not for a time. He wanted her for more than he dared to hope. It could go nowhere, he deserved nothing as amazing as she was and he had no life to offer her, but he would steal her for a little while. Would keep her to himself like a treasured secret. If she would have him. She still did not understand the scope of his crimes against her and all things living. Were he a more honorable man he would tell her and be done with it, but he didn't want the teasing light in her eyes to go away.

This was exactly the sort of selfish behavior that had gotten him into this mess in the first place. But clearly he had not learned his lesson well enough because he found he did not care. Truth would come to light in time. Until then, he would hold her to himself like a thirsting man would cradle a teaspoonful of water.

For Viève's part, she looked at him with consternation. He looked as though he had never even touched her . . . where she was certain there were his handprints all over her skin for all to see. She would be facing the world with the knowledge that she had been fundamentally changed in this short hour. She'd had her first lover. She could tell because of the slightly sore places she felt throughout her body. Otherwise there would be nothing but an all too brief memory to go by.

She bit her lip nervously. What did this mean for them now? These had been stolen moments away from the world, but now they were heading back into it and life would continue as before. Was this all there would be? Was this all she would have? Oh, if that were the case she wished that she had paid better attention! She had been so overwhelmed by his passion that she'd been swept up more than she'd been a true participant. Now it was over and she had only memories to go by. Not nearly enough memories. She hadn't even really gotten the chance to touch him. Not in all the ways she wanted to.

She found herself reaching out to him, her hand touching his biceps through his shirt, feeling the play of strong muscle there. He reached out for her, ringed his arm around her waist, and dragged her up against his body. Startled, she looked up into his eyes.

"We shall discuss this some more at our next opportunity," he said, his voice a low growl of feeling.

"You mean . . ." She was almost afraid to ask. "You mean you wish to do this again? Another time?"

"And another. And another. As long as you will have me." He frowned then. "But Viève, there are things about me, about my past, that I am afraid will take you away from me eventually. Know that, even though I am too cowardly to tell you what they are, I do not mean to purposely deceive you. I simply . . ." She watched him swallow. "I simply need, for a moment, to be with someone who does not see me as the villain that I am. It is selfish, I know, and I fear the way this may come to make you feel, but I am hoping this moment of honesty will be enough for you to realize I would never mean to cause you any pain, and so perhaps you will be better able to bear my deception."

"What is it you think you have done? I cannot imagine it being as bad as all that. You do not seem to be a villain to me."

"The words of a naïve woman. But," he said quickly before she could take offense, "I like that you are so able to see a part of me that might yet be redeemable."

"I see a great many parts. Any man who works this hard for the benefit of his people is more than redeemable and not a villain." She smiled at him when he shook his head. "We will agree to disagree on this matter. For now, bring your spell and let's find the Phoenixes."

"Very well. But remember this. I am not worthy of you. A better man would not touch you, knowing this. But I am not a better man," he said, reaching to caress her at the line of her jaw, "for I cannot help my desire to touch you."

Viève flushed warmly in already warm places. She reached to grasp the wrist of the hand touching her face and drew his touch away from her.

"We will never leave this room if you do not stop doing so for the moment."

He flashed a grimace, becoming infinitely more serious—if such a thing were possible from a man as serious as he was. He picked up the book with the spell in it and using his finger as a placeholder, he carried the book in one hand and reached out to her with the other. He cupped her elbow and turned her into step by his side. He opened the door and let her pass through before him.

# CHAPTER 10

They found the Phoenixes with Marissa and Jackson in the kitchen. Both were in clothes, after a fashion. The female was dressed in a wispy sort of cocktail dress made of chiffon and drapes of fabric that ended at mid-thigh. The male had donned a pair of loose-fitting cargo pants and nothing else. He was bare chested, the play of muscles beneath his dark skin obvious for all to see. He was not a weak man by any stretch of the imagination, and Kamen suspected he was purposely showing that fact off. He wanted others to know just how strong he was. Either that or he was simply showing off his beauty. Like a bird might do. Preening his feathers about.

The female was no less beautiful, the midnight blue of her dress contrasting with the fiery red of her hair in a most attractive manner. Viève thought she was beautiful—just as Marissa was beautiful—and she began to feel self-conscious amongst such elegant specimens of femininity. Marissa was a redhead too, though hers was a more coppery red. She was tall and classy in a black pencil skirt that hugged her curvaceous hips and a pretty emerald colored blouse.

Viève tugged on one of her dull gray locks and bit her lip. She would bet any makeup she'd applied earlier was either long gone or in need of a touch-up. She looked at Kamen from beneath her lashes. What did he think when he saw her up against such beautiful, vibrantly colored women when she was as washed out as any colorless Wraith? Marissa had blue-green eyes that virtually shone from her face. The Phoenix's were a fair lavender color. Her eyes were a flat, unexciting gray. With women like this to choose from, she would be picked last every time.

"We've found the spell I need," Kamen said to Jackson.

"Explain this spell to me," Jackson replied, placing his coffee cup down on the kitchen counter. "I want to know what you have planned before anyone risks taking part in it."

"It's a simple spell really," Kamen explained. "It allows me to take one person into the memories of another person to 'witness' an occurrence firsthand, as if they were there experiencing the situation themselves. I plan to take the Phoenixes into your memories," he said, nodding to both Jackson and Marissa in turn, "of what happened the last time we faced Apep."

"It sounds simple enough," Jackson said hesitantly. "But what's the catch?"

"Catch?" Kamen echoed.

"There's always a catch to these things."

"Not always. It's a pretty straightforward spell. The only catch would be . . . I don't know how real it will feel to the watcher. They might experience every bit of the pain you felt in that situation."

"I don't like the sound of that," Jackson said with a frown. He remembered the pain of that encounter all too well.

"I am not afraid of a little pain," the male Phoenix scoffed.

"It wasn't a little," Jackson bit out.

Cordo scoffed again. "Take me into his memories," he said. "Use your magic. I am not afraid."

"And what of you?" Kamen asked, looking at the female Phoenix. "Marissa did not experience physical pain, but the emotional devastation was crippling."

"I am hardly afraid of emotions," she said with a laugh.

"You should be," Marissa whispered softly. "I would never wish to relive that moment again if I had any choice in the matter."

"Well, there's your 'catch,'" Kamen said. "You will relive all of your pain right along with them as they experience it in great detail."

Marissa frowned and shuddered. "If it is what I have to do, then so be it."

"Then let's find somewhere comfortable to do this."

"My rooms?" Jackson offered.

"Yes. A bed for our guests would be best and we can pull up chairs for you and Marissa. You need to be in physical contact with the vessel receiving your memory."

They moved into Jackson and Marissa's suite and the Phoenixes laid down on the freshly made bed, side by side. Jackson pulled up a chair to the left side of the bed where the male lay and Marissa to the right where the female lay.

"Take hands," Kamen said, opening the book in his hands to the proper page. Jackson and Cordo clasped hands and Ceara and Marissa did likewise.

"Jackson, Marissa, take your minds back to that moment, just before Apep arrived on the grounds. Remember what you were doing."

"I was gardening," Marissa said.

"I was drinking a beer, sitting on the porch."

"Good. Hold those images in your mind." Kamen looked at Viève. "Step back a little. I don't know how this is going to manifest."

Viève obediently stepped away from the bed, walking backward until her back hit the wall. Then she stood and watched with rapacious curiosity.

Kamen cleared his throat and then began to recite the spell in perfect French.

*Take us back to the time, make one's memory mine, find me there, in the moment, to feel, to see, to witness all that came to pass as if it were my own.*

Then Kamen reached out and touched the foot of first Cordo and then Ceara.

Cordo found himself sitting in a rocking chair on the front porch of the house they were presently in. A bottle of beer hung from his fingers and he was watching the back of a man sitting not too far away from him. A friend. This man was his friend, and he was in trouble. Not immediate danger, but emotional pain, and he was wondering how he could help his friend.

Leo. His name was Leo and they had been friends since they'd been boys together. Leo was a simple human male, and he had been through a lot lately.

"Leo," he said, making the other man turn to look at him.

They exchanged words. Angry words. Leo was in so much pain he lashed out because of it. Cordo tried to be patient, but his friend tested him.

Someone joined them on the porch, a male he knew as Ram. His presence seemed to only worsen Leo's mood, but there was nothing he could do about that.

As they spoke he found himself looking across the yard to where Marissa was sitting in the garden, playing with a mound of soil and smiling absently to herself. She was beautiful. Breathtaking. He had known Hatshepsut, her Bodywalker, since the beginning of time it seemed, but he had only known the woman Marissa Anderson for a short while. And yet together they formed a creature of perfection he knew met his souls' needs in every way possible. He felt replete just looking at her. He remembered their lovemaking that evening just before they had risen to begin their day. It had been long and slow and tender. She had been everything a woman should be. And yet now she played in the dirt like a child.

He loved her beyond reason.

"I'm out of here," Leo snapped angrily before getting up and walking into the house. There was nothing he could do about it. His friend would have to come to terms with his anger in his own time.

He exchanged more words with Ram. They spoke of Kamenwati and their differing opinions on the man. Cordo held out more hope for the redeeming qualities of the man's character than Ram did. Even so, it would be some time before he could fully trust him.

Docia came out of the house next. His sister. He loved her. Her adorable face never failed to make him smile. This time was no exception. His dog, Sargent, came over and he scratched the canine behind the ears. He was surrounded by love and loyalty, and it felt good. As dangerous a time as they were living in, it felt good. He had never been happier.

And then, just like that, the feeling was gone, replaced with a sense of dread and foreboding unlike anything he'd ever felt before. The beer bottle dropped to the floor and he was on his feet. He was shouting for Marissa. He had to get to her, to get her to safety.

*"Marissa!"*

He broke into a dead run, his long legs eating up ground. Not fast enough. Not fast enough! He ran up the drive for her and suddenly a crackling beam of energy came screaming out of the sky, cutting across his path, spewing up dirt and rock, and driving him to a halt. He looked up to the sky, searching for a target, but there was nothing there. Nothing yet something. Something deadly and dangerous beyond the pale. Another powerful bolt of energy, this one at his back. The message was clear. Move forward and die, move backward and die.

Ram had come down off the porch and was running for him. He knew this because another bolt of energy came out of the sky and struck his friend square in the chest, sending him flying.

Leo came running from the house and he shouted for him to stay back. Or at least he thought he did. Then Leo was firing something, a gun, in the direction the bolts came from.

And just like that a woman appeared in the sky. A woman in white with long auburn hair. Blood began to stain the white of her clothing . . . bullet wounds. Leo had hit her. Hurt her.

It was Odjit, the leader of the Templar Bodywalkers and the bane of his existences for reincarnation after reincarnation. Only, it wasn't Odjit anymore. Odjit had been replaced by a god—the god of mischief and mayhem. Apep.

"Very well," she said to Leo. "If you wish to die first, I can oblige you."

"No!" Cordo cried, and then he felt power punching out of himself. His telekinetic power. He sent it ramming into Leo, shoving his friend out of the way as best he could.

His actions drew the attention of the creature in the sky.

"*You* are dangerous," she said, her voice echoing all around him, battering down at him from all sides.

He instinctively lashed out against her, calling on every bit of power he had. He shoved at her hard, a power that had ripped trees from the ground and moved them at will. And yet all it did was force her into a little mid-air tumble. That was when he knew just how powerless he was. It was when he knew there was nothing he could do to protect his best friend and the woman he loved. It was when he knew he was going to fail.

"You," she said again, "might be troublesome, given enough time. That thought makes us most unhappy."

"We know what you are," Cordo said with virulent anger. "A two-bit monster calling itself a god. If you think we're going to let you run amok in this world you have another—"

"Silence!" Cordo's adversary hissed. She flicked her hand, a discus of energy suddenly appearing in her fingers; she flung it at him. It all happened so quickly, the move lightning fast, the distance between her hand and his throat far too short. He threw up his hands in defense, but the disc whipped right through them and then straight through his neck.

The pain was blinding; it felt as though something was ripping his souls right from his body. The agony was too much. He lost consciousness.

Ceara saw her beloved husband get hit, watched him crumple to the ground as if his clothes were suddenly empty of their wearer. She screamed, the pain of loss suffocating, clawing through her.

*No!* They had only just found each other again! This wasn't possible! How could the world be so cruel to them? What had they done to deserve this?

Leo was shooting at the woman. *Good! Kill her! She deserves to die!*

Ceara went running forward, heedless of the danger it put her in. She needed Jackson! Needed to know he was still alive! It couldn't end like this. It just couldn't!

All the while she ran, inhuman screams could be heard. They were her screams, she realized. They were coming from her. The screams of a woman losing her soul mate.

She reached Jackson and fell to her knees, her hands clawing at his clothing as she dragged his head into her lap. Cradled him to her breast. She looked up for help. She saw a black-skinned woman throw up a barrier of some kind just in time to protect Leo from another one of those bolts of energy. The energy bounced off the shield and deflected back onto the god in the air, making the god scream in agony and fury.

"*You!*" It reached out a shaking finger, pointing at the black woman whose electric blue wings were taut and tense. "You will pay for this meddling. These are not your affairs! Be warned!"

And then the god disappeared.

All else faded away. She screamed Jackson's name over and over again, willing him to hear her. Willing him to awaken.

He did neither.

Ceara came out of the memory with a gasp. She lifted her hand to her cheek and found it was wet with tears. Her whole body felt wrung out, the emotions she had felt still solid in her heart. She was having trouble breathing, having trouble separating herself from the emotions of the memory she had just shared.

She realized everyone was looking down on her, including Cordo. He sat up beside her in the bed and his eyes looked haunted. He looked the way she felt.

"This is a terrible thing," she whispered to him.

He nodded. He looked to Jackson. "How did you survive?"

"With a lot of hard work," he said grimly. "Next thing I knew I was waking up in a bed surrounded by my loved ones. Although, in between all of that, I felt like I was floating away. Like I no longer had anything to tether me to this plane of existence. The only thing that kept me here was . . ."

He looked over at Marissa, love shining in his eyes. Marissa crossed the room and they met in a hard embrace. Ceara felt her throat tightening up once more with emotion.

"We must tell our Chieftain of this," Ceara said. "Of all of this. Including the beauty we have found here. You are not what we were told you were."

"What you were told we were?" Kamen echoed.

"Once long ago we used to live in this civilized world. Our leader was called something else, a Tsar, and we would ally ourselves with other races for various reasons. In the end it brought us nothing but trouble, so centuries ago we absented ourselves from the world of Nightwalkers and the world of men. Now we live in peace and quiet and we will not have that changed. Our Tsar is now our Chieftain and he rules with the assistance of a ring of elders, of which Ceara and I are two."

"No one has had contact with your species of Nightwalkers for centuries," Kamen said. "We had no way of knowing you had done this. No way of knowing the changes you have gone through."

"This is the way we preferred it to be," Cordo said. "The elders of our people told us contact with the outer world was a dangerous thing. And you see that is the truth of it. Your own memories show that to be true." He paused. "However, it is clear that this s a concern great enough for all of us to take heed of. I would have said this was just a Bodywalker problem, but the ease with which you were cut down . . . a man of such incredible power. The ineffectiveness of your best attack against the god . . . it must be noted. It must be heeded. If, as you say, Apep will not stop until he has destroyed us all, it must be heeded. We will go back and tell our Chieftain what we have discovered. Then we will return and be liaison between our tribe and your court."

"Thank you," Viève said with relief. That was one down, now one to go! If they got the Mysticals on board, then the Wraiths would follow.

But no sooner did she have the thought than she realized that once that happened there would no longer be a reason for her to be here. She would be expected to leave.

But she couldn't leave yet. Not when so much had changed. She needed more time. She needed . . . she needed to feel what she was feeling for just a little while longer. She had been made to feel special for the first time in her life, and she didn't want that to end.

"I will bring you home and then back again," Kamen said. "Are you prepared?"

"We are."

Kamen turned to Viève. "You will be all right while I go?"

His thoughtfulness made her throat tighten. He was looking out for her. No one ever looked out for her.

She nodded to him even though everything inside of her was screaming not to let him out of her sight.

He reached out, took the two Phoenixes' hands, and disappeared from sight. That left Viève alone in the room with Marissa and Jackson, who seemed to be wrapped up in each other for the moment. Not wishing to intrude, she inched toward the door.

"Viève."

She froze when Jackson spoke her name.

"Yes?"

"Stay a while. We wish to talk with you."

"Oh. Well . . . what could we possibly have to say to one another?" she asked with an uncomfortable laugh.

"You can tell us about the Wraiths."

"Oh. Them." She must have looked as disappointed as she sounded, because Marissa laughed.

"You do not seem particularly impressed with your own people."

"They're hardly my people," she said as explanation.

That made Marissa frown. "What does that mean? You are a Wraith aren't you?"

"Well yes. Mostly. Partly."

"Partly?"

"I'm half Wraith, half human."

"Oh. But half is still enough, isn't it?" Marissa said.

"Depends on who you ask," she muttered in reply.

"I see. So some would say you aren't Wraith enough?"

Most. But she didn't want them to think she wasn't a proper representative of the Wraiths.

"The Doyen thinks I'm Wraith enough for this assignment, and that is all that should matter."

"True," Marisa said slowly. "But why do I feel like there's more to this story?"

"I wouldn't know," Viève said, trying for a careless shrug but ending up with little more than a hunched shoulder.

"You know, before I was a Bodywalker, I was a psychiatrist," Marissa said, moving away from Jackson and coming to take Viève under her arm. Viève stiffened at the contact, but didn't want to seem rude so she allowed it. "If there is something you wish to talk about, I'm here to listen."

"No. There's nothing," Viève assured her. But she was grateful for the offer. It was a kindness and she had had very few in her lifetime. "But I'll keep it in mind. In case something does come up. But I'm not anticipating anything will," she added quickly.

"All right. But I would like to talk about something, if that's all right?" Marissa said.

Viève was leery, but she said, "Oh?" It wasn't often that people sought out conversation with her. She was a little rusty. She only hoped she didn't do anything to embarrass her people. If she did and it got back to the Doyen . . . there was no telling what the punishment might be for something like that.

"I want to discuss Kamen."

Viève blushed before she could stop herself and her hands flew up to cover her cheeks.

"W-what about him?"

Marissa exchanged a look with Jackson.

"I just want you to be careful. You do not know the kind of man he is. Be certain you learn of him before you decide to trust him."

Anger instantly overcame her. How dare they talk ill of Kamen? He was bending over backward to put this peace accord together! Didn't they see that?

But Viève was not able to express her anger like others might. In fact, the emotion felt alien to her. She hadn't experienced it in such a long time. She had grown so used to simply accepting things, then moving on to quietly live her life. When she grew frustrated, her only outlet was her gardening. Since there was nothing she could do about such emotions, she would simply weed or plant flowers until the feelings passed. It was hard not to find peace when working in the garden.

"Is there something you are trying to tell me?" she asked directly. Perhaps if they explained why they felt the way they did . . .

"Only that our experiences with Kamen throughout the ages have not been . . . in accord. Kamen is a Templar; we are Politic. The two have been enemies for quite a long while."

"But you work with him now?"

"Yes. On the surface it appears that Kamen's motives have changed. Whether it is actually true is something we are still waiting to discover."

"How long has he been here with you?"

"The better part of a year," Jackson said.

And still this wasn't enough for them to realize he was on their side now? What more did the man have to do? Perhaps that was why he was working so hard to obtain this peace. To prove to these people that his loyalties had changed.

"Do you have reason to believe he is insincere?" she asked.

"Only our experiences with him thus far. Kamen has sided against the body Politic quite resoundingly. He is deeply rooted in Templar ways. Do you remember the Gargoyles you met?"

She nodded.

"Ahnvil was forged by Kamen to be his slave."

This shocked her. Was this the thing he had been dreading her discovery of? Was this why he thought himself to be a bad man . . . a villain? Because he had created and owned slaves? But surely that had been some time ago!

"So he was his slave up until a year ago?" she asked with dread and confusion.

"No. Ahnvil obtained his freedom several hundred years ago. But for all we know there were others up until the moment he defected to our side," Marissa said.

"Why did he defect to your side?" she thought to ask.

"Ah. I think that is something you need to ask him," Marissa said.

She would. She would ask him as soon as he returned.

"Now enough talk of dreadful things," Marissa said. "Let's talk more about you."

"Me! There's nothing interesting about me," she demurred instantly.

"Surely you're mistaken. Tell us, what is it you do in the Wraith world?"

"I don't do anything. I'm really quite useless. I try to make myself useful, but I don't often succeed."

"In what ways do you make yourself useful?"

"I garden," she said. "But it's a trivial thing really. Anyone could do it."

"Gardening! I love to garden. Although gardening here in the Southwest is a very different affair than what I was used to in New York."

"New York! I always wanted to go to New York," Viève said wistfully.

"Where are you from?"

"Iowa. My cell is in Iowa."

"Is that where the Doyen is?" Marissa asked.

"Oh! No! The Doyen would never be part of such a small cell out in the middle of nowhere. Although, he does live in the middle of nowhere but not around the likes of me."

"The likes of you?"

"Like I said, I'm a half-breed," she said.

It made perfect sense to her, Marissa realized. Being a half-breed somehow made her less than her brethren. But from what she could see, Viève was more than any Wraith Hatshepsut, her Bodywalker soul, had ever seen. Over the generations Hatshepsut had had more than one encounter with the Wraiths, none of them good. In fact, one of Menes's deaths had been due to a Wraith deathtouch. But that had been many years ago. She was giving Jackson a lot of credit though. She knew he was uncomfortable being around the Wraith because of that fact, but he was being as open as he could be when dealing with her. He had to be. They all had to be. Including the Wraiths. Things were only going to get worse from here on out. They had to get along or the consequences would be dire.

If only they could break the curse. She knew Kamen and the Druid Bella were working day and night to find a solution, but Marissa feared it wouldn't be enough. She feared having to relive moments like the one she had just relived in her memory. She feared that this time . . . this time she would lose Menes for good. Not just for another hundred years, but for good. Who knew what power this god had? What if he had the power to obliterate souls entirely? How would she ever go on without Menes?

And Jackson would not be able to reincarnate. That part of him would be lost to the afterlife for good, his soul moving on, away from hers. Marissa loved Jackson. The separate soul that was Jackson and the separate soul that was Menes. She loved them both. She couldn't imagine having to live without either one of them.

Marissa wanted to go to Jackson, who was following behind them as they walked out into the hall, but she had to focus on the little Wraith.

"Well, just so you know, there are a lot of half-breeds here, and they all fit right in. So you should do fine here. I guess in a way, Jackson and I are half-breeds too. Two different halves coming together to make a whole."

"I never thought about it like that."

"You should. There is not really anyone on this planet who is a pure blood. I'm sure if we look far enough into everyone's past there's a little bit of something somewhere that dilutes the blood."

"I find that hard to believe with Wraiths," Viève said wryly. "We do have a distinctive look."

"Indeed you do. But someday you'll have children and I'm sure they'll look like full-bred Wraiths if their father happens to be a Wraith as well."

"Oh, that will never happen," Viève said dismissively. "No Wraith male will ever mate with me and so I will never have a full Wraith's child."

"You can't say never. In species as long lived as we are surely at some point someone—"

"No. Never," Viève said definitively.

"But your mother mated with a human . . . so it's not impossible that someone would want to—"

"No. Just . . . trust me. The odds of a male Wraith wanting the likes of me are astronomical. I think they'd rather cut it off."

It was blunt and crude, and it was clear she meant every word of it. This fair, pretty little Wraith honestly believed herself unworthy mating material. And probably not with just a Wraith. Viève's low self-esteem ran deep. It radiated from her like a dark sun.

"Well then, it is their loss and I feel very sorry for them," Marissa said, hugging Viève around her shoulders tightly.

It was very kind of her to say such things, but Viève understood it was just politeness. Still, it was nice to be on the receiving end of it.

However misplaced the sentiment might be.

# CHAPTER 11

By the time Kamen returned to his rooms, he was completely exhausted. He had expended a great deal of magic that night and the sun had since risen outside of the polarized glass windows of the house. He was weary right to the bone, but he would not rest unless he had Viève well taken care of.

"Where are Viève's rooms?" he asked Jackson once he found him.

"She doesn't have any," Jackson said with bemusement.

"Why would you not give her rooms? Is she any less worthy than the guests I just brought whom you have situated comfortably?" he asked, his voice sharp with his mounting anger.

"Kamen, she is more than worthy and we tried to give her her own rooms, but she insisted on staying in your rooms with you." Jackson frowned. "If you do not want her there then I will have her taken to her own rooms immediately. I figured we would sort it all out when you got back. Perhaps you should go and talk to her."

"Yes," he said absently. "Perhaps I should."

He was more than a little stunned as he climbed the stairs toward his rooms. They had not discussed where she would be spending her days, but he found it hard to believe his shy little Wraith had just boldly decided she should sleep in his bed without so much as talking to him about it.

But as he entered the outer room of his suite, he was presented with something that must have made perfect sense in her mind. She was sleeping on the couch, a nice, tidy little bed made up of sheets and a blanket on the cushions. She stirred when he entered the room and then was awake an instant later, sitting upright quickly.

"I hope you don't mind. If you do I'll just get my own rooms. I just . . . the thought of being all by myself in this big house was a little overwhelming. Especially knowing that most of the people here don't like Wraiths. At least I could be sure you like me a little. I thought so anyway. But I can move any time if—"

She broke off when he rounded the couch and came toward her. She braced herself, thinking he was going to kick her out and telling herself this had been a very foolish idea from the beginning. What had she been thinking? Just because they'd had one sexual encounter didn't mean she had any right to commandeer his couch!

He reached out to grab her hand, then jerked her out of her makeshift bed.

"I'm sorry. I shouldn't have—"

"Shut up," he said sharply.

She shut her mouth with a click. Tears welled in her eyes, more emotion from her human half, more weakness. She had known she was going to end up causing trouble somehow. She was famous for it. She never did anything right.

He swung her up into his arms so suddenly it made her dizzy. She was wearing a nightgown she had borrowed from the enormous wardrobe of women's clothing they had in the house. Was he going to put her outside in nothing but this thin pink silk gown?

He took two strides and she suddenly realized he wasn't heading for the door leading into the hallway, but was moving toward the one leading into his bedroom. It stood slightly ajar and he kicked the door open. The light flashed on and in four steps he was beside the bed and lowering her down onto the coverlet.

"Oh no! I can't take your bed!" she cried. "Thank you for the offer, but you don't have to be polite with me. I'm used to just—"

"I said shut up," he said sternly.

She did. She fidgeted with the lace on her gown as he pulled the tails of his shirt free of his pants then unbuttoned the cuffs. He stripped it off, revealing a beautifully broad chest shaped with incredibly delectable muscles. Her mouth went dry, then began to water as she envisioned herself running her tongue over each and every one of those muscles. Wouldn't that be nice?

His hands dropped to his belt and her eyes dropped with them. He kicked off his shoes as he worked his belt free. It slid off his waist, out of the belt loops of his pants. He curled it up and put it on the top of a nearby table. Then he unbuttoned and unzipped his pants.

"If you don't want to sleep with me, now is your chance to say so," he said quietly.

"You told me to shut up."

The corner of his mouth twitched. "You may speak for this purpose. Do you want to sleep with me?"

Her throat went dry. "Yes," she whispered. "But I didn't think . . . that is, I'm not expecting you to do this."

"That much is clear," he said grimly. "Viève, you and I are going to come to an agreement."

"What kind of agreement?" she asked as she watched him slide his pants down over his hips and thighs. He did this so slowly it was almost like a tease. But she knew he wasn't doing it on purpose.

"You and I are going to agree that, until one of us plainly says otherwise, we want each other. And with that want will come some certainties."

"Okay . . ."

"Certainty number one. You can tell me anytime, anywhere, and anyhow you want me. I will not become angry, I will not become offended, and I will not shut you down."

"But surely—"

"Certainty number two. You are to consider yourself wanted at all times. As such you hold an incredible value. Call it currency, and you can cash in any time you like."

"Any t—"

"*Any* time," he said firmly.

"All right," she said, something fluttering to life inside her chest. He wanted her. Until he said otherwise, he wanted her. He sounded so sure of it.

"Certainty number three," he said, folding his pants neatly and draping them over a chair back. "If you ever devalue yourself in front of me there will be a swift and severe punishment."

"P-punishment?"

He stood before her wearing only his boxer-briefs and yet it still felt as if he had on more clothes than she did. His presence was a self-assured and commanding one. One not to be argued with.

"Yes," he said as he bent down and climbed over her body. She laid back on the pillows, her hands fluttering against his chest. "It will come in the form of a sexual encounter that will put all others to shame."

"I've only had the one," she said, amusement creeping into her voice.

"For now. I'm about to double your experience."

"You are?"

"I am," he said. Then he caught up her mouth in a blistering kiss that left her absolutely breathless. "Now, this doesn't mean you can denigrate yourself just to get this experience. Remember certainty number one?"

"Yes," she breathed.

"You can simply ask for it any time you want it."

She blushed and covered her cheeks with her hands. "I wouldn't know how."

He bore his gaze into hers. "Learn," he said.

"All right," she whispered.

Then he was kissing her again, the heat of it scorching her, just like the heat of the nearness of his body was scorching her. It penetrated through the flimsy fabric of her nightgown as if it wasn't even there. He slipped a hand under her waist and pulled her body up into tighter contact with his. She arched into him even as she allowed him to devour her like a starving man devours a buffet. He started with her mouth, then broke from it to catch the skin of her throat between his teeth. He nibbled at her there a moment then licked his way down to her collarbone. He drew his mouth against her, sipping at her and nipping at her and then suddenly closing his whole mouth to her skin and sucking. He did this all down the plane of her chest until he reached the fabric of her gown where it covered her breasts.

His hand came up and he slipped a thumb under the spaghetti strap of the gown and slowly drew it down her shoulder and arm. Then he paused, seeming to second-guess his strategy.

"No, take it off. I'll not have it in my way."

He moved to her side and waited expectantly.

Even though she had technically been naked in front of him already, she had never stripped for a man before. She covered her cheek with one hand and reached for the hem of the gown with the other.

"Why do you do that?" he asked suddenly, making her freeze.

"Do what?"

"Cover your face every time you blush."

"Oh." She fiddled with the hem of her gown self-consciously. "Wraiths don't blush. Every time I do, it just reminds everyone how different I am. So I guess I try to hide it."

"But you wear blush," he noted.

"Yes. To try and cover up the fact that I blush naturally. I guess I figure maybe they'll just mistake it for makeup."

"Does that work?" he asked, bemused with her logic.

"Not really. But I do it anyway."

"How about you not worry about it with me," he said, taking her hand in his and drawing it away from her face. "Don't try to hide it. I actually enjoy your blushes. They make you very pretty and very tempting."

"Oh no. Not pretty," she said, blushing again and trying to lift her hand. But it was caught firmly in his and he didn't let go of it.

"Yes, pretty. You are not among Wraiths here. Here no one is judging you based on anything but what they see before them. And what they see is a very pretty woman with a very pretty blush on her cheeks."

Tears pricked at her eyes and she blinked them away. She wasn't going to cry just because someone had finally called her pretty. She simply wasn't.

"Okay," she whispered.

"Good. Now let's take this gown off. As much as it complements the color on your cheeks, I would have you naked for me."

This time when she blushed she didn't even try to cover her face. If he said it didn't bother him, then she would take him at his word.

She reached for the hem of the gown again and he reached with her. Together they pulled it up her body and then over her head. It fell to the side of the bed and now she was completely naked beside him.

She could hear the deep sound of his breaths as they moved in and out of his body. She watched as his eyes drank her in. He reached to drift soft knuckles over the rosy tip of her right nipple, then ran his fingers down her body until they were caught up in the little gray curls hiding her sex from him. Her breaths quickened, but he did nothing more than toy with the curls slowly, watching his fingers as he did so.

"You're perfect," he said, then before she could argue he caught up her mouth in a kiss that, had she been wearing socks, would have blown them right off. Then his fingers slid down and dipped between her damp thighs. "So welcoming already," he observed. He caressed the ready folds of her womanhood. "Good gods you're hot," he said heatedly.

She could only respond by letting her thighs fall open for him, giving him free access to whatever he wanted. Whatever it was, she would give it to him. Just as long as he kept making her feel like this. Like she was special, and sexy and hot. She hoped the feelings never stopped.

She touched him on his chest, tracing the muscles she had longed to map. She had imagined him as a bookworm, but his body did not suit the image. His body was thick and strong and physical. It was battle-ready, muscle roped with veins that gave life-giving blood to them. Her fingertips coasted over his nipples and he hissed in a breath. She repeated the caress, this time using the edges of her nails. He rewarded her with another blazing kiss. She clutched at his sides, feeling dizzy as his fingers delved deeper until one found her clit and began to circle around it flirtatiously. The touch enlivened every nerve she had. She gasped softly against his mouth and he growled with pleasure.

"There it is, yes? Right there?"

She could only nod.

"And what of here?" he asked as he thrust his finger inside her suddenly. He left his thumb to toy with her clit, refusing to abandon it. She moaned and nodded again.

"Good," he said. "So long as I am doing it right."

She had to laugh. "You have doubts?" she asked breathlessly.

"Not one. But it never hurts to check in with one's partner when it comes to these things."

"You are most considerate."

"Now you do the same. Ask me what I like."

She regarded him shyly, but his fingers inside her emboldened her. She drew her hand down a set of rock hard abdominal muscles and touched the elastic waistband of his underwear. Then she dipped her hand beneath and found her fingertips brushing against hard heat. She stroked the head of his cock gently.

"Do you like this?" she asked.

He shook his head and she bit her lip. She reached down and wrapped her hand around his length and stroked him root to tip. He growled softly, his hips surging forward.

"This then?" she asked.

He shook his head again. She frowned. He liked it. She could tell. They both could. So what was it he wanted?

She ran her hand down his length toward his body and cupped the soft sac beneath the rod.

"This?"

"Very close," he said tightly.

"Well, what is it you want?" she asked with no little pique.

"I want it all. Everything. I am selfish and voracious. I will not be satisfied until I have you wrapped around me any and every way imaginable."

"Oh," she breathed. "Then let's get rid of these." She reached to snap the band of his underwear.

"As long as you can do it without me having to let go of you."

An intriguing trick, but she thought she could manage it. She slid the material over his hips and pushed them down as far as she could without breaking his hold on her. He shifted and kicked them away. She immediately caught him up in her hands again, stroking him thoroughly, listening voraciously for every catch in his breath, for every low groan that escaped him. All the while his hand worked magic inside her. She panted with pleasure, rolling her hips up into his touch. His head dipped down and he took her nipple in between his teeth. He sucked it into his mouth again and again until the sensation combined with the stroking of his hand to bring her to her first blinding orgasm.

Her cries filled his ears and her hands clutched at his body. He was hard as nails with his want of her and he would not wait any longer to have her around him. He removed his fingers from inside her and pressed her legs further apart to make way for his hips. He slipped himself out of her hands and with a single thrust he sank deep into her body. He didn't miss the slight wince that crossed her features.

"I've used you too well?" he asked, concerned.

"No. It's nothing. A passing thing. I do not care so long as you stay inside me."

"But you would let me know if I hurt you? Ever?"

"I would let you know," she assured him.

"Good. Because I would not have you harmed in any way."

"You do not harm me in any way. You pleasure me beyond all reason."

He smiled at that. "Good. That's as it should be."

"Seeing you smile gives me pleasure as well," she said.

"For you the effort is easy. And now . . ." He thrust smoothly into her and she smiled at the pleasure of it. "I wish to make you smile."

"For you the effort is easy," she said on a low purr.

"There will be nothing easy about this effort," he promised her.

But all the same, he watched her carefully for the first few strokes to make sure she wasn't in any pain. She didn't reflect any on her face, so he had to be satisfied with that and the belief that she would keep her word and tell him if she was in any.

He reached to touch her breasts, his hand gliding over first one then the other, his fingers pausing only to tug gently on a nipple. When he had her purring like a kitten, he bent his head to her and took her mouth so he could catch her moans and sighs against his tongue.

He made love to her slowly and thoroughly, leaving no part of her body untouched. Later he would leave no part of her untasted. He vowed it to himself.

"Gods you're so hot," he growled against her ear.

"And you're so hard," she growled right back. It made him smile, hearing her so bold. He knew it didn't come easy for her, but she was relaxing in his company and allowing herself to stretch her wings. Given a little time, her confidence would improve. But it would be a long road. The Wraiths had done quite a number on her, battering her down until she barely thought she had a right to any enjoyment in the world. Yet he saw her as strong. One had to be strong in order to survive. To survive and carve out a little place of pleasure. Her gardens were her haven and she had crafted her world to suit her so long as she was out there. Now she needed to realize there was far more to the world than just a little plot of flowers and a house full of mean-spirited people.

He wouldn't let her go back there. Whatever happened, however all of this panned out, he would make her see that her little cell in Iowa was not the be-all and end-all of the world. That there were other places that would accept her for who she was without tearing her apart in the process. Whatever happened to him, he would see her have a better future.

Perspiration dampened his skin as he quickened his pace. Pleasure zinged through him in hot streaks, lighting his nerves on fire. He wondered at himself. Here he was having sex for the second time in a matter of hours after so many years of nothing. He should be exhausted—and he was—but his energy with her seemed to be boundless.

He rolled with her, flipping himself onto his back and having her straddle him. She raised herself up, her hands braced against his chest as his hand gripped her hips and moved her against him. He picked a rhythm to suit her and before long she was moaning in earnest. Every upward thrust set her breasts to shimmying and he longed to taste them. But he stayed focused on her impending orgasm. She began to ride him with energy, taking her pleasure instead of just allowing him to give it to her. It was a wondrous sight to behold, to see her grow so bold as her pleasure unfurled before him. She threw her head back and came hard.

It was impossible for him not to join her. She looked so glorious, felt so incredible. He gripped her hips so tightly he may have bruised her as he emptied himself inside her in long, hot pulses.

She collapsed onto his chest, panting hard for breath, her silvery gray hair tumbled all about his chest and shoulders. After a moment she sighed.

"I think that was better than the last time!"

"Imagine how the next time will feel," he said.

She sat up a little and looked down at him, bracing a hand against his shoulder. "Surely you don't mean tonight."

"Not if you don't want to," he amended.

"But you can't possibly . . . aren't you tired? It's been such a long night and you've used a great deal of magic. Don't you ever get tired?"

"I do," he admitted. "And I am. But something about you rejuvenates me."

"Really?" she asked shyly.

"Really. I can't remember the last time I wanted a woman with such appetite."

"You don't have to say that," she said, biting on her lip.

"I do not lie," he said sharply to her, making her startle.

"I did not say that you do!"

"You implied it. That I would speak words I do not mean would be the same as lying. I mean what I say, Viève. It has been almost a century and a half since I have taken a woman to my bed. True, one hundred years of that was spent in the Ether, but to go from one lifetime to the next without craving another and then suddenly there was you . . . I am still blown away by my reactions to you. I had not intended to take a lover today. It was the furthest thing from my mind. But I could not resist you."

"I wasn't trying to seduce you or anything," she said softly.

"You did not need to try. This came naturally to both of us, and that is something to be treasured. I will not take it lightly or for granted."

"I won't either," she vowed. "I never thought I would be so lucky. I never thought I deserved a lover."

"I hope now you see the error in your thinking," he said.

"I think I do," she said with a little lift to her chin. "Everyone deserves a lover. Even me."

"Especially you," he said firmly.

"If you say so then I must take you at your word because, as you said, you do not lie."

"No, I do lie. We all do. But I will not lie to you. Can we be agreed on that much?"

"I think I'd like an agreement like that. I will not lie to you either."

"Not even a little?" he teased her.

"Not even a little. Now come on, let's get some sleep. It's been a long night. Many things have happened and I need time in which to process it all."

"So sleep," he said, easing her down onto his chest. He pressed a kiss to her hair. "Know I will watch over you now."

"Mmm. What a nice thought," she said with a sleepy yawn. "But you need to sleep too. I will watch over you."

He chuckled. She wasn't making much sense and was probably half asleep already. He should not have made demands on her. She had clearly been weary. As had he. But they had each found energy in each other.

"Shh shh shh," he hushed softly.

His lids grew heavy, and within minutes he too was asleep.

# CHAPTER 12

Sagan awoke the next evening with a huge yawn. He rolled over and found his wife's warm body not too far away. He drew her in close, thoughtlessly waking her up.

"Mmm," she murmured.

The room was pitch black as always. It needed to be. The slightest bit of light could kill Sagan. When they were awake, Valera could cast a spell that blanketed him in darkness allowing him to go out amongst the others, but he did that very rarely. All it took was one little accident to disrupt her concentration and the spell would dissipate, leaving him vulnerable to whatever light there was. Luckily the Nightwalkers had excellent night vision, so it was easy for them to shut off all the lights and allow him to walk about without risk.

Still, there was always the danger of someone accidentally flicking on a light switch. In all of their training drills, the first thing they did was hit the main breaker and kill all the lights. This would allow for Sagan to come out into the darkness and use his deadly kurkuri blade in battle. The curved blade was his favored weapon, a katana coming a close second.

Valera ran her hand up along his arm as he kissed her ear.

"Sweet dreams?" he asked.

She sighed. "Not really. I don't think I'll have sweet dreams until this is all over and we're back in Alaska with nothing but darkness around us. I have this continual nightmare that someone somewhere is going to flip on a light switch and that will be the very last of you, my love."

"That isn't going to happen. We spend most of our time in this room. And when we leave it they shut off the main breaker to the house. Plus we cast your spell to protect me at the same time. There's no way any light is going to touch me."

"That doesn't help you in the thick of battle. According to Marissa and Jackson, Apep throws beams of *light*."

"I'm not going to engage Apep, and neither are you. You and I are limiting ourselves strictly to ground forces."

"The Curse of Ra that Templars use is a red light beam of energy. It's just as bad."

"Your spell will protect me. That's why it's important you stay back and focus on protecting me while I do the fighting."

"I still don't like it."

"We'll keep practicing until you are confident."

"We may not have any more time to practice."

"Valera, would you prefer if we returned to Alaska? They sent us because you're the only one that can protect a Shadowdweller in the world of light. If it's too much—"

"No. No, we have to stay. Remember what they said earlier? They need all twelve races in order to have any hope of breaking this curse."

"That's if they can break the curse. There are no guarantees, love."

"There never are. No," she said with another sigh. "We have to stay."

He bent his head and kissed her again. "I'll make it worth your while," he said on a teasing growl.

"Last night wasn't enough?" she teased.

"It will never be enough," he vowed to her. "It's been years now, yet I still feel as if we are at the start of it all."

"Oh, not the very start. The very start was hard." She thought about how they had once thought they couldn't bridge their two worlds. He had been a penance priest at the time, sworn to uphold a duty bound by the laws of his god and goddess. But they had left all that behind when he had resigned and they had gone to live together in the underground Shadowdweller city in Alaska. Away from light, away from the outside world. Just them and their three cats. She'd had to leave the cats behind when they moved out there, but Daenaira, a close Shadowdweller friend, was watching over them.

"True," he said. "I was talking to Chancellor Tristan yesterday."

"How is he?"

"He's fine, as is Malaya." Malaya was Tristan's twin and also Chancellor of their people. They shared the title in much the same way they shared everything else. "He mentioned coming down here to be with us."

"Oh no! He shouldn't do that! I can't protect you both!"

"I know," he said, calming her. "I told him as much. He just feels that he should be doing something to help us."

"Staying home would help us. Tell him to watch the cats. That'll be a big help to us."

"Val! I can't tell the Chancellor of my people to watch our cats! Besides, Dae is already doing it."

"Well, tell him anything, just keep him home safe."

"I already said as much. Give me some credit. But he does want to be apprised of the situation at all times."

"Well, we'll do that then."

"I said that too."

"Okay good." She reached up and kissed his lips. "Now move. I gotta pee."

He laughed. "All of the romance has gone out of our relationship."

"Ha! Tell that to my sore thighs," she said as she scrambled over him.

"Your thighs are sore?" he asked with concern. "I was too rough on you?"

"No!" she called out from the bathroom. "You were just rough enough!"

That made him grin a wolfish grin. His fiery little redhead had always been hot to the touch. And there was nothing he liked more than seeing his dark hands on her pale white flesh.

"Ah! That's better!" she said, coming out of the bathroom and sitting on the edge of the bed. He reached for her hand and began kissing her fingers. She didn't seem to notice as she said, "You know, I think we should have another one of those training sessions this evening."

"We're having one later on tonight."

"Well, I think we should have two. One in the evening and one later in the night. I feel like we need to be doing more."

He frowned. He understood the feeling. It was one he shared. He was a warrior. He was meant to be in the thick of battle. He exercised his skills every day, that wasn't the problem. The problem would come when people started hurling bolts of light at him. He felt restricted by his vulnerability to light. The only solution was to not be a target. To sneak attack. Move in and out before anyone saw him. Using shuriken, saw stars, and glave to hit from a distance. At home, in the dark.

"Then we'll go to Jacob and tell him how you feel. I'm sure everyone can agree there is no such thing as too much battle-readiness."

"All right." She nibbled on her nail a minute. "My protection spell has gotten stronger, and I think the spell that blocks light from touching you could work in tandem with it to protect you against the Curse of Ra. But the only way to know for sure is to have someone throw the Curse of Ra at you and see if it works and I'm not willing to take that risk."

"I think we might have to. It's the only way we'll know. If we don't know for sure then I shouldn't go out in the thick of it."

"Well, we can't test it on you! What if it doesn't work?"

"That's it!" he said, brightening suddenly. "We won't test it on me. We'll test it on someone else."

"But light doesn't hurt anyone else."

"Wrong. Sunlight burns Vampires. The Curse of Ra is a concentrated beam of sunlight. That's why it hurts Nightwalkers so much. Now all we have to do is figure out how to get the Curse of Ra on this side of the fence."

"I could cast it and—"

"No! It's an aggressive, antagonistic spell. It's just the kind of magic that can turn a human magic-user into a necromancer, poisoning you from the inside out. I won't have you doing it. We need a Templar—Kamenwati or Tameri."

"But the same problem as always applies. We can't see them and they can't see us."

"On the plus side, with the curse in place we aren't threatened by the Templars and the Curse of Ra. Again, they can't see us and we can't see them.

On the negative side, if they have necromancers that can cast it or something like it, we're screwed."

"So what do we do?"

He reached up and stroked a thumb across the sensitive, delicate skin beneath her eye. "I have no idea, baby." He sighed. "I have no idea at all."

Kamen awoke with a start, feeling something was out of place. He went to move, but something on his chest weighed him down. That was when he looked down and remembered what had become out of place. He wasn't used to sleeping with a woman. Even when he had indulged in sex it had been a rather cool exchange, certainly nothing worthy of having a woman sleep by his side. There had also been trust issues. The Templars were a sect known for its power-hungry ways; there were many who were willing to do anything to get it, and it would've been unwise to place trust in any of them for any reason—especially as a high ranking officer. It was also rather akin to a boss sleeping with one of his underlings. Never a wise choice. Not if he wanted others to take him seriously.

But anyone who was in the Templar sect had known to take him very seriously. He had proven himself time and again, in ways he was now not proud of. He had let himself be swept up in the coldness and callousness of Odjit's way of handling things, had kept his mind free of guilt by justifying it as a necessary evil.

He had many sins on his head, and he did not deserve forgiveness for them. Not yet and maybe not ever.

And he certainly didn't deserve her.

He reached up a hand and brushed back one frosted gray strand of hair from beneath her nose where her breath was stirring it. He traced the apple of her cheek with the lightest touch he could manage. He didn't want to wake her. He didn't know what kind of sleeper she was. Was she one that slept so heavy a freight train could come through and she wouldn't even stir? Or was she one of those who slept fairy light and stirred at the slightest disturbance?

He wasn't of a mind to find out just yet, so he spoke a Word and she slowly levitated into the air. As soon as he was able he slipped out from beneath her and then lowered her back down onto the bed in ginger increments. She settled and with a little snort she grabbed the pillow her head was on and hugged it closer to her cheek.

"Kamen," she said on an exhale of breath, then slept on.

He smiled. He liked the sound of his name on her soft lips. Hell, he liked everything about her. Except for her low esteem of herself. The thought wiped away his smile, replacing it with a dour frown. One of these days he was going back to that cell in Iowa and he was going to have a long talk with some Wraiths about the way they had treated her.

But he was treating her almost as badly. By continuing to be her lover without coming clean about who he was . . . it was a low thing to do. But he was a low creature and clearly that had not changed. He was just as selfish as he had been before. He could only hope that this time his selfishness would not have such a horrific impact as the last time. The last time he had wanted things his way, he had created the means for Apep to possess Odjit's body.

No. This time his selfishness was bound to hurt only one person. He touched her cheek again and tried to will himself to do the right thing. As soon as she awakened he would tell her everything. It was the right thing to do.

But it would mean the end of what he had found with her and he could not bear for that to happen just yet. Not just yet.

But he had to be the one to do it. The longer she spent in this house the more likely it was that someone would tell her what he had done.

Yes. When she awakened, he would tell her. And he would watch the light go out of her regard for him and she would look at him the way everyone else in this house looked at him.

Like the criminal he was.

Kamen stood up, walked into the bathroom, and stepped into the shower. His thoughts churned around and around as he tried to come to grips with what his next step would be.

Unable to agree with himself about things as far as Viève was concerned, he decided to plot his next course of action for the task of getting all of the Nightwalkers to come to the table. The only holdouts now were the Wraiths and the Mysticals. If he could get the Mysticals on board, the Wraiths would follow. But that was a pretty big if in the grand scheme of things. He had no idea what his reception with the Mysticals would be. He wasn't even sure that the Empress was of sound mind.

The Empress of the Mysticals was, in her Mystical form, a winged horse. Apparently she had been held captive for a length of time by the Wraiths. He didn't know why the Wraiths would want to hold the Empress prisoner, but it did not bode well for them getting along in the future. The Empress may not want anything to do with any agreement that involved the Wraiths.

But perhaps here he could use Viève. She was a kinder and gentler face for the Wraiths. Maybe if the Empress got to know Viève it would make her look more kindly on the idea of peace with the Wraiths.

But it wasn't only the Wraiths involved here, and the Empress must be made to see that as well. The idea of facing an enemy of the caliber of Apep was no easy thing. He was amazed he had gotten ten races to the table already. They had been fortunate in the fact that the First Faction of Nightwalkers had already shared a certain unity between the races. It was a unity the Second Faction lacked. But hopefully the future held better things for them. All they had to do was—

His thoughts were interrupted with a start when he felt a hand touch his back. The shower stall was a walk-in without doors, a small room of marble. She had walked in without him even hearing her. He turned under the spray to face her and she pushed at his chest so he took a step back. That allowed her to get completely beneath the spray of the shower and the water darkened her hair as it got wet. She washed her hands up over her face, basking in the shower as a lizard might bask in the sun. She was beautiful and he couldn't resist her. He ringed a hand around the back of her neck and pulled her up into a wet, heated kiss.

Her hands came around his back, clutching him to her. Their tongues danced against each other. After a long pair of minutes, he let her up for air, blocking the spray with his body so she could look up at him without getting water in her face.

"Hi," she said, beaming at him.

"Hello," he returned. "I thought to leave you sleeping."

"I woke up when you were no longer there."

"I see." There was no describing the pleasure those words sent singing through him.

"Do you mind me sharing your shower?" she asked shyly. "I should have asked first. I'm sorry. I've just never done this before and I—"

"Do you remember last night?" he interrupted her.

"Well, yes . . ." She blushed but, he was pleased to see, did not try to hide it from him.

"We discussed certainties."

"Yes." She brightened. "Yes! I'm supposed to assume you want me until you tell me otherwise."

"Very good. You remember."

"Yes. And I'm sorry. I just need to get used to all of this. I've never done this before, remember?"

"I remember. And if it makes you feel any better, I am not used to doing this either."

"Sharing your shower?"

"Exactly. But it doesn't follow that it is unwelcome. None of this is unwelcome. Change, I am discovering, is good for the soul."

"Have you done a lot of changing lately?" she asked.

"More than you can know." He reached out and traced a rivulet of water that ran down the slope of her breast. He brushed his thumb over her nipple and he heard her breath catch.

Damn she was so responsive. He was learning that it didn't take much to stir her passions. He wondered how she would feel if she knew . . . It would all go away. All of it. Damn him.

Damn him.

One last time. Before he had to face the world and the truth, he wanted her one last time.

Viève gasped when he suddenly reached out and grabbed her by the waist, jerking her into hard contact with his body. Her breasts were crushed to his chest, her hips were connected to his. She was on her toes because of their disparate heights, but she was there all the same.

But then clearly it wasn't enough for, as he swooped in and took her mouth, he gripped at her thighs and dragged her feet up off the floor. He managed her weight as if it were nothing, bringing her legs to wrap around his waist and hips, her ankles locking in the small of his back. He turned and pressed her to the tiled wall of the shower and she squealed at the cold of the marble against her skin. He kissed the sound away, feasting on her lips. All the while the hot water rained down on them.

He felt her hands alternately gripping his shoulders and caressing his chest. Then her touch followed the water down his body until she had her hands wrapped around his cock, embracing and stroking him with both hands at the same time. Stroking and cupping until he was hard as nails. Not that he hadn't already been immediately hard for her, but this made him all the more so. All he kept thinking was that this would be the last time she would let him love her so freely, and it spurred him to ever more heated passion. He jerked her hands away from his body, aimed himself at her and with a single thrust found his way inside her. She was so wonderfully hot and tight around him. Such wet flesh. It was astounding.

He was not gentle with her. The time for gentleness had passed. He wanted her with a fervor he couldn't contain. He thrust hard into her as he pinned her to the wall with his hips. He mauled her breast, brought it to his mouth and sucked hard on her nipple. His teeth came into play and she cried out. But he knew he had not hurt her. Hers was a cry of passion. He could feel it in the answering slickness of her body. He thrust harder . . . faster . . . working himself into a frenzy as pleasure gripped him. But this wasn't just about his selfish needs. There was plenty of that, yes, but there was more than that. There was her pleasure too. He wanted to make her scream his name, wanted her to remember this pleasure well into her years to come.

To that end he pushed his fingers between their bodies, found the nub of her clit, and stroked her in time with his thrusts. She reached orgasm the hard way, with savagery and heat. He kissed her cries away then removed his hand so he could grasp her hips with better traction. He fucked her to within an inch of her life, wrenching a second orgasm from her . . . and then a third. Still he would not finish. He wanted the sound of her cries emblazoned on his memory for all time . . . from this lifetime and into the next.

He pulled out of her, placed her wobbly legs on the ground and turned her roughly about, so now her front was to the tile wall. She gasped as he jerked her bottom up to meet his searching thrust through her wet folds. He found her easily and filled her again. Their cries and moans echoed into the shower stall as he found a new, tighter rhythm into her. This was slower, more intense, and he reached around to work her pleasure spot even as he continued to push inside her.

He bit her on her shoulder, then her neck, then the lobe of her ear. He wanted to make her come one more time . . . just once more to feel her tighten around him. She began to crescendo again, her wet head arching back, and then she burst apart, clenching around him like a fist, milking at him in unbearably sweet tension.

He came with a roar, his hand gripping her hair, his body emptying into hers almost violently. She had her hands pressed to the wall and now collapsed against it. Her legs gave way, but he held her up. He left her body with regret, then lifted her into the hot spray of water. Her head came forward to rest on his chest and she murmured something nonsensical to him. He reached into the little alcove and came away with a bar of soap. Slowly he began to wash her, every inch of her, his hand turning over each curve lovingly. She would not smell of strawberries tonight. Tonight she would smell of his soap and his scent and his shampoo. Whatever else happened, that would be the way of it for this night. She would be marked as his, whether she remained so or not.

Once he was certain every last crevice had been attended to, he put the soap aside and got his shampoo. He manipulated it into her long hair, working up a lather in the silvery gray strands. He massaged her scalp and the back of her neck, rinsed her free of every last bubble. She sighed in contentment as she leaned her weight into his body. He liked the feel of it, their naked bodies slipping against one another.

He had already washed by the time she had entered the shower, leaving only his hair to be done. But when he went to do his own she snatched the bottle away from him and poured the shampoo into her palm. She crooked her finger at him, beckoning him to bend down so she could more easily reach his head. He closed his eyes as her small fingers worked their way through the strands of his hair. He kept it reasonably close cut these days, preferring the wash-and-go style. But there was enough of it to enjoy what she was doing. It was pure decadent pleasure. A luxury. One he wasn't sure he was going to get to experience ever again. Not from her. And for some reason that hurt. It caused a physical pain in his chest when he thought of her turning against him.

But she would have every right to. Especially since he hadn't been forthright with her from the beginning, before they had become intimate. If he could change it . . . he wouldn't. He wouldn't deprive himself of the last twenty-four hours. He was just that selfish.

His thoughts dampened his mood as he helped her rinse his hair. When they were done they stepped out of the stall and he retrieved a big, fluffy towel.

He had this to say about the body Politic, they lived well and bought the best of everything, from designer clothes to designer sheets. They had housekeepers that kept all three of the houses on the property pristine at all times. Although they tended his rooms as little as possible, so he made his own bed every day. They came to change out sheets and towels once a week, but otherwise . . . it was clear he was something to be avoided.

He focused on drying her, running the thick towel up and down every pale limb, around each generous breast and the tempting swell of her bottom. Once she was dry he wrapped her up in the towel and then grabbed another to dry himself with. He tucked his around his hips, took her hand and walked into the next room with her.

# CHAPTER 13

"We're going to have to get you some clothes while you're here."

"Oh, I already got some!" she said with a bright smile. "Marissa took me to this huge closet—they have it stocked with all kinds of things in every size you can dream of. She said it was the 'just in case' closet. She said it gets a lot of use. Anyway, I found some jeans and a pretty blouse. I got panties and a bra too." She sighed. "It was very kind of her."

"Marissa and Jackson are very kind and considerate people. You will find a lot of people like that here. They should all treat you very well. However, they may not treat you as well if you let it be known we are . . . intimate with one another."

"Why not?" she asked as she moved into the sitting room and found the clothes she had folded neatly on the coffee table. She slid on the panties without taking off her towel, but dropped it a second later to put on the bra. It was a matching set, a dark lavender purple with provocative black lace at its edges.

"People here do not trust me."

"Why not?" she asked as she pulled on her jeans and zipped and buttoned them.

And here it was. The perfect opportunity to tell her the truth. The entire truth. And he had sworn to her that he would not lie to her. But he would not have this conversation naked.

"Finish dressing. I will tell you about it when we are both done."

"All right," she said as she reached for her blouse.

He went back into the bedroom and over to his dresser drawers. He opened them and decided to follow her example and wear a pair of jeans. They were pressed and free of any tears, but they were jeans. He was not normally a casual dresser. He was not a casual man. But he wore the jeans anyway because they were durable and comfortable. He went to his closet and fetched a button-down shirt.

When he was finished, he returned to the sitting room and found her putting on lipstick using a compact mirror. She had already applied eye shadow and a light touch of rouge.

"Let me guess, the magic closet had makeup too."

She smiled at him. "It does. Along with all the other toiletries. Including a toothbrush, which I used before getting in the shower with you."

"I thought you tasted minty," he said with a small smile.

"So did you."

"All right, now that we are agreed we are followers of proper hygiene, we need to have a very serious discussion."

She pouted a little, her newly pink lips looking plump and delectable. He had to shake himself to keep on point.

"I don't know if I like the sound of this," she said as she closed the compact with a snap.

She may very well not hear anything she liked for quite some time, he thought.

"There are things about me you need to know. Things . . . I'm afraid will more than likely turn your opinion of me upside down. Things that may have you looking for a new place to sleep tonight and I would not blame you in the least if you felt it necessary to do that. As it is I have been very unkind to you by not telling you these things from the outset. However, I've been quite swept away by you. I wasn't expecting you, nor the way you make me lose control of my common senses."

"I wasn't expecting you either. But that doesn't mean it's a bad thing, right?"

He began to pace, a nervous habit he was not prone to. But this conversation was sitting very ill on him. Still, he must face up to the truth. He must tell her everything.

"It is bad because you went into this uninformed. Had you known better, you probably would not have been swept away."

She smiled at him, the expression making her pretty features seem all the sweeter to him.

"I highly doubt that. Now, tell me what it is that's so bad about you. I can see it's upsetting you."

It *was* upsetting him. More than he would have thought possible. He was normally so calm, so matter-of-fact about the good and the bad things that happened in life. But this . . . this was hard. Hard on him . . . hard on her.

"What do you know of the Templars?" he asked her.

"Very little. All the Wraiths know is that your people are embroiled in a civil war. The Politic versus the Templars."

"And it has been thus ever since the first Gargoyles were freed from slavery. And that is one of my crimes. I have created many Gargoyles. One of whom I believe you have met. Ahnvil. I kidnapped him as a mortal man and forged him into a Gargoyle without his permission. I forged him for the express purpose of serving me and my needs."

"I know this. I was told yesterday," she said.

That took him by surprise. "And it does not bother you? That I would do such a thing?"

"It would bother me if you were still doing it. But clearly you are not. I doubt the Politic would allow you to live here if you were."

"There is more . . ."

"Go on. You won't upset me. I can see you are worried that you will."

"I had a man living under this roof tortured by a psychopath."

This seemed to give her pause, to make her uneasy.

"Why did you do that?"

"Does it matter why? It will not change the doing of it."

"No. But I would like to know just the same."

"It was vengeance," Kamen said. "I felt he had done me a wrong . . . done someone I loved a wrong. He had hurt her, nearly killed her. Put her in a comatose state."

"Why did *he* do that?"

"Because she tried to kill someone close to him."

"Who was it?"

"His name is Leo," he said.

"Oh, I met him yesterday. He's human."

"Yes, he is. And he was tormented at my command in a way that would have broken most people. I am quite certain it haunts him even now."

"But he is living under the same roof as you. How did that come to be?"

"Let's say I used him as a peace offering. I rescued him from the torture I inflicted upon him in order to gain access to this house and the body Politic."

"And why did you do that?" she asked.

Here it was. The moment of truth. Kamen swallowed, his mouth and throat dry.

"Because when I tried to rouse Odjit from her comatose state, I inadvertently resurrected the god Apep who now resides within her body. This situation we find ourselves in is my fault. It is of my doing. My selfish desires to see my mistress whole again resulted in loosing hell upon this earth."

She looked stunned, her jaw having dropped open a half an inch.

"You did this?" she asked. "You're the reason Apep is here?"

"Yes," he said tightly.

Now she would turn from him. He would never touch her again. The thought left him bereft in a powerful way. A way he had not thought possible in so short a time.

"But it was an accident, right? You didn't do it on purpose."

"Does that matter? It was done."

"It does matter. There is a huge difference between accidentally doing it and doing it on purpose."

"I resurrected the imp god and when I realized what I had done I took Leo from his torture and brought him to this house as a way of bargaining myself inside. When I realized the magnitude of my fault in this, I knew I had to use every skill I had, every resource available to me, to see this undone. That is how I came to be here today and that is why no one will thank you for being my lover.

"I am sorry," he said softly. "It was wrong of me not to tell you sooner, but . . ." He shook his head. "No. I have no excuse. Count it among my many other crimes."

"How long ago did this happen?" she asked.

"Almost a year ago. Why?"

"And in all that time, you have been here trying to undo what you did?"

"Yes, but—"

She held up a hand to silence him. "I get it. You've done terrible things. Made terrible mistakes. But what is important to me is what you have been doing about them. You have been trying to make things right."

"Nothing can make right what I did to Leo."

"No. Perhaps not. But you regret it now. That's what matters."

"Is it? I don't think it matters at all."

"It does. It matters a great deal. As does all the work you have been doing to try to rid the world of Apep."

"The mistake *I* created."

"Mistake being the key word," she argued stubbornly.

"Clearly you aren't understanding me," he said with frustration. Didn't she get it? He was unworthy of her. He was unworthy of everything.

"I understand you better than you think I do. I understand that you have dedicated yourself this past year to making things right."

"I released a god on this earth! That god has tortured, raped, and killed. All because of me!" he railed at her.

"And it's eating you up inside isn't it?" she shot back at him.

"Yes!"

"Good!"

*At last,* he thought. At last she was seeing that he needed to suffer penance for his crimes.

But then she said, "Because if it wasn't, then you wouldn't have changed at all. But you have changed, haven't you? You don't keep slaves anymore. You don't torture innocent people anymore. You don't do whatever reckless things it was that led you to bring Apep into the world. *You don't do it anymore.*"

"That doesn't matter," he said quietly. "The crimes are done and my current behavior doesn't erase them."

"I agree. It doesn't erase them. But it atones for them." She stood up and walked until she was standing toe to toe with him, looking up into his eyes. "You think you have done unforgivable things, and I agree, they were very bad things, but forgiveness isn't about abusing you for making terrible mistakes. It's forgiveness or it isn't. I think you deserve forgiveness. Maybe others in this house won't agree with me, but I don't care." She took his hands in hers. The contact was like a soothing balm to him. He had thought she would never touch him again. "I forgive you, Kamen."

"You don't know what you're saying," he said stubbornly.

"I'm saying that I forgive you. No ifs, ands, or buts about it. And I think you need to be forgiven. You deserve it."

"I deserve nothing."

"I disagree."

"But—"

She touched her fingers to his lips to silence him. "No buts, remember?"

Kamen didn't know what to say. He didn't know what to think. He didn't know if he thought she was a complete idiot or potentially the kindest heart in the known world. If she was the latter, he certainly didn't deserve her.

But she was staying. She knew the worst about him and she was staying.

"I will not have you be an outcast in this house. It is better if you—"

"I am very much used to being an outcast," she said firmly.

"You've done nothing to deserve it."

"Exactly. I've done nothing to deserve it. So if I am shunned, the fault lies with them, not me."

The insight surprised him. She was used to taking the blame for things. She usually agreed with people's poor perception of her. For her to think in this manner, it was positively revolutionary.

"I would not have you harmed," he whispered, touching his forehead to hers and squeezing her hands. "I would not have the stain of my crimes rub off onto you."

"It won't," she assured him. "I am not responsible for your crimes. For them to treat me as if I am . . . that would be wrong of them. And somehow . . . somehow I don't think these people are capable of being that judgmental. Not against me anyway. I can see they judge you and I can see why. But they're going to have to decide if they will forgive you for these crimes or not. That's on them. Not on me, and not on you. You just keep doing the right thing and the rest will fall into place eventually."

Kamen sighed and looked into her pretty gray eyes. "Where did you come from, little dove? And what did I do to deserve you?"

"I'm sure it was something very wicked. You are saddled with me now. You could not get rid of me."

"I thought I would never touch you again," he said as he drew her closer. "I thought you would hate me."

"Surprise," she said, reaching to touch her mouth to his.

He pulled her up into the kiss with the fervor of his relief. He kissed her as if it were the last time, even though he realized it wasn't.

He vowed to always kiss her as if it were going to be the last time.

# CHAPTER 14

Apep was sitting up in bed with an IV dripping into his veins. Pitocin. It was meant to start his labor, but it didn't seem to be working. He impatiently drummed his manicured nails against his thigh as he read a trashy little Hollywood insider magazine. Really, he'd grown quite addicted to hearing about these stars' lives.

The doctor was nervously pacing the room, biting his nails in a disgusting little habit. Ew. Maybe he should get a better doctor.

No. There wasn't time for that. There wasn't time for any of this.

"Oh, let's just cut it out of me already!" Apep cried in frustration.

"We don't have a surgery room!" the doctor said. "You'd risk infection or—"

"I'm not going to get an infection, I'm a god!"

"A . . . a god?"

"Yes! A god. A god who's tired of this whole pregnancy business. Get this fucking thing out of me—yeow!"

Apep ended on a cry when a sudden cramp seized his belly. He froze. Was this it? Was it starting?

"What was that?" he demanded of the doctor.

"Your labor has begun!" he said with relieved excitement. "It's only a matter of a few hours now."

Or at least the doctor hoped. He knew better than anyone how long a labor could last. If it didn't progress fast enough for this—this *god*—there was going to be trouble. He and his poor frightened nurse would be in serious danger. He didn't doubt that in the slightest.

"Rose, put the external fetal monitor on. I want to track the baby's heart rate."

"Oh, it'll be fine," Apep said, waving them off. "It's part god after all."

"Well, even so . . . just to be safe," the doctor urged. God help them if something went wrong with this birth or with the child. He had to take all of the precautions he could. "Ms. Odjit, really, you should let us."

"Oh well, all right. If it'll keep you from whining about it!" A second labor pain lanced through Apep's belly. That one was a bit stronger. Hmm. He wondered just how painful this business was going to be. Surely not that bad, otherwise humans wouldn't be doing it over and over again, polluting the earth with their inferior progeny. Now his progeny . . . his progeny was going to be great. Superior. By far. It was almost worth all this waiting for him to make an appearance.

The nurse put the monitor around his belly and immediately the machine registered the baby's heartbeat.

"It's a good, strong beat," the doctor said.

"Of course it is. I told yeoooowww!"

Okay, now that one was particularly uncomfortable. He was a god. This shouldn't hurt so much. It was this inferior human body he'd been resurrected into. It must be broken. It was bad enough there were two other souls clamoring around inside his head, the one called Odjit and the body's original soul before the Bodywalker had taken possession of it, but now a broken body on top of it? It was really too much.

Well, at least he had his worshippers to help him. Actually, the Templars were Odjit's worshippers, but that was just semantics. Once they realized how glorious a god he was, then they would truly be followers of Apep.

If only they would take this thing out of him.

Another pain came and he was encouraged. This would be over in another hour or two. Then he could go about his business of conquering these little people. After he got rid of the Nightwalkers. They were the only thing that could stand in the way of his total domination. Of course, they didn't know that. If they did . . . well . . . But they didn't. They didn't even know the others existed, thanks to his ingenious curse. Of course, he might have to dispel that curse if he was going to use the Wraiths to help him destroy the other Nightwalker races. But dispelling the curse was just as dangerous as leaving it be. All they had to do was get in the same room together and . . .

Well, that wasn't likely to happen now was it? No sense even thinking about it.

Instead, he was forced to focus on the pain that was creeping up on him in increasing intensity.

Yes, this should be over any time now. And once he had his son by his side, he would be unstoppable.

Viève refused to hide in Kamen's rooms, although he was very reluctant to have her go out amongst the others. They called a gathering of all the Nightwalkers presently on the property, just as they did every night, and introduced the Phoenixes around using the human mediators. Kamen then spoke about his next plan of action.

"Kat," he said to Ahnvil's wife, "I will need you to make contact with Grey."

Grey was the most powerful Djynn in the United States. No one knew exactly where he was located, but he always seemed to come around when he was needed most. But this, Kamen feared, was going to take a bit of coaxing.

"I can do that," Kat said readily. "He gave me the means to contact him any time. He taught me how. Djynn 101." She was proud of her accomplishments as a Djynn, especially since she hadn't even known she was one until a few months ago.

"Good, because the Empress of the Mysticals is in his care and if we are going to get their cooperation, we're going to have to go through her," Kamen said.

"All right. Let me try while we're all here."

Kat stood up and walked to the center of the room. She sat down cross-legged and closed her eyes. She went quiet and seemed to focus for a minute. After a while she began to frown.

"I know I'm doing it right. But he's not answering."

"Grey doesn't seem the type to be summoned," Kamen noted.

"But he's always answered me before. I kinda thought he liked our lessons. But maybe he's grown bored of me. You know how capricious Djynn can be."

"I am well aware," Kamen said. "Can you try SingSing? Maybe she knows how to get to Grey."

"Oh great. SingSing is just as hard to contact. But I'll try."

Kat closed her eyes and did her best to focus on calling SingSing. Grey had said it was just a matter of envisioning the Djynn she wanted to contact and calling out a hello. "Oh, SingSing . . . where are you?" she called out.

"I'm right heeeeeree! Tada!"

With a snap, a diminutive little woman appeared practically nose to nose with Kat. Startled, Kat jerked back.

"Hey, Kitty Kat, what's shakin'?" SingSing asked.

"SingSing, we need your help locating Grey," Kat said.

"What? No hello? No how are you? Just straight to business?" SingSing frowned.

"No no," Kat said quickly. "Of course, you are right. That was terribly rude of me. Hello, SingSing. How are you?"

"I'm spectacular! That is my word of the week," SingSing said in a loud aside. "Spectacular!"

"What have you been up to?" Kat asked.

"Oh, I just acquired this spectacular nik! Looky here." SingSing produced a little ceramic cat out of thin air. It looked like a cheap statuette one might find in a secondhand store.

"Are you sure that's a nik?" Kat asked doubtfully.

"What's a nik?" Viève asked in a whisper to Kamen.

SingSing disappeared and reappeared right under Viève's nose. Holding out the statue, she whispered, "This is a nik! A niknak to be precise. It is an object that holds magical energy. Energy Djynns use to fuel their magic abilities. Inanimate objects like this one are called niknaks. Animate ones, like my dragonlets"—she shook her corkscrew ginger curls and three little dragon heads poked out of them, the dragons' eyes blinking blearily as if they'd just been woken up—"are nikkis. So that's a nik. And this is a nik." She showed the statue off with a flourish of her hands. It levitated and began to turn, an unseen light highlighting all its features. And yet it still looked like a cheap little ceramic cat. A black one.

"Are you sure that thing is magical?" Viève asked doubtfully.

"Of course it is, ghost girl!" SingSing snatched the statuette out of the air and hugged it close to her chest. She shot a sidelong glance at Kat. "And don't you even try to steal it." She leaned back toward Viève. "Keep an eye on that one," she whispered loudly. "She steals niks."

"Hey! I do not!"

"Then how'd you get that necklace?" SingSing asked. "And that bracelet?"

"Oh, well I . . ." Kat flushed.

"See? She stole them."

"I *found* them," Kat corrected.

"Also known as stealing. See," SingSing explained to Viève, "all a Djynn has to do is touch a nik and it becomes theirs, so long as another Djynn isn't touching it at the time. I'm sure those niks she's wearing belonged to some Djynn somewhere and she just walked off with them."

"I did not! These were a Templar priest's!"

"See! She stole them."

"I didn't steal them I—Oh never mind! SingSing, can you help us or not?"

"Of course I can." SingSing poked at each little dragon head until they disappeared back into her curls. "The question is . . . do I want to help you? After all, you're a common thief."

"Stop calling me that! You know, we're just going to have to wait until Grey answers me. She's no help at all," Kat said.

"Of course I can help!" SingSing disappeared and reappeared back before Kat. "All you had to do was ask." She paused a beat. "Now what is it you want exactly? Did you have a *wish*?"

"No, I do not have a wish!" Kat exclaimed.

SingSing disappeared and reappeared under Viève's nose again. "What about you, ghost girl? You got a wish?"

"Do not, under any circumstances, make a wish," Kamen warned. "There's always a price to pay for making a wish with a Djynn."

"You're no fun," SingSing said with a pout. "Little ghost girl's just brimming with wishes. She wishes she was liked by the Wraiths. Wishes she wasn't a half-breed. Wishes this and wishes that. She even wishes she'd had another orgasm with you this morning."

"I do not!" Viève cried, her hands coming up to cover her cheeks as she looked at Kamen. "That's not true!"

"Oh, so who cares if you want another orgasm?" SingSing said with a careless wave of her hand. "All women wish they'd had another orgasm. Nothing wrong with that. I've had several women wish their men were better lovers." She snorted a laugh. "They just forgot to wish their men were better *loyal* lovers.

Loyal to them. Men being men, you make them a better lover and they're in demand all over the place."

"That's terrible!" Viève cried.

"Them's the breaks, kid. If you're gonna make a wish, you gotta think it through." She stared intently at Viève and tapped herself on the side of the head. "Use the old noggin." A little dragon head stuck out. It hiccupped a little fireball, singeing one of SingSing's curls. The smell of burnt hair wafted over Viève.

"Well, I'm not going to make a wish. I don't want anything that badly."

"Hmm. Veeeeery interesting," SingSing said, eyeballing Viève a moment. "Anywho! Back to my spectacular day!"

"Wait!" Kat cried before SingSing could finish her flourish of hands and disappear.

"What now, little thief?" SingSing asked.

"Grey?" Kat prompted her.

"Oh yes! Almost forgot. Who wants to go?"

"Go?"

"To Grey's! I can't have you all go!"

"We will," Kamen said quickly. "Viève and I."

"Hmm. So ghost girl wants to see the big bad Djynn, eh? Well, be careful what you wish for!"

SingSing clapped her hands and said, "Tada!"

Kamen and Viève disappeared from the room.

Kamen and Viève suddenly appeared in a golden room. The walls were beaten gold, the floor was golden tile. There were piles of gold coins everywhere and golden jewelry was strewn about. There was even a golden throne at the head of the room.

They were just getting their bearings when a handsome man with dark skin and jet black hair appeared on the throne, sprawling indolently over the arms of the giant chair. Then he narrowed his eyes at them and sighed in frustration.

"Oh. It's just you. What do you want?"

He stood up and snapped his fingers. The golden room disappeared and gave way to an opulent library. Grey walked over to the desk and poured himself a drink from the decanter sitting on its edge. He swirled the liquor in the glass, sniffing it a moment before tossing back a large swallow.

"Ah! Good stuff. Sorry about the golden room thing. Gotta give people what they want and everyone who rubs the lamps or whatever expects to see the Djynn in a golden room or some such nonsense. What can I do for you?"

"We're here to gain audience with the Empress of the Mysticals," Kamen said.

Grey burst out in a hard laugh. "And why would I let you do that? Especially with her." He pointed rudely to Viève. "Do you have any idea what the Wraiths did to the Empress?"

"Wraiths?" Viève asked in confusion. "What did the Wraiths do to her?"

"They held her captive for months. They tormented her and fed her eggs so she would be stuck in her Mystical form and couldn't escape, keeping her trapped in a room in a house. I think they tortured her. I'm not quite clear on all the details. She doesn't exactly speak to me about such things."

"But she does speak to you?"

"She does. She's been recovering here where she knows she's protected. She knows I would never hurt her. That I'm not just using her because she's a very powerful nikki."

"And how is her recovery going?" Viève asked.

"Between you and me, she's more better than worse. She spent a lot of time being threatened with the possibility of a Wraith using their deathtouch on her. It's the equivalent to a human being held constantly at gunpoint. She's been traumatized." Grey leaned in and narrowed eyes on Viève.

"That's terrible," Viève whispered.

"Indeed it was. So I ask again, what makes you think she's going to want to talk to a Wraith?"

"Then let her talk to me," Kamen said.

"You're not much better. Everyone knows what you did."

"She knows about Apep?" Kamen asked.

"I may have let something slip. But I've protected her from the goings-on in the outside world. She's a very delicate creature."

"Delicate creature or no, she's the leader of an entire species of Nightwalkers. She needs to come to grips with this situation and lead them," Kamen said.

Grey seemed to think on it a moment. "No," he said then. "I don't think I'll let you see her."

"Please," Viève spoke up. "We just want the Mysticals to join in our fight against Apep. If they don't then the Wraiths won't join. And if the Wraiths don't join we'll never be able to fight off Apep."

"What makes you so sure you'll be able to fight him off anyway?" Grey asked.

"We're not sure. But it's better than doing nothing and letting him run roughshod over us. We're the last line of defense between Apep and the mortal world and I think you know that."

"What do I care about the mortal world?" Grey asked carelessly.

"No mortals, no wishes," Viève spoke up quickly.

That made Grey go still. "Hmm. Hadn't thought about that. Still, if Apep does try to dominate the world, there'll be a lot of people *wishing* for a solution."

"One you can't provide. What happens, exactly, when a Djynn can't fulfill a wish?" Kamen asked.

Grey paled a little. "It's not a pretty sight," he admitted. "But that's why every wish is open to interpretation. So we can avoid the ones we can't fulfill. Not every Djynn is powerful enough to fulfill every wish. Power comes with time, training, and niks. Take your little Kat for instance. She shouldn't even ask for a wish because she's a half-breed with no power yet."

"There's nothing wrong with being a half-breed," Viève said defensively.

"No indeed. But it does make her less powerful than most . . . for the time being. I have hopes for your little half-breed Djynn."

"Let's get back to the Empress," Kamen redirected. "It's crucial you let us see her. Or at least point us in the direction of someone who can make these decisions for her."

"Oh, she can make these decisions. She's been ruling her people quite nicely from here." He seemed to think on it a moment. "Very well. I'll allow the visit. But only because she doesn't look so much like a Wraith. Those ghouls still give her nightmares."

"I don't understand what the Wraiths would have wanted with a Mystical," Viève said with a puzzled frown. "It's not like it is with Djynn. The Djynn can get power from a Mystical . . . if it's a nikki . . . right?"

"Right. Mysticals by nature are nikkis."

"But what would a Wraith do with a nikki?"

"That is a very good question. One you might pose to the Wraiths who held her captive."

"Does she know which cell it was?"

"I know which cell it was. I transported Leo and Faith there to retrieve her."

"Well . . . I'm not certain they would tell me. I'm only . . ." She stopped short of saying the words "a half-breed."

"It makes no difference. She's safe now and that's all that matters."

"Perhaps," Kamen said. "But it does make this more difficult. The Empress of the Mysticals is not going to want to strike an accord with the Wraiths."

"You will have to ask her about that," Grey said. "She may yet surprise you."

"We hope so," Viève said.

"Well then, come with me." Grey paused a moment and eyed Viève. "Perhaps . . . yes, at least for the beginning we should color your hair so it doesn't look so . . . so . . . Wraith."

Grey lifted a hand and touched Viève's hair. Kamen felt a visceral twinge at the sight of another man touching her in what could be described as an intimate way. As Grey stroked her hair he found himself fighting the urge to strike his hand away. The feeling shocked Kamen, disturbed him deeply. *What is this?* he asked himself. The last thing he should be doing in this situation was considering something so aggressive toward the man who was their only access to the Empress. He struggled with himself for that brief moment, and controlled the sensation. Still, it left its mark on him.

Viève's hair changed color under Grey's stroking touch. It felt odd to have another man's hands on her. People just didn't voluntarily touch her where she was from. Being with Kamen was the most she had ever been touched in her life. It was why she was so hungry for it. Starved really. But she didn't want Grey's touch the way she wanted Kamen's.

When Grey was finished her hair was a luscious red color, with golden red highlights. She fondled the locks for a moment, touching the vibrant color.

"Why red?" she asked.

"It goes with your complexion." A mirror suddenly appeared before Viève and she was shocked to see herself looking so different. Even her brows had been colored to match. Wraith hair did not take color using human coloring methods. It was gray or white and there was no changing it. She had always wished she could have another color, just to see what it was like for a little while.

But a little while was enough.

"Change it back," she said firmly.

"But don't you like it?" Grey asked.

"It's very pretty. And I appreciate the effort. But I won't go before her disguised as anything other than what I am. She may look upon that as a deceit on our part and that will not help our cause."

"Hmm." Grey seemed to think on it. "Perhaps you are right," he said. He looked to Kamen. "Your little Wraith is really quite clever."

"I know she is. But she is not mine."

Kamen's words hit Viève like a slap. Of course it was silly. She wasn't his. He was just speaking the truth. But hearing him deny her just stung for some reason.

"Are you certain of that?" Grey asked him.

"She belongs to herself and no one else, and that is as it should be," Kamen said.

The distinction helped ease the sting of his words a little, but still she felt hurt. It was ridiculous of course. She'd only known him twenty-four hours, if that. There was no reason for her to believe he would have developed any kind of possessive feelings where she was concerned.

"Oh, but look," Grey said, touching her chin and turning her face toward Kamen. "You have hurt her with your words."

"No!" Viève denied quickly. "He hasn't. He's right. I am my own."

"Are you certain?" Grey asked dubiously. "I could have sworn differently."

"Can we just get back to what we were doing," she said uncomfortably.

Grey seemed to shake himself to attention. "Yes. Of course." He filtered his hand back into her hair and she watched in the mirror as it changed back to its original, flat, uninteresting gray.

She sighed as Grey's hand left her hair. She reached out for Kamen's hand and took it between both of hers.

"Take us to her," she said, moving closer to Kamen. She felt as though she needed the comfort of his nearness, even if it was an illusion solely for her own benefit.

Grey nodded and then led the way out of the room. The area outside the door immediately opened up into a huge atrium with soaring windows. They were apparently on the second floor; there was a banister right before them that curved along the balcony and led to a grand, sweeping staircase in the center of the atrium. Grey guided them to the stairs and began to lead them up. With each level the stairs seemed to curve in all kinds of serpentine directions, sometimes moving to the right side of the atrium, sometimes to the left, and sometimes completely around the circumference. By the time they reached the fifth floor, looking down the full distance of the atrium left one feeling a little dizzy.

Grey led them all the way down a wide hall toward a rear window at the end of the long corridor. The house itself seemed huge. They walked for what felt like half a football field's length. Then, at the last door on the right side, he turned the knob and entered the room. The room was enormous, like the rest of the house seemed to be, and looked like a well-appointed sitting room in the style of Marie Antoinette's royal rooms in France. Everything was trimmed in gold.

And there, sitting on a chaise lounge reading a book, was a woman of delicate structure, her hair swept high from her face only to fall in a riot of ringlets bouncing down over her shoulders and back. She was as petite as Viève and looked very fragile in her gossamer white gown with its lace bodice and full-length skirt. With her porcelain pale skin, she reminded Kamen very much of Viève.

She looked up when they entered and smiled at Grey.

"Grey, my angel, what have you brought me to relieve my boredom?" she said in a voice with a thick French accent.

"Ma petite, this is Kamen and Geneviève."

Viève was surprised. She had never told him her name.

"You may call me Viève," she said to the Empress shyly.

"Do you speak French, Geneviève, to go with your French name?" she asked Viève in that language.

Viève answer in kind. "Yes, I do."

The Empress clapped her hands together in delight. "It always pleases me when someone speaks my native tongue."

""Then . . . you are not offended by my presence?" Viève asked.

"No! Why would I be?"

"Because I am a Wraith."

The Empress paled. She jumped up and backed away from Viève. "Grey! How could you? How could you bring one of those vile creatures into my presence!" she cried out in French.

"Please, I mean no offense, and I mean you no harm," Viève said quickly, refusing to hide behind Grey or Kamen. She held out a placating hand. "I am not one of the ones who kept you captive. I would never do something like that."

"As if you would tell us so! Grey, she is not to be trusted. Leave my sight! Leave my sight at once!" Her voice grew shriller as she spoke.

"We will not go until you have heard us out," Kamen spoke up firmly. "You can come to no harm with Grey standing right here. After all, that is why you stay here and do not return home, isn't it? So Grey can protect you? We all know he is the most powerful Djynn in the United States. We wouldn't stand a chance against him."

This seemed to give her a moment's pause, but it was clear to see she was trembling, her hands shaking.

"Do you know what those monsters did to me?" she asked, tears in her voice.

"I only wish I knew why," Viève said with regret. "It makes no sense that they would capture you and treat you in such a manner."

"Did they need a reason?" she asked sharply. "They did it for sport. They knew I had to do whatever they asked or risk being put to death with just a touch of their hands."

"It was cruel of them, but one bad cell does not make all of us the same."

She seemed to think on that. "Very well. I will listen to what you have to say. But you will stay there, at a distance."

"Of course," Viève said. "Whatever makes you most comfortable."

"It would make me most comfortable if you left. But in lieu of that, a distance before me will do. I am not like the dragons or the fairies, I do not have magical powers that do damage. My only ability is to fly. That and to commune with all things in nature,."

"Dragons and fairies?" Viève echoed.

"Yes. Other Mysticals. Don't you know anything of my people?"

"I'm afraid I don't," Viève said. "I've lived a very sheltered life. A very short one compared to most Nightwalkers."

"We are made up of all things mystical. Unicorns, Pegasus, dragons, fairies, brownies, elves, hippogriffs, centaurs . . . the list goes on. If it has been mentioned in a fantasy story, odds are it was real . . . and a Mystical."

"That's a lot of species for one race," Kamen noted.

"We are not a very large population in spite of that. Many of us have been hunted to extinction. Either that or we are held captive by Djynn for use of our powers as nikkis."

"And yet you willingly play the role of a nikki for Grey?" Kamen asked.

"I am not captive. He uses me as a nikki and in exchange he protects me here where no one can reach me."

"It sounds like a prison," Viève said. "To hide where no one can get you means also that you can get to no one."

"What would you have me do? Go out in the world where another Wraith could get hold of me?" she snapped.

"No. I understand why you are afraid. But you cannot live your life in fear," Kamen said.

She relented. "Perhaps not. But I will leave in my own time. Now, tell me what you want."

"It is about Apep." Kamen's mouth formed a grim line. "Any day now we are expecting an attack by him and his forces. And even if he does not attack us, we must find him and put him out of this world before he can do any more damage than he has already done. He is pure evil and must be destroyed if this planet is to have any peace."

"Yes. I have heard of this Apep. But I do not see what any of this has to do with *me*."

"Not with you so much as with your people. I have found ancient writings that indicate that all twelve Nightwalkers races must work together in order to fight this evil."

"Yes, Grey has told me of these other six Nightwalkers you have discovered. I find it most intriguing." She frowned. "Tell me about these writings."

"Well, it was hard to find much since it seems we can't read each other's writings, but I found a little indication of this." Kamen explained what he had found.

"And based on this you feel we should all work together? How many races do you have now?"

"All except yours and the Wraiths, but the Wraiths will join if you do." He told her of their meeting with the Doyen.

"The Wraiths are not to be trusted. They say one thing but could well mean another. They may already be in league with Apep and are simply toying with you."

"That may be true, but what other choice do we have but to trust them at their word until they prove otherwise?" Kamen said.

"I will not risk any of my people on such an unknown." She anxiously nibbled at the tip of one tapered nail.

"We cannot do this without the Mysticals," Kamen said gently.

"I will not risk my people, but I . . . I will risk myself."

"Paulette, no," Grey said suddenly. "You have been through enough. There are those who are stronger, better able to defend themselves."

"No. It must be me. All of these other leaders have sent their best and I should do the same, but . . . no one mistrusts the Wraiths more than I do, and it seems to me you need someone with a good dose of caution where the Wraiths are concerned. You are all too willing to believe them. It is a deadly, dangerous thing. One that could mean the end of you."

Viève didn't know how she felt right then. She was glad that the Empress was willing to help them, but she felt like a pariah. Like she would not be included in this venture as long as the Empress was there to whisper bad things about the Wraiths in people's ears.

But was she wrong to do so? She was just one little half-breed from one little cell in the middle of nowhere. What did she know about the machinations of the Wraith court? Still she hoped Paulette was wrong. She hoped that the Doyen meant what he said about joining the Nightwalkers against Apep.

"Will you come with us now?"

"Not just now. I have to get some things together first. I will come and I will see what is happening for myself before I talk to my captains and have them lend forces to your cause. Now, please go. I need to relax and pack. Grey will bring me when I am ready.

"Very well. Grey, will you send us back?" Kamen asked.

"Of course."

And just like that, they disappeared from Grey's mansion and reappeared in the common room of the Bodywalker house.

# CHAPTER 15

Apep screamed.

"Get it out!" he cried. It wasn't supposed to hurt this much! He was a *god*! Gods did not feel pain!

Well, that wasn't true. But it took a lot for a god to feel pain. Like when that Night Angel deflected his power back onto him. That had hurt. Come to think of it he still owed that bitch for that little infraction. He gritted his inferior mortal teeth together and rode out the next wave of pain. He was dripping with sweat and he was pretty sure his beautiful hairstyle was a thing of the past. The bedding was rumpled, but at least it was dry now. It had been a wet mess when his water had broken.

This giving birth thing was a messy business. He would have to remind himself in the future to never do this again. What had possessed him to think this was a good idea?

Oh. Right. A godly son to sit at his right hand. Yes. That would be worth it. Between him and his son he would rule this world and the Nightwalkers would be a small footnote in history.

"It will be any time now," the doctor said.

"Why are *you* sweating?" Apep growled when he saw the man mop his damp pate for the dozenth time. "I'm the one doing all the work! You're lucky I need you or I would have killed you and your sniveling nurse by now!"

The sniveling nurse released a frightened little sob. Her hands were shaking as she set a glass of water beside the bed.

"Get this away from me!" Apep picked up the glass and hurled it into the wall. It shattered and water sprayed everywhere. "And you said it would be 'any time now' two hours ago!"

"You're nine centimeters dilated," the doctor said in a placating tone. "One more centimeter and you'll be ready to push."

"Why can't I push now?" Apep wanted to know. "I could push nowwww!" Apep squealed as a contraction hit him hard.

"It doesn't work like that," the doctor said, mopping his brow again.

"I'm a god! I can do anything I want!"

"You'll just tire yourself out for nothing. You should conserve your strength for when it's time to push."

"Gah! You humans are useless!"

Apep flung out his hand releasing a discus of energy. It struck the nurse, slamming her back against the wall. She crumpled to the floor, dead.

"Get that thing out of here," Apep growled to one of the Templars hovering anxiously in the doorway. Two Templars hurried in and gathered up the nurse's body, dragging it out of the room.

The doctor had gone a deathly shade of pale, the liver spots on his hands and scalp standing out.

"You didn't have to do that," he said meekly. "We needed her."

"I have Templars that can do what she did without all of the whining and crying. Besides, she's out of her misery now, isn't she?"

"She had children!"

"Well so will I in a minute! And I'm far more important than she was!" Apep sighed as another labor pain passed. This whole business had grown old hours ago.

"You have one more hour," Apep warned the doctor. "If it's not out of me by then I'm going to get a knife and cut it out myself!"

"You'd risk harming the child! And what about you? You'd die of severe blood loss!"

"I'm a god! I can't die!"

The doctor wasn't about to argue. No normal person could do what he had just seen her do. He had thought she was just a dangerous and violent woman with delusions of grandeur, but that bolt of power and his nurse's death had proven her to be every bit the dangerous thing she claimed to be. What if she was a god? She certainly had god-like powers. What would that make the child that was about to be born? He should do something. He should do anything!

She had an IV. He could always inject something into it. He hadn't been able to do an epidural because he wasn't an anesthesiologist and he didn't have the equipment needed to do so anyway. Perhaps he should dope her up. She obviously didn't care about the health of her child. But he cared. Whatever it was, it was an innocent until it proved otherwise. And who was he? He was just one little man in the face of this deadly creature. Maybe he could do something to her after the child was born. Yes! Immediately after he would inject an overdose of morphine into her IV. He might go to jail for murder, but it was better than dying himself. Anyway he doubted he was going to get out of there alive. Once he killed their mistress, these followers would turn on him like rabid dogs.

Or they would hail him as a hero. They looked just as scared of her as he was. He had tried talking to them, but they had shut him down at every opportunity. He was there for one purpose. When that purpose was fulfilled, his life would mean nothing to them.

Yes. He had no choice but to make his move immediately after the birth.

He hoped it was enough.

Viève was in the kitchen making something to eat for herself and Kamen. Neither of them had eaten anything in almost twenty-four hours. She was starving.

The refrigerator was huge and it was full of food so there was plenty to choose from. She decided to make sandwiches. They required very little cooking skill so she couldn't screw them up. No one in her cell had liked her cooking so it was best she not risk it. She only wanted to make good impressions on Kamen and everyone else who was there.

She licked mayonnaise off her finger and began to hum as she folded meat onto the bread. Ham and cheese. Simple. Until she went to slice the tomato and ended up slicing her finger in the process. She cried out and stuck her finger in her mouth. Kamen heard her cry and came rushing in from the next room.

"Here let me see."

"No. If nuffing," she said around her finger. "I'm fine."

"Let me see," he said firmly.

She popped her finger out of her mouth and showed it to him. Blood immediately welled up at the tip.

"Leave it to me to screw up a sandwich," she said dejectedly.

"It's an accident. Everyone has them."

"I'm a Nightwalker. I'm supposed to have preternatural abilities and senses and I can't even slice a fucking tomato."

Her swearing made him smile as he led her to the sink and held her finger under water. Then he wrapped it up in a paper towel.

"Keep pressure on it. The bleeding will stop soon."

"I know," she said grouchily. "I'm a klutz, not stupid."

"You're not a klutz," he said admonishingly.

"You don't know me well enough to say that."

"Well, I'm learning. I know others have made you feel like you're inept, but I'm not going to do that and I'm not going to allow others to do that to you. Including yourself."

She grinned at that, feeling somehow special because of his words. It wasn't something she got to feel very often but she seemed to feel it a lot around him.

"I'll finish making the sandwiches. You sit right there," he said, pointing to a stool at the breakfast bar. She obediently got up on the stool and watched him complete what she had started. He cut the sandwiches, notably without cutting himself, and handed her one. Then he sat down on the barstool opposite her and began to eat.

"Gods I'm hungry," he said between bites. "I didn't even think to feed you last night."

"That's okay. I wasn't even thinking about food."

That made him grin. "What were you thinking about?"

"You know the answer to that. I was . . . I was feeding my soul." She lowered her lashes coquettishly. "You didn't eat either," she pointed out.

"Yes, but *my soul* was quite satisfied."

She laughed. "I'm very happy to hear that." She paused a beat. "But you would tell me, right? I mean, if you weren't. Satisfied." She blushed and covered it by dipping her head and taking a bite of her sandwich.

"I would tell you," he assured her, reaching to touch a finger to her flushing cheek. "And you will do the same, yes?"

"I don't think there's any fear of that," she said.

"Just the same. I want your promise. If there is anything not right for you, you will tell me immediately."

"I promise. I will tell you."

"Good. This is young yet and we do not know each other well enough to read all the outside clues. Honesty is the only way we will learn."

"So . . . there's nothing I'm doing wrong? Nothing I should be doing but I'm not?"

"Nothing I can think of right now. But if something occurs to me you will be the first to know."

"Thank you," she said, feeling pleased with herself for being so bold with him. She wanted to handle this relationship like a mature woman, with realistic expectations. It was wrong of her to feel hurt by a simple slight of words. As he said, the relationship was young yet. Meaning came with time.

It was just that it seemed to come so easy with him. She had never once felt awkward or gauche; he had made her feel like she was normal. Maybe even special.

And while she was happy with the way everyone was treating her—being very friendly and trying to engage her in conversation—she wasn't good at conversation so she felt awkward. But if it was just him, it was different somehow. *He* was different. She never felt like he was judging her. He was the only one in the world she felt that way about.

"Hey you," Marissa greeted as she walked into the kitchen. She disregarded Kamen and stood between their stools so her back was to him. "Viève, we're going to play a game of Nightwalker capture the flag. Want to play?"

"Oh, I couldn't," she said. "I'm not good at games."

"Well, it's more of a drill than it is a game. We're using the game to hone our abilities as a cohesive unit."

"But my ability is a deathtouch. I can't practice using that on any of you because you'd die or become extremely ill."

"Wait, you mean your deathtouch doesn't always kill?" Kamen asked from behind Marissa's back.

Piqued, Viève reached out and gently moved Marissa aside a pair of steps so she could see Kamen and include him in the conversation.

"The deathtouch has degrees," she explained. "It can be like giving someone a dose of the plague or it can be instant death. We can choose how extreme it is. Just like we can control when to use it."

"That's a very handy skill. You can incapacitate without killing. That could be important," Kamen said. "Sometimes the less casualties the better. Remember, the Templars think Apep is still Odjit. They are following her out of loyalty and the dedication she had built up over generations and generations of lives. These are misguided Bodywalkers. Some may not even want to fight, they just don't know how to defect safely."

"We can't think like that or it will make us hesitate when we should be striking hard," Marissa said with a frown.

"I know these people. Many of them are following her because she has promised unity between the warring sides of the Bodywalkers. By now they must be realizing something is very wrong with Odjit. Apep is bloodthirsty and cruel. Odjit was cold and could be cruel, but there was always a purpose to what she did. An explanation for why she was doing something. Apep is just mayhem for the sake of making mayhem. I'm sure they are puzzled as to why she got pregnant. Odjit was never a mother. Not since her original life. She had no tolerance for kids and she made no secret of it. If one of her trusted aides became a parent, she would demote them so they were at a distance from her. There are no children in Odjit's immediate camp."

"So why don't they just leave if she's gotten so bad?" Marissa asked.

"Did it not occur to you that they stay out of fear? If Apep caught someone trying to sneak out of camp what do you think would happen? Probably *has* happened. And those who were caught were no doubt made an example of. Fear is a powerful motivator."

Marissa frowned. "We want unity. We want to end this civil war. But it's gone on so long and people are so inured in their ways . . . including us. We have thought of Templars as 'the enemy' for so long but you're saying many of them are just misguided. What about the souls they suppress? Once a Templar Blends with its host it suppresses the host soul. Templars are not going to want to change that. To 'share' their bodies. They prefer things the way they are."

"Not all. Not all suppress. We are told to by Odjit, but there are those who don't agree and allow an equal Blending to take place."

"What about you? What have you done?" Viève asked.

Kamen frowned. "I have suppressed my host. I have never wanted to do otherwise . . . until recently. I want to put us on equal footing again, but it will have to wait until after this threat is dealt with. I need complete control of my body and my conscience."

"That sounds like an excuse to me," Marissa said harshly.

"It is a truth. The fact is I am far more succinct and cutthroat than my host is. My host soul has also witnessed the things I have done. That has no doubt caused damage to his psyche. There will be a time for reconciliation, but that time is not now."

"I understand," Viève said. "But you will reconcile after?"

"I will," he said with a nod. "It will make me a different person; one I hope you can give the benefit of the doubt to when the time comes," he said to Marissa.

"I'll worry about that when the time comes," Marissa said coolly.

"You're not being fair!" Viève said with frustration.

"Viève . . ." Kamen said.

"No! You're trying. You're making an effort here. And you have been for the better part of a year. You're doing more than anyone else to put this all together. I think you deserve a little bit of consideration for that!"

"You say this after only being here and knowing him for a day?" Marissa said, her tone tightly curious.

"Yes. He's told me what he's done. I understand people were hurt—"

"People were *tortured*," Marissa interrupted. "One of them is living under this roof and still having nightmares because of it!"

"All right I get that!" Viève cried. "But are you going to torture him in return to make up for it?"

"Of course not!"

"Then as I see it that leaves you only one other option. Forgiveness. And you can't just give lip service to it. You have to mean it and start treating him with a modicum of respect. At least do him the courtesy of including him in a conversation. It's just like with the Wraiths. You're going to have to forgive them for their past deeds if you are going to move into the future with them with any semblance of unity. You're willing to do that, aren't you?"

"Of course, but—"

"No! No buts. It's either forgiveness or it isn't. Make up your mind."

"Maybe you need to talk to Leo before you start talking about forgiveness," Marissa said in a hard tone. "Every individual here is going to have to decide for themselves whether or not they think he's worthy of forgiveness. I can't speak for all of them. I certainly can't speak for Leo. And I've died on the other end of the Curse of Ra thrown from his hands." She jerked a thumb at Kamen. "Do you know what it's like to be killed? To be torn apart from another soul and then thrust into the Ether where you have to wait around for a hundred years before you're able to reincarnate? To be deprived of the man you love because you've been hunted down by this Templar and his queen? Until you do, don't talk to me about forgiveness."

Marissa turned her back on them and stormed out of the kitchen.

Kamen sighed. "Thank you for the effort, but they have every right to feel the way that they do. I have caused a great deal of pain. I was sorely misguided for many generations."

"You've made mistakes," she said with a frown. "We all make mistakes."

"Mine were very serious ones."

"I get that. I do. But I've seen Wraiths use their deathtouch like it was nothing. It's so easy to take a life with just a touch. A Nightwalker life. And while the actual death part of the deathtouch doesn't work on humans, the plague part does. We can make a human being very ill—so ill that it can easily lead to death. It manifests as pneumonia or Ebola or anything in between. Humans put it down to chance, bad luck. But I know Wraiths who don't think twice about making a human sick. They make a sport of it. Enjoy watching them suffer. It's horrible. And I'm certainly not proud of being a Wraith when it comes to things like that.

"Do I think they're sincere about this whole idea of unity with the other Nightwalkers? I don't know. But if this is going to work, we have to forgive them for those sins and make an honest effort at working together, at putting past transgressions in the past. It has to be done with the Wraiths and it has to be done with you. Otherwise all of this is just talk and it will never go anywhere." Viève looked down at her half-eaten sandwich. "I've lost my appetite," she said, pushing away from the counter. Kamen reached out and took her arm in his hand, stopping her from going.

"Don't. Don't leave because of this."

"I just need some time to clear my head. I'll be back in a little while."

"All right," he said with reluctance, letting her go. "I'll meet you in our rooms in an hour."

"Okay." She smiled wanly at him. "I'll be there."

She left the kitchen.

# CHAPTER 16

Viève walked outside and found a gathering of Nightwalkers on the lawn. The Phoenixes were there as well as Kat, the Djynn, and Ahnvil, her Gargoyle husband. No one knew exactly where the Gargoyle fit in with all the prophecies and such floating about. But the odds were pretty damn high the Templars would show up with their Gargoyle slaves in tow, ready to do their dirty work. Having their own Gargoyles to combat them was extremely important.

Marissa and Jackson were there as well. And there was the Night Angel, Faith, and other Gargoyles and Bodywalkers Viève did not know. There were also the humans, watching from the sidelines.

They split into teams and began to play, each using their abilities to try and capture the flag from the opposing team.

It was the first time anyone got to see the Phoenixes use their ability.

And what an ability it was. They could throw fire. In many different forms. They could form balls, arrows, darts—all made of fire. They could form a lasso of fire and throw it around an opponent. It had no ability to actually hold the opponent, but it was still encircling the opponent with fire.

It was very powerful.

But the Bodywalkers innate abilities were just as impressive and were quite varied. There was Jackson's ability to move tremendous things with the force of his mind alone. And there was Tameri's/Docia's Templar abilities that, like Kamen, could cast spells such as the Curse of Ra. Although it was obvious she was using a watered down version of the red energy bolt for the sake of the games, as no one was truly injured by it.

Ram's ability was control of the weather, but since there was no real practical use for that, outside of a lightning strike which he could not use to practice with, he relied on pure strength. He could pack a punch that would rock his opponent's world. One strike of his fist could shatter a boulder into tiny smithereens. An interesting ability to have when up against Gargoyles, who were made of stone.

As the two teams fought against each other, Viève walked down the sidelines, making a beeline for Leo. He was watching his wife with a measure of frustration; it was clear he wanted to be out there by her side. But he had to realize that even if he was armed, there was little he could do in this kind of fight.

And it was clear that fact burned him.

"Go get 'em, babe!" he shouted out onto the field. Then he saw Viève and gave her a guarded, "Hey."

"Hello. I was wondering if I could talk to you for a minute."

"Sure. About what?"

"Kamen."

Leo stiffened. He gave her a hard look. "What about him?"

"I know that he hurt you—"

"You know that, huh? How well do you think you know that? Do you know what it's like to have strips of your skin peeled off you? To have your belly cut open and your insides taken out and shown to you? To watch a psychopath play in your blood? Do you know that?"

Viève paled. "No," she whispered.

"I didn't think so."

"But . . ." she said gingerly, "are you going to make him pay for it forever? Is there something you can do that will make you feel like the scales are balanced?"

Leo frowned. "I wouldn't even do that to my worst enemy. I guess my worst enemy is a lucky fellow." He eyed her critically. "Very lucky. I didn't think anyone could stand his company, let alone be touched by him."

"He's not the monster you think he is. Not anymore."

"And you know this after what . . . a day of fucking him?"

She flinched but said, "Yes. It's only taken me a day to realize there is a good man trying to get out from under his deeds of the past."

"It's hard to look beyond those deeds and see what you think you see."

"Hard, but not impossible. If you try."

"So you want me to just forget everything that happened to me? Forgive and forget?"

"Forgive, yes. Forget . . . I only wish that you could. I'm sure you do too."

Leo toed a clump of dirt on the ground. "Yeah. More than you know." He looked at her. "So you think I should hold hands with him and sing 'Kumbaya'?"

"No. But maybe everyone could stop punishing him and start helping him as he tries to do the right thing."

"We are helping him. Look out at this field. This is us helping him get everyone working together."

"Yes. And this is great. A real achievement—one that wouldn't have happened without him. The Empress of the Mysticals will be here soon and then you will have all twelve Nightwalkers under the same roof. Finally. Thanks to Kamen."

Leo was silent, his jaw working a moment. "I do give him credit for that."

"You do? How?"

"What? You want us to hug it out?"

"No, I just want you to start treating him with the respect he's earned. And he has earned it, hasn't he?"

"Some," Leo admitted. "But it doesn't erase the past."

"Nothing can erase the past. But the best thing for all of us is to leave it behind. The only way we'll move forward is if we forgive the crimes of the past. For Kamen. For the Wraiths. For the Templars and the Gargoyles who fight with them. If we want true unity, it has to be done."

Leo tapped out a rhythm with his fingers against his thigh. It was quick and agitated.

"I suppose you're right about that," he said reluctantly. "No. You're definitely right about that. Damn it. And maybe it's the only way for me to move on from this. To find a little peace with it. Peace I would desperately love to have."

"I think we all could use a little peace right about now. This accord . . . it's very important."

"Yes. It is. Listen, let me think about this a little. Let me think about . . . about how to come to terms with this. With Kamen."

"Of course. I'm not here to force you into anything. That isn't going to help at all."

"You couldn't force me even if you wanted to," Leo said. "But you do have me thinking. I'm not an ignorant man. A stubborn one, but not an ignorant one."

"I would never accuse you of that."

"But I'm running the risk of being that, aren't I? Being closed-minded. Prejudiced. You're right. That's not going to fly if we're to make any kind of peace with each other."

"Thank you," she said softly. "Thank you for at least thinking about it."

"You're welcome. Now c'mon. You gonna get out there and play or what?"

"Oh no! I can't. I can't use my deathtouch."

"No, but you can touch. We'll use the honor system. If you touch someone then they're out of the game until that round is over. C'mon, it'll be good practice for everyone."

"Well . . . all right."

Viève walked out onto the field and played.

Kamen came out onto the porch and watched.

He sat with a cup of coffee in one of the rocking chairs facing out toward the front of the property where everyone was gathered. He rocked the chair in an absentminded fashion, his attention trained on Viève and the group of fighters out on the lawn. She looked so small compared to everyone else out there. The thing about Bodywalkers was that they got to pick and choose who they were resurrected into, whose body they were going to share. True, the human had to be on the brink of death, but there were plenty of beautiful people dying all the time. So, every last one of the Bodywalkers out there were tall and beautiful, save Docia. Tameri had chosen a simple, pretty girl with extra curves to be reborn into.

As the only other Templar there, the first of their kind to defect to and be accepted by the Politic side, Tameri was the only one out on the field wielding the Curse of Ra. He should really join them, give them two targets to work against, one on each team. This way both teams got a taste of what it felt like to come up against the Curse. When they met up with the Templars, the Curse was going to be their main weapon and it was important they were battle-ready against it.

But he stayed where he was, sipping his coffee and watching Viève play. In the beginning she was withdrawn and shy, looking very awkward out on the field. Until Jackson flung a boulder the size of a Buick at her and she reacted instinctively, phasing so that it passed through her harmlessly. She took it personally. He could tell by the expression that immediately crossed her face. But then she seemed to shake herself up, she set her chin and launched into the air. Apparently, while she was phased, she could fly. It hadn't even occurred to him. But it should have. How else had she gotten them in and out of the Doyen's stronghold? They had "flown" up and down through the earth.

She flew straight at Jackson and before he could dodge her she solidified and touched him.

"Aw, man!" Kamen heard him cry. When she had joined the game Leo had outlined the rules. If Viève touched the player he was out of the game until the next round.

Before long she was caught up in the nature of the game. Yes, they were practicing battle techniques, but they were having fun while doing it. Before long she was laughing and joking with the rest of them.

They had accepted her.

Good. He had been worried about that. Worried that her association with him would taint her. Still, it hadn't kept his hands off her, he thought grimly. He'd been too selfish. He'd wanted her too much.

He was touched by the way she leapt to defend him, but he could have told her it was a losing battle. He didn't deserve forgiveness, couldn't she see that? This business with the Wraiths and Templars was different. That was about forgiving a people as a whole; not about forgiving specific crimes of an individual.

Right?

He frowned to himself. Wait. That didn't make sense. A people as a whole was made up of individuals. Each of those individuals had committed heinous acts against others and yet, if they were going to be given forgiveness as a whole . . . then that meant his crimes should also fall under the title of forgiveness.

But did the Templars and the Wraiths truly deserve that forgiveness? Did they deserve it any more or less than he did?

He could think himself in circles about this. In the end it came down to what he personally felt he deserved. And he did not think he deserved the forgiveness of people like Leo, whom he had wronged so egregiously.

He watched her play for a little while longer, then he went back into the house. He didn't know when the Empress was going to make an appearance, but he wanted to be ready for her when she did. He might only have all twelve races together in the same room for a short time. Since he could not find anything about reversing the curse, his only recourse was to make something up on his own. He would draw in components from other similar spells and create a new spell, honing the magic to a specific task. He might just be powerful enough to do it. If the second most powerful magic-using being on earth couldn't bring this to fruition, then no one could. No one on their side anyway. Perhaps Odjit could have, but she was clearly not going to be casting any spells any time soon. Certainly not to their benefit.

He found his journal and began leafing through the pages. He looked up some time later when Viève sat at his feet with a flounce and rested her chin on his knee as she panted softly for breath.

"I'm pooped!" she declared.

"You've only been out there a few minutes."

"I've been out there for over an hour!" She pointed to the clock and he was surprised to see how much time had passed while he was studying his journal. "What are you doing?" she asked him.

"Looking for answers," he said with an exhalation of breath. "I'm constructing a spell I hope will lift the veil between the First and Second Factions of Nightwalkers."

"Well, I won't bother you then," she said, moving to get up and leave him. But he caught her shoulder in his hand and with a gentle press kept her at his feet. "Don't go," he said quietly.

She gave him a half a smile. "But you'll study much better without me to distract you."

"That may be true, but the studying will be far less enjoyable."

"So what am I to do? Sit at your feet and watch you?" she asked, indicating her position on the floor with a sweep of her hand.

"No," he said with a twitch of his lips. "The idea of you on the floor at my feet will definitely not be conducive to me concentrating."

Her smile turned sly as she got up on her knees and moved around his feet until she was kneeling between his legs, her hands running up the length of his thighs. Her hands felt hot through the material of his jeans. All of the concentration of the past hour flew right out the window. Thoughts turned numb as sensation took over. She leaned forward, her breasts a warm weight against the fly of his jeans. Her touch drifted up the ridges of his abdomen until her flat palms were running over his chest.

"Are you concentrating now?" she asked.

"Yes. On the wrong thing, however," he said. He reached out and traced a thumb across a cheek that was ruddy with her outdoor play in the cool night air.

"Whatever do you mean?" she asked coyly. Her hands reversed direction and drew down his chest, rode over the hard bumps of his belly muscles and she reared back to make way for her hands to rub right down the length of his fly. He sucked a breath in through his teeth. She found him hard beneath her touch and she rubbed at him some more.

"There is no time for this," he murmured tightly.

"Yes. You are right," she said contritely, once more rising to get up. Again he stopped her from doing so with a firm hand on her shoulder.

"We will make time," he said.

She smiled and leaned forward, pressing her breasts against him as he leaned forward for a kiss of great depth and greater heat. All the while her hands worked between them to unfasten his jeans, pulling the zipper down. With a few tugs she pulled his jeans down past his hips. Then she dipped her hand into his underwear and wrapped her fingers around his hardening shaft. She licked her soft pink lips and his whole body tightened with need and want. His hands had gone to her shoulders, and now his fingers tightened around her flesh. She pulled him free of his boxers and stroked him from root to tip.

"Are you concentrating still?" she asked him, doing that provocative licking of her lips again.

"Very much so," he said raspily.

"Good. Now try and stay focused," she said, the light of mischief in her eyes.

"I shall do my level best," he said.

She laughed at him and he smiled as she dipped her head down and blew a soft, sustained breath across his heated flesh. Then she took a deep breath in.

"I love the way you smell. Like bergamot and man and sex all wrapped up into one." She leaned forward and touched her tongue to the tip of his cock, giving him an experimental lick. Then she regarded him with serious eyes. "You'll tell me if I'm doing this wrong?" she asked him.

"You're already doing it right," he said huskily.

She smiled at that. Then she dipped her head again and this time she danced her tongue all around his glans. She picked him up into her hand and stroked him as she closed her mouth fully around him. He sucked in a sharp breath between his teeth and she hesitated, looking up at him with question in her eyes. He shook his head. Content, she swirled her tongue around him again and sucked him deep into her mouth.

There weren't many places for him to put his hands. What he wanted to do was to bury them into her hair and guide her while he thrust into her mouth, but he didn't want to control this. She was in control. She needed to be in control. It was important to her and therefore it was important to him.

So he gripped the arms of the chair he was in and forced himself to relax, to take deep, even breaths. But that was hard to do when in the voracious mouth of a woman bent on pleasing every last one of his senses. His every nerve ending seemed to come alive, the electric sensations riding over and through him in wonderful waves. There was a thump of sound and some distant part of his brain registered that it was his journal hitting the floor. He couldn't care less. Her mouth was hot and wet around him, first pulling him in, and then slowly sliding away. She employed one hand to stroke him whenever she receded, while her other hand curved around his hip, her fingers digging lightly into his left buttock. He had the inane thought that she was left-handed. He didn't know why that should matter.

She moved her hand aside so she could lick him from tip to root and back again. The act was slow and tortuous and he groaned in relief when she took him in her mouth again. He loved everything she was doing, every single slow stroke and sensual tasting, but a sense of urgency was beginning to build in him. He gripped at the arms of the chair, willing himself into submission. And yet he couldn't seem to stop himself from thrusting against her palate.

"Gods, Viève, stronger," he begged her. "Faster—yes!" He threw his head back and felt her obey his commands, let himself fall dizzily into the sensations she was providing for him. Need clawed through the seat of his sac, building up tightly there, readying for release. It wouldn't take much longer. She was working him in earnest now, her mouth stroking and gliding and oh so heavenly sweet.

"Viève! Viève, I'm going to come!" It was more a warning than a pronouncement. He didn't want her to experience anything she wasn't ready for. But she absorbed the announcement by redoubling her speed.

Pure lust screamed through him. He shouted out and began to come in hard, pulsating bursts. Now his hands found her hair, his fingers boring through the fine strands. He gripped at her, trying to will himself into calming. But his heartbeat thundered on and on. He blinked his lashes, trying to clear his vision of the bursts of color he had seen so brightly.

She let go of him and he sagged back into the chair.

He tipped her head back and looked into her smiling eyes. They were the eyes of a woman satisfied with her accomplishment. And she should feel satisfied. She had wrung him out, made him lose even the smallest ounce of control.

All focus and all thoughts of his magic had been shot straight to hell.

# CHAPTER 17

When the Empress arrived, it was with Grey in tow. He had vowed never to leave her side during all of this, to protect her with all that he could. After all, she was his most powerful nikki. It was in his best interest.

Kamen and Viève didn't realize she had arrived at first. Kamen had gone back to studying his spell journals, carefully crafting together what he thought he would need to break the curse. He took portions of other curse breakers, a portion of reveal spells, and a little bit of truth spells. He drew them all together and thought he had come up with something that could work.

When he and Viève went downstairs, it was with all the supplies he would need to cast the spell. He walked into the large common room and found almost everyone from the Second Faction sitting in the room. Apparently they had called a meeting of the groups to welcome the Empress. There was also Max, Angelina, and Leo, the three humans who had been acting as go-betweens between the two worlds. It was just what he needed. Everyone. Together. And he told them as much. Told them of his plans and his concocted spell. He could tell it didn't go over well with many of the people in the room, but as Marissa said:

"What other choice do we have?"

"All right," Leo said. "Everyone from both factions is in this room. And let me tell you, this whole sharing space thing is unnerving. From my perspective I see two people sitting in the same chair but it looks like they're sitting inside one another. Very creepy."

"For the spell I am casting," Kamen said, "we all need to occupy our own space in the room. If we suddenly become visible to one another we don't want to be occupying the same space, just in case."

It took some rearranging and communication through the humans in the room, but eventually they were all in their own individual space.

"Now I want to clear any extraneous people from the room. All I need is one person from each race in here at the same time. Choose who stays and who goes."

After Leo relayed this message, the Second Faction cleared the room except for Viève, the Wraith; Paulette, the Mystical; Grey the Djynn; Kamen, the Bodywalker, Faith, the Night Angel; and Cordo the Phoenix.

On the First Faction's side it was Sagan, the Shadowdweller; Bella, the Druid; Jacob, the Demon; Jasmine, the Vampire; Jinaeri the Lycanthrope; and Windsong, the Mistral.

"Leo, you and Angelina and Max are going to serve as our links. Everyone is to hold hands with each other using our human friends as the link between First and Second Factions. While you are doing that, I am going to get everything ready."

Everyone in the room linked hands. To those on the Second Faction's side it looked as though Leo was holding hands with thin air on one side and Faith on the other. The only one not connected was Kamen, who was preparing the components of his spell. Viève stood on the end of the line of linked hands, waiting to take his hand in hers.

"I hope like hell this works," Leo said, his mistrust of Kamen and all things magical coming through in his voice and his expression. "This is starting to piss me off. We need to be able to connect with each other." He held up his hands, one of which held Faith's, the other of which held Bella's. He could see them both, feel them both, and yet they were not able to see each other even though they were so close. It was frustrating. They needed to come together. It was the only way.

"I am ready to begin," Kamen said as he lit a sage wand and burned it until the smoke filled the air. He set it down in a dish and let it continue to burn. Then he opened his journal to the page he had used to craft the spell on and laid it down on the coffee table next to the burning sage. There were other herbal components strewn out on the table. Rosemary for remembrance. Thyme for constancy. Saffron for awareness. Paprika for harmony. He had brought every herb he could think of that had to do with awareness or remembrance. The sage was just to cleanse the room of any residual magic, if there was any. That meant dispelling the darkness spell Valera used to protect her husband, Sagan, so he had seen the main breaker shut off first.

"This may feel strange, it may even manifest violently," Kamen said. "It is imperative that no one breaks the circle at any time." He looked to his left at Angelina who stood waiting with her hand held out and Viève on his right doing the same.

He took their hands simultaneously.

The room exploded.

Or that was how it felt. Lightning struck in the center of the living room, wind began to blow violently around them, whipping at their hair and stinging their eyes. A clap of thunder was heard all around them and the room began to shake violently, as if there was an earthquake. Angelina fell to the ground, but Kamen gripped her hand harder.

"Don't break the circle!" he shouted to all of them. Leo echoed the warning to the First Faction.

"What did you do?" Leo shouted accusatorily.

"I didn't do anything!" he shouted back. "This is happening on its own! I never got a chance to even try to cast my spell! I think the curse is breaking on its own because—!"

He was cut off when a growl tore through the room, then what sounded like a feminine scream of rage.

"Noooo!" it cried angrily.

Then there was another blinding flash of lightning and when everyone's eyes recovered . . .

There were fifteen people standing in the room.

And they could all see each other.

The first thing they realized was that one of them was screaming in agony.

The Shadowdweller. The lightning strikes had burned his retinas, blinding him, and it had seared his flesh so that his exposed skin was a raw, open burn filled with blisters oozing pus. Everyone ran to him.

"Get back!" Kamen commanded in a booming voice. Everyone immediately obeyed. He kneeled before the Shadowdweller, who was on the floor writhing in pain. He laid a hand on top of his shoulder, a part of him that had been covered by clothing and unexposed to the lightning so it would not hurt him.

He chose his healing spell very carefully. It had to be a spell that didn't give off any light at all or it could do even more damage . . . potentially even kill him. They were fortunate he was still alive as it was.

Kamen spoke the words of the spell quietly and strongly, ignoring the clamor of voices and concerns going on around him. He bathed the Shadowdweller in lightless, healing energy; dulled his pain until the screams died down.

"Sagan!" Valera cried.

She and many others had rushed into the room the minute they had heard the screams. Now she ran to him, wanting to throw herself protectively over him, but knowing that she would only harm him further if she did. She settled for sitting on the floor beside him and placing her lap beneath his head. She shushed him gently as his cries of agony quieted down.

Silence gripped the room, except for Kamen who was continually speaking the words of his spell, over and over again. Valera knew healing magic of her own, but she didn't use it for fear of disrupting the Bodywalker's work.

Kamen followed his healing spell with another spell. A quick Word that put the injured Shadowdweller into a deep sleep.

"We should bring him to a bed," Kamen said. "Somewhere he can rest comfortably while I continue to heal him."

"Take him to our room," Jackson said. "It's better than carrying him all the way to the other house."

Kamen nodded, then cast a levitation spell, which lifted the Shadowdweller into the air without need of any hands to touch his injured body. He followed the floating man as he directed him up the stairs and into the master suite of the house. He waited for Valera to enter, then shut the door behind them. He lowered Sagan onto the bed and immediately Valera moved a pillow to place under his head.

"Take off his shirt," Kamen instructed.

She nodded and gingerly went about taking his shirt off. It made her cry to see the painful burns on his flesh. Belated fear gripped her. He could have died. He could have been gone in an instant and she never would have had the chance to . . . oh, the list of things was endless. To say she loved him one last time. To go back home to Alaska. To give him a child. There were dozens of things they hadn't done yet that they had wanted to do one day.

One day almost hadn't come. For good.

No. She wouldn't think like that. He was there now. She would protect him. He would be healed and she would protect him until her dying breath.

Downstairs, in the living area, almost three dozen people stood around looking at each other. Confident that Kamen was caring for the injured Nightwalker, they now were able to take stock of themselves and each other.

Bella was the first to speak.

"Hi!" she said, waving. "I'm Bella! This is Jacob and . . ."

The introductions flew around the room, First and Second Factions no longer existing as they all became one. Nightwalkers. Once everybody was introduced, a slightly overwhelmed Viève said, "I don't know about you all, but I could use a drink."

The sentiment was echoed all around. Most of them took to the liquor cabinet, the Demons went to the fridge.

"So that's why there's zebra milk in the fridge!" Viève exclaimed when she was told a Demon's alcohol was animal milk. Different animals equaled different "proofs" of liquor. Cow's milk had the potency of grape juice. Zebra milk was like a fine whiskey. "When I saw it I thought it was a joke. Say, how does one get zebra milk exactly?"

"Very carefully," Bella and Jacob said in unison.

The room erupted in chuckles.

"Well, the curse is broken obviously," Jasmine said. "What do we do now?"

"We train," Leo said. "Together."

"Wow, our teams for 'capture the flag' have just doubled in size," Faith said.

"And that's a good thing. Now we train as a cohesive unit instead of split factions," Jackson said.

"Did anyone else hear that woman's scream?" Viève asked hesitantly.

"I did," Leo said, "and what's more, I think I recognized it."

"What are you thinking, Leo?"

"I think it was Apep. And I think he knows the curse is broken," Leo said.

"I can't decide if that's bad news or good news," Jackson said grimly.

"When it comes to Apep, it's all bad news," Leo said.

"True," Jackson agreed. "Well, now that I can properly welcome you all to my home, welcome to Portales. I hope we've been seeing to your every need."

"Not quite. There's no delivery in this town. What do I do when I get the munchies in the middle of the night?" Jasmine asked. They all laughed as Jasmine licked her fangs and said, "Nothing beats a pizza delivery guy for a midnight snack."

"Other than that?" Jackson asked with a chuckle.

Everyone agreed that they were quite comfortable.

"Great. Now that that's settled, I'm up for a game of capture the flag. And everyone's playing," Jackson said sternly. "Well, except for the humans that is."

"Thank god," Angelina said. Her sister, Marissa, had signed her on for all of this when she had told her who and what she had become, but she wasn't going to stick her delicate human neck into the fray. She wasn't stupid with a cup of crazy on the inside.

That was Leo.

He may not be playing, but he was watching. He shouted tactics from the sidelines, and cheered and jeered when necessary. He kept them all motivated. He was walking around armed, an automatic on his hip with a backup strapped to his ankle. He wouldn't know how much damage a bullet could do until the time came, but he'd be damned if he was going to stay on the sidelines when the real thing came down on them.

"Max, come spar with me," Leo said.

If he got his hands on someone, Leo would need to make the most of the situation as quickly as possible before their disparate abilities kicked in. Between his gun and a body honed for fighting, he had a fair shot at it.

Maybe.

But he refused to count himself out until he was lying dead on the floor.

His wife, Faith, was of a different mind-set. She knew that Leo was outgunned and outmatched. Maybe he could cause some damage to a Templar, but there would no doubt be a wave of Templars, not just one. He wouldn't have a prayer. She needed to convince him that his place was protecting the lives of the humans on the property and getting them to safety. He had to have a role—an important one—or he wouldn't be satisfied. Now that they were a cohesive bunch, Corrine was happy to hand over her duties to Leo and become a follower.

"Leo, can we talk?" Faith asked him as they walked outside.

"I know what you're going to say," he said with a frown.

"You need to see reason!" she said with frustration. "Someone needs to see Max and Angelina and the non-offensive members to safety when this all goes down! They can't do it themselves. They need a stone-cold killer to help them and someone who knows how to move with a fair amount of speed and stealth. They will become targets instantly if they are seen."

Leo's jaw tightened and released. "But I can't just turn my back on you. I can't just leave you and not know what is happening to you."

"I will be fine and you know it. My innate ability to reflect spells back on the caster will protect me more than you ever could."

"Gee. Thanks," he said sullenly.

"Leo, please . . . I won't be able to concentrate on the battle if I think you are at risk."

"All the more reason why we should be taking the fight to them instead of standing here waiting like sitting ducks."

"We don't even know where they are," Faith said.

"I know," Leo said dejectedly. "This really sucks. I don't like it."

"But you'll do it?" Faith asked hopefully.

Leo grumbled. "I'll do it. But Angelina should leave now. She has no fighting skills whatsoever and now that everyone can see each other we don't need her to act as a go-between."

"I'll talk to Marissa about that. Angelina may not want to go. Marissa is all the family she has."

"All the more reason. When the shit hits the fan I need to know she's not going to linger, to fight me taking her away so that she can see what happens to her sister."

"Just as you would fight to see what happens to me?"

"Exactly like that. But if you give me a job and I say I'm going to do it, it'll get done. I'll get the others to safety no matter what."

"Good. There's a storm cellar in the far back of the property. You're to take them there and wait until one of us comes to get you."

"Provided you win. If you lose we'll be stuck there and you can bet Apep isn't going to abandon a perfectly good property once he has it."

"Another reason why they need you. If that's the case they are going to need you to get them off the property as soon as the sun rises. No one will be able to stop you as long as the sun is out. The sun will turn the Gargoyles to stone and it will paralyze the Bodywalkers. The only one that leaves is Apep, and he can't be everywhere at all times."

"Yes, he can. He's a god," Leo said.

"Not an omniscient one. He has limitations. Otherwise he would have known we were trying to break this curse and thrown everything he had against us by now."

"Everything but himself. But he's waiting. I can feel it. And as soon as he gets whatever it is he needs, he's going to come at us," Leo said.

"I think he's waiting for the birth of this child. It must be taxing him in some way. If only we could attack him now, while he is so obviously weak . . ."

"But as you said, we don't know where he is."

"Maybe we can change that," Faith said. "Kamen has been able to locate the two Nightwalker groups using a spell. Why couldn't he do the same for Apep's stronghold?"

"I don't know how the spell works, but you have a point. If he can find one why not the other? And why hasn't he made the suggestion himself before now?" Leo asked with suspicion.

"It would have been useless with us not being able to see each other. Give him a shred of the benefit of the doubt. Let's approach him with the subject and see how he responds."

"You're right," Leo said. "It's not as though he hasn't been busy. You know, the little Wraith said something to me tonight . . ."

"What did she say?"

He reached to touch the ebony skin at the side of her neck, stroking her there in a familiar way he knew she loved. "That none of us were going to be able to make it if we didn't forgive the transgressions of the past. For everyone. The Wraiths. Any Templars who wish to defect. Including Kamen."

"She makes a good point. But forgiveness comes with trust and trust must be earned."

"But hasn't he though?" Leo asked tightly. "Hasn't he earned it? When I look at all he's done this past year, the effort he has made has been tremendous. He's almost been trying too hard."

"He is passionate about correcting the mistakes of his past."

"Yeah, I can see that." Leo ran his fingers down the long length of her arm until he was linking his fingers with hers. "It's hard to shake the injuries of the past," he said quietly.

"It's up to you, Leo. You have to choose to do it for your own reasons, not for anyone else's. Viève's a sweet thing really, and her heart is in the right place, but she doesn't get to dictate when you should be ready to forgive what was a truly heinous act."

"He didn't do it himself," Leo heard himself saying, much to his shock. "He was responsible for what happened to me, but he didn't actually stick his hands inside my body and root around. That was Chatha. And Chatha is gone now."

"Yes. He is. But as you say, Kamen was responsible. He sent Chatha on you like a master commands a pitbull to attack an innocent bystander."

"Yes. But maybe that distance is what I need to come to terms with this. And maybe if I come to terms, the damn nightmares will stop."

"They have gotten to be less and less ever since Chatha was released from this earth," Faith pointed out.

"Yeah. It helped knowing he was gone. Knowing he wouldn't somehow find me and put me under his knife again."

"No. He is gone and it is over for good," Faith said, stepping into his arms and giving him the comforting nearness of her body.

"Come on," he said after clearing his throat. "Let's go play." He kissed her on her temple, turned her away from himself and propelled her forward with a smack on her ass. She yelped and then purred, rubbing the spot suggestively. "Why do you always tease me in public?"

"Because it makes the private so much more fun. Now get going, dirty girl."

She shot him a smoldering glance, then moved out of the house and onto the playing field.

# CHAPTER 18

Kamen left the Shadowdweller sleeping peacefully, and shut the door behind him. He was surprised to see Viève standing in the hall waiting for him. One look at her tension-riddled face and he knew something was wrong.

"What is it?"

"Is he going to be all right?" she asked.

"Yes. He's already almost completely healed."

"Good. That's good," she said, rubbing her palms together anxiously.

He took her hands in his and met her eyes as he squeezed calmness into them. "What troubles you?" he asked directly.

"Time. Time troubles me," she said. "If what we suspect is true, then Apep knows what has happened and that the curse is broken. He could attack at any time."

"Yes, this is true. Are you frightened?"

"Yes, but that isn't what troubles me. If time grows short then we have to go back to the Doyen as quickly as possible. We need to tell him what has happened and secure more Wraiths for the coming battle. With Wraiths on our side the odds will shift considerably in our favor. Especially if you want to try to keep the body count low, to give Templars a chance to redeem themselves. We can incapacitate with just a touch, without the need to kill. Because they are Bodywalkers and have advanced healing abilities it is less likely that the plaguetouch will actually kill them. And, if necessary, the deathtouch is still an option. But we must secure them as soon as possible. We must see if the Doyen is willing to keep his word."

"You do not believe he will?" Kamen asked her.

"I . . . I do not trust my own people to do anything that isn't selfishly motivated. If what he says is true, if Apep has approached him to fight on his side and he doesn't want to get caught up in all of that, then he may believe that siding with you is the better option. But he also may just want to see if he can stay out of the altercation entirely. He may want to sit back and let us do all of the dirty work for him."

"If what he says is true, he may not have that option. Apep will not take kindly to a refusal."

"Perhaps. But he might just be willing to take his chances. I don't know. The only way to know is to meet with him now."

"All right. Let me tell Valera that I will be back shortly and then you and I can go to the Doyen. Go find Jackson and Marissa and tell them where we are going."

She nodded and hurried to do so. He found her outside a short while later, talking to Jackson and Marissa on the sidelines of the game that was being played.

He came up behind her and placed a hand at her small waist. She looked up at him at his touch, worry etched into her features.

"Has she told you where we are going?" he asked Jackson.

"She has, but I was just telling her that I'm not certain I like the idea of you going alone."

"It has to be alone. Any more than just the two of us and the Doyen might feel threatened," Viève said.

"She has a point," Kamen said. "The Doyen is a little on the slippery side. I wouldn't want him to escape us on the basis of a technicality."

"If he is that touchy, then perhaps we don't need his help," Jackson said. "Thanks to our own little Wraith, the curse has been broken. Perhaps we no longer need the Wraiths for the battle to come."

"You know that we do. Every advantage on our side makes it more likely we will be victorious over Apep. Also, I am afraid it is just as likely the Doyen will side with Apep if we do not secure him first."

"All right. Go to him," Jackson said. "Come back quickly with his answer. Viève . . ." Jackson turned to her and rested his hands on her shoulders. "You have been invaluable to us. We could not have broken this curse without you. I hope that you will return with Kamen regardless of your Doyen's decision."

Viève looked surprised.

"I had not thought to do otherwise," she said.

That made both Jackson and Kamen smile. "Good," Jackson said. "Come back quickly. Very quickly."

Viève walked away with Kamen, her mind spinning. They wanted her to come back. They wanted *her*. She had been stressing out, trying to think of a way to make herself useful to them so that she would be allowed to stay, but then Jackson had asked her to come back.

Tears threatened and she didn't know why. No. Wait. She did know why. No one had ever wanted her before. No one had ever gone out of their way to request her presence. No one except maybe Kamen. But Kamen wanted her for sex. It was great sex and more than she had ever hoped to have in her life, but it was still just sex. And that was the way it should be after only a day of knowing one another. She couldn't possibly ask for more. But what a day it had been. Twenty-four hours had changed her life so dramatically. The lives of all the Nightwalkers had been changed so dramatically.

But here now was an opportunity to maybe make things . . . more. Maybe she could find a place here. A wanted place. Maybe one day Kamen might want her for more than sex. She didn't see how, seeing as though he was so driven to do other things and . . . well . . . she was who she was. But at least there was a chance she could maybe make herself useful to him to the point where he might not want to let her go. Not any time soon. Oh, she had no doubt that it would come to an end at some point. She would invariably do something stupid or wrong and it would piss him off enough that he would be done with her. But until then she wanted to live this life of feeling like she was wanted. However long or short a time as it was, she wanted to live this life.

And who knew . . . maybe when Kamen was done with her she might still find a place here among these people. They had all been so kind and accepting so far. Again, she had not had the opportunity to screw up yet, and that was only a matter of time. At least they had found her useful so far. Now all she had to do was keep being useful to them. And she could be. If there was a coming battle, her deathtouch could make a difference.

If she was able to do it. She had never used her deathtouch before. Not to pass plague or to kill a Nightwalker. Her cell members had sneered that she was a coward, that she didn't have it in her to be a true Wraith. That she was watered down by her half-breed genes.

But she would be able to do it. She would continue to play their games and become more comfortable with the idea of touching someone in a fight. When Apep came she would be unafraid to do what she had to do.

Or at least that was what she hoped.

"You're deep in thought," Kamen remarked to her.

"Hmm? Oh. I . . . I was just thinking of what we will say to the Doyen."

"We will simply tell him what we have done and that it is time for him to hold up his side of the bargain."

"I pray it's that easy," she said wistfully.

"Come." He came to a stop and held out his hands to her. She took them readily. "Ready?" he asked.

She nodded. She had learned it was best to close her eyes during the streak. It made it wholly less disconcerting. She closed her eyes and focused on where they had to go, just as she had the first time. She didn't know if he needed her to, since he already had been there and knew where it was, but she did it all the same.

The streak was hard and fast. They left it with a jolt and when she opened her eyes they were once more inside the wire fence in that desolate desert area. She was still holding his hands, so she was easily able to phase them together and pushed them down into the rock and soil. They appeared in the same room as before, only this time it was by design rather than happenstance.

However, the room was empty. They moved toward the door and peeked out of it. There was a large hallway just beyond the door and they could hear people talking. They slipped out into the hall quietly. They had to find the Doyen without running into any of his subordinates first. To be safe, Viève made sure she had tight hold of Kamen's hands. As long as he was phased, no one could use their deathtouch on him. She would not see him harmed through some sort of misunderstanding.

The hallway emptied out into a large living area, a well-appointed room with marble tiled floors, thick Persian rugs and old restored antiques. The artwork on the walls was large and, no doubt, expensive.

There were three men in the living area. Each was seated on different chairs, all facing one another. None of them was the Doyen. They were Wraiths in business suits, their gray hair and faces standing out sharply against navy blue and black fabrics.

Viève and Kamen snuck back into the hallway. There were several doors leading off it that might lead them to the Doyen. They phased through one of the doors and found themselves in a large bathroom with shining black marble and brushed nickel fixtures. Luckily it was unoccupied. The thing about phasing was it was easy to phase into someone else's privacy.

There was a second door adjoining into the bath and they moved toward it, their feet floating six inches off the floor. This time when they phased through the door the room was very much occupied. They stumbled right into a large office that had at least four Wraiths in it.

Someone caught sight of them right away.

"What the hell?"

Viève panicked as all four Wraiths turned to face them. She went to push off. To get them out of there.

Three of the occupants of the room came rushing toward them.

"Viève, wait!" Kamen said.

"No! I have to get you out of here!"

"Viève, it's the Doyen!"

Viève stopped moving and turned to see that the fourth person, sitting in a relaxed pose behind the desk, was the Doyen.

The other three Wraiths reached them and formed a wall between them and the Doyen.

"I can't get to him," Viève whispered. "Wraiths can't phase through one another!"

"Gentlemen," the Doyen spoke up, "let the half-breed through."

The Wraiths cast doubtful glances between each other and the Doyen. Then they stepped aside and let Viève and Kamen move forward. They came to a stop on the other side of the desk.

"Well now, I really hadn't thought I would see you two again," he said.

"We've done what you asked!" Viève blurted out. "All eleven Nightwalkers are joined together. The Wraiths are the only holdouts."

The Doyen absorbed this news slowly. Then he stood up and came around the desk to face them.

"All eleven? Even the Mysticals?"

Paulette had not said she would or she wouldn't join them, but she had attended their game play all night and did not seem to be in a hurry to leave.

"Yes," Viève said uneasily. Why did it matter to him if the Mysticals in specific were joined? Why not ask about the Phoenixes or some other breed?

"All have joined and we can now see and connect with one another. The curse that separated us has been lifted."

"Ah. I'm sure our master would be most displeased to hear about that."

"Master?" Kamen echoed suspiciously.

"Apep," the Doyen said. "Or so he claims to be. Our master, that is. He says he created our race from the dust of the earth and now we owe all that we are to him. That we are bound to serve him."

"And will you? Serve him?" Kamen asked, his tone hard.

"I confess I had not decided. I was trying to figure out what would cause the least amount of damage and inconvenience to my people. Do we serve the whims of an egomaniacal lunatic, or do we stand alone against him and his wrath and watch him cut a swath through our numbers. But now here you are presenting me with a third option; to join a rebellion against the god; perhaps defeating him and chasing him from this plane of existence.

"I admit, I find that idea intriguing. But a rebellion will cost lives as well. So, as a leader I must ask myself this: which way will allow for the least loss of Wraith life?" He regarded them a moment. "You really have the Mysticals on board?"

"Why do you keep asking about them?" Viève asked.

"Silence, half-breed!" one of the other Wraiths snapped. Kamen watched her cringe and immediately shrink back. It angered him. Angered him like nothing had angered him since the day Odjit had been put into a coma. But this anger seemed hotter . . . more pure. He tried to school himself. The last time he had let his temper have free rein, people had been hurt and a god had been unleashed.

But to see her so abused made him burn.

"I will have your answer," Kamen said recklessly. "We have done as you asked. An honorable man would adhere to his part of the bargain."

"The flaw in that," the Doyen said smoothly, "is the assumption that I am an honorable man."

"He isn't going to help us," Viève said in a small whisper.

The Doyen smiled. "On the contrary. I am going to help you. Why, I will send a troop of Wraiths with you right now. How many do you require? A hundred? A thousand?"

Kamen suddenly had a feeling they had been led into a trap. A feeling that the Doyen's offer was not to be trusted.

"We will contact you with that information," Kamen lied.

"I insist you let me send some with you now. A small contingent of men. Felix, Darius, and Raymond will accompany you and will send word back to me as to what more is needed," the Doyen said. He turned to his men and said, "See to it our interests are served well."

"I cannot bring them all with me," Kamen said. "I will give you the location of our base of operations and you can join us there."

The Doyen frowned. "Surely you can take at least one with you?"

"One," Kamen agreed tightly.

"Excellent. The rest will join you by conventional means. Felix."

Felix stepped forward, a toothy grin on his long face. "I am ready," he said.

"Viève, I need to touch him," Kamen said quietly.

"No," she whispered.

"Viève, release me from the phase. I'll be safe, I promise you."

"Is there a problem, half-breed?" the Doyen asked her.

She quailed. "N-n-no."

"Well then, let's get on with it."

"Touch him only on his clothing," Viève whispered to him anxiously.

Kamen nodded and she released her phase so that Kamen might reach out and touch the Wraith on his suit jacket. They entered the streak instantaneously.

The moment they exited the streak, Viève yanked him out of contact with the Wraith who, predictably, became sick to his stomach. He vomited in the grass.

They were standing off to the right of the field where the Nightwalkers were running their game, their skills being used to the utmost as each tried to best the other's side.

Standing on the sidelines, not too far away from them, were Max, Leo, Angelina, and Paulette. Apparently Paulette was not interested in playing the game, but she was watching Grey attend them. Grey was a significant advantage over the opposing team. His magic seemed boundless and he was creative and powerful. He could conjure almost anything he desired. Most recently it had been three suits of armor that fought as though men were inside of them . . . yet they were empty of anything living.

Viève had a death grip on Kamen, ready to phase him away from the Wraith's touch if necessary.

"I don't trust him," she whispered against his ear.

"Neither do I, but aren't you the one preaching to everyone about second chances and forgiveness? We must extend trust . . . until that trust is broken."

"But at what cost?"

Kamen didn't respond because the Wraith was recovering, standing up dizzily and taking deep breaths.

"What the fuck was that?" he ground out angrily.

"It's called a streak. It is not the most pleasant way to travel, but it is the fastest."

"Go back and bring the two others here as well," Felix commanded him.

"I'm afraid I can't do that. My magic has limitations and this spell has exhausted me," Kamen said.

Viève knew it to be a lie. Kamen was more than capable of going back and getting the other Wraiths. She felt relief that they would only have one Wraith to contend with . . . at least for now. Which was no doubt Kamen's design.

The Wraith looked around, and took in everything going on around him. He saw Paulette and immediately made a beeline to get to her. Kamen was a half-step behind him. He quickly cast his protection bubble, and then took the man's arm in hand, pulling him to a stop.

"Allow me to introduce you to everyone," he said, turning Felix toward the playing field. "Jackson!"

Jackson looked up at his name being called and upon seeing the Wraith immediately left the game. Marissa followed him.

"Jackson, this is Felix. Felix, this is Jackson and Marissa, Pharaohs of the Bodywalkers."

"*Half* the Bodywalkers," Felix said with a derisive snort.

"True," Jackson said carefully, "we are not united. But every day I hope we will be."

"Not with Apep leading the Templars you won't. When Apep comes for you—and he *will* come for you—he's going to use the Templars as cannon fodder. You will be forced to kill your own kind. There will be no unity."

"That remains to be seen," Jackson said, his eyes washing over the business-suited man. "What about you? What do you do for the Doyen?"

"Whatever he asks me to do. Right now, he wants me to check out your story about having all of the Nightwalkers joined."

"As you can see, it is a truth, not a story," Jackson said, indicating the field of players.

"I would have you introduce me to all of the players in the game against Apep. One of each race. Then I will tell my Doyen that your tales are truths. Let's start with her."

He turned hard and pointed to Paulette. Paulette paled, going a sickly shade of white.

"Grey!" she cried as the Wraith took two steps toward her. But Kamen was there again, holding his arm.

"This is Paulette, a Mystical, but you already know that, don't you?" Kamen said.

"What if I do?" The Wraith tried to shrug off his touch.

Viève watched the struggle with bated breath, her skin cold and clammy, her palms sweating. Kamen was so close to danger. So close to death. All the Wraith had to do was touch him and he would be dead.

She clung to Kamen's free arm and stared hard at every move the Wraith made. She didn't even notice that though she was holding on to him, her hands didn't actually 'touch' his skin and clothing.

If Felix so much as changed the slightest bit of color, Viève would phase Kamen. For when a Wraith was about to use his deathtouch, his hands turned a venous blue. But it could happen in the blink of an eye, so it was barely enough of a warning. She wanted to phase Kamen anyway, but Kamen was keeping the Wraith away from Paulette with the presence of his solid body.

"What is it the Wraiths find so interesting about the Mysticals?" Kamen asked him, still keeping hold of him. The Wraith could have phased right through him, he realized. He was allowing himself to be held. Why?

"Why, their sheer beauty of course," the Wraith said, giving Paulette a long once-over.

By now Grey had come off the field and went to stand in front of her, placing his body between her and the Wraith. Grey was not a small man and his body adequately sheltered Paulette.

"You aren't like the Djynn. You can derive no power from them as nikkis," Kamen said.

"As I said, it is their beauty which lures us. As you may have noticed, Wraiths lack color in their looks. And diversity. The Mysticals are always beautiful in both their forms. And we can see their aura. It shines . . . warms us. Adds color to a drab, colorless existence. And it's addicting. Strengthening. It is like a drug that makes us feel all-powerful, as if we cannot be stopped and can conquer anything."

"*I* can't see an aura," Viève said.

"You're a fucking half-breed," he snapped.

Kamen saw red. "Speak to her in that tone of voice and in that derisive way again," he said through his teeth, "and I will rip out your tongue."

The Wraith snorted out a laugh. "You would break our fragile peace accord over a disgusting little half-breed?"

"Yes," Kamen hissed. "We have many half-breeds here and we treat each and every one of them with respect. You will do the same or find yourself removed from our company. In what manner you'll be removed will all depend on my mood at the time."

The Wraith sucked at his teeth and gave Viève a derisive once-over.

"Fine," he said. "I'll make nice with the half-breed."

"I would prefer you avoid her altogether," Kamen said. "Now we will continue our introductions."

Kamen slowly introduced the other members of the Nightwalker clans.

"What of the eleventh race? I count only ten," he said.

"The Shadowdweller is inside the house. He was injured during the stripping of the curse."

"I will meet him." The Wraith broke away from the group and marched toward the house. Kamen kept in stride beside him and said, "You will allow me to see if he is up to it. He may not be well enough yet."

They went inside the house and the Wraith indicated that Kamen should show him the way. Kamen led him upstairs. The Wraith seemed to notice every detail, took everything in. When they stopped outside of Jackson and Marissa's suite, Kamen held up a hand to stop him from entering. "I'll be only a moment."

"Very well," the Wraith said.

Kamen disappeared into the room, leaving Viève, Jackson, and Marissa outside. The Wraith folded his arms across his thin chest and peered down at Viève.

"So your mother couldn't control herself around one little human?" he said.

Viève blanched. She didn't know all the details of her mother's indiscretion, only that she regretted it and the result of it.

"A fact she regrets," Viève said in a whisper.

"And so she should. Look at you. You're too fleshy. Your face is round and fat. You have makeup on. Any decent Wraith woman wouldn't be caught wearing makeup."

"That's not true. All the women in my cell wear makeup. They like the color."

His frown was dour. "Perhaps," he said. "Where is your cell?"

"Plainsboro, Iowa."

"Iowa! Well that explains that. Your cell can't be very big. How many get together at your Kinua gatherings?"

"Our cell has twenty people in it. Our gatherings are over one hundred and fifty strong."

"One hundred and fifty is nothing. But," he eyed her, "surely they don't allow you to go to a Kinua."

"No," she said in a small voice. "They don't."

Felix huffed out a breath. "Well, at least they are doing something right. The idea of you breeding and putting more of your tainted blood into our numbers is appalling."

"I know," Viève said miserably.

"Hey, that's enough of that!" Jackson said.

"I only speak the truth," Felix said. "Look at her. She knows it's true."

Viève wanted the earth to open up and swallow her whole. She didn't want to be there. She didn't want to be anywhere near Felix. He was ruining this place for her. Here she had found a brief respite of acceptance. Now he was here polluting all those good feelings. And if more Wraiths came it would grow even worse.

"Perhaps I should go back to my cell," Viève said in a small voice.

"If they'll have you. Better to stay here where no one knows any better," Felix said. "But if this peace is going to work, having a half-breed around won't do you any favors," he said to Jackson. "A lot of Wraiths will be offended."

"Then they can go home," Jackson said firmly. "We don't need that kind of prejudice around here. We all accept one another. You better start doing the same or you can leave too. Viève belongs here. We like her just fine."

Viève felt as though the whole world had suddenly brightened around her. Her heart swelled in her chest, and she had to take a deep breath. She had never had anyone stand up for her before. No one except Kamen. Now here was Jackson standing up for her and she hadn't even done anything for him. Except be instrumental in breaking the curse. She had to give herself credit for that. She didn't see Felix being the sort who would readily give himself over to the ceremony that had broken the curse.

But still, Jackson had said that he accepted her. Liked her. It was more than she'd ever gotten before. Maybe . . . maybe she had done something to deserve that. She had fit in with these people really well. She didn't see Felix being able to do the same. In that she had advantage over him.

"Don't say I didn't warn you," Felix said.

Kamen came back through the door and closed it behind him.

"He's resting. I need to stay here. Some of his wounds have reopened. He will need a healing spell to close them."

"I thought you were too tired to do more magic," Felix asked suspiciously.

Kamen took the observation in stride. "The streak is far more taxing than a healing spell."

"Well, make sure you get plenty of rest. I expect you to go back for more Wraiths tomorrow."

"We will see about that," Jackson said with a frown. "Space here is limited. There are a lot of people here."

"I suggest you make room. You are going to need an army against Apep. All I see now is a piddly little cell of misfits."

"These misfits can do a lot of damage," Jackson said.

"Against what? Against each other? I saw the games you were playing. That is nothing like what the real thing will be. Apep laid waste to continents the last time he was incarnated into mortal form."

"He hasn't had time to grow that strong. Unless he gets the Wraiths to fight on his side, all he has are Templars and maybe a few misguided humans. The Templars are only a few hundred strong."

"Well then, I suggest you keep us happy," Felix said with a grin that bared his teeth. "You wouldn't want us changing our minds."

"Do that and it will go ill for you," Kamen said ominously. "Not only will you be subject to the whims of a maniac, you'll have made an enemy of every other Nightwalker breed there is. And there's a lot of us."

Felix took that in for a moment, sucking his teeth briefly. "Where will I be staying?" he asked finally.

"I will show you the way," Jackson said, leading Felix down the hall toward one of the back bedrooms. Marissa followed and Kamen and Viève stayed behind.

"I was wrong," Viève said in a small voice.

"About what?"

"We can't trust them. We can't forgive them."

Kamen put an arm around her shoulders and drew her into his body for a hard hug. He kissed her against her temple. It was practically affection in public, something he had not done before then. It made her flush.

"Maybe not. You have to give them a chance though. Just like you've given me a chance."

"I don't see how such closed-minded people can possibly fit in well with such diversity," she said.

"It is true, they are very closed-minded. I especially don't like his treatment of you. But they will have to play by our rules or find themselves facing Apep's wrath alone. And believe me, when he hears the Wraiths will have nothing to do with him, he will be feeling a great deal of wrath."

He began to lead her down the hall toward their rooms. "Now I want you to stay in our rooms until I am through healing the Shadowdweller. This last time should be enough."

"It sounded much worse when you . . ."

"A little bit of creative truth telling," he said. "I don't want him to think he can have his way in everything the moment he demands it. He has to answer to the needs of the household just like anyone else does; that means respecting the wishes and situations of others. Never fear, we will have him well trained before long."

She gave him a doubtful frown. He laughed at her. "Don't you trust me?" he asked.

"I don't trust him."

"You've made that very clear. But don't let the personal pain you feel color your judgment. He needs to be assessed as an asset to this situation, not based on how he and his race treat their half-breeds. One is certainly telling of the other, but it's not the whole story. That being said, I don't want you alone in the same room with him."

"You don't trust me with him?"

"I don't want him to have the opportunity to spew poison at you," Kamen said firmly. "You've heard more than enough of it throughout your lifetime and I won't have you hearing any of it here. If he is an indication of how the others in your cell treated you . . ."

"He is exactly how the others treated me," she told him.

"Then I am glad you are here. Glad it was you I ran into outside of your cell that night. On so many levels and for so many reasons, I am glad."

Warmth infused her. She smiled at him. "I am glad too. More than you'll ever know. If I'd had any idea what kind of an adventure I'd be going on . . . well, I don't know if I would've been brave enough to embark on it knowing it was coming. But I'm glad it happened as it did. I've never met anyone like you before. No one's ever treated me the way you do."

He stopped before their bedroom door and turned her toward himself, reaching to brush warm fingers along her jawline. "And no one's ever treated me the way you do. Even when I had a position of power and respect, no one was ever warm and kind to me just for being myself. And I was never able to be myself around anyone then. Not even with Odjit. She was a draining personality. She always wanted more. Even when I had already given her everything. You . . . you seem content with whatever I give you. This is a flaw of your self-worth, but at the same time it is somewhat relaxing to know you expect nothing of me."

"I don't expect anything. I just hope for things. Things like your time, your consideration, your touch." This last she said on a whisper. He cupped her cheek and she turned into the caress, nuzzling him warmly.

"You may have all three whenever your heart desires it," he said softly.

"I desire them all, especially the latter, as soon as possible."

He smiled at her. "I will come to you as soon as I am done with Sagan."

"Thank you," she said with a smile.

"For what?"

"For telling Felix you would throw away the peace accord if he didn't stop treating me the way he was. I know you wouldn't really do that, but he didn't and he believed you. That might make things a little better, though I won't hold my breath."

He frowned. "I think you should know, I was entirely serious. I would break this accord in a heartbeat if he treated you ill again. But in the end it isn't up to me. This is a joint effort. Inclusion or exclusion of a race is something that would have to be decided by all. But, as you said, he doesn't know that so perhaps he will take it to heart."

Viève didn't think that he would, his behavior afterward when Kamen wasn't around a fair indicator, but it was the gesture that had touched her. Deeply.

"Hurry back," she whispered to him. "I would have you naked and in my arms."

He smiled again. This time wolfishly. "A most favorite place to be," he said. He dipped his head and caught her mouth against his, kissing her deeply. His tongue touched hers and she sighed with pleasure. He kissed her so deeply she grew dizzy . . . perhaps from lack of oxygen. Definitely from the intensity of the passion that swam between them.

He separated from her mouth reluctantly, and then pushed himself away.

"Go on." He nodded toward the bedroom door.

She smiled and went inside the room.

# CHAPTER 19

Apep pushed with a fury. The pain meant nothing, he told himself. He was a god. The pain would pass as soon as this was over.

What did not pass, however, was the rage he felt. His curse, his beautiful curse . . . ruined! Destroyed! The Nightwalkers had done the one thing that should have been impossible to do: get all twelve races together, form a circle of connected hands. They couldn't even see each other, never mind be tangible enough to clasp hands!

And that meant the Wraiths had been a part of it. After he had gone to them specifically and told them they would be fighting on his side. That they were his minions and that he had created them just for that purpose. The betrayal infuriated him even more than the broken curse did. He would have to lay waste to the ingrates as soon as he was done dealing with that puny little gathering of Nightwalkers in New Mexico. That had to be where they were. Where that traitor Kamen had gone after resurrecting Apep to this world.

He had attacked them there once before but he had been unprepared that time. This time he would not underestimate them. He would attack them in force, bringing his army to bear, starting there in his obliteration of the Nightwalker races. His original intention had been to use his Templars to destroy the first half of the Nightwalkers, the half they could see. Then he would lift the curse and set them on the second half. The tactic would have been far wiser than facing them all down at once.

But he had to start eliminating them before more of these little cells of Nightwalkers began to form, creating what might be an army of resistance against him. Not that they could win; but it was best to nip it in the bud before it got out of control. Especially since they could potentially do him the worst kind of harm. They might even be able to defeat him if they but knew the way. What if they did know the way? What would he do then?

He couldn't worry about that now. He had to push. Get this parasite out of him. Only then could he regain his strength.

He pushed with a scream and suddenly . . . brilliantly . . . the child slipped from his body. The doctor caught the baby as Apep lay back in the bed with a flounce. He gasped for much needed breath, his body feeling the relief of no longer trying to push a huge creature out of such a tiny orifice. Ugh! How did human women stand it? And to do it more than once? They were mad!

The doctor held up the child with a grin.

"Congratulations! It's a girl!"

"A what?" Apep cried, sitting up to take a closer look. Sure enough, his son was a girl! How did that happen? He was a celestial being and he had wanted a son—that should have made it so! A daughter? What the hell was he supposed to do with a daughter?

"Ugh!" he cried in disgust. "Take it away from me!" He snapped his fingers and two Templars hastened into the room to do just that.

"What shall we do with it, mistress?"

"Throw it out! It's of no use to me!" Apep watched them take the child and the doctor stood up and mopped his brow.

"Surely you don't mean . . . throw it out. It isn't trash after all," the doctor said as he fumbled around in his bag and gathered up a syringe and a vial in shaking hands. He pulled a large dose of the liquid into the syringe. Then, stumbling once over his own feet, he went to the IV and put the syringe in the port.

"Yes, I do mean throw it out! Find a dumpster and be rid of the thing." Apep glared at the doctor. "What is that? What are you doing?"

"V-v-vitamins," the doctor stammered. "T-to help with the healing."

"I don't need vitamins! I need a son! To think, I went through all of this for nothing." Apep reached for the IV and ripped it out of his arm.

"No!" the doctor cried.

Apep narrowed his eyes on the doctor. "What kind of vitamins?" he asked.

He held out his hand and the vial the doctor had used floated out of the bag and into his palm. He read the label. Succinylcholine.

"This isn't vitamins," Apep said dangerously. "This is poison. You were going to poison me."

"N-no I wasn't!"

"You were!" Apep laughed. "I didn't think you had it in you. And here I thought you were just a sniveling little cowardly, good for nothing human. Of course, I can't possibly trust you, but I do admire you for having big brass hanging balls. Throw him out too!"

Apep used the power of his mind to bash the doctor against the wall, the floor, the ceiling, and then the wall again. Spots of red splattered against the surfaces, and finally Apep released the doctor and his broken body crumpled to the ground.

"Well? Go on! Do it!" Apep roared at the Templar minions who stood frozen in place. Then one of them went to fetch the doctor's body while the other carried the baby out of the room.

Filomena, the Templar woman who held the baby in her arms, felt her heart pound and her stomach turned sick. The baby was screaming and crying, but it was so small and wrinkled and helpless. How could anyone wish harm on an innocent little baby? She hadn't signed up for this. Not for any of it. Their mistress had clearly gone out of her mind. Kamen, their mistress's most beloved pet, had disappeared and ever since that day she had not been the same. She had changed in appearance, her size and stature having enlarged considerably. Ever since then the woman who had once been cruel alone had become vicious and intractable. Nothing seemed to please her, and when she was displeased she usually ended up killing something. Or someone. Usually someone. No matter how hard they struggled to serve her, it was never enough. A life could be forfeit just because the wind blew the wrong way in that moment.

No. It was not what she had signed up for and there were many who felt the same way. Only they were too frightened to do anything about it. Odjit had caught Templars trying to defect in the past and had made examples of them. Oh, she had not caught all of them. Some had escaped unscathed. Most since the pregnancy had grown heaviest on her; almost as though her power had waned the more she had quickened with the child. Filomena had been too afraid to try escape before this, not willing to risk her life.

But to obey her mistress now meant she would have to kill this baby.

If there was ever a time to escape, now would be it. But she would have to leave right that very instant, no packing of her belongings, nothing of the kind. Her heart pounded with fear. Fear for herself and, mostly, fear for the life of this child.

"I . . . I'm going to dispose of this baby in a dumpster in the heart of the human town not far from here. That way no one will find the body here and call it into question," she said.

It was lame and it made no sense but it was all she could think of.

"Make sure you break its neck first before you leave it," her male counterpart said as he hefted the weight of the dead, slightly obese doctor. "We don't need some human finding it and getting all sentimental over it. If the mistress wants it dead it better be dead. And you know she'll know."

"Of course! Do I look stupid to you?" she snapped.

"Just do it!" the Templar huffed and puffed under the weight of his burden.

Filomena hurried away and headed straight to her room. She hastened to put only the smallest bag together in as quick a manner as she could, then she looked up the location she wanted on a map.

Without another thought she stepped into a streak.

Viève felt like she was hiding out in her room.

She didn't mean to, she was just afraid to go out and face the possibility of running into Felix.

Okay, so she did mean to. But she had to stop. Other Wraiths would be coming soon and they'd all have bad things to say about her. The only way she could countermand those bad things was to go out into the house and prove to everyone that she had some kind of value. Besides, she wanted to keep an eye on Felix and any other Wraiths that came. She didn't trust them at all.

She finished putting on her makeup and looked in the bathroom mirror. She wasn't going to do this. She wasn't going to hide.

She touched a pinky to her frosted pink lip at the corner, tidying up her lipstick. Satisfied with the way she looked she checked her braid to make sure her hair was all tightly bound within. If they played capture the flag today she wanted to be able to move without her hair getting in her way.

She turned away from the mirror and taking a deep breath she left the bedroom. She headed down the stairs looking for Kamen. He had woken up earlier than she had and been gone before she'd even opened her eyes.

She probably should have checked Marissa and Jackson's room. Maybe the Shadowdweller was still there and he had gone to heal him some more.

She went into the kitchen and the first person she ran into was Paulette. To her surprise, Viève did not see Grey anywhere. Usually the two were inseparable. And with there being more Wraiths in the house, she would have thought she would feel all the more insecure. Conscious of this she apologized to Paulette and went to leave the room.

"No. Please. Stay. I wish to speak with you."

Viève was surprised, but she came into the room fully and took a seat at the breakfast bar, a full countertop away from Paulette, who was standing in the heart of the kitchen with a coffee cup in her hands.

"I'm sorry about last night. If the Wraith scared you," Viève clarified.

"Yes. He did. Does. But it made me realize how different you are from them. I heard some of the things he said to you. They were very cruel things. Do they do that to you often? Treat you with such little respect?"

Viève could only nod.

"It is very wrong of them. I find you to be quite unique. And uniqueness should be treasured, not shunned."

"Thank you for saying that, but that is not how my people feel."

"Your people have been wrong on many an occasion. They have done me wrong."

"You don't know how sorry I am for that. It must be difficult to be in the same house with . . . with Wraiths like Felix."

"It is. I did not sleep here because of it. I had Grey take me back to his home for the daytime. But as you see, I have returned."

"I still don't understand why the Wraiths find you so addicting. I mean, not that you're not a fascinating woman . . . you are. But . . ." Viève floundered.

"I know what you mean," she said with a little laugh. "I wish I knew how it all worked. But theirs is a cold, colorless world, as you well know. We have color and life to us that the Wraiths cannot understand, but they covet it like nothing else. As he said, it is like a drug."

"I cannot see your aura. As Felix said, it is probably because I am a half-breed."

"Better to be half-bred than full in this case," Paulette said bitterly.

"I am beginning to see that for myself. Before I was ashamed of my human side. But since coming here, I am ashamed of my Wraith side."

"You should not feel shame for either side. You are not the sum of your heritage. Your life is what you make of it. You are what you make yourself to be. You can either choose to be like a Wraith or you can choose to be like a human. Or you may be as your heritage is . . . a little bit of each. Either way you must accept who you are and determine what you will allow others to see you as. No one can think badly of you as long as you do not think badly of yourself. If you think of yourself as less, then others will as well."

What the Mystical said made sense, but it was easier said than done. Still, Viève vowed to take the advice to heart. She would try to think better of herself and would not accept the criticisms of others. Not anymore. Not from Felix, not from any Wraith. She was special. She had done extraordinary things these past two days. If she could do so much in just two days, imagine what she could do here in the future.

"Paulette, are you going to bring any other Mysticals here?"

"I have already sent for some dragons. They are the most powerful and nothing beats their size in a battle. They should be here soon. Grey has cast magic on this house expanding the inside of it to twice the rooms as before, although it will look no different on the outside. It will allow us to house many more people. It will provide an extra kitchen and more bathrooms as well."

"I didn't know he could do that!"

"Djynn are used to making the most of cramped or confined spaces. It was an easy bit of magic for him. In fact, he should be here shortly. He does not leave me for long, but as Felix was outside on the grounds he felt it was all right to leave me for a brief moment to take care of a personal matter. He has asked more Djynn to come. I think he is looking for a response. SingSing has arrived as well and is residing in a canteen, I believe. It's hanging on the door over there."

She pointed to a door which did indeed have a canteen hanging from the doorknob.

"She's *inside*?"

"I told you: Djynn can make the most of cramped places. In fact, they prefer them. Lamps, bottles, canteens, and other such strong but hollowed-out containers. If she brought you inside the canteen, however, it would probably be like walking into a mansion, depending on the Djynn's power. Weaker Djynn cannot cast and maintain such powerful magic. But for Djynn like Grey, there are almost no limits to what they can do."

The Mystical's eyes were a little dreamy as she said this. It led Viève to wonder if there was more to Grey and Paulette's relationship than she had thought. But she wasn't about to ask. It was really none of her business. Still, it would be such a sweet story. Powerful Djynn rescues captive Mystical Empress from the clutches of a vile enemy and love blossoms between them as she recovers from her ordeal.

Viève sighed. It sounded so lovely. She actually hoped it was true. Paulette deserved something nice after all she had been through. She certainly didn't deserve to be pawed or leered at by a Wraith.

Then Grey appeared in a blink of an eye. His appearance at Paulette's back was so sudden that Viève gasped in surprise. Paulette chuckled.

"You get used to it eventually. He is so quiet. Like a little church mouse."

"I have been known to be quite loud," Grey said, his rich voice flowing smoothly into the room. There was no mistaking the suggestiveness of his statement and Paulette clicked her tongue at him and gave him an admonishing swat. Grey's grin was unrepentant. "Are you okay?" he asked of Paulette. Her smile faltered.

"Yes, but do not leave me unless you must. I fear there are more of them coming. I heard mention of Kamen going to retrieve two others."

Grey frowned. "I do not like the idea of you being here any longer. The others will act just as Felix did, gawking at you, trying to touch you."

"The dragons are coming. I have come to see that Mystical presence is sorely needed here. Once they are here I will leave. The dragons can take care of themselves against the Wraiths, unlike me. I will send others as well. Griffins, maybe. Or centaurs. More soldiers for our little army."

"This is all good," Grey said. "But it can all take place without you."

"No. I will stay and make proper introductions for the dragons. We will lose much in this coming battle. Hopefully manners and politeness will not be the first to go."

Grey smiled at her and pressed a kiss to the hair at her temple. It was such an easy sign of affection. Kamen gave her such indications of affection in the privacy of their rooms. They were hers to hold on to, not to share with others, and she liked it that way.

As if her thoughts had conjured him, Kamen entered the kitchen. When his gaze rested on her his lips tipped upward into a small smile, but the expression did not reach his eyes. She knew instantly something was wrong.

# CHAPTER 20

"Viève, could you come with me please?"

Viève nodded and hopped down off the barstool. She fell into step beside Kamen, and she felt his hand settle at the base of her spine. He led her out of the front door and into the cool, crisp night. There were people sitting on the porch and some gathered on the front lawn, but Kamen steered her away from them, taking her for a walk down the drive.

"Felix has asked me to fetch two more of the Wraiths to come and stay here."

A cold sensation settled in the pit of her stomach, but she tried to smile her way through it. She had made a promise to herself that she would not let the Wraiths get to her and she was determined to follow through.

"When will you go?"

That gave him pause. "You do not mind them coming? They are bound to be as bad as Felix is toward you."

"I realize that. And I am used to it, actually. The difference is I no longer feel it is my due to be treated in such a way. Yesterday I was shocked into awareness again of how the Wraiths treated me. I didn't know what to say or do other than to just accept it. But now, after spending the day in your arms, learning what it means to have value in the eyes of another, it has changed me. All of this has changed me. I want to deserve to be here. That means making myself as strong as everyone else here."

This time, when he smiled, the light of it warmed his eyes. He pulled her to a stop and very publicly took her into his arms. He held her close, touched his forehead to hers in affection. Then he pulled back and looked into her eyes.

"I am really quite proud of you," he said fondly.

She smiled back at him as a warm, bright sensation filled her chest. "Are you?" she breathed.

"Very much so. I was worried. I was worried they would beat you down with their words until you felt like you deserved it."

"I don't deserve it. I've done nothing wrong. All I did was be born. If they don't like my being here . . . well they can leave!" She lifted her chin strongly and nodded her head. "So there you have it."

"Are you sure you can do this?" he asked a little skeptically.

Viève's expression became grim. "I'm not saying it won't be hard. And maybe I might get a little beaten up in the process. But all I have to do is think of you or Marissa or Jackson and the way you treat me like I'm worth something and that will help me to pull through."

"Good," he said, tipping her chin up and placing a warm kiss on her lips.

"What do you think you're doing!"

The booming, acidic statement was followed up by an iron hand wrapping around her arm and jerking her away from Kamen. Startled, they both automatically tried to remain connected, their hands catching.

Felix jerked harder, trying to pull her away from him completely.

"Get away from him you, little mongrel!" he spat. "Bad enough your mother polluted this earth with you! I won't have you compounding the mistake by allowing you to mate with this . . . this . . . human!"

"He's not human! He's a Bodywalker!" she spluttered, the response the first thing she could think of as she tried to jerk free of him.

"His *soul* is a Bodywalker, his body is human. I'll not have you spawn any more diluted mongrels!"

"Enough! Take your hands off her or so help me I will cast a rending spell that will sever your spine into two parts!" Kamen growled out.

The threat didn't seem to faze Felix in the least. He pulled harder.

Unable to bear his blistering disapproval and rude behavior a second longer, she lifted up the arm he held captive until his hand was at her lips then she bit down on him as hard as she could.

Felix yowled in pain, finally letting go of her, rearing back from her as if she'd suddenly turned into a venomous creature.

"You bit me!"

"You deserved it!" she shot back. "Never *ever* touch me again. If you do I'll bite off more than just your finger."

Kamen drew her close, holding her protectively.

"The Doyen will hear of this. He will command you to—"

"The Doyen can't command me to do anything!" she spat. "I am a free being, with the right to do anything I choose. And if I choose to mate with a Bodywalker, then that is what I am going to do. And anyway, you're too late. I've been fucking him for two days now," she said crudely.

She heard a snort and realized Kamen had just kept himself from laughing. She looked up into his eyes and saw pride and delight dancing in them.

"You mean you're pregnant?" Felix said, horrified.

"So what if I am?" she said, even though she knew she wasn't. "There's nothing you can do about it now. Wraiths can't get abortions."

"That may be true, but don't expect your child to ever be accepted by decent Wraiths."

"I wouldn't want it to be accepted by Wraiths. And I have yet to meet a decent one!" she shot back.

"You are an ungrateful female. Your mother gave you life. Your cell tolerated you. And this is what you give us in return? Do not ever think you can come back to your cell. We will see to it you are never allowed back."

Tears stung at Viève's eyes as she thought of losing the only home she had ever known. But she realized she didn't care. These were tears of liberation, of finally feeling of value. Kamen had given her that. He had shown up in her garden and changed her life.

"I don't want to go back. I'd rather live life as a human than ever go back."

"You'll have no haven. No funds." Felix was growing shrill as he realized she wasn't at all fazed by his threats.

"No derision. No scorn," she retaliated.

"It's what you deserve."

"No one deserves that. Not me, not anyone," she said. "Come on, Kamen. Let's go back to the house and fuck like bunnies."

She tugged his hand and pulled him forward and this time Kamen didn't hold back his laugh. It belted out into the air and made her smile. He fell into step beside her and dropped his arm around her shoulders. He hugged her so tight she couldn't walk straight.

"I'm so proud of you," he whispered fiercely into her hair.

She laughed shakily. "Yeah. Except now I have nowhere to go."

"You'll stay here. With me. You'll always have somewhere to go as long as I am alive on this earth."

The words pleased her so much she could hardly contain the feeling. "But you hardly know me. I wouldn't want to saddle you with me the rest of your life."

"Saddle me? Viève, you breathe life into me!" He stopped and turned her toward him so she could look into his eyes. "Before all of this . . . before Apep . . . all I wanted to do was figure out a way to die. Not just die so I could come back again, but to end it all once and for all. I was trying to figure out how I could remove my soul from this endless cycle of life and death. I remember every life I've had, every death I've had. After all of this time it weighs on me like a thousand elephants on my chest. Or at least it did. I had purpose in trying to rectify the mistake I made with Apep, but when I met you . . . you gave me life. Joy. Pleasure I haven't known for many lifetimes now. In two short days you've changed me in such a fundamental way. There's nothing I can ever do to pay you back for that."

Tears threatened her eyes, but they were good tears. He made her sound so wonderful. Made all of this sound so wonderful. Of course, he wasn't promising her his heart or anything like that, and she shouldn't expect it after only two days, but perhaps one day . . .

It gave her a hope she had never known before.

Kamen had never been one to wax poetic, but he had been unable to help himself. It was important to him that she know what changes she had wrought in him. He didn't know how—didn't know why—he just knew it in the depths of his soul. He had found something special in her. He wasn't going to let go of that feeling any time soon.

"Come. Let's go fuck like bunnies," he said to her, amusement tickling every part of him. She laughed, a beautiful sound to his ears. She seemed so much lighter than she had when she had first come there. She was learning her true value in the world. Learning to measure herself by her own yardstick and not that of the Wraiths. He truly was proud of her.

"Is there a problem?" Jackson asked as he hurried up to them, clearly having seen the altercation.

"Not anymore," Viève said as she hugged Kamen to her side.

Jackson watched the easy affection between them with bemusement. Kamen had changed these past two days. Viève had brought something out in him that hadn't been there before. Or maybe it was just that he seemed so much more human, more approachable because he was attached to her.

"If he's giving you trouble, Viève, we can petition the Doyen to send someone else."

"It would only be more of the same," Viève said with a shrug. "I am simply less to them, and they can't see past it."

"If they can't see past it for one of their own, how will they be able to see past it for the rest of us?"

"That's a very good question," Kamen said. "One worth considering seriously."

"We're going to need them. Our deathtouch is going to be crucial. It will even the odds considerably."

"If we didn't need them I would have kicked them to the curb already," Jackson said. "I don't like to see anyone treated badly."

"We're bound to have friction with this many people. They are so varied and their mind-sets so differing. I'm amazed it hasn't happened before this," Kamen said.

"So far I've seen a lot of mind-sets turned to the same direction. To getting along and working as a cohesive unit."

"We've been lucky so far."

"Until now," Viève said grimly as she cast a glance back at a fuming Felix. "What do we do when he reports back to the Doyen?"

"As you said, the Doyen has no power over you."

"He may not see it that way," Viève said anxiously. "What if I become a point of contention?"

"You aren't the first to 'spawn' with a human and you won't be the last. They'll realize there is nothing they can do to stop it," Kamen said.

"I hope you're right."

"I'm right," he assured her. "Anyway, we'll find out soon enough," Kamen said.

"Do we really know for certain what side they are on?" Jackson asked.

"We have to give them the benefit of the doubt until they give us cause to do otherwise," Kamen said.

"I only hope it doesn't cost us in lives later on," Jackson said uneasily.

"All it takes is a touch," Viève said softly.

"Let's just stay on our guard. Trust is earned and so far they haven't been earning much in my opinion," Kamen said.

"They're just being what they've always been. We have to give them a chance to prove they can be something different. Or rather, different enough to be of use to us," Viève said.

"Us. I like the sound of that," Kamen said, giving her a smile. "Jackson, I told Viève that she would always have a home here with us. I hope I did not overstep myself, but I felt that you would agree."

"Of course I agree. Viève, we haven't known you long but we know enough. You have a good and true heart. You will always be welcome here."

"Thank you so much," she said, flushing warmly under the acceptance.

"Any time. Any time at all." Jackson's head went up and his gaze narrowed on a point over their shoulders. "What's this?" he asked curiously.

Thinking Felix had done something, she turned to take him in. To her surprise, she saw someone walking slowly up the drive; coming in starts and stops, carrying something in her arms. It was a female. She had long brown hair blowing loosely in the night breeze.

"Templar," Kamen hissed suddenly, pulling Viève behind himself.

Jackson stepped forward and put a calming hand on Kamen's arm. "She's alone."

"It could be a trick."

"My instincts are screaming at me to not trust, but haven't we been saying that trust has to start somewhere or this won't work?" Jackson stepped forward to greet the Templar female, Kamen following quickly behind him.

"I . . . I couldn't find you," she said hesitantly. "Please don't hurt me. I wish to defect."

"We won't hurt you," Jackson assured her. "All Bodywalkers who wish to come and follow the way of the Politic are welcome here." He nodded to the bundle in her arms. "What is this?"

She pushed the fabric aside and revealed a baby. The infant gurgled in its sleep then settled down.

"Is this your child?" Jackson asked gently. "She looks newly born. Are you well?"

"It's not my child. The child is Odjit's. When she saw it was not a boy she ordered me to kill it and dispose of it as if it were trash. I could not bring myself to do so, so I risked all to come here."

Jackson went very still. "Odjit has given birth?" he asked, needing to hear it again.

"Yes."

Kamen stepped forward and held his hands out for the child. The Templar held on to it more tightly. "I need your word that you will not harm her. I would rather live in the wilds of the humans if that is what I must do. Only . . . Odjit has discovered a way, I know not how, of tracking those who would try and defect from her. I will need your protection in case she comes for me or the child."

"You have my promise that no harm will come to her from us," Jackson said, making Kamen give him a hard look. But Jackson remained firm. "She is safe here."

The Templar struggled visibly for a moment, clearly trying to decide if they should be trusted. But she must have realized there was no choice for her in the matter really, so she handed the baby to Kamen.

Kamen took the child and inspected her. She had the black skin of a Night Angel. Her hair was a deep, dark blue, almost black as well. She couldn't weigh more than seven pounds and on close inspection she looked just like any normal Night Angel child.

"Viève, go get Faith," Jackson instructed her. Viève wasted no time running to get the Night Angel.

Kamen and Jackson focused on welcoming the child and its rescuer.

"What's your name?"

"Filomena," she said. "But most call me Mena."

"Well, Mena, we appreciate that you have come here and brought the child to us. You will be under our protection from here on out."

"I've wanted to come before this, but we're so afraid of the mistress." She looked at Kamen anxiously. "Ever since you left she has been . . . she's always had a cold streak in her, as you well know. And you . . . you were just as cold." She cleared her throat of its fear for talking to him so bluntly. "But since you left she has gone through such drastic changes. She's been vicious and cruel. And she never even speaks of the goals that made us loyal to her in the first place. The unification of the Bodywalker race used to be everything to her. Now all she talks about is destroying you all."

Jackson and Kamen exchanged a look over her head.

"She has always plotted the destruction of the Politic, but she used to couch it in lies about unification," Kamen explained to Jackson. "That is how she led so many Templars to her side. That and the promise of power through magic. She was a powerful priestess and tempted others to follow her by promising to teach them the power she knew. Even those who did not have an aptitude for magic.

"But Odjit would promise that she could teach anyone to cast magic with power. It was a lie I never refuted. I wanted the same thing she did or what I thought she did. Unification through any means necessary. If that meant telling a few lies, what did it matter?" He looked at Mena. "I have since learned the error of my ways."

"A lot of the Templars are fed up with Odjit's volatile temperament," Mena confided in a whisper, as if Odjit might hear her even now. "Some have tried leaving and some have been killed for doing so. Has no one made it here to you?"

Jackson shook his head. "No. No one. But that doesn't mean they did not make it away from her. They might just be lying low for the time being. You say many of the Templars are fed up. How many would you say are willing to put an end to this constant bickering and come to the Politic side?"

"At least half," Mena said. "But they are too afraid to do anything."

"Not now perhaps. But in time they might be able to do something about it," Jackson said.

The baby began to cry.

"Come on. It's too cold out here for the child. Let's go inside and then we will see about getting her some food."

"She hasn't eaten once since she was born and that was a few hours ago." Mena gnawed at her bottom lip. "They've surely noticed my absence by now. And they know I have the baby. They may even suspect I have come here."

"Try not to worry about it," Jackson said, leading her toward the house.

They were almost to the porch of the main house when Faith came bolting out the front door. The Night Angel stopped in her tracks and stared at the baby in Kamen's hands.

"Oh my gods," she whispered. Then she came closer and looked down on the little face. She reached out and touched the tuft of midnight blue hair on its head. "It's Dax's hair," she said with awe. "I'd recognize it anywhere." She swallowed noisily. "I'm an aunt."

"Faith, there is still the matter of the child's maternity," Kamen warned. "Or should I say, other paternity."

"I don't understand," Mena said.

"I will explain it to you," Jackson said. "Kamen, Faith, take the babe inside. Have someone run into town for supplies."

"I have to call my brother," Faith said.

"Should we do that right away?" Kamen asked skeptically. "We don't even know anything about the child."

"My brother is this child's father. It was done by force, but it's still his daughter. He has a right to know and the right to come and see her," Faith said sternly.

Kamen subsided. "Of course. You're right. Go and call him. Viève and I will watch over her."

Viève and Kamen walked into the house with Faith, but then she pulled a cellphone out of her back pocket and went off to call her brother in private.

"I don't understand," Viève said.

"Dax is Faith's brother. He is a very powerful Night Angel. Apep raped him in order to father this child with him."

"Oh my god, that's terrible. Now he's the father of a child he never wanted—that was gotten by violence. How will he feel about this baby?"

"That's something only he can decide. He knew it was conceived, knew it would be born. He has had all these months to come to terms with it. Hopefully that was long enough."

"Can one ever come to terms with such a heinous act committed against them?"

"I'd imagine you'd have to, otherwise there would be no moving on from it. If he is as strong as Faith has led us to believe, he will have done so." Kamen cradled the baby in his hands as though he were quite expert at it, seemingly unafraid to be holding an infant as fragile as this newborn was.

"Have you ever had children?" Viève asked him.

"I have. In my early lives before I joined with Odjit. But I stopped once I realized I would always be leaving them behind. Either I would die or they would die and I'd move on to the next life without them, the pain of the loss mine to carry with me."

"If you had a child with a Nightwalker they would most likely become immortal."

"I suppose that would depend on how strong the Nightwalker genetics were in the child. This child is half Nightwalker, but clearly its Nightwalker traits are dominant. It is also half god. No one knows what that will mean for her. It seems reckless of Apep to discard her in such a way. Perhaps only a male child could be imbued with the power of a god. Who knows what that demented mind is thinking. It could just be a very old prejudice from a god born in times when male children held all the value, while daughters were deemed to be of little worth."

"What does this mean for us? If Apep suspects we have his daughter, couldn't that propel him into action?"

"He's given birth now. The burden on his powers has been lifted. Once he regains his strength you can bet we will be the first thing on his to-do list. We cannot sit here and wait for him to act against us. I must use my location spell, find Apep, and bring the battle to him before he is expecting it or is prepared and recovered from giving birth. We must do this right away. I must speak with Marissa and Jackson right away."

"Here. Give me the baby and go speak to them," Viève said, holding her hands out. He gave her a dubious look.

"Have you ever handled a child?" he asked.

She hesitated. "Well, no. They wouldn't let me touch the babies in the house."

"All right, I will show you," he said, gently handing her the baby and showing her how to support its head in the crook of her arm. She cradled the baby to her breast and the warmest sensation slipped through her. She had never thought to ever hold a child. Would she hold one of her own? she wondered.

It would most likely be a half-breed like her—even more diluted than she was. But, she realized, that wouldn't matter in a place like this. Here where everyone was accepted. She could easily raise a child here. And she wouldn't have to do it alone. There would be any number of people to help.

But there was a lot that had to happen between here and there, and thinking of children with a threat like Apep around was not a good thing. But it was nice to dream all the same. She had never been much of a dreamer, her world based in a very hard reality, but now she had the freedom to hope and dream and it was a good feeling. She'd been having a lot of good feelings since coming there.

For now, she basked in the warmth of the child. Kamen seemed reluctant to part from her at first, and she didn't know why. Perhaps he did not trust her?

"I'll be fine. I won't hurt the baby," she said in a whisper.

"I am more worried about the baby hurting you," he said.

"She's just a baby," she said with surprise.

"She's part of a malicious god."

"She's innocent of that for now. And here we give people the benefit of the doubt, remember?"

He sighed and nodded. "I'm going to talk to Jackson before I gather the components of my spell. He will have to coordinate troops from all of the Nightwalker races and get them to converge at the same place at the same time, which is no small undertaking. But we need to strike now. We needed to strike yesterday when the god was still weak."

"And do what? Kill him with a baby inside of him? No, we couldn't do that."

Kamen frowned. "Better one life than hundreds."

"That is a very cold way of thinking," Viève said, matching his frown.

"But it is a practical way of thinking. Do you disagree with me? One life versus hundreds?"

"No. I don't disagree," she said quietly. "Anyway it's a moot point now."

"Indeed it is. Go. Sit down. This house has grown so big inside that I fear it will take some time for me to find Jackson and then our rooms again."

Kamen walked away, leaving her alone with the baby. Viève walked into the living room where Faith had gone to have her phone conversation.

"I love you too," she said into the phone, then she hung up and stuffed the device in her back pocket. She looked up at Viève. "He's on his way. He's not far from here. He should be here in a few hours."

"Would you like to hold your niece?" Viève asked, holding the baby out to her. Faith hesitated, but then she took the child in her arms. She cuddled her close, cooing at the child when she fussed.

"She must be starved."

"I'll go find someone to go to the market. Maybe Kane. The Mind Demon that can teleport. Walmart should still be open at this hour."

"All right. We'll need formula, bottles, diapers, wipes . . . the whole shebang.

She doesn't even have a diaper on," Faith said after a quick check. "She's barely been cleaned off. We'll need something to bathe her in and some infant soap. Powder . . . clothes. Oh my gods, we need it all."

"I'll go with him. Together we should be able to get everything relatively quickly." Viève brushed a thumb over the baby's cheek. "I'll be right back."

Viève went in search of Kane.

# CHAPTER 21

Dax arrived about three hours later. They were having a gathering outside in front of the main house, each race reporting in about the readiness of their people to join in an attack against Apep and the Templars. According to the Templar defector, Apep had been gathering human magic users as well. Necromancers, as the First Faction called them. Like a cult they had gravitated to him, having Templars teach them in the ways of magic. The Demons were used to dealing with these people. Magic corrupted humans, even making them smell like garbage to a Nightwalker nose.

They could only hope that the necromancers didn't have any Demons on their side. Necromancers had spells that could "summon" a Demon if they knew the Demon's power name. Then they could bring that Demon's power to bear against his compatriots. A Demon that was summoned could not be recovered or cured. Once it was corrupted it remained so until the Enforcers, Bella and Jacob, destroyed it. It was a waste of life and a tragic loss. It also meant that they could end up fighting against any of the elements, except Fire. There were only three Fire Demons in existence and all were accounted for. The Demon King Noah being the most powerful Fire Demon alive.

And Noah was on his way there.

Dax flew on electric red wings and lowered himself to the ground. He was an imposing figure, broad in the shoulders and narrow in the waist. Muscle defined every inch of his naked body.

"I never realized so many Nightwalkers eschewed clothes," Viève whispered to Kamen.

"As far as I know it's only the Phoenixes and the Night Angels," he replied.

Jackson stepped forward to greet Dax, but Dax's attention went straight to his sister, who was holding a fed, cleaned, clothed, and diapered infant in her arms. She held the child out to her brother.

For a moment it looked as though Dax was going to shun the child. There was definite emotion working its way through his tense body. But then Dax held out his arms and Faith gently laid the baby in them.

"She doesn't have a name," Faith said quietly.

"I will give her one," Dax said, his deep voice rolling over them. Then he held up the child for all to see. "This is the daughter of Dax. She is destined for great things."

It was clearly a ceremonial act, something from the Night Angel culture. A show of acceptance and responsibility for the child. There was no telling what the future held for the child, no telling who and what she would become, but that was true of any child. What was clear was that she would need guidance. She would need strength. Dax would be exactly the one to give her both. He was a powerful and important Night Angel. He stood high in his father's house—his father being the ruling Night Angel of the North American continent.

"Congratulations, Dax. You're a father," Faith said proudly.

"Let's get this child somewhere safe," Dax said.

"I believe the safest place for her is here. In the middle of all of us. There's no telling if Apep can track her. At least until we move against him once and for all. Which will be very soon," Jackson said.

"How soon? I want her safe," Dax said, holding the baby tighter.

"I'm hoping tomorrow at dusk. As soon as the sun goes down," Jackson said. "We could use however many Night Angels you can spare."

"I'll put a call out, but on such short notice I don't know how many you'll be able to get," Dax said.

"We'll take what we can get. Mena's been telling us how many strong the Templars are and it sounds like they aren't more than three hundred. The human necromancers are much less than that. But I'm not as worried about them as I am about Apep. He's the great unknown. All we can do is hope he is still weakened by the birth," Jackson said.

"Noah and Gideon, the Ancient Body Demon medic will be here shortly," Kane said. "Gideon is bringing more medics with him. He and his medics will be able to handle any injuries that come our way. At least for the Bodywalkers. They have human bodies and Demons can heal humans. Whether they can heal the other Nightwalkers remains to be seen. So far healing across races has proven difficult for them."

"We'll take whatever we can get. Felix, you've been in contact with the Doyen via phone, what does he say?"

Felix had been leaning indolently against a column on the porch but perked up when he was addressed.

"The Doyen can't possibly mobilize any reasonable force on such short notice," he said, his smile sly. "But if the Templar Kamen were to transport them, we could provide six more Wraiths."

"Kamen needs to conserve his magic. The Mind Demon Kane can help you, provided they are not too far away."

"That depends, is Nevada too far away for you to travel?" Felix asked.

"No. I can do that," Kane said. "But I can only transport one at a time. If we had a stronger Mind Demon here they could transport more people more efficiently."

"You'll do fine," Jackson assured him. "How many can you get?"

"I'd say four . . . maybe five. It'll wear me out. I'll be shot for the day," Kane warned.

"Will you be rested for tomorrow night?" Jackson asked.

"I should be."

"Good. Because I think I'm going to need that little teleport ability you have. I'll talk to you about it later."

"Kamen, how long will it take you to cast the locating spell?" Jackson asked.

"Not long at all. The trick is getting a hundred fighters to the staging area as fast as possible. There's no telling how far away Apep is from us. I can only take two at a time in the streak and I don't have the strength to do that fifty times. No one does."

"I can cast the streak spell too," Docia said, bringing her Bodywalker Tameri's abilities to the fore. "If Kane could contact more Mind Demons we could use them to teleport us all there in waves."

"That's too slow. We will be in threat of discovery every moment. And it's hard to say where exactly we'll be able to gather that will keep us concealed until the last minute. No . . . a mass teleportation spell is needed," Kamen said.

"A spell of that magnitude could drain the caster to the point of barely being able to survive," Docia said worriedly.

"It is a chance I am willing to take."

"It would count you out for the duration of the battle. We are going to need you on the front lines, Kamen. Your skill with offensive spells far exceeds mine," Docia said. "No. It makes more sense that I cast the mass teleportation spell."

"Docia, no!" Ram said.

"Ram, it has to be done."

"Not by you."

"Yes, by me! You are going to need Kamen in the battle if you are to have any hope of destroying Apep. Kamen, tell them what you told me earlier."

Kamen had everyone's attention. "I think I found a way to banish Apep from this plane of existence."

"What?" a chorus of cries went up.

"I found it in an ancient scroll. It's not actually about banishing Apep, but about moving energy from one plane of existence to another. It's a very complex spell, but if we can get Apep into the circle that I will draw out to act as a portal, I think I can push him through it. But that requires holding him in place for as long as it will take me to cast the spell. So far I have timed myself at three minutes."

"That's not too long," Kane said.

"It's a long time to hold a god," Kamen said. "I am researching a binding spell, but there's no telling if it would be strong enough. How are we to know what will work against a god until we try it in the thick of battle?"

"There's no need for that. I can bind him," Grey said. "I think. As you say, there is no way of knowing for certain."

"All we can do is have a plan and execute it. That means practicing it. I have a few ideas but as you said, it's hard to know what will work against a god until we're actually in the thick of the battle," Jackson said. "I'll need Grey and the Phoenixes and Viève."

"Me? What can I do?" Viève asked.

"That deathtouch of yours is bound to at least weaken a god. He is in a mortal body after all."

"But that means I'll have to get close enough to touch him!" she said, panic rushing over her.

"That's what I need Kane and Grey for. Trust me, Viève, we won't leave you hanging out there."

"Why use the half-breed?" Felix asked snidely. "Has she ever even used her deathtouch before? How do we know it'll even work? Why not use me?"

"He's right. I've never used my deathtouch before. And it's not like I can practice on just anyone!" Viève cried.

"Viève, we will be able to test it. That night. The first chance you are able to, I want you to use your deathtouch against an enemy. If it works then we'll use you, if it doesn't then . . . we'll use Felix." It was clear they didn't want to depend on Felix. Viève couldn't blame them. Felix just shrugged.

"You're wasting your time with her. Best to count on me. I've used my deathtouch before. It works quite well."

Jackson didn't want to know who had fallen victim to Felix's deathtouch. But the knowledge that he was able to use it effectively couldn't be ignored.

"Yes. Just use Felix," Viève said as she nervously clutched her hands together before her. She didn't want them to depend on her for something so critical when it wasn't clear if her half-breed genes could perform.

"Very well," Jackson said reluctantly. "I won't make you do something you don't feel you're ready to do. Felix, you can come out on the field and practice with us."

"Tameri," Kamen said to Docia, "we need to prepare you for the mass teleportation spell. I'll cast the location spell now. Then you will know where you'll be sending everyone. We cannot practice the full spell, but we can prepare you for it as best as we are able."

"All right," Docia said, rubbing her hands together anxiously. "I can do this."

"I know that you can," Kamen said. "You are a powerful priestess. I have seen you do many incredible things. This is well within your range of ability. But, as you said, it will drain you until you are flirting with death. Someone will have to stay behind to care for you."

"I will care for her," Ram said tightly.

"Very well. Come with us, Ram. I will show you how best to care for her once the spell has drained her."

Ram nodded tightly and went to follow them into the house.

"Everyone else needs to be contacting more forces or practicing on this field," Jackson said.

"I'll be with you in just a second, Jackson," Kane said as he hurried into the house after the others. "Kamen!"

Kamen stopped halfway up the stairs and looked down at the Demon. "Yes?"

"I need you to take me to the Doyen's headquarters. I can only teleport somewhere I've already been. I'm not able to take the place out of someone's mind like a stronger Mind Demon could."

Kamen nodded. "Meet me in my rooms in ten minutes. I want to get Tameri studying this spell first."

"Will do."

Kane turned around and went back outside. The gathering had broken up, most of the people going out onto the field to practice their offensive and defensive abilities. Jackson had pooled together his little contingent, which was made up of Felix, Viève, Kane, the Phoenixes, and Grey.

"I don't know why I'm here," Viève was saying hesitantly.

"You're backup, in case something happens to Felix."

"Nothing is going to happen to me," Felix drawled. "I've been in a battle before. I'm six hundred sixty-two years old. I've battled Nightwalkers before and I've certainly taken down humans."

"Still, I like to play it safe," Jackson said. "My plan is simple. Ceara, Cordo, you're going to distract Apep with sheer firepower. Kane, while Apep is distracted, you're going to teleport Felix to within touching distance of Apep. Felix, you're going to use your deathtouch on him to weaken him. And, Grey, you're going to bind him and get him into the circle Kamen will be drawing."

"Sounds simple enough, provided everyone can do their part," Felix said, eyeing Grey.

"I can get him to the circle; it's keeping him there that'll be the problem. Hopefully Felix's deathtouch will make it all the easier," Grey replied.

"Viève, I still want you to execute your deathtouch as soon as you can. If something should happen to Felix I need to know I have a backup."

"All right. I will."

But the idea of touching another being with death was a hard pill for Viève to swallow. She knew she would have to do it if she was going to be a part of this battle. And she did want to be a part of this battle. She would have to get over it. She wanted to prove her worth to these people more than anything.

"It would be better to use one of the other Wraiths that are coming as backup," Felix said. "Wraiths with experience."

"I think Viève will do just fine," Jackson said.

"If you insist. If that is all, you must excuse me," he said.

"That isn't all. We need to practice these maneuvers."

"We can't. You heard him," he said nodding toward Kane. "Transporting the other Wraiths is going to wear him out. He doesn't have the energy to put into practice."

"He has a point," Kane said.

"SingSing can do the teleporting. She's really quite good at it," Grey said. "I would do it myself, but I fear all of my energy is going to have to be on holding this god in place."

SingSing was also unpredictable. It was exactly why Jackson hadn't asked her to be a part of this from the beginning. He had carefully chosen participants based on what he had seen during their capture the flag games.

"All right, if you think you can corral her," Jackson said. "Now we need someone strong to play the role of Apep. Someone with a lot of firepower."

"Did someone say they needed firepower?" a strong male voice asked from the left.

"Noah!" Kane exclaimed, going up to the Demon King and shaking his hand.

"Kane. I heard you needed some help. So, Gideon and I came. Legna stayed behind, however. She is watching over the children."

"With you and Gideon here, we don't need anyone else."

Jackson took in the sight of the brawny, black-haired Demon King and the taller, leaner built Gideon whose silver hair and eyes gave him a startling appearance. He was as young looking as his ruler was, but there was something very aged in his eyes and demeanor.

"Anyway, if you need firepower . . ." Noah held out a hand and a ball of flame appeared. He pitched it hard against a group of landscaping rocks and they burst into cinders.

"Nice," Cordo said.

It figured the Phoenixes would like the Fire Demon.

They moved to an area of the lawn separate from where everyone else was practicing and, after Grey fetched SingSing, began to practice their skills, their timing, and what it would feel like to take a hit in the process.

SingSing kept entertaining herself by disappearing and reappearing, a delighted "Tada!" accompanying each appearance. It grew old fast for everyone except SingSing.

"SingSing, take this seriously," Jackson scolded from the sidelines. "If Kane can't do this for whatever reason, we may need you as a backup."

"Oh, I'm taking this very seriously." She scrunched up her face and pointed to it. "See? This is my serious face."

Jackson sighed.

"Let's do it again."

# CHAPTER 22

Kamen was pacing. It was so out of character for the serene man she had come to know. He usually dealt with the world in such a calm and confident manner.

Except when it came to her. He was confident, but he was also turbulent. Passionate. She liked it that way.

But she didn't like seeing him stressed out. Yet she knew there was very little she could do about it. Her odds of getting any sleep today were probably just as low as his.

Tomorrow night would tell the tale. They would finally face this terrible enemy and the truth was . . . the truth was they weren't all going to come back alive and intact. There were going to be casualties. On one side or another, there were going to be casualties.

"Kamen, what can I do to help you?" she asked, moving to stop him in his circuit across the floor.

He gave her a small smile, reached to cup her face in his hand, and ran a thumb over her frowning lips.

"There is nothing to be done. Tomorrow people are going to die. Because of me. Templars, Politic, Demons, Djynn . . . I have wrought this terrible circumstance and others are going to pay for it."

"Blaming yourself isn't going to solve anything. It isn't going to help. If you spend all your time these next hours fretting about what guilt you bear, then you won't get the rest you need and you won't be as sharp as you need to be to stop people from getting hurt."

He sighed and pulled her in close. Held her tightly to the hard planes of his body and pressed his mouth down on hers.

"Would that it were so simple," he whispered against her lips.

"I'm not saying it is simple or easy. But sometimes forgiveness has to start with the forgiven. You need to let go of the reasons why this has come to pass and focus instead on what you can do to stop it from getting any worse."

He looked down into her eyes, letting her see deep into the startling blue of his. She saw his pain there. His guilt. And she saw him suffering because of it. She didn't want him to suffer anymore. She couldn't wait for this to finally be over, for him to be free of this enormous weight that was dragging him down. She wanted Apep gone from their existence once and for all.

"It will all happen as it is meant to," she said softly.

"I feel as if I am meant to die tomorrow. Oh, don't worry. In another hundred years I'll be back to cause more chaos again," he said dryly. "But this life, I fear, is almost at an end. And there is nothing I will regret more than leaving you behind."

Fear gripped at her chest. "You're not going anywhere! You're not leaving me behind! Don't even think like that. If you think that way then it is bound to happen. You cannot die until you have rectified this mistake, right?"

"Right."

"And once the mistake is rectified, there will be nothing left to kill you. So you will be fine."

"Destroying Apep will not end the battle," Kamen said. "There will be others to contend with."

"And they will be dealt with. By our others. You need to just focus on Apep. Tomorrow we will drag him down into that circle and you will purge him from this world."

"If all goes well," he said with a sigh. "I'm not even sure—"

"It will go well," she said, silencing his fretting with a kiss. Then she deepened the kiss, taking his flavor onto her tongue, drawing him into her, coaxing him into being present in the moment with her.

He lifted his knuckles to the rise of her cheek and pulled back to watch himself caress her there. She was so beautiful and he knew she had no idea that she was. Which somehow made her twice as lovely. She had come into his life two short nights ago and changed his world. With her forgiveness, her unabashed kindness, her damaged ego. But she had come a long way in just those two nights. All she had needed, he had come to realize, was some perspective. She had needed to draw breath in an environment other than her cell where she had been raised to believe she was nothing. Now she was growing confidence. It was still only just germinating inside of her, but she had stood up to Felix and that had been a major step for her.

And now there was a chance he wouldn't be able to watch the rest of her development. There was a chance one or both of them could die. For the first time he was grateful for Felix. He would much rather have Felix trying to touch that deadly monster than Viève. The closer she got to Apep the more chances she wouldn't survive.

"I want you to stay away from Apep," he said suddenly.

"But if Felix falls . . ."

"There are other Wraiths. Jackson can use them. I don't want you anywhere near Apep."

"All right," she said, relief washing through her. She didn't want to be anywhere near Apep either. She would much rather contend with the Templars. But could the Wraiths be trusted to do their part? That was the question. One that wouldn't have an answer until they were in the thick of battle.

Tomorrow night. A few short hours away.

"I don't want to talk about it anymore," she said fiercely, fighting back the sting of tears. "I want to be with you. If this is potentially our last day on earth, I want to spend it with you."

"And I you," he said fondly, his knuckles stroking her. "I never thought I would find someone to be with. Never thought I would even want something like this. But now it is all I want. It is what will make all of this worthwhile. Before it was a duty, now destroying Apep is paramount to my . . . my heart. I need to make room for you, and the only way I can do that is by lifting this burden of guilt. I will feel every loss of life tomorrow, but it will be easier to bear knowing you are here to forgive me. Please . . . be here for me."

She knew he was asking her to survive. Even though he didn't believe in his own survival, he was asking her to survive.

"I am here for you and I will be here until you get sick of me."

"That will be a very long time from now," he said, for the first time thinking like a man with a future. A future he had to have only if it could be with her. He had been going through the motions of life for so many centuries now and for the first time in a long time he wanted to be alive. He wanted to tell her, but he could not. Not until the burdens of guilt were lifted from his soul. She didn't deserve him, but he was going to subject her to himself all the same.

She looked pleased by his words, and so she should be. She should be made to feel special every minute of every night.

He leaned down and kissed her pale pink lips. He savored the feel of her, the way she sighed with pleasure, the sweet strawberry smell of her. She had gotten her own toiletries from town the night before and included in that was a strawberry scented body wash. It took the mystery out of how she managed to smell so sweet, but he didn't care. It was still uniquely Viève. And she added a warmth and depth to it that mere fabricated scent could never accomplish.

He deepened the kiss, drawing her body into his. He was much taller so she had to perch up on the tips of her toes to meet him better. The feel of her lithe body against his took his breath away. Made him hard. He wanted her more and more with every passing hour it seemed. She had the power to ease his mind of all the weight it bore. A tremendous ability to be sure. Perhaps he shouldn't allow it; perhaps he didn't deserve to be unburdened, but he selfishly could not see himself bear any punishment while she was around.

He cupped her head in one hand, noticing how small it was in his large palm. He was tall and strong and athletic but he was not an overly large man, and yet he was still much larger than she was. She had the ability to make him feel as if he were a giant. Not just in size but in ability. With her he felt as though he might be able to conquer the world tomorrow.

Her hair filtered between his fingers, the slippery, silvery strands soft and silky. Her hands had been clinging to his arms but now climbed up to his shoulders, then one wrapped around his neck, her fingers toying with the crisp ends of his hair at the base of his hairline. All the while their kiss grew deeper and deeper.

His free hand moved suddenly to her breast, cupping her through the soft cotton material of her nightgown. Her unfettered breast filled his hand perfectly and his thumb brushed over the bud of her nipple that was pebbled beneath the cotton. He didn't know which was sweeter, her mouth or the feel of her.

He began to feel a growing sense of urgency. She felt it too. He could tell by the way she clutched at him with increasing strength and the way she was starting to devour him with every clash of their tongues. He had wanted to make love to her sweetly . . . slowly . . . radiating every ounce of his feelings for her into her, saying with his body all the things he didn't have the right to say with words.

But as was often the case with her, it would not be that way. It was becoming torrid and hot, threatening to consume them. His knees bent, his hands went to her thighs, dragging up the skirt of her nightgown before grasping hold of the bare thighs beneath and hauling her up off her feet. She flew up, her legs wrapping around his waist, her ankles latching together in the small of his back. They seemed to favor this position. He liked it because all he needed was to put a wall to her back as a counterpoint and he could thrust up hard into her, all the while looking deep into her eyes, all the while watching emotion play over her features. And she was so very expressive. He could see, and therefore feel, every single thing that she felt. Every single moan of pleasure was punctuated by the intensity in her eyes and then he was lost.

Just as he was losing himself now. He broke from her mouth, panting hard for breath while he searched the room briefly for what he wanted. There. There it was.

A wall.

He walked them over to it in three steps, her back hitting it an instant later, his mouth crushing down on hers again. He broke away only long enough to divest her of her nightgown, leaving her naked in his arms and against his bare chest. He had changed into a pair of silky pajama pants earlier, and now they rode low on his hips, leaving his chest bare to feel the warmth and sultry softness of her skin against his. He could feel the tough little points of her nipples brushing over him and the sensation of all of it, on top of her blistering kisses, made him so hard he could hardly see straight.

"Gods how I want to be inside you," he groaned against her lips.

"Come inside me," she invited in a soft little panting of breaths. "I'm wet and waiting for you."

He groaned again at the erotic invitation and all the images it conjured for him in lightning fast succession. She had grown into quite the confident seductress in their time together. This fact was highlighted by the way she arched her back so her nipples rubbed enticingly over his chest and the way she trailed searching fingers in a line down his belly, below his navel, stopping only when she reached the edge of his pants. Then she found the drawstring, pulled it free with a simple tug, pushed his pants down past his hips until they pooled down around his ankles. He took only a moment to kick them away. He then planted his feet and sought upward with his hips. The head of his cock drew wetly along the seam of her outer lips, parting them around him. He hungrily lifted a breast to his lips then slid his hand down to where their bodies made contact, and through her damp curls, sought out the hard nub of her clitoris. He sucked on her nipple in time with his touch and she cried out with pleasure, her voice ringing in his ears. It wasn't enough of course. That one little cry would not satisfy him. Not by half. He undulated his hips, drawing himself through her wet flesh. He was there . . . right there. A single thrust away from burying himself deep inside her. He released her breast and found her mouth, sliding his tongue against hers with wild abandon.

"Do it," she panted, her body squirming in his arms.

"Are you rushing me?" he teased, prodding at her playfully but refusing her any satisfaction other than what his fingers were giving her.

She groaned with frustration, but then suddenly began to rethink her position. A mischievous light entered her eyes. "Of course," she said breathily. "You're right. We have as long as we like." She pulled his hand away from her body and slid hers in between them instead. She slowly wrapped her fingers around his jutting length and began to stroke him tightly. He hissed in pleasure, thrusting up into her strokes until he was so hard and so needy he was dizzy from the speed of his pulse.

"Enough," he growled.

"Never," she growled back. "It will never be enough."

She was so right. It would never be enough. He could have her a thousand times and he knew it would be just as intense the thousandth time as it had been the first. And he wanted her a thousand times. Ten thousand times. More.

The thought gave him a moment's pause, causing him to go still. She looked at him with curiosity. "What is it?"

It was the knowledge that he wanted his life to go on. He wanted his life to go on, but only if hers were to be in tandem with it. He didn't think he could bear life without her. It had been so cold before. So long and lifeless. So devoid of any passion. Now he had passion in spades. All because of her.

"I want you more than I've wanted anything in all of my lifetimes," he said fiercely, his voice barely a whisper. But she heard him well enough. He could tell by the warmth of red that suffused her already pink cheeks.

"I want you too," she said, and he knew it was meant to be more than want of just the moment. But of course she would want him. He was the first passion she had ever known. One day, when she was stronger, she might not want him any longer. She might want to move on and experience the variety life had to offer her.

The thought angered him. No! He wouldn't allow her to want anything more than him. He would be everything she needed and more.

He jerked her hand free of his body, and with a punishing thrust he rammed himself into her. She gasped, her body barely having a moment to adapt to him before he was thrusting into her in earnest.

He rode her hard, forcing cries of passion out of her, forcing pleasure out of her. She was innocent of the mood that had fallen on him, yet he could not hold himself in check. The idea of her giving herself to anyone but him had him acting with fire and haste. He pinned her against the wall and wrested her first orgasm out of her.

"None but me," he growled against her cheek as her cries deafened him in his ear. He didn't realize he had spoken aloud until she said, "None but you."

This mollified him a little bit. He slowed, moved with a more aching passion. He needed her and he let her know it in the movements of his body connected to hers. She felt the difference and he saw tears shining in her eyes.

"Shh," he soothed her, kissing her lips.

"You feel so good," she whispered. "I don't want this to end."

"It's just the beginning," he promised her.

And he kept to his promise. He loved her long and sweet, hard and fast, shifting moods and speed as fast as lightning. When he had wrested her third or fourth orgasm from her—he'd lost count because they seemed to blend together—only then did he allow himself to come into her. He came so hard he could barely stand. She had drained him, taken every part of him.

They leaned there gasping for breath for a long minute, then he pushed them away from the wall and walked them to the bed. He laid her down and then pulled the covers over her.

"Come with me," she implored, holding out her hand to him.

"I just did," he teased her, amusement twitching at his lips.

"Come to bed," she said, pulling back the covers in invitation.

"No. I can't. I have to study this spell so I know it backward and forward. I need to be able to cast it quickly and accurately. One mistake can mean the difference between life and death. Success and failure. And I will not fail."

"You need sleep as well. You can't go into this unrested."

He reached out and petted her hair. He gave her a small smile. "I won't be sleeping today. But you should rest."

"Without you?" she pouted.

"I'll come back to you in a little while. I plan on making love to you again before the day is done."

The announcement made her smile. But it was a sleepy smile. She was fading fast.

"Promise?" she said, laying her head down on the pillow.

"You have my word," he said.

And later, after he had memorized the spell to the best of his ability, he kept his word. He came to her, woke her up, and made love to her slow and sweet, kissing every inch of her body he could find, licking her into delicious madness. He was completely unselfish, and so was she. She touched him, loved him, gave him everything she had. And when they came together this time, she cried.

She held on to him, and cried.

# CHAPTER 23

Kat was fondling the necklace around her neck. She was lying in bed, naked, next to her Gargoyle lover and husband. Ahnvil had chosen not to sit out in the sun regenerating this day, wanting instead to spend it with her. He could do this for several days without it affecting him, but eventually being out of contact with his touchstone, the stone that regenerated his life force and strength, would drive him mad and could even end in permanent being . . . turning to stone once and for all with no hope of turning back into the flesh and blood man she loved.

She poked her lover in the shoulder, waking him from his light slumber. None of them were sleeping well that day. Certainly not the Gargoyles who were sworn to protect their Bodywalkers with their lives. Jackson was Ahnvil's Bodywalker and tomorrow, he knew, Jackson would be in the thick of the battle. That meant her husband would be right by his side, protecting him.

"What is it?" he asked, no trace of sleep in his heavy Scots burr.

"I've been thinking."

"Always a dangerous pastime."

"Stop it. Will you be serious?"

"I think things are far too serious as it is," he said grimly.

"True. But remember that passage you told me about regarding Adoma's Amulet?" She held out the amulet that had started their adventure together and had led her to discover it was a powerful nik and she was a Djynn. All her life she had thought she was allergic to the sun, only to find out it was because she was a Nightwalker that she burned in sunlight. Once she had learned to turn to smoke, the way Djynns kept from burning in the sun, she had never had to worry about it again.

"I do. 'The slave, born of the infinite Nightwalkers, will set free the power within. The one that harnesses Adoma's Amulet will have such power as to make a god weep.'"

"Now see, it's that last line that gets me. Maybe this is meant to be more than just a nik. Maybe there's something about it—about me—that's meant to go up against Apep. To make a god weep."

Ahnvil sat up like a shot in bed and glared at her.

"There is no way I'm letting you get anywhere near that homicidal bastard!"

"Calm down!"

"Doona tell me to calm down! Listen to yourself! You are thinking about pitting yourself against a god!"

"Not pitting myself against him! But being somehow instrumental in weakening him so that Kamen can work his mojo."

"Like what? What could you possibly do that would make it reasonable for you to go up against a *god*?"

"Stop saying that. I'm not going up against him. Just . . . sort of around him."

"Explain yourself, Kat, for you doona make much sense right now."

"Grey has been teaching me all about being a Djynn. And I've been learning. A lot. He taught me what he called 'arresting' magic. It's meant to paralyze an object. Freeze them in place."

"You want to cast magic like that against Apep?" Ahnvil scoffed. "He can probably break through something like that easily."

"Maybe. But maybe if I draw all the energy I need for it from Adoma's Amulet, maybe there's something special in it that can give it a unique kind of strength."

"That's a pretty goddamn scary maybe! What if you just succeed in making yourself a target and pissing him off?"

"Well, it's worth a try!"

"No, 'tis not. I doona want you anywhere near that god tomorrow. Hell, I doona want you there at all!"

"You're not leaving me behind. I can be useful. I've learned how to cast energy blasts, how to phase through things. I've learned to arrest things in place! All of which can be key tools when battling the Templars. I've got some good tricks up my sleeve."

"You're a novice at being a Djynn. You only learned what you are a few months ago. You are not near good enough to go into battle. When people are getting hit, dying all around you . . . 'tis hard, Kat, and I would spare you that. I would spare you from the danger as well. I canna fight for my Pharaoh if I'm worried about you."

"I'm not staying behind. You have to trust me to know what I'm doing. To know what I'm capable of."

"How can I when you're talking abou' going up against a god?"

"It's going to be chaos, Ahnvil. He won't even know it's me."

"He's a fucking god! He'll know!" he roared.

"Stop yelling at me!"

"Then stop being so bloody stupid!"

She gaped at him, shock and hurt striking through her. His expression became instantly contrite. "I didna mean to say it like that."

"You said exactly what you were thinking! That I'm stupid!"

"I doona think your stupid, Kat lass," he said gently. "I'm just . . . I'm bloody fucking scared. Tomorrow we're going to lose a lot of good people. I doona want you to be one of them. I want to be able to come home to you tomorrow, on safe, sound ground."

"No ground will be safe or sound if we all don't pull together to fight this monster. You can't exclude me because you're afraid for me. I'm terrified for you. I know you're going to be with Jackson, leading the charge. I don't want you to go. But," she said with a hard swallow, "I'm letting you go. I'm not going to ask you to stay behind. You wouldn't be able to grant a request like that and you wouldn't want to. It would be an unreasonable and selfish thing to do."

"But, Kat lass, there's a big difference between a battle-hardened Gargoyle and a novice Djynn half-breed."

Again his words stung her. "Stop that! Stop making me out to be less than you are!" she cried, leaping out of bed and quickly slipping on her robe. He caught up to her just as she was striding into the sitting room connected to their bedroom. He hadn't paused to put on something and so he stood naked before her as he stepped into her path.

"You're no' less than me, Kat! I doona think that at all!"

"You do! You just said so. There's a difference between a Gargoyle and a half-breed Djynn. A large enough one to make the difference between me succeeding tomorrow and me possibly failing."

"We're all in danger of failing tomorrow. Individually we're all weaker than someone else out there. None of us is so powerful that we are not in danger of failure."

"Just some of us are weaker than others."

"Aye, 'tis true and I willna say otherwise. And if you were looking at this logically you would say the same. But you're taking this personally."

"Damn right I'm taking it personally!"

"Kat, I doona want to fight."

"Then stop saying mean and stupid things."

"Aha! There now you said it. Called me stupid," he shot back.

"I said the things spewing out of your mouth were stupid."

"Those things are created by my mind so therefore you're calling my mind stupid."

"'The one that harnesses Adoma's Amulet will have such power as to make a god weep'! That's what it says! I can't ignore that and I won't!"

She marched for the outer door and he again stepped in her way.

"Where do you think you're going?"

"Away from you! I'm going somewhere where I can practice that paralyzing spell. Whether I use it on Apep or just on a Templar, I want to be ready."

"You're not using it on Apep!"

"We'll see what Jackson has to say about that!" She ducked under his arm and shot out the door, slamming it in her wake. He couldn't immediately follow her because he was stark naked and while that didn't bother him, it might bother someone else if he accidentally ran into them in the hallway. He hurried into the bedroom to grab his robe, but by the time he got out into the hallway, she was gone and he didn't know where she had headed. His first thought was Jackson and Marissa's room. Sagan was healed now, so he was no longer using their room. It was likely they were in their own bed. Still, it was a while before sunset and they were probably still asleep.

If they were asleep.

Odds were, they were having just a difficult time of it as he and Kat were.

Jackson heard a door slam in the hallway, the punctuation to a shouting argument not too far away. He looked down at his wife and soul mate; it was clear what she was thinking. It was a wonder they all weren't having arguments. The tension in the house was so thick it could be cut with a knife.

"It sounded like Kat," she said.

He nodded. He thought he'd recognized the cadence to his lead Gargoyle's speech.

"Likely he doesn't want her in the middle of the danger," Jackson said.

"She could be very useful. Unlike myself."

Every Bodywalker had a special innate ability—like Jackson's telekinetic power. But Marissa's power was as benign as it got. She was an empath. She could divine people's emotions. She could feel the pain in the argument that had just happened.

Which meant she would be useless come the morrow.

"Marissa, you'll be better off here."

"I know that," she said quickly. "I'm not going to argue otherwise."

"Good," he said with relief. "The last thing I need before this battle is to have an argument with my wife."

"I am aware of that. That's why I've taken a whole 'make love not war' approach to our past few hours." She ran her hand along his chest, down to his abdomen, over the mark of his ouroboros tattoo that marked him as a Bodywalker. She had a similar tattoo. They all did. It appeared the moment their Bodywalker soul joined with its host soul in the same body. "But you should try and get some sleep."

"That's not likely to happen," he said, bending down to kiss her with fiery heat. "So let's continue to explore the 'make love' part of this approach of yours."

She laughed and let him kiss her. She let him fill her senses because, if she didn't, she'd begin to think about the coming night and the fact that her lover was going to lead the charge against a maniacal being of unfathomable power. And she couldn't bear the thought of it. She wouldn't bear the thought of it until she absolutely had to. So if he wanted to make love until they were both overly sated, then that was exactly what she was going to do.

By the time dusk came, the house was already buzzing with life and activity. No one had slept well—if at all—and so they'd taken to wandering the house. They filtered into the main living area, an impromptu gathering of first one couple, then another, then another person and another until every seat was taken and they realized they were waiting for their leader to waken and join them.

Jackson came down the stairs a short time later and found them all waiting for him expectantly.

"Hey. Waiting for your fearless leader?" he quipped. "Someone should have come and got me."

"We knew you'd come eventually," Ram said. He clasped hands with Jackson and brought him in for a masculine hug and a thump on the back. They had been the best of companions throughout their many lives together. Each had been pharaohs in their own right during their original lives, but since then Ram had deferred to Jackson, letting him take on the role of leader for their people. But Jackson could never have done it without Ram. He and Docia managed all of the little things in the household, leaving Jackson to deal with the heavier problems.

Like an imp god let loose on the world.

"All right, I'm going to make this short and sweet," Jackson said. "We have to work together from beginning to end. We've been practicing for months now. We can do it with our eyes closed. But . . . some of us aren't going to make it out of this, and we're going to see friends fall. Just remember you can't let it distract you. Keep your eye on your goal. Keep the Templars off Kamen so he can cast his circle and support us in any way you can. Once we get Apep in that circle . . . if it works . . . it still won't be over until every last Templar is either dead or dealt with."

"And what about the ones who want a way out?" Mena asked anxiously. "Do they deserve to die just because they are fighting with no choice?"

"Oh, they'll be given a choice," Jackson said. "I promise you that."

"So . . . don't get killed . . . don't let anyone else get killed . . . and keep away from the killer god. Everyone got that?" Ram said.

They all nodded.

"Good. We'll leave as soon as Docia is ready to cast the mass teleportation spell. I'm going to go to the other houses and give them the same speech. Ram, are you with me or Docia right now?" Jackson asked.

"I'm going to stick with Docia, help her any way I can."

"Good. Docia, how long do you need?"

"Let's make it an hour from now. We'll meet on the front lawn. All of us."

"All right. Everyone good with that?"

They all nodded.

"Good," Jackson said. Then he got up to leave, ready to head for the other houses to make the same speech.

"Jackson, I need to talk to you," Kat said, moving out of Ahnvil's grasp and heading for him.

"Kat!" Ahnvil warned.

"No!" she snapped at him. Then she softened. "Please. Don't let the last thing we do before this be an argument."

He subsided immediately. And, though he didn't like it, he allowed her to go to Jackson.

Kat told Jackson about the Adoma's Amulet prophecy and gave him her take on it as they walked toward the house where the First Faction of Nightwalkers lived.

"And you think you can do that? Paralyze him?"

"Maybe. For a little while. I'm not sure. But I figure it's worth a shot right?"

"Right. The question is when to do it. Grey is going to bind him into the circle and that will take all of his energy and focus. But you . . . maybe we could use you right before Felix touches Apep. To hold him in place for the touch. Otherwise it's going to be very chaotic. You could make things much easier on us if you are able to do that."

"I can certainly try," she said.

"But she's a novice," Ahnvil blurted out in spite of himself. "You could just be drawing Apep's attention to her."

"Maybe. But we're all taking that risk," Jackson said.

This was what it meant to be a leader to these people, he thought. The ability to make the hard choices when no outcome seemed to be a good outcome. He knew he was sending people to their potential deaths. He did not welcome the thought or the responsibility. But someone had to do it.

"Kat, practice that paralyzing spell on one of the more powerful Nightwalkers. Noah, perhaps. Come with me and we can ask him for his help."

Ahnvil did not say another word as they walked, but Jackson could feel a world of anger, worry, and pain radiating off him. Jackson was sorry to put Ahnvil in such a position, but they were going to need everyone's help in this. No role would be too small although some would be greater than others.

When they reached the second house, Noah was addressing the household much in the way Jackson had just done. The room turned as one when he entered.

"Ah, Jackson," Noah said, reaching to shake his hand. "I was just about to send someone to get you. After all, you're the one with the experience dealing with the Templars. Any advice for the troops?"

"The Curse of Ra is their weapon of choice. If the priest wielding it is powerful enough, it can kill. When it hits, it hits hard."

"We were practicing against it with Tameri. I mean Docia." Adam smiled grimly. "Sorry. Still getting used to this whole two souls one body thing. Don't know what to call you half the time."

"She prefers Docia. I prefer Jackson. It doesn't matter. I answer to Menes as well. Are there any questions I can help you with?"

"Other than the Curse of Ra, what else can we expect?" Adam asked.

"Some paralyzing spells. Some elemental spells. Those are their go-to spells."

"Jasmine, maybe you ought to sit this one out," Adam said worriedly.

"Oh, I know you did not just say that," she said with rising indignation.

"Babe, it's just that with your—"

"Don't finish that sentence," Jasmine said quickly and harshly. "I'm going. End of story."

Adam knew when to argue with his wife and when not to. If he fought with her on this she would just dig her heels in harder. He let it go and prayed for a miracle. Prayed she wouldn't get hurt. Prayed to Destiny that their child was meant to be.

Jackson fielded a few more questions, then told everyone to meet out on the front lawn of the main house by the end of the hour.

Jackson wrapped up the meeting by going to Sagan.

"The Curse of Ra is a light spell. One hit and you're literally toast. You might want to—"

"No. I'm going. Valera can protect me from light. We'll work in tandem. As long as she is conscious and focused, I'm good to go. I've beat worse odds in worse situations."

"Worse than this?" Jackson said skeptically.

"Well, not worse than this. But pretty close." He exchanged knowing glances with Valera.

"All right, if you insist. I can see I can't talk you out of it."

Sagan shook his head.

"Well, I'll see you on the front lawn then."

Jackson left the house and went walking toward the third house on the property where he would do it all again. By the time he was done it was almost time to meet on the front lawn. He had just enough time to find Marissa and pull her into a hard, fiery embrace. He kissed her so deeply her toes curled. She clung to him, her hands trying to hold him closer . . . forever . . . but she knew she had to let him go and that he might not make it back.

"Come back to me or I'll kill you," she said illogically.

"If I don't see you again in this life, know that I'll be waiting for you in the next one. Only . . . you have to promise me something."

"What?" she asked, tears in her eyes.

"You won't go the route I took last time. You'll be brave and lead our people for the next hundred years until I come back. Someone is going to need to lead them if I'm gone and it has to be you."

The route he took last time. He had lost her so quickly after finding her again that it had devastated him to the point where he had taken his own life. They were soul mates and it was so hard for one of them to live without the other.

"But I can't—"

"You can. We'll have a divided people trying to come together and they need a strong leader for that."

She nodded and now her tears were tracking down her face. She knew how hard this was for him. She could feel his emotions as if they were her own. He wanted to be selfish, to tell her to come and be with him in the Ether rather than stay here where she would be without him. But they would be disembodied souls in the Ether and though their souls could occasionally touch, it was not the same as when they were physically present with one another.

"I will stay and I will wait for you. A hundred years or a thousand, I will wait for you."

Jackson breathed a sigh of relief. It would be a hard separation, but they had been through it before. But maybe now, after this was over, if he survived . . . maybe they would be able to finally live in peace, without the Templar threat hanging constantly over their heads.

He kissed her again, then moved away from her. Her hands clung to him for as long as they could, then fell away. She lifted her chin and followed him out onto the front lawn.

Docia was there, sitting in the middle of a drawn circle with the five points of a pentacle transecting into it. She had a variety of herbs strewn about in a way that would only make sense to a magic-user. Ram was standing just outside the circle watching her with a stern look on his face. He didn't like this. Didn't like what this promised to do to her. But they had no choice.

"They're in California," she said, "if Kamen's location spell is accurate."

"It's accurate," he said, sounding slightly affronted.

"Everyone should think about how you're going to get back. Some of you are going to have to take conventional means. Kamen can't bring all of you back."

"We'll have Mind Demons as well. They can teleport pretty easily," Noah said. "I'll have some standing by."

"All right then. I'm ready. Everyone, get as close together as possible. I mean a huge press of human flesh," Docia said.

They did as instructed, a little over a hundred bodies pressing into each other.

"Good luck," Docia said.

Then she began to cast her spell. It was a highly physical spell, her body twisting and folding and gyrating as she put every last ounce of energy into it. She could feel it draining her, but no one was going anywhere. They were still there. She was starting to panic when a sudden explosion of power burst out of her and everyone on the field disappeared.

She collapsed, her whole body going numb and weak. No, not weak . . . paralyzed. She couldn't feel anything. She couldn't even feel Ram's touch on her as he lifted her into his arms. It was a good thing he was as strong as he was, because he was lifting dead weight. She couldn't even hold up her head.

"It's all right," he said, holding her against his chest. "I've got you."

She tried to say something, but she couldn't speak. Her mouth wouldn't form the words, her throat wouldn't work. Panic infused her. She was a prisoner in her own body. What if this never went away? What if this were permanent?

"I've got you. You'll be all right," he said soothingly as he carried her into the house and to their bedroom.

He laid her down on the bed and, after a few minutes, the feeling began to return to her extremities.

She and Ram sighed with relief, but it was a measured relief. Their worries were now with the others.

# CHAPTER 24

The group appeared not in one place, but in several places, all within sight of each other. They got their bearings as quickly as possible, not knowing if they were going to find themselves dead center of Apep central or not.

They were in a vast field of grapevines. A winery, it appeared. There were many large buildings within easy sight of them and they knew this was where they would find Apep and the Templars. Jasmine took to the air, reconnoitering from above. Adam turned to mist and followed her closely. Noah turned to smoke and followed suit. There were others who could take to the air and they did, but most were left to run up the hillside toward the winery buildings. There were several houses on the property and a barbed wire fence had been erected around them. The Phoenixes burned through them in a heartbeat, leaving smoldering, molten edges in their wake.

"The main house," Kamen said. "I can sense his extraordinary power. But don't ignore the other houses. They too are filled with beings of power."

"How many would you say?" Jackson asked.

"We're outnumbered," Kamen said grimly.

"By how much?"

"I'd say two to one at least."

So everyone would have to do more than their share and they would have to do it quickly.

The Templars spotted them right about then, and an alarm raised up all along the property. Templars began to spill out of the buildings and the Curse of Ra began to burst out of them. The way they poured out of the house as a single entity, it was almost as though they were unsurprised to see them. As though they had been prepared for the attack.

The first bolt hit Jackson, who was leading the charge. It took him down, but only for a minute. It would take a much more powerful caster to bring down a man of Jackson's power.

Jackson retaliated by grabbing anything loose on the ground and using his power to fling it into the Templars from every direction. A pile of unused metal rods from unfinished fencing became a series of javelins, spearing through Templar bodies, maiming them but not killing them. He would avoid death wherever he could, but no fatalities was an unrealistic expectation. He knew that. He would give these people the chance to change loyalties . . . whether it be in this lifetime or the next. He didn't know how . . . but he would do it.

Sagan, protected from the Curse, drew his kukuri blade in one hand and the katana in the other. He too would only maim those who crossed his path. It was dangerous because even an injured Templar could still cast using magic, could potentially heal themselves and rejoin the battle. But Kamen had assured him that that would take monumental effort and no one could heal themselves in that amount of time in the thick of the battle. Also, Kamen said that mere pain would be enough to disrupt the abilities of the Templars. So, he began to cut down Templars, the muscles on his arms and back playing hard as he swung through bone and sinew, reaching low to bisect an Achilles tendon, crippling the victim, or reaching high to sever a limb completely. Maimed but not dead, and creating enough pain and debilitation to take them out of the fight.

Ahnvil turned to his grotesque state, the stone visage that most looked like a hideous Gargoyle, his wings sprouting forth as he took to the sky with the rest of the Gargoyles, leading the charge with a war cry. He kept close to Jackson's side; taking hits from the Curse whenever possible, lessening the possibility of injury or death to his leader. His big body was designed for taking massive amounts of damage. He was not invincible, however he did not hesitate nor flinch in the face of the Curse of Ra.

Viève did as promised. She hurried onto the property in search of someone to try her deathtouch out on. Her heart was thundering in her chest and she could feel Kamen protectively at her back. He used the Curse of Ra to beat back anyone who came near them. Only, with his power, his Curse did not simply stun. It killed. He sent Templar souls flying back into the Ether. Kamen had no problem doing so. He knew they would be reborn again in the next life.

"Let me touch one!" Viève cried in frustration when he refused to allow anyone close to her.

"Not until it is necessary!" he shouted back to her. He blasted away another Templar.

"It's necessary! Jackson wanted me to!"

But he stubbornly refused to heed her.

And that was when Apep arrived.

He exploded out of the house, shards of wood and beams blowing out all around him as he took to the air. Wind whipped through his long hair and he cut quite a beautiful figure in the air, looking like a virago of hate and power.

"You fools!" he cried. "You think you can attack me? You think your puny mortality can stop a *god*?"

"And we can succeed!" Jackson shouted back at him.

*"You!"* Apep said with disgust. "Didn't I kill you once already?"

"I'm not that easy to kill!" Jackson said.

"We'll see about that!"

Apep formed a discus of brilliant white energy in his hand and flung it at Jackson. Jackson went to dash out of the way, but Ahnvil was there, placing his body between Jackson and the strike. The discus hit him hard and flung his stone body back into Jackson. The two men went tumbling head over heels into the dirt.

"Who else wants the power of a god shoved down their throats?"

"We do!" the Phoenixes cried in unison.

Here it was. The beginning of their plan to engage Apep. Only Kamen had been so busy protecting Viève that he hadn't drawn his circle yet. Jackson shoved his way out from under the dead weight of Ahnvil and shouted out.

"Kamen, get ready!"

Kamen heard the cry and suddenly remembered what he was supposed to be doing. He pulled back, leaving Viève exposed, hoping she knew what she was doing. He landed not too far away and began to burn the grass in a circle and pentacle pattern.

Cordo lassoed Apep in a ring of fire while Ceara threw balls of flame at him. Apep lobbed them all back with frightening ease, sending them screaming back at her. She was hit hard by the impact, but the fire itself could not burn her.

Noah saw how ineffective their attack was and he moved up to the forefront. The plan wasn't that they were to defeat Apep in this way, merely distract him so that Felix could get behind him and touch him.

Only Felix was nowhere to be found.

At first.

Then Viève saw him. She saw him reach out and touch one of the Body Demons, the Demon crumpling to the ground.

"No!" she cried.

Felix heard her and turned to her.

"Yes, little fool," he hissed at her. "Apep is our master. You had better get used to the idea. He's going to rule this whole sorry world! Then finally the Wraiths won't have to hide away in their little cells. We'll be free to roam everywhere and anywhere we desire!"

That was when she saw the Wraiths. A small army of them, rushing forward into the fray from Apep's side. Clearly they had been in the house with Apep. It suddenly dawned on Viève that Felix and the other Wraiths Kane had brought had probably warned the god about their surprise attack. But it had to have been a recent development, or wouldn't Mena have noticed them and reported their presence? Felix turned to Apep and said, "Master! Do not be distracted! They mean to push you from this world!"

"Thank you for the warning, Wraith, but they are no match for me." Apep built a discus of power in his hand and flung it at Noah. Noah ducked and the discus flew past him and struck Cordo full in the chest. The Phoenix screamed as his flesh was seared off his bones and his soul was ripped out of his body. Cordo's lifeless body fell to the ground, smoldering. His female counterpart screamed.

"Focus, Ceara!" Jackson demanded of her, knowing by her body language that she wanted to go to her fallen comrade.

"There's nothing we can do!" she cried. "He's too strong!"

Jackson turned to find Kat, who was kneeling beside her fallen mate, tears tracking down her face. When he had been knocked unconscious Ahnvil had reverted to his flesh state and there was a huge burn on his chest from where Apep had struck him. It was deep and bloody and right over his heart, half cauterized by the searing heat of the strike that had taken him down, half bleeding heavily.

"Kat! We need you!"

Kat swallowed, rage building inside of her so fiercely she could taste the bile of it. She left her lover on the ground and grabbed the amulet in her hand. She tapped into the power she felt emanating from it. She had more powerful niks. One a bracelet she was wearing on her wrist even now, but she did not draw energy from that at all. The written passage had been clear. It was Adoma's Amulet that would have the power to make a god fall to his knees. She only prayed that she was Djynn enough to do it.

That was when Felix came out of nowhere and lunged for Kat. She was so focused on what she was doing that she didn't even see him. But just as Felix was about to lay hands on her, Noah sent a fireball full of fury screaming against him. It hit and Felix was thrown off his feet, back away from Kat. Set on fire, Felix was consumed by the flames until his screams could no longer be heard.

Viève realized that Felix's betrayal had an even more deadly aspect to it than his attack on his fellow Nightwalkers. It meant a key part of Jackson's plan to capture Apep now had a huge hole in it. A hole she would need to fill. But she hadn't even gotten a chance to touch a single person! She didn't even know if she was even capable of a deathtouch.

She had no choice but to find out the hard way. She would be phased until the moment she actually touched Apep, so she wasn't afraid he could hurt her. At least, she didn't think he could hurt her. But he was a god. Anything was possible. She prayed she could do her part. If not, all would be lost. She watched as Apep began picking off Nightwalkers one by one with horrible savagery, sometimes incinerating them into ash. She knew this plan had to work. She had to make herself do her part.

"Listen! All of you!" Jackson boomed out into the fighting forces. "Templars! Do not fight against us! You do not fight for the Templar cause but for the whims of a maniacal god! Odjit is lost to you. She has been ever since Kamen defected to the Politic!"

"They know who they fight for!" Apep announced with a crazed laugh. "I told them they are graced with the presence of a supreme being just last night. They now know how blessed they are."

"Do you feel blessed?" Jackson called out. "Or do you feel cursed? Cursed by the god who threatens you, who kills you based on whether or not he's in a bad mood? How has he made your life easier? How has he made it better since he stole Odjit from you? I know the Templars and the Politic have had their differences, but we can see an end to that once and for all!"

"Puny! Insignificant! Did you really think my Templars and my Wraiths would betray me?" Apep threw another discus of energy at Jackson, who dodged it. Barely. Then he sent an explosion of fire radiating out around him where it rained down on the attacking forces and his own forces alike.

"See how he has no regard for you?" Jackson shouted out. "If you join us, fight against your master, unify the two halves of the Bodywalker race. You do not have to die tonight! This is your moment of choice. If you choose to fight with us, you will have safe haven with the Politic. Let us put our differences aside once and for all!"

There were screams of pain elevating all around Jackson as Templars and Nightwalkers from both sides were burned by Apep's fire. Jasmine was one of its victims, her blouse having caught fire, burning on her body. But Adam was there instantly, turning his mass into a wave of water and washing over her. She was drenched from head to toe by the time he was done, but she was no longer on fire. He reshaped himself and wrapped his arms around her.

"Off!" she said, shrugging him off angrily. "I'm going to kick this fucker's ass!"

"Jas!" He jerked her around so she was paying attention. "You can't hurt him! Stick to doing what you know you can be successful at!"

Jasmine seemed to come to her senses and gave him a curt nod. "You're right. I'm sorry. But someone better do something about him soon. We can't take much more of that!"

Adam nodded grimly then tapped into the water in the soil and under the ground. He used his ability to manipulate it to send it misting up above the soil. The thick mist settled over the entire area, dousing any burning things or people, but also obscuring their vision. This debilitated both sides, so as soon as fire was doused, he lowered the mist back into the ground.

Viève looked for Kane. She saw him just as he saw her, and they ran to meet one another.

"Can you teleport me right behind him? It has to be lightning fast. I need to touch him before he can turn on me!"

"Will do," Kane said. He looked for Kat and saw she was standing nearby, focusing all of her will onto Apep, he assumed. Kane waited to see what she could accomplish.

Apep held out his hands and the ground roiled beneath the feet of the land-bound fighters on both sides. Huge fissures opened beneath them and bodies began to fall into the earth. All the while Apep laughed at his own destruction.

"This is actually quite fun!" he declared. "I didn't realize just how bored I was. Thank you ever so!"

Jacob quickly tried to counter the earthly attack, sealing the fissures, using the softened earth to catch the falling bodies and return them to their feet aboveground. It was a massive undertaking, even for someone of Jacob's skill and power. Bella protected him as he focused, leaping onto the back of a nearby necromancer who tried to stab him in the neck, snapping her neck with a quick, succinct movement and a crack of sound.

"That's what you get for trying to touch my husband!" she spat at the corpse.

Suddenly Apep released a scream of outrage. As they all watched, he seemed to be struggling in mid-air. He couldn't seem to lift his arms to cast his next bit of power.

"What is this?" he screamed shrilly. He struggled harder.

"It's Kat!" Viève whispered harshly to Kane. Kane nodded and grabbed Viève, holding her close.

"Hold on. Do what you do but make it fast!"

Viève didn't know if she could do what they were counting on her to do, and she didn't know if it would even have any effect on a god if she could.

"Make sure you let go of me right away."

"You'll fall!" Kane argued.

"Not if I'm holding on to him I won't. I don't want you anywhere near me when I go to deathtouch him. I'm not sure if I can focus it just to my hands. It might go all over my skin."

"Gotcha. Let's do this!"

Kamen watched as Kane grabbed her and they disappeared from the ground. When they reappeared they were in mid-air right at Apep's back. Viève leapt out of Kane's hold, latched onto Apep, and wrapped her hands around the god's throat. Trapped as he was, he couldn't fight, couldn't throw her off. From the ground Kamen could see the focus on her face.

Apep's struggles weakened considerably. It was working! It could all be over right then. Apep was in the body of a mortal Nightwalker, after all. Viève's deathtouch could potentially kill his host's body.

Tears were streaming down Apep's face as he fought for breath, fought for life, fought against the fury of his helpless situation. Finally he seemed to wrest free of Kat's mental hold on him. Kat collapsed onto the ground, all of her magical energy from the amulet depleted. Apep shrugged off Viève, turning on her with a snarl.

"You traitorous bitch! I'll see you dead!"

Viève phased out of instinct, but Apep could barely move, weakness infusing every molecule of his body.

"Grey! Now!"

Now it was Grey's turn. He appeared in mid-air behind Apep and used powerful magic to bind him once more. Then he teleported him down to the circle where Kamen was standing.

"You!" Apep snarled when he recognized Kamen's face. "You brought me into this world!"

"And I shall take you right back out of it," Kamen vowed.

Apep's scream was shrill and full of fury. "Wraiths! Come to me! I command you!"

But the Wraiths were all occupied elsewhere and could not attend to their struggling master.

Using the power of his mind to compensate where his body was weak, the god began to fling things at Kamen to try and disrupt his concentration as he began to recite the spell. Viève saw this and hastened to her lover's side.

She reached to phase him so that objects might pass through him instead of hitting him, but he quickly shook his head. His meaning was clear. He didn't think he could effectively cast the spell if he wasn't physically there. A large wooden crate came barreling toward Kamen, but just before it hit him it burst into flame and a wall of ash was left in its place, dousing Kamen in the warm gray dust. Viève looked up at the male Fire Demon gratefully. Noah nodded his head.

Jackson took over from there, using his telekinetic ability to protect Kamen from any further flying debris. Kamen spoke the spell as cleanly and as quickly as he could, his hours of practice and memorization serving him well. He couldn't forget a single word. And he didn't. He was a master at what he did.

Apep screamed in frustration and fury. He tried to fight against Grey's power, but the Djynn was too much for him in his weakened state.

In the end, it was a rather simple finale. Bursts of energy slammed into Viève, knocking her back on her butt, and Apep screamed one last time.

Odjit's body went limp in Grey's hold.

Kamen opened his eyes and Grey looked at him questioningly. Had it worked? Or was Apep simply playing possum? Kamen came forward and reached out two fingers to touch Apep's throat. There was no sign of a pulse. Apep and all the souls trapped in Odjit's body had been banished to another realm. What realm was anybody's guess, but as long as it was not there on Earth, it didn't matter.

"Are you sure he's gone? What if he just jumped bodies?" Grey asked skeptically.

"He's gone. If he had jumped bodies Odjit and her host would still be intact. I sent everything inside of her to another realm. It worked."

"As long as you're sure . . ." Grey said.

Kamen nodded. Grey released his hold and Odjit's body collapsed bonelessly to the ground.

"That seemed almost too eas—"

Grey broke off with a gasp and Viève and Kamen looked up from Odjit's body to see a Wraith wrapping its hands around Grey's throat.

"No!" Viève cried, leaping forward to try to touch Grey, to phase him away, but Grey disappeared before her eyes, leaving the Wraith to fall forward. Kamen blasted out the Curse of Ra against him and he was incinerated.

"What happened to Grey? Is he dead? Do Djynn just disappear when they die?" Viève asked, her tone panicked.

"I don't know. But come, this fight isn't over yet. Go see to it Kat's protected. She's helpless out there on the field. I'll come back for you once this is over."

"It's done!" Jackson shouted. "Your leader is dead! Stop fighting us or die by his side!"

Half of the field had already pulled out of the fight, not acting against the Nightwalkers any longer, but not acting with them either. When they realized what Jackson was saying was true, they began to kneel on the ground, one by one, and put their hands in the air.

The Wraiths screamed in fury.

"Cowards!" a Wraith cried. "Fight them! Come on and fight them! Do you want to live under their boot heels for the rest of your lives?"

"It's over!" Jackson said harshly. "Your master is dead. Unless the Wraiths want a war with the rest of the Nightwalker clans I'd call a halt if I were you."

"Maybe I'll just kill you and be done with you!" The Wraith phased and launched himself at Jackson. Jackson tensed, but suddenly Viève was in front of him, blocking his path. She grabbed hold of him, one phased Wraith grappling with another.

"Don't be stubborn!" Viève grunted. "Can't you see it's over?"

"Get your hands off me, you filthy little mongrel!"

There was a crack of sound as Viève hauled back and punched the Wraith in the face. He snapped back and fell to the ground, unphasing as he hit the dirt, unconscious.

"Call me a mongrel again!" Viève hissed. "I dare you!"

Then she phased back into solid form and went looking for Kat. She found her kneeling next to Ahnvil.

"If he just wakes up and turns to stone, he could heal," she said in a small voice. "Do you think he'll wake up?"

Viève looked down at the Gargoyle and the huge chunk of flesh that had been taken out of his chest. She had serious doubts, but the Gargoyle was still breathing and that was all that mattered right then. Maybe one of the Body Demons could help heal him. It was hard to say. She had heard that the Body Demons had trouble healing others outside their own species, except for humans. But as she understood it the Gargoyles had been human before they were forged. Maybe that meant they could be healed?

With Apep gone, the fight went out of the remaining Templars. Some who were die-hard met their ends the hard way. Gideon, the Body Demon, reached out and stopped the heart of one . . . then two . . . right in their chests. In the end Templar bodies were as fragile as any human's. They were susceptible to injury and even death. In spite of the havoc and death they had wrought, the Wraiths realized they were outnumbered and began to flee the scene, but not after taking a few more lives, including that of the Phoenix Ceara and a pair of the Mystical dragons. But the damage they caused before leaving was breathtaking. Many lives had been lost with just a touch.

The battle was won. They had taken heavy casualties, but the Templars had taken worse. The Templars that had given up came willingly to kneel before Jackson.

"Listen, all of you," he said vehemently to them. "This war is over. There will no longer be Templar and Politic sides. There will only be a Bodywalker side. Trust must be earned, but if you truly want to be part of a cohesive whole, you will earn it. And over time you may be forgiven the egregious sins you have committed. All you have to do is look to Kamen for your role model and your guidance. You looked to him as leader in the past, look to him now as you will look to me. He has worked hard to earn his forgiveness, and you must work even harder. It will not come easy, but it will come."

Kamen looked to Jackson in surprise. The idea of forgiveness from someone like Jackson, to whom he had committed so many ills, was shocking to him. He had not been looking for forgiveness, nor had he expected it. He had simply done what he felt was necessary to make things right.

Kamen didn't know what to feel. He still felt undeserving of such a thing. Defeating Apep had made it better, but that didn't change the fact that he had created the problem in the first place. He had made so many mistakes, caused so much pain. As he looked around at all the wounded and dead he knew he was responsible for all of it.

Viève walked toward him, her steps hurrying as she watched the tight play of emotions crossing his face. She reached for his hands, caught them up into hers, and squeezed them tightly.

"It's all right," she said soothingly. "It's over now."

"But the mourning has just begun," he said, looking at Cordo and Ceara where they lay dead. They had come to represent their people and they had paid with their lives. What would the rest of the Phoenixes think of them now? Would any hope of a lasting relationship die with their representatives? Kamen would have to return to the Brazilian rain forest and report their deaths. No other should do it. It was his responsibility.

"The reunification has just begun as well," she said, looking around at all of the Templars.

"I can see at least ten right now who will not come willingly to the side of good. They are vicious and brutal beings. It is they who should lay dead," Kamen said fiercely.

Jackson heard this and turned to him.

"We will discover who they are with your help. You know the Templars better than anyone. You will know who deserves a second chance and who deserves to pay for their crimes."

"As I have paid?"

"You have earned your redemption because you sought it out. Anyone who seeks the same will receive it," Jackson said. "All others will see imprisonment."

"And I am to judge who is sincere and who is not?" Kamen asked bitterly.

"You are to help us judge. This is a group effort, remember? You are not alone in this."

"Then why do I feel so isolated?" he asked painfully.

"But you are not," Viève said softly, leaning her body against his, giving him support and warmth. "You have me, for whatever that's worth."

He frowned down at her, reaching to touch a finger to her powder soft cheek. "It's worth everything. That alone has more value to me than anything else in this world. You have the power to make me feel as though . . . as though somehow I managed to be deserving of something good, even though I am at a loss as to how I managed it."

"You managed it because you have become a creature of good intent," Jackson said. "And that is worthy of good things."

Then Jackson turned and walked away, heading for Kat and her fallen Gargoyle.

"Have I?" Kamen asked quietly. "Have I become a creature of good intent, or have I just been trying to right a single wrong? What of all the other wrongs I have committed?"

"Remember them. *Learn* from them. Make sure you've left such behaviors in the past and move into the future without them," Viève said.

"I've been a selfish being for so many lifetimes now," he said to her, searching her gray eyes for answers, hoping she could provide them. "Am I suddenly changed?"

"What do you think? I can't stand here trying to convince you of your goodness. That's something that has to come from within. But I can tell you this. You have been good to me. So good. Better than anyone has ever been to me. No one told you to do that. You weren't trying to make up for past mistakes. You were unselfish and kind and so good to me."

"You are wrong," he said softly. "I was more selfish than I have ever been before. I wanted you. I took you. All without regard for the consequences of my actions."

"I'm so very glad you did," she breathed.

Kamen seemed to suddenly remember where they were and he drew away from her.

"Come. No one can heal a Gargoyle better than the man who created him."

He left her and walked over to Kat and Ahnvil. Viève watched him go and felt sorry for him. Sorry that he couldn't seem to come to terms with the man he now was versus the man he had once been. He saw no difference, though everyone else was seeing a world of difference.

Kamen knelt beside Ahnvil and laid a hand over the gaping wound that was on his chest. Kat looked up at him through tearful eyes and he saw hope spring up within them.

"I can heal him to consciousness," he told her. "Once conscious he can change to his grotesque state and it will accelerate his healing."

"He . . . he'll be all right then?" Kat asked. "He won't die?"

"I won't let him," Kamen said firmly.

Kat burst into fresh tears.

Kamen began to speak the healing words.

# CHAPTER 25

Over the years the Politic had designed prisons to hold Templar criminals if they were captured. There were several all over the world. Jackson sent groups of Templars to all of these prisons with the understanding that the prisons would become their homes temporarily. They would earn their freedom as any prisoner would. Through evaluation and good behavior.

It took some time before everyone made it back to the house in Portales. There they held one last meeting on the front lawn of the house.

"Thank you," Jackson said to them all, "for all that you have done for us. You have helped end a serious threat to us all and, in the process, ended a civil war that has lasted hundreds of years. We cannot possibly express appropriate gratitude. You are all welcome to stay for as long as you want, but I am sure many of you long to go home at last and would hurry on your way. I will not be offended in the least if this is what you choose to do. Please know that you take with you our wishes to see you well and safe wherever your travels take you."

The group then broke up and people began to go their separate ways. Viève approached Jackson.

"What of the Wraiths?" she asked him. "The Doyen?"

"I think we'll just let the Doyen stew in his own juices, wondering what the Nightwalker races will do in retribution for his bad choices."

"What *will* you do?"

"Nothing. As long as they get the message and don't move against any other Nightwalkers in any other way. But if they persist in harming others we will be forced to take a unified action against them."

Noah approached them and Jackson said to him, "I wish to have a meeting with all the rulers of the various Nightwalker races. A summit meeting, if you will. Do you think that can be arranged?"

"I think I can get the message out to the other rulers. Technology doesn't work so well with many of the races on our side, so we'll have to figure a way around calling. We've always sent ambassadors to foreign courts. Will you accept the same?"

"Of course," Jackson said readily. "Send whomever you like and all the other courts can do the same."

"I think I will leave one of the dragons behind," the Empress of the Mysticals said as she came up on them. "If that is suited to you?"

"Very much so. I will welcome all ambassadors from all courts and will arrange to send ones from our court if they are welcome."

"My father will be happy to send someone," Dax said. "And receive the same. There are different rulers for each continent with the Night Angels, but I am sure we can agree on one person that would suit them all."

"The same goes for the Djynn."

The group turned with a collective gasp to see Grey leaning casually against a wall.

"Grey! You're alive!" Viève cried out.

"I phased out long before the deathtouch could affect me," Grey said with a cocky smile.

"Oh, but I always knew you could not be dead!" Paulette cried as she threw her arms around him and hugged him. Grey grinned a bit sheepishly, but he didn't stop her display of affection in the least.

There was more discussion of ambassadors, and it was sometime then before Viève made a quiet retreat. She would let the rulers decide amongst themselves what their next actions would be. Her concerns were of a different nature.

She sought out Kamen.

It was a full hour before she found him. Actually, he found her, in their rooms. He streaked into them from wherever he had been.

"Where were you?" she asked him as she came up to him and tried to give him an affectionate greeting. He turned away from her.

"With the Phoenixes, returning the bodies of their dead."

"Oh," she said, suddenly understanding why he had rebuffed her. He had no doubt been through a very unpleasant experience. "Did they say anything?"

"Only that we should not bother them again. Contact with the outside world cost them too dearly. They prefer to remain in their wild habitat safe from all the machinations of the world."

"Who could blame them? I wish I could escape to the wilds with them. It would be so much easier."

"Would that I could live in such blissful ignorance," Kamen said softly.

Viève tried once again to move into his embrace, and this time he let her come. He tipped her chin up with a single finger and looked down on her face.

"Would you come live in the wilds with me? Away from all the rest of the world?"

"I would go anywhere with you," she said intently. "Anywhere at any time."

He gave her half a smile. "You need to live in a world where people are accepting of you. At least for a little while. You have lived too long in the dark of disapproval. You only love me because I was the first person to be kind to you."

Love? Had she spoken of love?

Did she love him?

Viève realized that she did. She loved the way he talked. The way he smelled of bergamot. The way he moved like liquid muscle. She loved the way he touched her and the way he made her feel. She always felt so special beneath his caresses. She loved the heat of their passion and the wildness that came with it.

"I love you for far more reasons than the fact that you have been kind to me," she said sternly.

He looked at her in surprise when she voiced the emotion for herself. He had not even realized what he was saying before, but hearing it from her lips changed everything.

He stepped away from her, leaving her cold.

"You cannot love me," he said.

"Why not?" she asked.

"You do not understand. You never have. I am not . . . I'm not worthy of anyone's love. Least of all yours."

"That isn't true," she insisted, trying to step back into contact with him. But he stepped away again.

"You aren't listening to me!" he said sharply.

"I am! And it sounds like you are saying you don't love me. Is that true?"

"That isn't what I am saying at all! My feelings . . . my feelings are beside the point!"

"What *are* your feelings?" she demanded of him. "Do you feel anything at all for me or are you truly so selfish that you cannot give love to someone else?"

"I have done nothing but give you love! Have you not felt my love for you in every little caress? Every little touch? I have tried to love you in the best way I know how!"

"You mean physical love. But have I touched your heart?" she asked.

He wanted to say yes. He wanted to tell her the truth. But that would be selfish because he would only be telling her to make her stay by his side for all the rest of his days . . . and she deserved better than that. Better than him.

And yet he couldn't make himself say "no." It would be a lie, and he was done with telling lies. If he were going to make any kind of a decent man of himself, he would need to be honest with others and with himself.

So he simply dodged the question.

"You only think you are in love because for the first time ever you have been exposed to kindness and gentility and acceptance. I am your first and all women fall in love with their first. Or they think they do."

"Do you really think I'm that simpleminded? Are my feelings truly that trivial?" She sounded hurt. He would be hurt too if someone trivialized his feelings. But she couldn't possibly love him. She simply couldn't.

"This changes everything," he said, backing away from her and crossing the room. "You can stay here. I will leave."

Shock left her cold.

"You mean . . . permanently? You're leaving altogether?"

"Yes. I'm no longer needed here and I need time by myself for a while. And it would be best for you if I—"

"Stop! You do not get to decide what is best for me! And you can't leave. You have work to do. A lot of work! There are prisoners to deal with. You are the only one who knows these people, what they are truly made of. They need your help."

"I'll . . ." he floundered. She was right. His work here wasn't done. "I'll come back. After a while. When you've had time to realize that what you are feeling is not what you think it is."

"Then you'll be gone a long time because my feelings will not have changed. And neither will yours!" she said daringly. "You love me. I know you do. Why else would you be so afraid?"

"It's not fear! It's knowing. I know I am not good enough for you and you simply will not see that!"

"I never have and I never will because it's not true! You are more than good enough. More than deserving."

"You are wrong. It only proves to me how much you still devalue yourself. I won't argue about this any longer," he said, turning on her and walking out the door.

She followed him immediately, shouting at his back as he moved through the hall and down the stairs into the main body of the house.

"Oh! I have never met such a stubborn man! *I* am not the one devaluing myself! You're the one who thinks he isn't worthy of love. And you are wrong. Everybody, even the lowest of creatures, is deserving of love!"

They entered the main sitting room, only to find a group of people, including Leo; his wife, Faith; Jackson; Marissa; Ahnvil; and Kat sitting in conversation. They looked up upon hearing their angry voices.

"You're wrong," he said quietly, searching for an exit. "Love is a sacred thing. Just as forgiveness is a sacred thing. But you are so willing to give both so easily that you don't see there are those who are undeserving of it."

"Well that's a real kick in the pants. You mean to say if someone goes through the trouble of forgiving you, you're not even going to accept it?" Leo said, standing up.

Kamen froze in place and turned to look at Leo.

"I'm not asking for—"

"But you have it all the same," Leo said quietly. Firmly. "I'm not saying we're going to be the best of buds, but I realize I can't move on from this if I don't have some closure. That and the fact that I've seen how hard you've tried over this past year to make up for the things you've done."

"I didn't ask for your forgiveness," Kamen echoed.

"No. But she did." Leo pointed to Viève. "And she was right to do so. It's time we all stopped playing kick the puppy around here."

"Aye," Ahnvil spoke up, though not too strongly at first. "I've been giving this a lot of thought myself lately. I find I doona hate you as much as I once did. These past months have allowed me to come to terms with the wrongs you have done me."

Kamen stood stunned. Here were two men he had wronged in violent terms, and they were saying they forgave him?

"You can't mean this," he said softly.

"Just because we've forgiven you doesn't mean you get to dictate our feelings to us," Leo said sharply. "And you don't get to trivialize this either."

Again, that word. Was that what he was doing? Making important feelings small and . . . less? But he couldn't seem to grasp such a weighty thing as forgiveness. Oh, he understood the essentials of it, but he wasn't certain he would be as capable of giving it as Leo seemed to be. Or Ahnvil, a man he had enslaved for decades.

But here they were, telling him he was worthy of it. He thought they were wrong, but it was such a profound thing that he dare not refuse it.

"I . . . I thank you," he said at last. "I feel myself undeserving of this, but I thank you for it."

"If you weren't deserving we wouldn't be giving it," Leo said. "You know, you sound like little Viève did when she first got here. In three days she's learned to stick up for herself. Perhaps you should take a lesson from that."

Kamen looked to Viève, who had a fairly smug expression on her face. She held out her hand to him. "Come on. Let's go back upstairs and talk about this like grown-ups. Like grown-ups who are worthy of one another."

"This changes nothing," he said, although he looked and felt a little at sea.

"It changes *everything*," she said. She stepped forward and caught his hands up in hers. "You're worth more than you know. And I'm not the only one who thinks so."

"Yeah," Leo said. "You're a jerk, but you have value to this household. To the people in it. We need you."

"Not any longer. Apep is destroyed," Kamen said.

"And who is going to help us wade through hundreds of Templar prisoners?" Jackson asked. "Kamen, you have made yourself invaluable in more ways than just your pursuit of Apep."

"Name one," Kamen said harshly.

"Healing. Whenever someone is injured you are there, without question, healing their wounds."

Kamen fell silent. His mind was working frantically, trying hard to piece together the meaning in what he was hearing. He was not a dense or stupid man, but he felt like both right then.

Jackson stood up and placed a hand on Kamen's shoulder. "You killed me once, remember?"

Kamen did remember. It had been lifetimes ago and he had used the Curse on him. It was a painful way to die. He swallowed and nodded.

"If I am willing to forgive you that, don't you think you're allowed to forgive yourself?"

Kamen's eyes widened slightly. He hesitated, and then gave another nod. He could do that, couldn't he? Could he do any less than what they were willing to do for him? It wouldn't be right to spit in the face of such gifts.

And yet, to accept it meant he had to accept his own worth. Or rather, he had to upgrade his own worth in his own eyes. That was not an easy task. But perhaps . . .

"Yes," Viève said softly as she watched the play of emotion that crossed his face so openly, for all to see and understand. "You see it don't you? You are worth forgiving and even more. You are worth loving."

"No one loves me here. None but you," he added hastily.

"Am I not enough?" she asked him simply.

He gazed into her dove gray eyes and knew he couldn't reject her. She had grown strong and sure these past three nights, but she was still fragile. She couldn't bear up under this continual rejection.

And he found he no longer wanted to reject her. Was it true what they said? Did he deserve forgiveness and love?

He stepped forward quickly, into her embrace, his arms wrapping around her tightly, his hug lifting her feet off the floor. He buried his face into her hair and breathed deeply of her. The scent of strawberries filled his senses.

"You are more than enough," he whispered against her ear. "More than I shall ever deserve. But I swear to you I will strive every day to make you feel loved beyond reason. You will ever be a treasure in my eyes and I will never take your worth for granted."

"What woman could ask for anything more?" she asked him fiercely. "Now take me upstairs and make love to me properly to make up for this foolishness."

"Yes, madam," he said with a smile before he kissed her lips, then bent and hauled her up over his shoulder like a sack of potatoes. She yelped in surprise, but the feel of his hand intimately on her backside quelled any complaints she might have had. As he walked, Viève took in the group of people they were leaving behind. She waved to them and mouthed the words "thank you."

Leo nodded to her. He had a great deal of respect for the openhearted little Wraith who was brave enough to turn her back on her entire species to stand up for what she believed in. She may not have seemed strong when she first got there, but he realized now she had a lot more strength within her than she had been given credit for. Now, in a place where that strength would be nurtured, she promised to do great and wonderful things.

Leo felt a sense of closure settling over him as well. That wasn't to say he would never dream of the horrors he had suffered again, but he realized he was going to sleep easier tonight, and it would be all her doing.

Viève allowed Kamen to carry her to their rooms without so much as a word. When he closed the door behind them, he slid her down his body until she was on her feet. But he did not allow her to put even the slightest millimeter of space between them.

"If I didn't know any better I would say you planned all of this," he said in a deep, rumbling voice. There was emotion in his tone. He was moved by what the others had given him. What she had given him. For he knew none of it would have been possible without her.

He tipped her chin up and bent to kiss her lips softly.

"I love you," he said simply.

"I knew that all along. I just wanted you to admit it. And I wanted you to be willing to accept my love in return."

"I still am not worthy, but I will do my best to learn how to deserve you."

"I do not love unworthy people. I will not tolerate you saying otherwise."

"Yes, my little dove," he said softly. "You are correct. Forgive me."

"Make me forgive you," she challenged him.

"Ah. So now I am to work for your forgiveness?"

"Mmhmm," she said, a twinkle in her eye.

He smiled for her and kissed the side of her neck. "I wonder how I will ever manage to do that," he said, his teeth catching her dainty little earlobe and giving it a tug.

"I'm sure you'll think of something," she said invitingly.

"I'm sure I will," he said right before swooping in and catching her up in a searing kiss.

He made love to her. It wasn't the blistering, rampant passion they had so often shared with each other. It was gentle and soft and needy, and he realized how starved he was for someone to love him. It had been like that from the beginning. It had been what had allowed her to sweep into his arms and turn his world upside down. He had taken her against all his better judgment, and was now grateful that he had. He would never have earned a place of true acceptance in this house without her.

He would never have known what love truly was without her. She had loved him unconditionally from the very beginning. She had a heart the size of a continent and as he made love to her he told her he was lucky to have found a place in it.

He touched every inch of her skin, treasuring every soft caress. Then, once he had stirred her with his touch, his mouth followed. He sucked on every finger and every toe. He nipped at her behind her knees, inside her elbows, at the small of her back. He was determined that by the time they were through she would feel that every inch of herself had been thoroughly loved.

And she did.

But she was not satisfied simply lying there being catered to. She wanted to make certain he knew he was loved as well so she matched him kiss for kiss, touch for touch. He chuckled at her determination to mirror him. Oh, how she made him laugh. Made him feel light. Took a world of burdens from his shoulders so damn easily. He would never forget the things he had done wrong, always reminding himself never to take that path again, but it would be easy to remember as long as she was with him.

When they came together it brought the heat back into their coupling. There would always be this burning heat, he realized. There was no changing that, no straying from it. He would always make love to her as if it were the very last time, because he never knew when the last time might be. But now that there was less threat hanging over them, he hoped they were safe from the threat of being separated. She was as long-lived as he was, so they had many years ahead of them . . . together. And the idea of moving through this world with her made it so much easier to bear. There had been a time when he had despised his every day, hated the torment of living life over and over with no end in sight. But now he found he feared losing this life before he was ready. He could not leave her. For selfish reasons and for unselfish ones. He would not leave her to navigate the world unprotected. He would not leave her so soon after finding her.

And in a hundred years, it would still be too soon.

"Are we children, to feel so much love in so little time? Isn't it the young who are reckless in such ways?" he asked her when they were cuddled up close afterward, the sweat from their rigorous lovemaking cooling on their bodies.

"Don't do that. Don't give it less value just because we *know* so easily."

"No. Never. I will never give this less value again. I swear to you."

"Good," she said, turning her head to kiss him. "I love you. I will love you a hundred years from now. It won't always be the same love; it will grow and mature and become something deep and steady, but I will still love you."

"Deep and steady?" He hummed. "I hope that doesn't mean you think we will not want to make love as often, because I do not want a deep and steady love if that is the case."

She laughed at him and he chuckled.

"Don't worry, we have no fears of that. I have not had sex for over fifty years. I have a lot of making up to do for the next fifty . . . and then some. And one day . . . maybe we will speak of having children. Not now," she said quickly when she saw the expression on his face. "I'm not ready either. But one day I would like to have a child. A pretty, perfect, half-breed child."

"I think . . . I think I would like that. One day. To see a baby with its mother's fair skin and maybe its father's strong countenance."

"It may look more Wraith than I do," she thought with a moment of worry. Then she put that worry aside. "Regardless, I will love it. I will not do as my mother did. My child will be raised with love. And a father. A whole and loving family."

"I wonder that your mother did not abort you," he said gingerly. "If you were such a disgrace to her. She had to know what her life would be like."

"Wraiths cannot have abortions. It kills the mother to kill the child."

"Ah. That makes more sense now. She was preserving her own life, rather than yours. Our child will never be an accident. We will plan very carefully when to bring it into the world. But it is a more peaceful world right now. More peaceful than I've known in a long time. I would not be afraid to bring a child into this world. But if there is one thing I have learned in my many generations, it's that peace never lasts. As long as there are people on this earth, peace will never last. Someone somewhere will take offense to someone somewhere else and then peace will be destroyed."

"Such a cynical view of the world. I am going to have to rid you of that problem."

He smiled at her. "Please do," he invited her.

She kissed him again and began to do just that.

# EPILOGUE

Bella looked down at the page in front of her and finished her inscription with a flourish.

"What are you up to?" her husband asked as he set their son down on the floor, letting him run wild.

"I am writing a prophecy," she said proudly.

"A prophecy?"

"Well, I am a prognosticator. Why shouldn't I write a prophecy of my own? My power allows me to see into the future. Maybe what I am compelled to write is something that will come true."

"I'm not sure it works like that," he said with a chuckle.

"Says who? Where do all these prophecies come from anyway? I say it's people like me who write them."

"All right then. What is your prophecy?" he asked, reaching for the piece of paper. She snatched it back from him.

"No. You'll just make fun of me."

He gave her a wounded look. "When have I ever made fun of you?"

"Well, there was that time when—"

"I meant about something that was important to you."

She had to acquiesce. "Never. You've always taken seriously anything I take seriously. And I do take this seriously."

"I can see that. So let me see your prophecy."

She handed him the paper and he read it. A smile grew on his face. He put down the pad and pulled her into a hard embrace, giving her a heady kiss.

"Now there is a prophecy meant to come true. And I have a prophecy for you."

"Oh?" she said, already knowing where this was going.

"I prophesize that you will be making mad passionate love to your husband after the children go to bed today."

"Well, what do you know! I had the same prophecy!"

"And what is your prognostication as far as Dax's daughter is concerned? Any thoughts there?"

"I predict that she will be greatly loved and that her power, whatever it may be, will be handled with loving wisdom and the strength of many nations to guide her."

"Say, you're pretty good at this prognostication thing."

She laughed as he swung her up into his arms and kissed her.

"Do you really think so?"
"Well, let's just say . . . I have great hopes that your fortune telling is accurate."
"So do I," she said with a sigh. "So do I."

*"And so it will come to pass, from this day forward, that the Nightwalkers will grow and flourish and live in peace. They will come to understand one another, they will come to love one another. A new era will be born, new generations will thrive, and all things will be possible."*

—Bella's Prophecy

# GLOSSARY AND PRONUNCIATION TABLE

**Apep:** (Ā-pep)
**Ceara:** (CĒ-ah-rah)
**Cordo:** (COR-dō)
**Docia:** (DŌ-shuh)
**Geneviève (Viève):** (JAHN-vē-ehv) (Vē-EHV)
**Hatshepsut:** (hat-SHEP-soot)
**Kamenwati:** (Kah-men-WAH-ti)
**Legna:** (LĀY-nuh)
**Menes:** (MEN-es)
**Ouroboros:** (You-row-BORE-us) A snake or dragon devouring its own tail; a sign of infinity or perpetual life.
**Pharaoh:** (FEY-roh) Egyptian king or queen. This is used in reference to both male and female rulers. In this case, the rulers of the Bodywalkers.
**Tameri:** (Tah-MARE-ē)

Note: All the *h*'s in the Gargoyles' names are silent unless the name begins with *h* or the *h* logically occurs in the name.

# ABOUT THE AUTHOR

Jacquelyn Frank is the *New York Times*–bestselling author of the Immortal Brothers series (*Cursed by Fire, Cursed by Ice, Bound by Sin*, and *Bound in Darkness*), the World of Nightwalkers series (*Forbidden, Forever, Forsaken, Forged*, and *Nightwalker*), the Three Worlds series (*Seduce Me in Dreams* and *Seduce Me in Flames*), the Nightwalkers series (*Adam, Jacob, Gideon, Elijah, Damien*, and *Noah*), the Shadowdwellers novels (*Ecstasy, Rapture*, and *Pleasure*), and the Gatherers novels (*Hunting Julian* and *Stealing Kathryn*). She lives in North Carolina and has been writing romantic fiction ever since she picked up her first romance novel at age thirteen.

# THE WORLD OF NIGHTWALKERS

FROM OPEN ROAD MEDIA

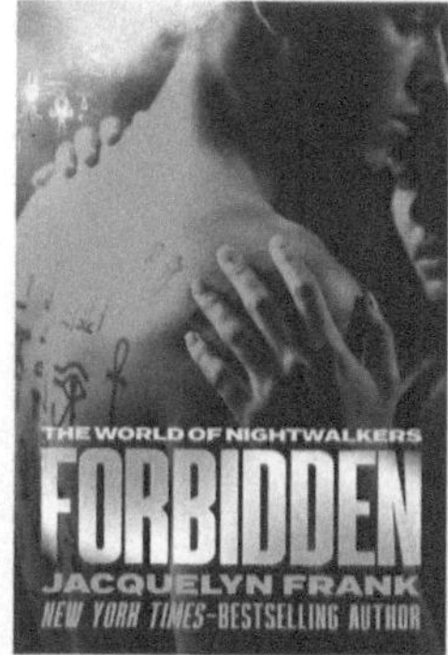

www.ingramcontent.com/pod-product-compliance
Lightning Source LLC
LaVergne TN
LVHW090603110826
845146LV00001B/237

* 9 7 9 8 3 3 7 2 0 5 4 9 6 *